The Iron Crown

Book Thirteen in the Iron Soul Series

J.M. Briggs

Contents

For my parents for always loving and supporting me
even when I first explained the stories and voices in
my head that were trying to come out.
Thank you for finding it more amusing than worrying.
And thank you for believing that I would finish the series.
I certainly didn't at the start of all this.

Dragon Filled Skies

Magic still shimmered beneath the surface of the world of Dragons, even after three days of rest and talking to their now much more gracious hosts. Every time Alex glanced around, she could see the flickers of power in the soil and plants that were coaxing the world back to life. The Iron Chalice had performed far beyond any hopes that she might have had when Bran suggested using it on the area damaged by the Darkness. With the sky clearing and the magic of the Chalice either strengthening or purifying the lines of energy in this world, things were looking up.

There was a myth of a Fisher King that was often connected to Arthurian lore that now came to mind. Alex had considered it before, mainly because the Iron Chalice had healed Bran's old injury in much the same way as that of the Fisher King. The king had been lame and the land he watched over had suffered. Given that Bran's last name was Fisher, Alex had always been amused by the similarities, but now she wondered if there was more to it. This seemed to be another story that had far more truth than it should have and echoed the future, similar to the Welsh story of a mountain opening and a bell leading a blond person to the entrance that had helped Alex find the Iron Chalice in this life.

It all made her wonder. The world that she was now seeking to protect stretched beyond the confines of the Iron Realm. She'd been forced in the past few years to accept that the universe was far greater and stranger than she'd ever imagined. It was humbling and terrifying, and worried her. Would they ever find the reason why so many stories held clues for them? And if they did, would she like the answer, and what would it mean for the Iron Realm?

Alex was standing atop one of the crumbling rock structures that made up the ruins over the cavern in which they were currently staying. This mountaintop overlooked a now lush valley, and overhead she could see Dragons in flight as they sailed on the strong winds of this world. She'd expected the stormy winds to die down once the Darkness was sealed, but they'd only smoothed out. Apparently, Dragons were aided in flight by the winds.

She marveled at it all for a few moments, letting the warm sun of this world shine down on her. It was warmer than she was used to, likely being closer to this sun than Earth was to Sol. Alex wasn't certain how this affected the Dragons. Aiden and Bran had been discussing if they were cold-blooded, warm-blooded or something in between last night. Nicki had called them nerds but listened with interest. How could she not when they were camping in a world full of dragons?

Behind her, there was a whoosh of air and the heavy sound of the wind catching on something. Alex didn't panic and spin around, but instead turned towards the noise calmly. Emrys was in the air above her, his great red wings spread. She hadn't realized that he was awake. He landed with a thump that was much softer than Alex would have imagined a Dragon could manage before this trip.

The only Dragon that Alex knew other than Emrys was Ty. The old Dragon had threatened to eat them at first but had carried Alex on his back to the Darkness to help, and since then had been helping Emrys as new Dragons arrived to find out what had happened. The hilltop ruin that they'd set up as their base was already a hub of activity. Though she had magic, the sight of so many hungry and worn-down Dragons still made Alex nervous. Her eyes scanned a group of new arrivals who had yet to be healed with the Chalice, and her chest ached with magical exhaustion prematurely.

As if summoned by Emrys' arrival in the ruins, more Dragons flew towards the mountaintop. Alex stayed still and watched their great forms move against the light of the sky and the backdrop of the clouds. The shifting of their wings was similar to a bird's on Earth, but slower, and she noted that they often held their wings open to catch air currents as the Gryphons had done.

Three young-looking Dragons with smooth shiny scales landed near Emrys and began talking all at once. They had so many questions about the 'Old Times' from whence Emrys had originated. No topic seemed to be taboo with them, asking about his long-gone family, his clan structure, the government, the fortress that had once stood here and a variety of things that meant next to nothing to Alex. When she had met Emrys, he had told her that Dragons were reborn after death and regained their old memories, but it no longer seemed to work. One more potential scar from the Darkness. Emrys was patient through all the questions, demonstrating the skill he had spent centuries refining in his underground prison. He answered most of them as more Dragons arrived, including a few older ones who landed with Ty.

Alex paid little attention to the Dragons, picking up bits of the conversation, and they took little note of her. She sat down on one of the rocks and exhaled slowly, trying to clear her mind and relax. They likely had another full day of healing and answering questions ahead of them.

The issue was that their food supplies from the Gryphons were running low, and they'd still made no progress in dealing with the source of the Darkness.

Figures appeared on the small trail that she and the other humans had created over the past few days. It zig zagged up the mountain around rocks and thick patches of vegetation, allowing them to get up here without too much exertion. Morgana was in the lead, with Bran, Nicki, and Aiden all following behind. The eldest of the mages relaxed the moment she caught sight of Alex. Her green eyes then narrowed and flicked between Alex and the Dragons. Shrugging, Alex gestured the others over and hoped that her calm would alleviate whatever concerns Morgana had.

"You were gone when we woke," Morgana said, coming closer. Her tone wasn't angry, but there was a hint of warning.

"Couldn't sleep anymore."

Alex left off the part about being tired of using sleeping bags on rock every night because they were all uncomfortable pulling up the new vegetation to pad their sleeping area and were too afraid to sleep outside in case new Dragons thought they were tasty treats. Her back was really starting to ache from night after night of sleeping on the too hard and bumpy surface of the cavern below them. It made her miss the nests of the Gryphons.

"I hear that." Aiden rubbed the back of his neck and rolled his shoulders. "Not so much fun."

The tone of the Dragons shifted, and Alex turned her attention away from her fellow mages. The high energy of the questions had faded and the young Dragons were moving back as more familiar Dragons landed near Emrys. The red Dragon laid down and crossed his front legs, calm and looking like a lounging king. Seeing that something more serious was about to take place, Alex waved off the others and moved forward to join in the circle so she could be sure of hearing and seeing what was happening. Dragons, in general, were too large for Alex to see around their wings.

Emrys noticed her coming and nodded to two nearby Dragons. They huffed a little but moved back to give Alex plenty of space. Morgana followed Alex. As the crowd of Dragons settled, Morgana took hold of Alex's left hand. Around her neck, Alex was aware of the weight of the Iron Pendant that she had forged before they left home. With the power to allow her and those touching her to understand any language spoken to them and be understood in return, it was proving itself to be a resounding success. It might lack the mythological grandeur of Cathanáil on her back or Mjǫllnir on her hip or the Iron Chalice, but Alex knew they wouldn't have gotten this far without it.

"Anything of interest to report this morning?" Emrys, the red Dragon formerly of Wales asked the Dragons as they gathered.

"The magic is spreading far," an enormous dragon that Alex didn't recognize said. The purple Dragon's green eyes were bright with glee. "I came from three valleys over and heard from family that further out the vegetation is springing to life."

"The Klaxeon Forest is regrowing quickly!" Alex remembered the wasteland they'd flown over to reach the Darkness. "The trees are growing so fast that the air is filled with creaking and groaning."

"The War in Reticallicon has ended," another Dragon added eagerly. "With food returning, the fighting Dragons have dispersed. There is more still alive than we'd thought possible. Animals are either being restored by the magic or showing themselves for the first time in years."

Emrys glanced at Alex, but she had no idea. It seemed impossible for the Chalice to have brought dead animals back to life, but the Chalice's power had unknown limits. Maybe it had reacted to the greater need here and poured out more magic than ever before, or perhaps, as Alex suspected, it had cleansed the natural lines of magic in this world and given them a jump start. Maybe the world had reacted to save itself. If that were true, she wished that she'd used the Chalice more often on Earth. Maybe when they were home, she'd take the Iron Chalice to pollution sites and see what happened. If Shiva met her there with the Iron Trishula and purified things, then who knew what they could manage.

"Should we reach out to the Gryphons?" one of the blueish Dragons asked. Alex didn't know how to pronounce their name and hadn't been given a nickname or short version to use. "It might be the best way to avoid a war."

"I'd advise against it," Emrys said. His rumbling voice seemed to enthrall all the Dragons present. While he was smaller than most of them, his bearing was regal and his calm soothed them. The knowledge that he came from a time when the Dragon world had been strong and united fascinated his fellow Dragons. "The Darkness there has been stopped, but travel between worlds can cause unexpected issues." Shaking his great red head, Emrys sighed loudly. "The Dragons who went there have already made enemies of the Gryphons. Us sending more will not fix the situation."

"I agree," Morgana added. If the Grand Mage was intimidated standing in a circle of Dragons, she did not show it. "Strange things happen when worlds collide. Both worlds are on the mend. I'd hesitate to risk that."

The Dragons nodded at Morgana's words. Despite not being a Dragon or being the person who closed the hole the Darkness had eaten into their world, the Dragons regarded her with respect. Emrys had commented that Morgana smelled old, and Alex could only imagine what 'old' meant to a Dragon his age.

"Then are we to stay in this area?" another Dragon asked. It studied Alex. "Will this magic heal the entire world?"

"This is the worst area," Alex pointed out. She did not know how far the magic would spread. "And the energy that feeds your world is shining brightly." That remark made Morgana's grip on her hand tighten. Keeping her smile closed mouth lest she show teeth to Dragons. Alex gestured out into the plain below with her free hand. "Healing this area is the most critical, and if hostilities stop, then more of the world will be able to recover."

"Fair points," Emrys agreed, "And we lack knowledge of the extent of the fighting. We must be grateful that the flow of poison has stopped. With care and cooperation, we can make inroads in giving the rest of our world the time it needs to heal."

There were small murmurs of agreement, but Alex was aware of the Dragons watching her. Nervousness churned in her stomach. These were Dragons, not humans, and she had to be careful. She and her fellow mages had managed something miraculous to them, but they'd also demonstrated power. That power might frighten some or make others greedy to use them. If they had been humans, Alex would have been worried about political machinations to use the mages, but again, she couldn't be certain of what to expect.

Besides, she was the Iron Soul. Her primary duty was to the safety of Earth, the Iron Realm, where they came from. Stopping the Darkness in other worlds helped them learn of the force they faced and lessened the likelihood that the terrified species would invade. And with what they knew now.... Alex pushed that thought away. Right now they needed to stay focused on the Dragons, but it reminded her that plans for departing needed to be formed.

"Thank you for your insights," Emrys said to all the assembled Dragons. "And you, good mages." He nodded to them and then turned to Ty and one other older Dragon, asking about the numbers of Dragons over the next mountain range.

Morgana tugged on Alex's hand, guiding her away from the gathering. Alex didn't protest and allowed herself to be led away without a fuss. Morgana was likely worrying about the same things as Alex. They'd gotten this far in the Dragon world with only one attempt to eat them and had successfully stopped the Darkness. Bran's suggestion about the Chalice had bought them goodwill, but they still needed to be careful. They reached the others, and Morgana pointed to an area beyond the ruins. Without argument, they headed over there to put some distance between them and the Dragons.

"How are things going?" Nicki asked eagerly. The redhead was watching the Dragons with excited eyes. "I wish I could understand them."

"Things are going well," Alex offered. She didn't extend her hand. Exhaustion still clung to her despite the slow regeneration of her magic, and she wasn't interested in using any more magic through the Iron Pendant. "They're just hammering out some details."

Nicki eyed her hand and then shook her head, apparently deciding not to use Alex as a translation conduit for the time being. Alex was grateful and couldn't help but notice the small headache building up in her forehead.

"How much longer are we staying?" Aiden asked. He paused and glanced at a nearby Dragon. "Not that I don't like them or anything, but I don't think we can afford to stay long enough to heal the entire population."

"That's a fair point," Bran agreed. "We are regaining magic each day, but it's slower here than on Earth. We're more limited here in what we can do."

"I know." Alex held back a sigh. "I know. We need to make plans of our own." A slight smile appeared on her face. "But we've done a lot of good here. The Darkness has been stopped and the world won't die." Gesturing around, Alex struggled to wrap her head around the change. "The magic will slow down and the Dragons will need to be careful for a few generations while things recover, but I'm confident that this world is saved. Provided that the Darkness doesn't return."

"And the Darkness was spilling from this world into the Gryphon world, which means that their world is safe now too," Nicki added. "So it's all about the source."

"Exactly." Alex looked upwards, but it was just the open sky, free of the purple storm caused by the Darkness. She couldn't see the Tree of Reality beyond this world. "I'm afraid that... I think it's unlikely that the worlds further up the branch can be saved." She hated the words as soon as they were out of her mouth, but they were the truth. "The best thing we can do now is try to find the source of the Darkness and seal it."

Easier said than done.

2

Dreaming of Sídhean

She was dreaming of Sídhean again. The dark, violet sky filled with debris and the windswept, burned-out landscape always gave it away. Above her head the sky churned, and she searched for the source of the Darkness, but it was difficult. This entire world had been consumed, and it was hard to tell what might be the natural color and what might not be. It wasn't like on Earth or the Dragon world, where the Darkness had been a sharp contrast.

"It's awful," a voice said behind her.

Alex turned in surprise, but not panic. The wind tugged at her long, braided, blonde hair, but there was no pain or discomfort. Her gray eyes landed on a figure standing a few feet away. He was tall with brown hair, and was studying part of a stone ruin that was partially buried in dirt and ash. The man was dressed in a woven tunic and had a few golden decorations in his shoulder-length hair. A familiar sword with a golden hilt was strapped to his back, and the sight of it made Alex feel naked in her jeans, t-shirt, and boots.

"Arto." His name hung in the air. "Why are you here?" she asked. This was a new variation in the dream about Sídhean. "Whispering not enough anymore?"

"You called me," Arto answered. He shrugged and gestured around. "Why do you dream of this?"

"It's a dead world. That bothers me." Alex scanned the surroundings. It wasn't the same place she'd been before. There were always ruins and dunes of dark soil and ash, but she was in a slightly different place each time. "This is a dream, my subconscious at work. Well... it is now." When she'd spoken to the dying Queen, that had been different. "Unless you have a theory?"

"You plan to come here."

"Maybe." Alex shrugged. "We need to go into the Sídhe branch. I know that much." A soft sigh escaped her. "Everything always seems to go back to the Sídhe, doesn't it?"

"In a way." Arto walked closer to her, his footfalls making no sound and leaving no footprints. "You left Luegáed and Gwenyvar on Earth."

"I did. I miss them," Alex defended. "But they aren't mages. Bringing them here would have been dangerous and if... if things go badly for us, it's good that they'll be able to help Avani and Robin contact the Old Ones and any other living magicians."

"I understand." Arto sighed, "Though the idea of being without them is painful to me." He stared into the sky with a neutral expression. "I fear that it might have been my magic in my grief that trapped them in the cycle of rebirth. I didn't seek to punish them: I just... I missed them, at the end."

Alex nodded. Memories of that last day flickered through her mind. Arto had only been a little older than her, though he'd been a much more experienced mage, and everything had happened quickly at the end of his life. Everything had tried to fall apart all at once.

"It doesn't matter anymore," Alex said. "It's over now. I'm confident of that. When I die and am reborn, they will not follow me."

"When you die..." Arto's lips quirked, but he wasn't smiling. "Merlin is gone. There will be only Morgana."

"I know." Alex's stomach turned, and a wave of disquiet washed over her. They were standing on the surface of a dead world, and yet that wasn't what made her ill. "I'm worried too." There was an echo in her chest. The others were worried; even those who had never met Morgana and Merlin were worried about her going on alone. "But that's not something we can change. If we can reach the Darkness-"

"What will you do?"

"Depends." Alex looked up again, wishing that she could tell if the Darkness had come through the sky here. "On what we learn. We don't know what the Darkness is; not really. Maybe it was a weapon that got out of hand, or maybe when they first tried to jump worlds, they... hit something else." Alex wasn't sure. Her mouth was dry as she spoke. "What we find will determine what happens next. Maybe I can cut Sídhean off from the rest of the Tree of Reality, to cut off the Darkness' path. Then we could close the breaches on the individual worlds. It's a lot, but it's the whole of reality we're talking about."

"But it spreads through all branches, not just this one, Alex." Arto's voice was gentle, and Alex tensed at the tone. She was not a child to be coddled. "The whole sky of the Tree, where the branches grow, has been corrupted."

"I know."

And she did know. The wind howled around them. Alex closed her eyes for a moment. She knew she was dreaming. Arto standing before her was proof of that, but that wind sounded so real. The empty space around Alex weighed her down, and the chill in the air sank into her. It was real somewhere in the Tree of Reality, just not where she was in the waking world. Alex wondered once again if she was truly dreaming or if she was reaching out with her magic.

"Do you have any advice?" Alex asked. "Any kernels of wisdom to share?"

"You have my memories, my knowledge."

"I have it," she agreed, "But I'm not going to pretend that I'm always aware of your memories or know what to do with them."

That was the truth. The memories of the others were always there, manifesting as the voices in her head that even two years ago would have had Alex checking into a mental health center. It was just something she had to live with. Exhaling softly, she looked around at the landscape. There was nothing for her to learn from here. This dream was just her worry haunting her even while she slept.

"Your fellow mages are tired," Arto observed. "You have to be careful about how much you push people. Even the greatest warriors falter in the face of the unknown, especially when exhausted."

"I know." Alex sighed and rubbed her eyes. The sensation was muted: it was her merely imagining what it felt like. "But if we go home... I'm afraid that we might not push again. This is exciting and scary and... Morgana will struggle to go into Sídhean."

"Yes, she will, but she will go with you if you insist." Arto frowned in disapproval. Alex wasn't sure if he disapproved of her putting Morgana in that position or Morgana's stubbornness. Maybe both. She thought it was both.

"I have faith in the others," Alex said. Her throat tickled, but she pressed on. "They trust me when I say that this is important. If we can stop the Darkness, maybe we can stop the invasions."

"I hope so." Arto shook his head. "The raids of my time seem so small now, but what I did bound you and the others to this course."

"You didn't know. And who knows what may happen when this is all over. But there isn't a future for the branches if we can't stop the spread of the Darkness." Memories of the thick shadow the Darkness cast over the whole Tree of Reality flickered through her mind. "I have to go. It's dangerous, I know that, but I have to try. I don't know what will happen to the Iron Soul if I die away from the Iron Realm, and I'm sorry that I'm putting all that we have ever been at risk, but I have to go."

"Be careful," Arto said. "Not just for who you once were, but for yourself." His expression was thoughtful, and he seemed older than before. "You will not be the same at the end of this. It is too far and too grand for you to be unchanged at the end of this journey."

"I'm pretty sure that's how life works in general."

Alex tried to smile reassuringly. Something shifted in the air. Magic mixed with worry and was twisting into a shape that she couldn't see. No matter how calm she might try to be, Alex was growing nervous and a little scared at Arto's words. They rang with a hint of prophecy.

"I know not what you'll face," Arto continued. He stayed a foot away from her, making no move to touch her. "But you are the Iron Soul."

"I'm aware." Alex smirked, not bothering to keep the dryness out of her tone.

However, Arto's brown eyes were fixed on her with a weight to them that Alex could feel settling on her shoulders. They were the same person, in reality, and yet she couldn't read that expression. She didn't like that and heard the others stirring. Soft whispers washed over her, comforting and worrying all at once. The loudest were familiar to her. Their stories were ones she knew well, but there were others who had lived quiet lives without magic who nonetheless offered their support.

"Alex!"

A voice that was not one of the Iron Souls cut through the dream. Alex grimaced, and the landscape faded away. Someone called her again. It was a familiar voice. She groaned and her body became heavy. Alex shifted, but she wasn't standing anymore. She was laying down. Opening her eyes, Alex peered up into the darkness. For an instant, she was terrified by the blackness stretching around her.

"Alex," Morgana called gently. "Alex, are you alright?"

"Huh?" Alex blinked and turned her head.

Then there was a soft light beside her as the solar-powered lantern was switched on. Morgana was lingering beside Alex, her hair in slight disarray and worry in her green eyes.

"Alex, are you alright? You were..." Morgana hesitated for a moment. "You were talking in your sleep. It sounded like-" Morgana stopped herself, but Alex could see what the woman wanted to say in her eyes.

"I was talking with Arto," Alex confirmed for her.

Sitting up, Alex tried to remember all the details of the dream, but it was already fading. Arto had been there, and she replayed parts of their conversation. None of it had been truly helpful, but a warmth lingered in her chest. At least her other selves didn't think she was insane for all of this, even if she likely was.

"Did he have any advice?"

"No." Alex shook her head. "I was in Sídhean again. He thought it looked horrible." She tried to chuckle, but the sound was weak and twisted itself into something tragic.

"That's not surprising."

Morgana leaned back, sitting on her sleeping bag. The others were still sleeping peacefully, though Nicki's head had completely vanished into the bag and the only reason Alex knew she was still inside was the shape of Nicki curled up and the soft snores.

"We need to go there," Alex said. "We can't stay here much longer. Things need to stabilize on their own. Us staying will only make more and more Dragons wonder about other worlds."

"I agree." Morgana nodded, and Alex nearly sighed in relief. "The issue is, do we return to Earth first? We could rest and resupply."

"I'm not sure." Alex reached beside her sleeping bag. Cathanáil was right where it should be. "We know that while traveling through a branch is the most natural path, it isn't the only path."

"You want to jump branches?" Morgana raised her eyebrows with clear surprise. "That's dangerous."

"I know making the holes is dangerous," Alex agreed, "but the Dvergr and Jǫtnar made it through without difficulty. The Iron Realm was fine. I know I can make a path using the Sword and-"

"The path you made was to the next world. We followed the flow of magical energy, according to you," Morgana reminded her in a low voice. She pointed to Aiden, who was rolling over in a silent reminder for Alex to watch her volume. "Going sideways through the emptiness of the Tree is something completely different."

Morgana had a point there, Alex had to admit. They didn't know what might happen, and the source of the holes that the Dvergr and Jǫtnar had fallen through was a bit of a mystery. There were theories, but nothing absolute. Alex still wasn't even sure what branch or branches they had come from.

"If we go back to Earth, we have to open a path to the Gryphon world," Alex pointed out. "And while the Chalice has helped, there's nothing to say for sure that we wouldn't weaken what defenses might be rebuilding. Some Dragons would be more than willing to go to the Gryphon world rather than put the work into this world."

"That's a fair point," Morgana conceded. "But it isn't our concern."

There it was. Alex had been waiting for it, in a way. She loved Morgana; she truly did. Alex carried not only her own fondness for her mentor but also Arto's deep love and respect for his elder sister. She loved Morgana, but Alex knew the old mage could be set in her ways. She was loyal to the Iron Realm and, in many ways, only to the Iron Realm. The Darkness was a threat to everyone and everything in the Tree of Reality, and it was likely that many worlds were dead and gone; that whole worlds had been consumed and all life on them extinguished as it was.

"If we make war more likely on the Gryphon world, then they might push through to the Iron Realm," Alex said. "Yes, we have the Iron Gates to help defend it, but if too many species and worlds start pushing against them, they will crumble. They have limits. It's better to draw as little attention to the Iron Realm as possible."

Morgana hummed thoughtfully and Alex resigned herself to a back and forth on the issue for a bit. Hopefully it wouldn't take too long, because they couldn't stay here much longer. Besides the issue of Dragons and Gryphons, they still had no idea if being in these other worlds was going to have negative consequences on them. The Sídhe on Earth had lost their horns and lived in constant pain, for example, and Alex wasn't looking forward to finding out what might happen to her.

"Besides," Alex added, "if we go sideways, as dangerous as it may be, it's more likely that we'll reach Sídhean faster. If we go back to Earth, we'll have to pass through the conquered areas of the empire. We don't look like Sídhe and we're likely to run into trouble. The fewer worlds we have to go through, the better."

"That... that is a valid point." Morgana sighed loudly, and Bran stirred. "We know nothing of the current political climate."

"Yeah," Alex said. When she'd been taken into the tunnels, all she'd heard was that different princes were in power. "Things could be in a state of civil war."

"Likely."

That didn't seem to bother Morgana at all, and Alex barely held back a frown. Morgana had suffered at the hands of the Sídhe, and it was unlikely that she'd ever see them as anything other than monsters. Alex couldn't help but feel a little sympathy now that she knew their culture had been built on conquests as they ran from the Darkness.

"I don't think we can wait," Alex offered softly. "We can't spend time going through every branch to stop the Darkness, even if we wanted to. The Old Ones come from a branch with less matter than ours, so I don't even want to risk going there."

Morgana nodded again, and Alex could see the wheels were turning. There was an urgency burning beneath her skin, one that Alex didn't fully understand herself, but they needed to keep moving. Backtracking to the Iron Realm, while it would let them restock, would slow them down. Alex might not know why she was so anxious, but at this point, she'd learned to trust her instincts. Maybe in one of her visions, she'd seen something that hadn't fully settled yet or-

"What's going on?" Bran's sleepy voice asked.

Alex looked over and smiled, holding back a chuckle. Bran's dark brown hair was in disarray and his green eyes were barely open. He seemed much younger than he really was, and Alex allowed a wave of fondness to wash over her. Morgana openly chuckled.

"We're planning our next move," Morgana said gently. Her eyes shifted over to Alex. "Go back to sleep, Bran. We'll need your strength to make the trip to the Sídhe branch."

Bran nodded, clearly not really understanding what Morgana had just said, and laid his head back down. If he had understood her, Alex knew that he would have asked for more details and instantly been wide awake. Aiden rolled over in his sleeping bag, muttering something in his sleep, and Nicki remained unmoving. Across the cave, Alex could hear the deep breathing of the sleeping Dragons. She longed to curl back up in her sleeping bag and get some more rest, but there was too much to think about. There was planning to do.

"Details can wait until morning," Morgana said, as if reading Alex's mind. She reached for the lantern and shifted back into her own sleeping bag. "Try and get more rest. If you speak with any other past selves, do see if they have any advice."

The words were teasing, but there was an undercurrent of desperation to them. Then the light was turned off and Alex heard Morgana sigh once again. Laying back herself, she adjusted the sweatshirt she'd been using as a pillow and stared up into the blackness overhead. Sleep did not return easily to Alex, but sometime later, after she'd started making lists of things to do, it did finally find her once again.

3

End of the World

542 C.E. Constantinople

The world was ending. That was what the children whispered, what the men on the streets were screaming and women were crying as they held their dying children. Morgana had seen many horrors over her long years. She'd seen children taken by Sídhe warriors and nobles to be their sexual slaves, seen her fellow humans whipped for minor offenses, and seen men cut down in war after war. Disease was familiar to her and Merlin: it was a fact of human life that haunted the steps of humanity as they tried to walk into the future. A looming shadow over their path that had sent many empires crumbling.

She'd seen death before. Morgana was familiar with its patterns, and too many faces had long since faded from her memory. They were ghosts on the winds. She and Merlin had long ago gained confidence that their magic protected them from the diseases that struck down so many other humans. Consumption had never touched them, despite the white death stalking humanity since before Morgana and Merlin had even been born.

This was something else. This plague was more than anything Morgana had ever seen before. She'd heard the rumors of a plague in Egypt and hadn't given it much thought beyond hoping that Merlin was safe in Alexandria. Illness occurred all across the world. More stories had reached the great city of Emperor Justinian as more and more outbreaks had occurred.

Now this new sickness was master of the city. Thousands were dying every day, and despite the Emperor's best efforts, too much of the city was grinding to a halt. Businesses everywhere were closed as the owners or their families fell ill. Fields outside of the city were going unharvested. Trade was at a crawl as only the brave and desperate left their homes. Even Emperor Justinian had not been spared. News from the palace said that he was in a coma, and his wife, Theodora, was barely keeping the political wolves at bay. Morgana wished her luck. Constantinople hadn't become this powerful without making enemies.

Staring out the window of the small home she rented, Morgana's eyes traced the streets. They were empty of living people going about their business. Instead, there were bodies piled for collection. It was a good thing when the families got them to the street rather than the rotting setting in within a building. There was a lot of that out in the city. Loyal loved ones tended the ill and fell ill themselves, with no one to help them.

There would be more bodies to come. Morgana could not see them clearly from her window on the second floor of the building. Most had been wrapped up, but she knew they would likely have the bulbous areas on them and blackened tissue. Everyone knew the symptoms, even if there was some variation in how the plague killed. She wasn't sure which was the worst way to die. Falling into a coma and dying without awareness seemed best to her, but it meant that those who fell into comas without family to care for them died slowly of starvation or thirst. They'd found a body two days ago in a nearby house who died of starvation. He'd only been found when the stench of his corpse became too pungent.

Guilt clawed at Morgana. Their magic was weak. The world was at peace, except for the native creatures who made war and fell ill. They could not heal this, and the scope of it made her wonder if their magic would be strong enough to protect them. Serving as a nurse would do little at this point for anyone, but part of her felt that she should under the circumstances.

A figure appeared on the road, carrying a frail corpse in their arms. They paused and looked at a pile of corpses, seemingly debating if they should keep going with the body or relinquish it to the pile. She couldn't see their face, but the choice was made, and they surrendered their burden to the mound.

No one walked on the street without a corpse, it was said. That wasn't completely true, but it was quickly becoming so. Not long after the figure vanished back into a building, a cart rolled into view. The back was already half full of corpses, but it stopped and two men loaded up more of the bodies. Morgana knew they would be placed in one of the mass graves outside the city. The office that the Emperor had established to help with funerals had long since been overwhelmed and the graveyards were full.

They were digging pits outside of the city walls in the open land now, but the rate of death would quickly fill those. Morgana's stomach turned in revulsion. Even now, the air stank with decay. She pulled the shutters closed, unable to look out at the suffering any longer now. The question of what to do lingered in the air. The bakery she worked at had been closed for a week now as grain prices rose and the plague limited the number of people shopping. No one was worrying about rent right now, but eventually she'd have to worry about paying the landlord and finding a new job.

A knock on her door made Morgana jump in surprise. The sound was loud in the quiet building. There was shuffling on the other side of her wall and Morgana hesitated. It was hard to understand why someone would be trying to visit. Checking that her dagger was still secured to her belt, Morgana moved to the door and braced herself for bandits or the awkwardness of a brave neighbor checking on her.

The door opened with a long and loud creak, but it wasn't a looter looking to take advantage of weak residents or one of her neighbors. Standing in front of her, looking exhausted and leaning heavily on a walking stick, was Merlin. His gray curls were a mess and dark bags under his normally sharp eyes made him look decades older. A bag was slung across his body and back, but otherwise he was carrying nothing.

"Merlin?"

His eyes met hers, and there was a rush of familiar images. They'd been apart long enough for their magic, as weak as it was, to rise and form a Connection. It was silly given that she knew him as a fellow mage already, but the sight, sound, and smells of a great forest were enough to pull her out of her shock. This was Merlin, and a rush of relief and fondness hit her hard in her chest. Then the vision faded and she was confronted once again with the bedraggled and exhausted figure.

"Morgana." His voice was weak.

She moved forward, linking an arm under Merlin's left elbow and taking on some of his weight. He sighed in relief and let Morgana lead him into her small home. She kicked the door closed behind her, reminding herself to lock it as soon as she could. What was important was making sure that her partner was alright. What was he even doing here? Had this plague gotten worse in the west? Or had he come because of rumors of the state of the city?

Merlin's body was frail, thinner than she'd ever seen before, and for one horrible moment Morgana feared her partner had the plague. She nearly dragged him to the bed and laid him back on it after wrestling off his bag. Before Merlin could protest, she tossed aside his cloak and pulled up his robe. Merlin chuckled softly, but didn't stop her as she exposed his thighs. They were clean. There were no buboes in sight. She checked his neck next and then his armpits. Merlin drifted in and out of consciousness. There was no sign that he had the plague and Morgana finally allowed herself to relax a little.

"I'm not sick," Merlin said. He sounded terrible. "Just exhausted. Everything is falling apart out there."

"I noticed." Morgana left the bed and went to the door to secure the bolts. To be extra safe, she hefted up the length of wood that she occasionally used to bar the door and slid it into place. "But I think you came to the worst place in the world at the present moment."

"I came to find you," Merlin groaned. "Alexandria is in chaos, but I think things are worse here."

"That doesn't surprise me."

Morgana went to the jar of water she'd drawn earlier that morning and used magic to clean. Given the state of the city and the bodies being dumped, she hadn't trusted the well. Filling a small glass, she listened to Merlin's breathing even out and carried the glass over to him.

The older mage sat up a little and took slow and long sips from the glass. It was a good sign. Then he laid back down and exhaled loudly. His death grip on his staff eased, and Morgana gently took it from him. Propping it up against the wall, she stayed silent and gave him some time to breathe. Reaching out, she brushed a strand of sweaty hair from Merlin's face.

"I'm amazed you found me with the city in such a state. Scrying was never your talent."

A soft chuckle escaped Merlin. "I did have your letters."

That was true enough. They wrote to each other every half a year or so to check in. Morgana hadn't thought that she provided enough details for him to find her with the city in this state, but apparently, it had been enough.

"How did you manage to get here? Please tell me you didn't use a water tunnel?"

"No, I didn't," Merlin promised. "A few short trips on ships and a lot of hiking. It wasn't easy or cheap. Everyone is terrified of leaving their homes."

"Well, I am glad that you made it," Morgana confessed. "I was wondering about you earlier." Merlin smiled in response, and Morgana decided that would not do. "Of course, I didn't expect you to be so foolish as to come across a plague-ridden empire to find me."

"It was just across the sea."

"You're a fool." The words rang with more affection than she'd expected.

He was already looking a bit better now that he was off his feet. The heat and the stress of travel had taken their toll, but Morgana's confidence that he'd be alright was returning. Anger and irritation took its place. How dare that fool worry her!

"Why are you always so difficult?" Morgana muttered. His eyes were dropping closed, and she was certain that he'd fall to sleep soon. "Honestly, Merlin, this is exactly why we parted ways."

"That's what we do," Merlin sighed. His lips curved into a small smile. "We argue too much, separate for a little while, start to miss each other, and come together once more."

She was tempted to argue with the old man, but there was no point. He wasn't wrong. Sometimes, when things were quiet and there was no threat, it was hard to be around him for too long. When it was just her in some new place, it was easier to forget about the past for a little while. But it never lasted.

"I'll be alright," Merlin assured her. "I just need to be off my feet for a bit. I'll be fine. I'm certain that I'm not ill."

"I'm starting to worry that we might not be as safe as we think from this plague," Morgana murmured. She stood and moved back to the window. Nothing had changed outside. "But where will we go? From all the news I've gathered, this plague is all over."

"It is," Merlin answered. His voice was low and sorrowful, and Morgana wondered what horrors he had seen in his frantic dash to Constantinople. "This is worse than anything I've seen before. It was bad in Alexandria, but here... it might be worse here. Maybe there are simply more people to watch die."

Morgana made a sound of agreement. "I'm glad you came here."

"I fled from Alexandria," Merlin scoffed. "Coming to find you was only natural."

They let the silence surround them. Morgana had enjoyed a reasonable life here. It wasn't perfect, but thanks to the efforts of the Empress, it wasn't a terrible place for women. Still, they had no way of knowing how long this would go on, and the daily sight of the suffering was taking its toll. Morgana nodded slowly and moved to the table. Slumping into her seat, she folded her hands on top of the table and tried to ignore the way they were shaking.

"Where do you want to go?" she asked.

"Maybe north. I don't dare board a boat across the Black Sea, but we could follow the road to the west and then swing north towards the Danube."

"Into Goth territory?" Morgana scoffed. "Merlin, reports say that the plague is strong there, too."

"Then maybe Africa. Perhaps it has burned itself out in Egypt. The empire's war with Persia and campaign into Italy make those areas far too dangerous. And I can tell you for certain that the plague is all across the Empire. The Mediterranean is full of plague ships. I barely made it here."

She wanted to ask, but it was unfair to force him to re-live such things so soon. His eyes were dark and haunted. Morgana reached out a hand and covered his, squeezing it gently, suddenly grateful for the small space of her home. The contact was brief and she soon pulled her hand back as Merlin's eyelids drooped. Hopefully, he'd recover quickly.

"I'm fine," Merlin said. "Really, Morgana. I'm fine."

"We'll go north," Morgana said. "Give me a day or two to collect some supplies while you rest."

Merlin made a soft sound of agreement, but it was weak. His breathing was smoothing out as he drifted off. Shaking her head, Morgana watched him for a long time, reassuring herself with the soft rise and fall of his chest. Strange and miraculous as it sounded, Merlin was here. In the middle of a crisis, that was swallowing the entire Empire and beyond.

"Old fool," she whispered. Still, at the end of the world, he was the one she'd want to face it with. Or run from it with.

Standing up, Morgana dismissed the dark thoughts and turned her attention to her shelves. She'd been avoiding going out into the market, so her stock of food was low. Morgana had some water, but they'd need more. A soft sigh escaped her. This was going to be complicated and poorly thought out. But Merlin was here now. Leaving Constantinople would be bitter under the circumstances, but there was nothing for it. She wasn't interested in testing the limits of their immortality.

4

Patience and Preparation

Nicki really missed showers. There were no mirrors here beyond the small one that Bran carried for scrying and Morgana's polished bronze disk, but Nicki knew that her hair was greasy. A tight braid kept it out of her face and out of her sight, but she knew anyway. Her hair had always been a bit picky about her shampoo schedule. The feeling brought back very old memories of the car she'd lived in with her parents so long ago.

Being in another world brought strange things into clarity. It was odd the things Nicki missed and the things she didn't. On some level, she'd expected to become regretful and scared in the event they didn't make it back. That hadn't happened. She still felt fine about her parting from her parents and her choice to walk away from them, despite everything that had happened. There weren't regrets weighing her down or doubts about what they were going to do. She was just curious when they'd get back to work.

Anyway, she was considering digging out the bar of shampoo that she'd packed and hiking down to the water to at least wash out her hair when a dull roar echoed down into the cavern. She paused in her work and looked around the cave nervously. All of their stuff was near the doorway, so there was a little light from the entry and the solar lantern, but she still couldn't see very far. Nicki waited for a moment, but there was no more roaring. Hopefully, it was some Dragon just trying to make a point.

Shaking her head, Nicki finished securing Bran's sleeping bag to the side of his backpack and rolled her shoulders. It was surprisingly difficult to compress the gear back into its original size and shape. Difficult, but not impossible, even without using magic. She grabbed the lantern and turned it off as she headed for the doorway. Once she was outside in the sunlight, she set the lantern off to the side, away from the feet of any Dragon, so that it could recharge.

The sun was warm, and the entire atmosphere of the planet had been shifted. Clear skies that weren't the right color were dotted with small clouds that were also just different enough from what Nicki knew from Earth to be interesting. The red vegetation differed from the normal color of plants at home, and yet the structure was similar enough to be grounding. In many ways, it was exactly what Nicki expected alien planets were like. It just had Dragons.

Bran was sitting on a rock and drawing something in his notebook. Without noticing her, he reached over to a nearby plant and gently pulled one of the long red leaves towards him. He didn't pull it out or break it but left it intact as he studied it. Shaking her head fondly, Nicki moved over to join him and glanced around in search of Aiden.

"Hi, Bran."

"Hi." He didn't look up at her. "I wish I had a microscope. The texture is so similar to that of Earth plants that I really think the cells are structured the same way. I know that's a big leap to take, but it's just so-"

"I'll take your word for it," Nicki cut in. "Not a science nerd like you and Aiden." She leaned over to inspect the small drawing of the plant that Bran had made in the book along with his observations on the texture, color, and smell of the plant. He hadn't made any notes about the taste, which Nicki was grateful for. "Where is the other science nerd anyway?"

"He went with Alex and Morgana on the supply run."

"Ah." Nicki lowered herself to the ground beside Bran's rock and pressed her back against the sun-warmed surface. "Fair enough."

"Everything packed up inside?" Bran asked kindly.

"Yeah, I finished it up." Nicki glared at him. "You could have helped."

"I offered!" Bran took his eyes off of his notebook and released the plant with a pout on his face. "I asked you if you wanted help twice and you just brushed me off!"

"You know better than to assume I'm listening when I'm in the zone."

"Packing puts you in the zone?" Bran was clearly trying not to laugh at her. "Really?"

"I'm bored." Nicki let a long groan escape her and tilted her head back. "So, yes: Apparently packing our backpacks puts me in the zone."

"Well, then it's probably a good thing I didn't take any of the packing away from you as it is."

She would have hit him if it wouldn't be so much work. The sound of wings against air made her look towards the top of the mountain. Another Dragon was landing, this one bright green with hints of red at the tips of the wings. She smiled at the sight. It didn't seem as injured or damaged as some of the others. Hopefully, they wouldn't be called upon to use the Iron Chalice again today.

"What are you thinking?" Bran asked gently.

"About how tired I am of using the Chalice." Nicki turned her head so she could look up at her friend. "Does that make me horrible?"

"No," Bran assured her. "I am too. I'm grateful we've been able to help, but... but there are other things we need to worry about. For what it's worth, I think that's part of what is pushing Morgana and Alex to prep us for leaving."

"For Sídhean."

"Yes."

"Does that scare you?"

"It does," Bran admitted.

"Me too." Nicki paused, letting the apprehension surround them. "I'm worried about Morgana. How is she going to react to being back around the Sídhe, being back in their empire?"

"Hopefully she'll be alright. She'll never let Alex go without her, and Alex is certain that is where we have to go."

"Yeah. Doesn't mean I'm not worried."

"It's not going to be easy on any of us. The Sídhe have always been our greatest foes. Yes, we've had to fight the Demons too, but it all comes back to the Sídhe." Bran's voice was distant, and Nicki knew that he'd been thinking on this. "I've thought about Sídhean a lot; what the Empire looks like, how it's fared over the centuries. I mean, Morgana was last there three thousand years ago."

"That's assuming that time works the same way," Nicki pointed out. "Though, it might."

"Maybe." Bran hummed thoughtfully. "But how might the tunnels impact that? Does time run the same if two worlds are connected, but different if they aren't?"

"Don't," Nicki said firmly. "Do not put scary ideas about when we'll get home into my head."

"Sorry." Bran grimaced, and she reached up to pat his leg. "I didn't think about it like that."

"Let's try to stay positive."

"And not panic."

"Definitely not panic," Nicki agreed.

Nicki felt she should make a reference or a joke, but she just didn't have the energy. Sitting on the ground wasn't comfortable, but the sun was warm on her skin and she was tired. Sleeping on the floor of a cave wasn't helping her temperament. She listened to the scratching of Bran's pencil on the paper of the moleskine journal and almost smiled. It was relaxing in a way. A loud grumbling sound from the top of the mountain made her eyes swing up. No Dragons were taking off and there was no fire in sight, so they were probably just having a heated debate. She giggled at her own joke.

"What?" Bran asked.

"Heated debate," Nicki said. She gestured her hand at the mountaintop. "Dragons. Fire."

"Maybe we should pull up some plants tonight to pad our beds," Bran teased. "You're sounding a little crazy."

"Hopefully this will be our last night here," Nicki sighed. "Or maybe we'll leave this afternoon."

"I hope there's more planning than that." Bran sounded horrified at her suggestion. "We can't plan for a lot, but I'd prefer to try at least."

"We know Alex wants to jump branches," Nicki said. "Not much more to really plan beyond trying to resupply." She cleared her throat and finally shifted so she could look at Bran properly. "So, we're going sideways?"

"We're going to try. I have no idea what the ribbon of connecting energy does when you make a path, so I don't know if it'll work."

"Morgana must think it will, or at least that won't harm us," Nicki pointed out. "Given that she's agreed."

"I suppose so."

"What do you think?"

"I don't know. I wish I knew more about how the Tree of Reality works. There's something around the worlds; it isn't just empty space, but it isn't energy like what connects the worlds." He shrugged, but the tension in his limbs was apparent. "But I understand their concerns about going home and then opening another path out of the Iron Realm. That wouldn't help the defenses stay strong, and with us not there..." Bran trailed off.

"Yeah," Nicki agreed with a soft sigh. "I hear you."

The wind picked up, tugging at some loose wisps of Nicki's hair and making the nearby leafy plants rustle. It was a pleasant sound, and if she ignored the color, she could almost believe they were on Earth. A hint of pollen hit her nose and Nicki curled it to avoid a sneeze. She could only pray to whatever entity seemed to be watching over them and nudging them that no one was allergic to anything on any of these worlds. They did not have any allergy medication, which suddenly felt like a major oversight.

"Hey, that idea of yours to use the Chalice was a good one."

"Thanks," Bran replied. She could hear the unease in his voice. "I was thinking about the Fisher King story."

"You mean the guy with an injury that is healed by the Holy Grail and restores the land?" It was more of a statement than a question. "The guy who has a shockingly similar name to Bran Fisher?"

"That's the one."

"Fair enough." Nicki sighed loudly. "Things like that make me wonder."

"How sentient magic is?"

"If there isn't someone, not just magic, tugging at our strings," Nicki responded. "I mean... maybe it's like the Force with a sense of purpose, but some of this just feels like someone planting a specific story in someone's head so that we can take a clue from it years, even centuries later. It makes me uncomfortable."

Bran said nothing. Nicki didn't expect him to. Visions weren't her thing. She was good at water, some other spells, and was a decent healer, even if the Iron Chalice meant she didn't have to do that much anymore. Bran, on the other hand, had been saved by a vision. If he hadn't pulled on the steering wheel of the car he'd been in after a vision then he might have died. Instead, he'd been injured until the day when his connection to his prior incarnation as another mage named Bran led them to the Iron Chalice and he'd been healed. Just thinking about it made Nicki want to laugh.

"There's nothing we can do about it," Bran said. "At least the Force, be it just magic or an intelligence, seems to be on our side."

"I hope so." Nicki shivered. "Let's hope if it is an intelligence that it can keep watch even in the Sídhe branch. I hate not knowing what to expect. Morgana's knowledge is so out of date. I'm imagining a medieval world, but that was thousands of years ago. Maybe they have spaceships and their own internet by now."

Bran chuckled. "Maybe, but if they'd come that far, I would have hoped that they'd stopped having slaves." He paused. "Given what we know, they either live a lot longer than us or time is different there. The Sídhe nurse Alex killed in the tunnel was known to Morgana, remember?"

"I'd forgotten that." Nicki hummed thoughtfully. "That leans towards the time moves differently or they live a lot longer. That might mean that they change slowly, which isn't good."

"We'll just have to see. Guessing isn't going to do us any good."

"I hate this." Nicki climbed to her feet and started to pace. She had to do something with the pent-up energy. "I hate not knowing. If something is trying to guide us, then why aren't there straightforward stories to help us figure out what to expect?"

"I don't know." Bran sounded far too calm and Nicki gave him a dirty look. "Nicki, we're getting ready to leave, and going sideways might not even work. We may have to backtrack to Earth and delay Alex's plan while we reinforce the Iron Realm. There's simply nothing we can do until Morgana declares us ready to go."

"It had better be soon," Nicki muttered. "No internet and no mission doesn't make for a good combination."

"We have a mission." Bran offered her a small smile. "This is just a pause in how things are working."

"Hey, guys!" Aiden's voice called cheerfully.

Nicki paused her glaring and swung around to look at her best friend. Part of his t-shirt was damp, but he seemed in good spirits. Holding up an armful of canteens, he grinned at Nicki and headed straight for them. Stepping forward, Nicki took two of the canteens from him to ease his load.

"Thanks."

"How did it go?"

"I got some berries for us to check over," Aiden said. Nicki noticed the pack around his waist at his words. "And some roots that looked vaguely like some of the stuff we ate in the Gryphon world. Plus, the water."

"It's a start," Bran said. "No trouble with Dragons?"

"None were down there. Which is good since I think the fact we can only talk to them with Alex around freaks them out a little."

"I'm not sure they get magic," Nicki said. "Not like we do, at least."

"Maybe not." Aiden shrugged and set down the rest of the canteens.

"Where are Morgana and Alex?" Nicki peered the way he'd come. "Didn't you go with them?"

"I did. They've got some more stuff, but a Dragon wanted to talk with them. I came ahead."

"We shouldn't go off alone," Bran said with a small frown.

Nicki and Aiden shared a look but didn't argue with him. He had a point.

"It wasn't far," Aiden said. "Just around the curve of the mountain. They should be along soon." Opening his pouch, he held out a small purplish berry. "What do you think? Looks a bit like a blueberry to me?"

"Any sign of animals eating them?" Nicki asked. She plucked it out of Aiden's hand and examined it. Not that a visual inspection could tell her much.

"No, but there's not much sign of animals yet most places." Aiden's smile faded. "It's going to take a long time for this world to recover. Honestly, I'm really concerned that they might invade the Gryphons no matter what Emrys says."

That was an unpleasant thought, but Nicki could understand his worry. The work the Iron Chalice had already done was astonishing. She hadn't had much faith in Bran's idea, but the results were clear. Nonetheless, sooner or later, the magic had to run out. There had to be a limit to what the Chalice could do. Animals would need time to grow up, breed, and raise offspring. There was plant life to support them now, but Nicki had trouble imagining Dragons as herbivores with their teeth.

Then again, they'd survived this long, so there must still be some large animals out in the world. Hopefully the Dragons would shrink a little in size over the next few generations. It seemed like a bad way to adapt:

becoming larger for fighting, but needing more of the precious food. She wished them luck either way. They were going to need it.

Two more figures appeared, coming around the mountain on a faint trail. It was Morgana and Alex, talking with each other. Thankfully, they both looked calm and Nicki relaxed. Each of them was carrying a bag that appeared loaded up. If even half of what they'd gathered was edible for humans, then maybe, just maybe, they could get this show back on the road. Whichever road it ended up taking.

5

Making a Path

The air was crackling with nervous energy, or maybe Alex's own nervous excitement was only making it feel that way. Beneath her feet, there was a low thrum of this world's magic. It was different enough that she'd never forget she wasn't on Earth, but welcoming in its own way. It was grateful, as if it had been aware of how close it had come to being snuffed out.

Pushing aside the dark thought, Alex fought the urge to speed up her climb of the mountain. She was almost to the top where Emrys waited for them. The others were following behind her on the small path they'd carved in the vegetation. Overhead the sun was beginning to sink towards the horizon, and Alex wondered what time it was at home. What were Avani, Lance, and Jenny doing right now? Was Timothy still at the house or had he gone to visit his family? She hoped that he was still looking after the others. She knew how much of a worrier Jenny could be.

Had there been any problems in Ravenslake so far? Had Robin needed to get involved with anything? It felt strange knowing that she'd entrusted the safety of the Iron Realm to two Old Ones and three magicians, though Jenny and Lance barely qualified yet as magicians. Maybe someday. She was sure that they were practicing and working on it as they could. She just hoped that they were safe. Glancing back, Alex confirmed that the others were still behind her and that she wasn't moving too fast.

They soon reached the top, and Alex's gaze fell on Emrys. The red Dragon was lounging in the sunlight, his front legs folded in front of him. His long neck was stretched out, and she was certain that he was enjoying his freedom from confinement. As usual, there was a small court of Dragons near him. Three young Dragons with small horns and brightly colored scales were pacing near Emrys. The older and more familiar Dragons were absent, and there was an undercurrent of excitement and eagerness that put Alex on edge. They were not familiar to her. She approached slowly, waiting for a signal from Emrys, but he was calm and his focus was on the Dragons. Nothing happened. None of them lunged at Emrys, tore at his throat, or attacked his wings. In fact, they didn't even enter his personal space, only coming up right to the edge.

"What can I do for you?" Emrys asked politely. He made no move to leave or attack the newcomers.

"You are from the Old Times," one of them said. Their voice was nearly reverent. "How do you survive, Elder?"

Emrys was startled at the use of the word Elder, and Alex wondered what the context was. Her pendant was warm against her skin, promising her that it was working. On Earth, Elder could be a title of respect. Judging from Emrys' reaction, she suspected that it might be here as well. The Dragon recovered quickly and cleared his throat.

"Travel to other worlds can result in physiological changes, I fear. In the Iron Realm... I was able to survive for centuries." Alex was grateful that he phrased it that way. "Though I do not recommend the experience." He shook his head. "You need not concern yourselves with it. Where do you come from?"

"We're from the Haligon Meadows," a young green Dragon said. This one eased forward into Emrys' space.

The other Dragons exchanged looks. There was something in their eyes that she couldn't pin down. Their expressions were too alien, and even the flicker of emotions in their eyes were distorted to her senses by the odd pupil shape.

"What was it like in the Old Times?" the greenish Dragon asked.

"Very different." Emrys' body language changed, sorrow weighing down the Dragon's wings and head. "There were many great structures then, carved from stone with fire, and the cavern tunnel network was a sight to behold. Many of us lived underground, though we frequently flew in the skies when we weren't resting."

"What of food?" Another Dragon pressed.

"There was much food " Emrys cast his eyes around the group. "I confess that I do not understand why you are so much larger than I. My growth was likely restricted somewhat in the Iron Realm, but you are all larger than any Dragon I knew in my own time. If food is a point of worry, then I am unsure why bodies would have become even larger."

"I don't know," one of the Dragons answered. "Some say it was the Darkness warping us." They shifted their wings as if to shrug. "There are many who can no longer fly. And the memories of lives past come much more slowly or never at all."

Alex frowned. It was difficult to tell how long the Darkness had been infecting this world, and nothing they'd encountered so far indicated that the Darkness had any properties that altered evolution. She heard Nicki mutter something to Bran and Aiden behind her, but didn't take her focus off the Dragons. Maybe the redhead had thoughts on the matter.

"I am sorry." Emrys shook his head. "It was not a perfect world. I do not wish to give you that delusion. The world was split into Clans who each ruled over a set territory. There were battles from time to time, but in general things were very peaceful."

"And you helped to keep the peace?" this question came from a reddish Dragon that must have been very young compared to the others, given that they were only roughly Emrys' size.

"I did. It was my role. It was in the fulfillment of that duty that I came to be in another world and imprisoned there." Emrys shook his head and caught sight of the mages. "Please excuse me. I must speak with the mages."

"Those are the mages?" a young bluish Dragon asked. It tilted its head. "I've never seen anything like them."

"What odd small creatures," the reddish one agreed.

"Peace, young ones," Emrys said. Amusement and a hint of affection colored his voice. "Please, head below. There is a cavern and other Dragons to speak to. I must speak with the mages. Please give us some space."

The young Dragons exchanged looks that Alex, again, couldn't read. Without any argument, they took off into the sky in a rush of air and slap of wings. Alex watched the small group swing up into the sky and then dive down into the valley below. It was effortless, and she knew that she'd miss the sight. Even the best special effects in movies couldn't capture the grace of a creature born to the air and yet was so large. Their bodies twisted, and the scales seemed to ripple as they cut through the wind.

Emrys didn't stand up. Instead, he relaxed and lowered his head closer to the ground. Alex crossed the distance, only about forty feet, and smiled in greeting. The wind blew through the ruins and ruffled Alex's hair. Now that they were alone, the mountaintop seemed much larger.

"Hello, mages," Emrys greeted warmly. There was an odd note in his voice. It wasn't surprise. He was worried about something. Alex's eyes traced the sky. "The Dragons agreed to give us a little time alone. Those young ones were new arrivals who had not made that agreement. We can speak."

"Ah, thank you." Alex shrugged off her heavy pack with a huff and glared down at it. "I really wish we'd figured out magical storage."

"I tried," Nicki sighed. Her bag thumped on the ground. "I really did, but folding space is complicated and I chickened out. I was worried that there'd be an explosion."

"Dimensional magic isn't something we have a lot of practice with," Aiden said. He put a hand on Nicki's shoulder and smiled. "Even water tunnels are weird... they're more like wormholes, but also not exactly."

"I know," Nicki groaned. "Still, it would have been useful."

"Sorry I brought it up." Alex turned to Morgana. "I think we're ready."

"Do we have everything?" Morgana asked. She was eyeing the pile of bags critically.

All of their gear was packed up in their backpacks, and the small pouches and side bags were filled with the food that they thought was safe for them. Water bottles and canteens were filled, and they were all wearing layers in order to deal with whatever weather they came across. There was nothing more they could do to prepare themselves for this. Alex studied the backpacks herself and double-checked that she had Mjǫllnir and Cathanáil, despite being able to feel their weight on her hips. Her belt wasn't really for holding up her jeans anymore. Now it was a way to store weapons. A quick check confirmed that the Chalice was secure with Bran.

"We've got what we can take," Nicki said. "All of our gear, restocked water, and some more food." She smiled a little too widely. "Let's get this show on the road!"

"Alex, I will not be accompanying you." Emrys' words were hesitant, but his expression was serious. "I do not believe it wise for me to leave this world at this time."

No one moved or spoke. Alex stared at the red Dragon. His gold eyes were sad, but determination shined in them. She would not change his mind, and honestly, Alex wasn't sure that she should. Emrys had been a huge asset to them in navigating the vast distances of the Gryphon world and helping them with the Dragons, but the Sídhe were a whole different branch. There was no way of telling what might happen to the Dragon if he went into another branch after his centuries in the Iron Realm. While part of her was nervous about not having Emrys to help them, she had to admit that taking him could complicate things.

Besides, there was a small voice at the back of her mind that didn't think he should come. Here he was mortal once again and amongst his people. Emrys' long and painful story might finally have a happy ending. His family was gone, but these Dragons needed leadership and advice. Emrys hadn't been a part of the wars and was a neutral third party with knowledge of old Dragon law. He might just be exactly what this poor battered world needed.

"I will miss you," Alex said. Reaching up, she gently laid her hand on Emrys' snout. The Dragon exhaled warm air over her that smelled a little like sulfur but was still comforting. "I know you want to take care of them, but please take care of yourself, too."

"I will. I meant to go with you all the way, Alex. I truly did, but..."

"They need you here." Alex offered the Dragon a soft smile. She did understand, and if she was honest, she was more than a little relieved.

At least one friend of hers would be in a better place than they'd been when they met. "We understand, Emrys." Tears pricked at her eyes, and Alex felt foolish for the overly emotional reaction. "I understand. It's better that life here finds a new normal, that your civilization is rebuilt peacefully." She didn't say anything about avoiding an invasion of the Gryphon world, as Alex knew she didn't need to. "Goodbye, old friend."

"Goodbye, Alexandra and Gofiben"

The sound of her former name called the voice of Gofiben to the forefront of her mind. Her former self said a soft farewell to the Dragon. They hadn't known each other very well; they hadn't spent much time together in the grand scope of things, but there was a bond there. Emrys' Dragon fire had helped form the Iron Chalice. Remembering that made Alex smile. It was appropriate that it had helped to save the Dragon world in the end. There was symmetry and poetry there that the literature student that still dwelled deep in Alex's heart approved of.

Brushing her hand over Emrys' snout, Alex allowed herself a moment to marvel at the sensation of his scales against her skin. The others waited patiently, but she quickly stepped back from the Dragon and gave him one more smile. Turning back to her bag, she hefted it onto her back with Bran's help and secured the front straps. There was a rush of movement as the others grabbed their bags and strapped themselves in for what might be a very long day of walking.

"Thank you, Emrys," Morgana said to the Dragon. "I am grateful that your people have welcomed you."

"Indeed. Thank you, Grand Mage Morgana." The Dragon briefly hesitated. "I hope you find what you are looking for in the Sídhe branch. For the sake of all life in the Tree of Reality."

"Stay safe," Alex said. She licked her lips, but wasn't sure what else to say. Memories rippled across the surface of her mind like waves on a pond after a pebble was tossed in. Gofiben's voice grew louder. "You were a good friend, true and compassionate always. You helped me when Morgana and Merlin- well, you helped end the plague."

"I could not save your life then."

"No, but that's not your fault." Alex touched his snout again. "But... you proved so many times that not all those who came into the Iron Realm wanted to cause harm. You stayed in that cave for centuries just to make sure that you didn't."

Emrys made a soft humming sound, and Alex's throat tightened. This was silly. She shouldn't be this emotional, but this was a parting. They would not be coming back here, even if they were successful in the crossing and in stopping the Darkness.

"Stay safe," she repeated.

Stepping away, Alex blinked rapidly to rid herself of the tears trying to gather. Fear, grief, and doubt swirled in her chest and there was nothing she could say to herself to stop it. Emotions were storming through her, and not all of them belonged to Alex. Bran walked over to Emrys and said a few soft words that made the Dragon nod. It reminded her that while Bran didn't exactly remember his past life, he did possess an awareness of it and knew the connection they'd had back then with Emrys.

Pulling Cathanáil free of the scabbard on her left hip, Alex almost dislodged Mjǫllnir on her right side. It was ridiculous and Alex almost started to giggle. Morgana gave her a sharp look and Alex shook her head as she tried to rein in the mess of feelings plaguing her. A weapon on each hip, a heavy pack on her back, and a magical mission. It was a video game without the benefit of a magical inventory system.

"Alex?" Morgana asked.

"Just give me a moment."

Closing her eyes, Alex pushed her mirth away. It was time to focus. Magic hummed in the air, but it had little strength to lend. This would have to be her with the help of the others. Cathanáil was warm in her grip. Alex swallowed down the nervous thoughts that were trying to take hold. She couldn't worry about failure now. They had to get to the Sídhe branch. They had to find the source of the Darkness and stop it once and for all before it swallowed everything.

"We're here, Alex," Bran's warm voice said. He took her left hand and magic flowed into her flesh. "Whatever you need."

Unable to form the words, Alex swallowed and nodded. More magic flowed. It rippled around her, and the bright outlines of her friends burned against her eyelids. They were lined up beside her, and magic flowed from each into the other and then into her. Adjusting Cathanáil, Alex pulled on the image of Sídhean that haunted her dreams. The Sword trembled. Ozone hit her nose, sharp and strong. Magic built in her chest, curling around her heart before she shoved it all into the Sword, leaving hot pangs radiating through her limbs. She sliced Cathanáil through the air, reaching out with her magic and pouring her will, her need to get to Sídhean into the blade.

Thunder crashed. A gasp shook Alex and her eyes snapped open as a whoop of victory shook the suddenly still air. She could smell nothing but the sharp tang of ozone. Electricity jumped across her fingertips, making Cathanáil's golden hilt glow in her hand. But all that went away as Alex's eyes found the hole she'd cut in the world. It shimmered in the air, two pieces of the world apart with a strange landscape visible between them. Rolling pale green hills and odd silvery trees met Alex's eyes. She had made the path.

Her knees trembled beneath her. Strong hands grabbed her and kept Alex upright as a soft victorious laugh escaped her. Someone pushed a pulse of magic into her body. Alex recognized it as Bran's power a moment later as her magic swallowed it up and Alex turned to smile at him. Soft green eyes met hers and he smiled back, but Alex could see the uncertainty in his eyes. She didn't blame him at all and knew that the same was reflected in her gaze. Still, all they could do was go forward.

6

Walking Together

5 42 C.E. Romanian Black Sea coast

Morgana had to admit that things were better outside of the city. Without the crush of bodies, the plague was spreading slower, though there were signs of it scattered across the farmlands. Fields sat unharvested, and Morgana and Merlin frequently stopped to harvest a bit of the fields they came across. They kept a fraction of what they harvested and left the rest at the doorway of the appropriate farmhouse for the family. Twice they had fled with all the harvest they could carry when the tell-tale stench of rotting flesh reached them out of a house.

Thin dogs wandered some small towns. Morgana couldn't be sure if the place was abandoned or if everyone was simply hiding. She hated all of it. This whole mess brought up bad memories of Gofiben and Badb's plague. Guilt still lingered over his death and Galath's anger. If that Chalice of his was real, this would have been a great time to find it.

They were resting under a tree. Bright green leaves sheltered them from the sunshine and kept them cool. Morgana sighed softly and tossed a berry into her mouth. The sweetness was a welcome distraction. It would be getting colder soon and they were heading north, which would only bring the change on faster.

From their place on the top of the hill she could see the Black Sea in the distance, and wondered how many ships piled with bodies were drifting on the water. It was a dark thought, but Merlin had told her enough about the things he had seen on his way to Constantinople. She'd been foolish to linger so long in the city, but was also grateful that she and Merlin had not missed each other.

"What has you so distracted?" Merlin asked.

Turning her head, Morgana checked on her partner. He was thinner than he had been when he arrived at her home, but his color was better and the faint fear she'd had that he had the plague was gone. His features were relaxed despite the stress of their flight.

"I'm thinking about what happens when we reach the north. We brought little to start a new life with."

"We have a few trinkets to sell." He sounded far too unconcerned about this issue. Morgana didn't demand jewels and silks, but in her opinion, a basic level of comfort was necessary.

"What if that isn't enough?"

"Morgana." Merlin shifted his body so he could look at her. "We have started over before, and we will survive doing so again. If nothing else, we can live together as husband and wife for a time while we establish ourselves. We both have plenty of skills that we can apply. It will be fine."

"The world has changed."

"Not that much." Merlin chuckled softly and leaned his head back against the tree. "People are still people. Society's values and traditions have shifted a little, but not beyond what we can manage. Besides, in some ways, this world is more like the one we grew up in."

"It is not!"

"Trade connects the world."

"Not completely."

Merlin sighed loudly, and she could sense his irritation. She understood what he meant. Trade helped; people moved around a decent amount, but it wasn't the same. It was all focused on the Empire, and trade was limited. In her youth, bronze had been shipped all across Europe. They had possessed trinkets and treasures from as far away as Rome. While the world might be impressed with their Byzantine Empire around the Mediterranean Sea, Morgana had an inkling of how large the world was. She wasn't all that impressed.

It would fall someday. The plague had made that all too clear. But then, that was the way of things. Rome had slipped from the Roman Empire's grasp, and now they were based in the east rather than their ancient home. She'd seen that empire rise and fall. She'd seen peoples and cities fall apart. Morgana did not have Merlin's faith, and while the idea of returning to their home, their true and ancient home, held some appeal, Morgana feared what they might find. What kind of culture, what kind of people awaited them there?

"I hope that if there is an Iron Soul living now, they are safe," Merlin said softly.

Morgana tensed, her mind conjuring images of the swelling and decaying bodies they'd found along their path thus far. She thought of the chaos and hunger in the city due to the fear of leaving the house. She remembered the starving dogs that attacked anything living that came too close and feasted on the rotting flesh of their dead masters. Surely such a thing could not happen to the Iron Soul. Fear churned in her chest, and she worried for a being that she did not even know for certain lived. It was an odd sensation.

"I hope not," Morgana managed. "If there is, I hope they are living a peaceful life far from here."

"I hope so too. They might very well be; after all, there has been no magical threat for some time," Merlin said quickly, likely aware that he had upset her.

"That only makes me worry more." Morgana shivered and looked out at the farms in the valley below them. "Merlin, do you think that this plague might be the result of magic?"

"No." Merlin shook his head. "Disease is a horrible thing, Morgana, but it is part of our world, I fear."

"What if it isn't? What if the root of all disease hails from-"

"Morgana."

Merlin's tone was gentle, and Morgana exhaled sadly, slumping against the tree once again. The wind brushed against her cheeks, and she realized they were wet. Bringing up a hand, she found a few stray tears washing over her skin. A soft shudder shook her body and she swallowed thickly. She knew that Merlin was right and she hated it. Why couldn't the world be peaceful and safe? It would make the battles they faced so much easier if they were truly stamping out the root of all that was bad in the Iron Realm.

She dropped her hand back to the ground and a moment later, Merlin's warm hand covered it. He did not squeeze her hand or say anything. He was just there, and Morgana smiled and closed her eyes. She had missed the old sentimental man. It was fitting that when the world around them was in upheaval, they found one another. Part of her was happy that this time he was the one that had sought her out.

"Why didn't you use a water tunnel to come to Constantinople?"

"There is so much water traffic there," Merlin answered. "I was worried about being seen, and with magic being so low, I honestly wasn't sure if the tunnel would make it the whole way."

"That's fair." Morgana nodded. It was, after all, why they had been traveling on foot. "But perhaps we should try to wake Cyrridven. Maybe she knows of a safe place."

"Maybe," Merlin didn't sound convinced. "But we should keep moving. We've been safe enough thus far."

Morgana scoffed. "We'll be approaching the war zones soon enough. I wouldn't count on us being safe there."

"We needn't go all the way to Italy."

"We will have to go west at some point if the plan is to go home."

"That is true, but I have a thought. If we keep going north, we can return to the Norselands. We haven't spoken with Sif in a long time."

"By design, Merlin."

Her partner laughed loudly, his body shaking with his mirth, and Morgana wondered just what memory he had let himself get lost in. There were many to choose from. Raising an eyebrow, Morgana waited impatiently for him to finish.

"Ah." Merlin rubbed his eyes and grinned. "You never did like her."

"It's not that."

"You never liked her marrying Thor then. He was a good incarnation of the Iron Soul, Morgana. He loved her and she made him happy. What more did you need?"

"I still can't believe that you consented to their match."

"My consent wasn't necessary to Thor. He would have married her anyway. That lad was stubborn. He was never inclined to idolize us as Arto or Gofiben did. He was older than them when we met him."

That was true enough. Morgana's lips quirked a little as a memory of Thor's bellowing laugh echoed in her mind. She did miss that life a little. Not with the desperation that she missed Arto, of course. None of the incarnations would ever replace her brother in her eyes, but Thor's happy nature and core goodness had been pleasant to be around.

"She might not be awake," Morgana reminded Merlin. "She and her family have always been careful about staying awake too long."

"That is true," Merlin agreed. "Still, it's as good a place to go as any. We can check in on the Fae communities there and make sure that everything is peaceful. If we push a little, we can make Tomis tonight."

"I suppose it is time to get a move on."

Morgana sighed again. It was tempting to stay here and let the world keep moving on. It always did. Going north wasn't very tempting to her. The Old Ones of the Norse lands were polite enough, and thanks to Thor, respectful towards mages. She had to give their late student credit for his drive to make peace in the region. But the Dvergrs were long dead, having sealed themselves in the mountain tunnels and died off within a few decades, and the Jötunn that had made such a menace of themselves were also gone. There was little to do in the north, but nothing to do behind them. Without a threat, without their magic rising, there was no clear path for them. Merlin's idea was good enough for now.

Merlin climbed to his feet, leveraging himself up on his walking stick with a huff. One of the metal necklaces around his neck caught the sunlight and glittered merrily. It wasn't a familiar ornament, but then again, there were few things that remained in their possession from their old lives. The brooch that Airril had given her so long ago was wrapped up delicately, and she occasionally pushed a little of her magic into the bronze to keep it strong. It was all she had now. This looked to be an iron piece in the shape of the triskelion and was fairly new.

"Morgana?" Merlin extended a hand to her and smiled. "Shall we?"

There was nothing for it. Morgana took his hand. It was warm and solid. She hadn't noticed how nice that felt before, touching another living person. How long had it been? There were people she jostled in the streets from time to time, but it had truly been too long since she had prolonged physical contact with another human being. She allowed Merlin to help her to her feet and promptly brushed off her skirt with her free hand. Merlin didn't drop her hand, and Morgana felt no need to pull away from the touch as long as he didn't comment on it.

Merlin didn't. Instead, he gave it a soft tug, and they headed back across the field towards the road. Their bags were heavy with their belongings and the fruit they'd harvested in this orchard. A small house was placed by the road, and Merlin led her towards it. Everything was closed up and there was no sound from inside, but also no foul smell. Merlin finally released her hand and they laid some of the baskets near the front of the house with most of the gathered fruit.

Then Merlin knocked on the door and announced that there was fresh food on the doorstep. Merlin was also honest enough to say that they were taking some themselves, as payment for harvesting. Morgana heard movement inside, but no one opened the door. A soft sigh of relief escaped Merlin at the sound, and he stepped away from the house. Snagging Morgana's hand, he squeezed it, and they headed for the road. After walking further away, Morgana looked over her shoulder and smiled at the sight of a woman with a child beside her in the doorway scooping up the first of the baskets.

"That's something," Merlin said. She looked at him and found him smiling. "I hope they'll be alright. I wish..."

"I know," Morgana said. "But we don't have the magic to stop this."

"Still, you'd think that someday it would be easier."

"This is the worst we've ever seen without it being magical," Morgana reminded him. "And... maybe it is a good thing that it doesn't get easier. We need to keep caring."

"Why, Morgana, such a sentimental statement from you!" Merlin was grinning now, and Morgana almost pulled her hand away. "But you are correct, of course," he added.

"We're helping a few by gathering food." Morgana glanced around at the nearby farmland and other houses. Clearing her throat, she gave her magic a small experimental tug. The spark of power was weak, but it was there. Thanks to the Fae and the Old Ones in their world, there was always a little magic being generated. "If we're careful and watch out for each other, I suppose it wouldn't hurt to use a little magic and pull in some more harvests."

"We'd still be risking traveling in the winter."

"It's not like we have to reach a certain destination," Morgana replied. "There's no war to fight and Sif or Odin aren't in the north waiting for us." She shivered and shook her head. "Besides, if I'm honest, I don't think that I really want to spend any of the winter so far north."

"That may be a wise choice." There was hesitation and hope warring in Merlin's voice. Morgana was glad that she'd voiced the option. "I suppose that if we are careful, we can help a little more here and there. Though, we need to be cautious in how much magic we use."

He was saying things she already knew, but Morgana knew it was nervousness and maybe a little guilt. Merlin had to be feeling too helpless in light of this plague. She squeezed his hand, and he coughed lightly before gesturing towards another nearby house and the unharvested grain in the large field next to it. There was also a small orchard built into a hill. Nodding in agreement, she allowed Merlin to guide them towards their next target.

The plague would pass. Morgana knew this to be true. She'd seen so much else pass that she knew even this horrible period would come to an end. The question would be the scale of the death and damage, and what came next? Which governments would survive? Which would crumble under the pressure? The world had changed much in the long years of her life, and this would change it again. There was nothing they could do to stop the tides of change. They kept living through it all. Sooner or later, another threat would rise and she would have dreams that led her to scry and find the latest incarnation of her brother's soul. They would train him, help him against the threat, and say goodbye when the task was done, or worse, they fell in battle. Such was the way of their lives now. Morgana squeezed Merlin's hand, grateful for his warm presence beside her. At least, she did not walk this long path alone.

7

Forest of the Sídhe

Alex crossed through the breech first with Morgana holding tightly to her hand. Darkness swirled around them, and flashes of the Tree of Reality lit up Alex's eyes. There were flickers of light from the dark between the worlds, but it all went by too fast. They were shoved forward, thrown through the void with pressure on their backs. It was a roller coaster, but there was nothing to grab onto: There was no cart to contain them and no track ahead to see.

Her left hand reached towards a glowing sphere that was growing larger and larger with each passing moment. Magic rippled around them, but she could not breathe. Her lungs were burning, and her skin was warming too quickly. Terror and regret blurred. The path had opened, but it was further than she'd thought. Was it too far? Alex slammed her eyes shut, blocking out the glittering lights and the looming blackness that taunted her.

She pushed with her magic, threw everything she had at the tenuous connection tying them to the distant world. Squeezing Morgana's hand, Alex flexed her left fingers as if she could physically pull them forward faster. Their speed increased like they were dropping from the high point on a roller coaster. Now she could only hold on. Magic snapped, and her eyes opened.

Her feet hit solid ground, and she stumbled forward as a vague awareness of the others behind her kept Alex moving. Cold air brushed over her skin, and she was pleased when her lungs expanded without pain. Air was good. Her lungs filled as Alex sucked in oxygen desperately. She'd known on some level that humans could breathe in the Sídhe worlds, but confirmation was good. Alex blinked to clear her eyes. They felt dry and crusty. Morgana had yet to release Alex's hand, so she had to use her left hand to rub at her eyes.

"Sound off," Alex croaked. Her voice was weak, as if she'd been screaming. She was pretty sure that she hadn't, but then again, their passage through had been rough. "Everyone okay?"

"I'm fine," Morgana said.

"Nicki, and I'm fine!" Nicki didn't sound much better than Alex did.

"Bran."

"Aiden."

All five of them had made it. Alex exhaled and released her grip on Morgana's hand. Weakness left her trembling, but she didn't collapse under the weight of her pack. Her mouth was dry, and Alex swallowed a few times as Morgana finally let go of her hand. Turning to the others, Alex chuckled when she found that everyone's hair was a mess, and all of them looked just as out of breath as she was. Her laughter spread to the others as they let go of each other and stretched out. Nicki covered her mouth to smother the laughter trying to escape her. Alex basked in the release of tension, but her eyes soon found the rippling air behind Bran. The path was still open, and she could see the mountain and the great red body of Emrys. They were hazy, as if being viewed at a great distance through a dirty telescope.

Drawing Cathanáil once again, Alex ignored the burning in her chest as she pulled on her magic. In her hand, the hilt began to glow and light glittered along the edge of the blade. Alex raised the sword to the rip and tried to recall what it had felt like to close the tear when they made it to the Gryphon world. A soft humming beneath her feet was reassuring, and Alex was aware of a slight amount of magic transferring into her body. She pulled it up, letting it transform into her magic, and closed her eyes.

The rip was a strange sight to her magical gaze. Along the edge, magic sparked and jumped across what appeared as an empty void. Focusing like this she could no longer see the Dragon world, but was instead aware of magic stretching out into the void. With the sword, she cut the thin connection and watched in fascination as the magic slipped back into this world like a retreating animal. She pushed out the last of the magic coiled in her chest and imagined the two sides of the rip knitting back together. She opened her eyes. The air sparked and small flashes of light left glowing spots in Alex's vision, but the two sides did as she commanded. A sharp scent of ozone made Alex smile in relief as the faint image of the rip faded away.

That sorted, Alex finally took a moment to look around them. The air tasted sweet. There was a sharpness to it that made Alex frown and lick her lips thoughtfully. The sky was a dark violet color, similar to the color of the Sídhe's eyes. It was similar to the sky of the dying world she'd seen in her dreams, but softer and far less stormy. Thick whitish clouds dotted the sky, and a distant, darker patch invoked thoughts of rain. She stayed still, giving herself and the others a moment to take it all in.

The world was very similar to the dead Sídhean world, except that it wasn't a ruin. Alex wondered if this was what connected the worlds in a single branch: Similarities in appearance, and the core fundamentals of their physics. The trees were a pale violet color, with silvery leaves that contrasted to the pale violet sky. Over the tops of the trees, Alex could see high mountains topped with off-white. It was similar to Earth, but the colors were off.

Nearby ferns were shades of violet to deep purple. The thin wisps of grass that covered the clearing were a deeper violet. Apparently the eyes of the Sídhe and the Fae reflected well the coloration of their home branch. Alex thought she heard the steady thrum of running water to her right in the trees, and could see deep purple and red berries dotting some of the thick bushes around them. Everything was bathed in soft, low light, similar to twilight, with a haunting quality that made Alex wish to close her eyes and sleep. It was beautiful; right out of a fairy tale, but of course, that was the problem.

"The Sídhean," Morgana breathed, with both terror and awe coloring her voice. The mage's green eyes were wide, and a slight trembling in her hands gave Alex pause.

"I thought Sídhean was the name of the homeworld," Nicki whispered. Her eyes were darting between Alex and Morgana worriedly.

"It was." Morgana cleared her throat and clutched the straps of her backpack to still her hands. "But the empire was collectively called the Sídhean as well."

"That sounds complicated," Nicki remarked.

"It was a little. For instance, Scáthbás actually ruled from a place called The Crossing. It was where the tunnels I grew up in met the true Sídhe world." Morgana shrugged, but no one was buying her nonchalance. "But again, even that was usually just called Sídhean. I'm afraid that I can't say for certain how many worlds there are to contend with before we can reach the homeworld."

"That's fair." Alex nodded and drew the other's attention. "The good news is that we made it." She tried to smile, but it wasn't exactly good news, because now they were in hostile territory, and they didn't have a Dragon to help them. And she's been aiming for the homeworld, so they weren't where she'd wanted to be. "Let's try to stay out of the way of the locals for now while we recover our magic. Once we're stronger, we can try and scry for the next world."

"IF we regain our magic," Aiden pointed out. He was eying the trees with a mixture of curiosity and worry. "We don't know that for sure."

"We will," Alex said with confidence. "I can see the magic. It's a little different, but it is reacting to us."

"Interesting," Bran said. He was looking at the ground, but Alex was sure he'd have to work to see what she was seeing.

"We must stay together," Morgana said firmly. "Trust me, you do not want to be caught alone by a Síd. And use deadly force to protect yourselves if seen." Her eyes took on a cold and hard appearance like jade.

"Are you okay, Morgana?" Nicki asked, voicing what they were all thinking.

"I will be," Morgana said. Her voice was guarded, but calm. "As I said, we need to stay together and be careful. The Gryphons were very reasonable despite how things turned out, and we were lucky that the Dragons were desperate enough to accept our help." Alex held back a snort. "The Sídhe... they are likely to be far more difficult to deal with."

Guilt flooded Alex. What was she thinking, bringing Morgana here, to one of the worlds held by the Sídhe. This species had done so much harm to Morgana, her family, and her world, and now she was back here. Swallowing, Alex tried to summon up the words to apologize to Morgana, but the older woman caught her eye and shook her head.

"This needs to be done," Morgana said softly. "Do not regret that which is necessary."

Nodding, Alex knew that following the advice wouldn't be so easy.

"Okay," Aiden said calmly. "Noted. But first thing, any advice on what is safe here?"

Morgana's expression shifted, becoming lost and confused as her determination slipped away. With wide eyes, she looked around at the plants and the soothing landscape. Then she shook her head and licked her lips uneasily. Alex tensed at the play of emotions across Morgana's features and felt protectiveness stir in Arto.

"No," Morgana finally said. "I was... I wasn't allowed outside of the tunnels and palace. There were scenes of the outside on the walls." Her voice was too soft.

Alex stepped forward and touched Morgana's shoulder. She would have hugged the woman had they not had their packs on. Morgana didn't even seem to notice. Her eyes were far away as she traced the outline of a nearby tree and turned her face up to look into the sky. Never before had Alex been so tempted to take a peek into someone's mind. But her chest was hot, and her limbs ached from using too much magic. It would be foolish to try more than she needed to.

The forest around them was quiet. There was no sign of animals, which could have been a good thing or a bad thing. Alex stayed close to Morgana and checked the sky once again. She saw no sign of the Darkness, which was both good and bad. It was good because it meant that this world wasn't dangerous in that way, but bad because it meant that they had further to go.

"This isn't a bad place to camp," Aiden suggested. "My magic is exhausted; I sent most of it to Alex."

"Me too," Nicki agreed.

"We need to figure out some basics of this world," Bran added. "Resting now is probably a good idea until we can figure things out."

"No," Morgana said. She came back to herself and shook her head. "Unlike the Dragons and the Gryphons, the Sídhe are aware of magic. Some among them can control it. If any of them are nearby, then they might have detected us."

That was not comforting, and any intention of camping here vanished. Everyone made sure that their packs were secure while Morgana looked cluelessly up into the sky. There was no sign of any cities, not that they would have wanted to go there, and no clear direction for them to go.

"Woods seem thickest this way." Aiden pointed off to the right.

It was as good as anything. Keeping Cathanáil drawn, Alex headed in that direction and heard the others fall in line behind her. A faint, narrow game trail led away from the clearing. It was a clear sign that life still existed in this world, but also meant that they were likely to run into something. The low light made it difficult for her to see in the shadowy trees, but it was their best option. It wasn't as bad as hiking through Wales in the dark during winter.

Someone pulled out a flashlight, Alex didn't turn to see who it was, and used it to illuminate some of the ferns and plants beside the path. Small animals rushed out, including a scaled creature that looked a bit like a squirrel. It all but slithered up a nearby tree. Alex shuddered, the sight of something so alien throwing her instincts into chaos.

A soft laugh filled her mouth, but Alex kept it contained. It would do no good, and if she started laughing, she would never stop. Putting one foot in front of the other, Alex kept moving and swept her eyes around for anything out of order. Despite the different color palette, the feel of the forest was familiar. Life was crammed tightly together and tangling around itself. There was a strange stillness that was only an illusion. A faint wind rustled the silvery leaves, and every so often, Alex heard something else moving through the underbrush.

Then something much larger came rushing through the undergrowth. It stopped on the path ahead of them and sniffed the air. It was a Hound. Alex stopped and braced herself for a fight. The creature looked over at them with bright violet eyes. The low light danced off its silvery fur. Here it was not as translucent as it was on Earth. The creature sniffed at the air, and a low growl escaped it. Alex heard the others moving behind her and knew they were preparing for a fight. But then the Hound moved off and vanished into the undergrowth.

"Stay on your guard," Morgana whispered. "It might try to flank us."

"Or it might be a wild Hound that doesn't want to take on such a large group," Nicki offered.

"Still, Morgana is right," Bran said reasonably. "If there is one wild Hound in the area, there are likely more, and I'd rather not become dog food."

"If it is wild, then hopefully we can find someplace to rest peacefully tonight," Morgana said. Nervousness still rang in her voice, and Alex knew it wouldn't fade anytime soon.

"Come on." Alex started walking again, slower this time as she eyed where the Hound had vanished.

The scenery did nothing for Alex's nerves. No one spoke loud enough for a conversation, but there were occasional soft warnings about roots and rocks. Birds or something similar swooped overhead, vanishing into branches before Alex could get a good look at them. She heard Bran and Aiden say something to each other, but it was brief.

The shadows grew longer as they walked. The sun was sinking and more clouds were rolling in. She had no idea how long they had been in this world. The weight of her pack was becoming painful. Alex was sharply aware of the growing ache in her legs. Exhaling slowly, she kept her breathing under control. They were approaching a ridge. Dark stone with a bluish tint was shimmering in the low light. Thick vines were splayed across the rock and cast shadows in a flat area below.

"Stop under the ridge," Morgana said. "It is getting too dark to keep moving."

"Right." Alex wasn't going to argue.

Approaching the ridge, Alex noted that the rock created a small outcropping with a protected section below. Her lips curled into a relieved smile. She wasn't an expert on camping, but she was pretty sure that it was a promising campsite.

"Excellent," Morgana said. "We'll rest here."

Alex's sweaty body was immediately cooled when she stepped into the shadow of the ridge. She finally slid Cathanáil back into her scabbard and then turned to help Nicki pull off her backpack. More packs were set on the ground with soft thumps, and the sound of grateful groans echoed against the ridge. Alex stretched her arms over her head and rolled her shoulders.

"We should use some branches to build a shelter," Nicki suggested. "That will blend in better than our tents."

"Good idea," Morgana said. She checked them over with a swift glance. "Stay close. We need to be careful."

It was a warning that no one needed, but Alex and the others nodded in agreement. There was nothing to say to that. Holding back a sigh, Alex grabbed Nicki's hand and pulled her towards the nearby trees to gather materials for a shelter. Aiden and Bran pulled out the collapsible bucket and headed out in search of water. With one more glance at Morgana, Alex told herself to set up camp now and worry later. There was nothing more they could do until their magic recovered. Tomorrow morning, the real work would begin.

8

Keeping Watch

Bran couldn't put his finger on what smelled wrong about this world, but it was nagging at him. Something in the air had a texture that made his mind whirl as he tried to figure out what it was. Now, with the others asleep and no one to talk to, he had too much time on his hands to sort through the various sights and smells that had been taunting him all afternoon. The fire was low beside him, barely crackling as the red-hot coals gave off waves of intense heat.

At least fire worked as expected, and the color here was even the familiar brilliant orange, hot yellow, and sharp red. The water they had found had passed Morgana's inspection, and she'd revealed more about her life while a prisoner of the Sídhe than Bran thought she'd ever discussed before. In the past, any mentions of her time in Sídhean had been brief and followed by a sharp look that warned them all not to ask questions. Bran was pretty sure the only reason they even knew at all was because of her close relationship with Alex.

The pair were sound asleep under the small canopy of sticks and downed branches that Nicki and Aiden had constructed. Before the fire had died down, he'd seen them pressed tightly together despite being in their individual sleeping bags. Not that Aiden and Nicki were any better. Those two were doing an impressive impression of a two-person puppy pile. Given that everyone was still in their clothes and had their daggers at hand, it was shocking how quickly they'd gotten comfortable. Cathanáil's hilt was just visible out of the top of Alex's sleeping bag, and Bran couldn't imagine how Alex was comfortable curled up around the leather sheath. Soft snores and the occasional grumble were his only company, and Bran wished that they'd decided on a two-person watch. Then again, he'd talk to them, and that would make extra noise.

It was just as well that he was on watch. Bran doubted that he'd have been able to fall asleep despite the ache in his limbs. They'd used a great deal of magic in the crossing, and here his power was slow to rebuild. He was confident that if he had to, he'd be able to use some magic, but he'd have to be careful and precise. And yet, his mind was too alive, too aware, and too on edge for him to have been able to fall asleep.

Another new world, and one that he felt he knew a great deal about and yet knew nothing. Morgana did not speak of her experience with the Sídhe often, but the forest was very different from her or Alex's description. This was the wilds of the Sídhe Empire, an area that hummed with life. It might be different forms of life, but it wasn't stone walls and slaves. Bran was grateful that the magic had brought them here rather than dropping them in the middle of a city.

Tapping his fingers on his knee, Bran swept his eyes across the area beyond their little camp. There was nothing to see. A twig cracked in the distance, and he tensed. A soft chittering noise followed the sound and then he heard scratching. An animal then. He relaxed and looked down into the smoldering coals. He'd have to risk putting some more wood on the fire soon. They had a pile of loose branches nearby, and Bran could just see the outline of their irregular and sharp shapes. His eyes had adjusted to the dark, and he had the odd sense that it was still brighter here than it ought to be.

Before tucking themselves under the rocky outcropping for the night, the mages had seen some stars appear in the sky. It was another reassuring similarity. All of the worlds were planets in their own universes. Then again, what little they knew about the homeworld of the Old Ones indicated that there might not be stars there. As fascinating as a world with less mass was, Bran wasn't interested in risking going there.

He clicked his tongue before catching himself. Licking his lips, Bran held back a sigh and fought to stay still. If he got the flames going again, he'd have enough light to see by, and he could do some work in his notebook. That would keep him busy, but that wasn't the point of standing watch. Bran reached for the woodpile, telling himself that he needed to feed the fire so it didn't completely go out. The solar lantern was by Morgana, and everyone had flashlights, but with the lower level of light here during the day, keeping everything charged could be an issue. It was better to conserve what they had while they could.

His hand had closed around a broken branch when a snapping sound caught his attention. It was loud, much louder than the small soft sounds he'd been hearing from the trees. Something heavy and large was moving. There was another noise. Pulling his hand back, Bran held his breath and tried to pinpoint the source of the noise. Another crunch came soon on the heels of the earlier sounds.

Staying perfectly still, Bran strained his ears and glanced nervously at the fire. Suddenly, he was very grateful that he'd hesitated to build it back up. The light being cast from it was low, but still fear swirled inside of him that they would see it. Voices echoed down from above. They were at the top of the ridge. Bran looked up, but all he could see was dark stone. With luck, they were truly hidden down here.

The voices washed over him, but he couldn't make them out completely. Bran was unsure if the distance, an echo, or language was the issue. Easing to the side, he moved as slowly and carefully as he could manage towards Alex's sleeping bag. He could barely see her. There was just a dark mass in the low light. His eyes struggled and he second-guessed himself. If he woke her up and she made a noise then-

Bran touched her hand carefully and braced himself. The voices were still too garbled, even with him touching Alex's hand. Did the Iron Pendant need her to be awake for it to work? Did she have to be thinking about them also understanding the language, or were these beings simply too far away?

"Huh?" a groggy voice said.

"Shhh, Alex," Bran whispered. "It's Bran. Something is close. Stay still."

Either Alex had woken up enough that she understood or she was too sleepy still to notice his alarm because she didn't move. Her head remained on the sweatshirt she had balled up as a pillow, and she didn't pull her hand away. Bran lowered his free hand to his waist and touched the hilt of his iron dagger just to reassure himself that he had it. For a moment, there was nothing, and he wondered if he'd only imagined it. But then the sounds of something moving above them through ferns and bushes became clearer.

"Are we close yet?" a high-pitched voice asked. Bran couldn't see the speaker, but he imagined a younger Síd. "There's been no sign of anything unusual."

"We have a ways to go still," another voice answered. This one was a little deeper, but still had that odd musical and otherworldly tone to it.

They were right overhead now. Noise was vibrating through the stone, and a rock hit the ground just beyond the camp with a loud thunk. He flinched at the sound and held his breath. Alex tensed and turned her hand, gripping his fingers, finally assuring him that she was awake. She didn't move. He didn't move. Morgana, however, shifted beside Alex, and Bran prayed that she'd either wake up silently or stay asleep.

"What was that?" a third voice asked with a hint of alarm.

"Just a stone going off the edge," the deeper voice huffed. "Be careful, you fool. If you fall, I will not be helping you!"

"Quiet," the first high-pitched voice hissed. "That surge of magic could have been anything. There could be something in the forest. Stay quiet and alert."

"What do you think it was?" Bran wished he could see the speakers and swallowed as he listened eagerly.

"If we're lucky, a new mage for the prince. He'll reward us well if we find such a prize. Something had to cause that surge. Come on and stay quiet!"

"What's going on?" Nicki's shape was moving, and the sleeping bag shifted around and rustled the leaves that they'd piled up to make a mattress. "Aiden?" She still sounded half asleep, and Bran hoped she'd spoken quietly enough.

"What was that?" the deeper voice asked.

It was too dark for Bran to see Nicki clearly, but he could see her form freeze as she sat up. She'd heard the voices and recognized that they were not those of her fellow mages. No one moved, and Bran swallowed nervously. He could hear the pounding of his heart in his chest and breathed shallowly, desperate not to make too much noise.

"I don't hear anything," a voice overhead said.

"I heard something," the deep-voiced one said again.

"What did you hear?"

"Not sure. Sounded like it came from down below."

"Below? There's nothing down there. It's not worth going down the hill. This path will lead us where we need to go."

"We can get there from down below," the deeper voice snapped. Bran could hear the scowl in its voice. "Might as well check it out."

There was grumbling, but the sounds of movement were sharp and clear. Bran eased his hand off of Alex's and slowly shifted back. He pulled out his dagger and bounced uneasily on the balls of his feet. Bran heard Alex move around in the sleeping bag, and the telltale sound of a zipper being pulled was too loud in the quiet cave.

Branches cracked outside of their camp, and Bran closed his eyes and inhaled slowly. This was happening. He didn't see any way for them to avoid this. When he opened his eyes, he leaned over to the woodpile and grabbed a log to put on the fire. Flames erupted to life with a little spark of magical help and bathed the small camp in light.

"Wake up!" Alex snapped. "Morgana! Aiden!"

The other two lumps that had been silent jolted awake as Alex and Nicki quickly unzipped their bags and sprang up. Both paused only for brief moments to shove their feet into their shoes. Bran rose to his feet as six Sídhe came rushing into view out of the trees. There was no golden armor. These Sídhe were tall, and leather-like wrappings covered their long and curving horns. Dressed in cloth with some pieces of armor protecting their chests and swords, they were not the terrifying and awe-striking figures they'd seen before. There were no horses or Hounds in sight. One of the Síd spoke. The words meant nothing to Bran, but Alex tensed and took a tentative step forward.

"We are here to help," she said. Cathanáil hung from her hip and Alex held her hands up where the Sídhe could see. "We don't want any trouble."

Bran didn't like the way that the Sídhe patrol or bandit party or whatever they were was eyeing them. Another Síd, this one dressed in armor that looked a bit like leather with a bow on their back, said something to one of the others. Violet eyes sparkled with excitement as another leaned closer to the Síd at the front of the group. The tone had shifted to something that made a chill roll down Bran's spine. His fingers itched to grab his dagger from its holster on his side.

"Yes..." Alex replied to something that a Síd snapped. Her hesitancy and worry were clear, and Bran wanted to know what was said. "But-"

It was Morgana who moved first. With a cry, she pulled her dagger and shoved a hand forward. A thin silver whip appeared and struck the Síd closest to her. The whip lacked the usual brilliance, but it was there. That was the only signal either side needed, and the gap quickly closed with the Síd and the mages lunging forward. There was a slick metallic sound, and light flashed off of Cathanáil. A light orb appeared overhead, dimmer than usual, but enough to help them see in the fire's glow. If the Sídhe were surprised by the show of magic, they didn't show it, and weapons were raised.

A sword came too close to Bran, being slashed wildly through the air. Another Síd was closing in with two long and wicked daggers out. Pushing his magic forward, Bran followed the wave of energy as it knocked the Sídhe backward. They didn't fall. His power wasn't strong enough for that, but it staggered them, and both blinked in surprise. Bringing up his dagger, Bran ignored the sick feeling already taking hold and drove the iron blade into the neck of the closest Sídhe. Its mouth opened and it gasped, pale blood spilling out around his dagger and from the creature's mouth.

It didn't vanish. It didn't turn to dust. Instead, one hand grasped at his clothing and wide violet eyes filled with surprise met his. Bran was frozen in place. Something moved beside him, and there was a shout. Still, he didn't look away from those eyes. A blur of red and Nicki's voice kept the panic at bay. Then the Síd released his arm and fell to the ground. It was unmoving, the corpse staying there amongst the fallen leaves and broken branches.

Taking a shaky breath, Bran looked to the others. Nicki was standing over the second Síd, her dagger grasped in her hand and staring down at it. Bran wondered if she was as stunned as he was that they were still there. Her hands were shaking, and he stepped forward. Finally, his mind started to work again, and he realized it wasn't strange that the bodies would remain. This was their world, or at least very close to their world. They were part of it. Bran and his fellow mages were the beings that didn't belong here.

A fearful cry pulled him free. Bran's head snapped up, and he found a Síd standing over Aiden. His fellow mage's hands were surrounded by red sparks, but a sword was already being raised. Nicki howled and crashed against the Síd, knocking it to the ground. Aiden rolled over and grabbed a dagger from the forest floor. Another Síd was stalking towards them, and Bran's feet moved before his mind caught up. As the Síd raised its blade, Bran found a point in its back where there was no protective covering.

The dagger slid in roughly, scraping a bone as it tore through tissue. Flinching at the creature's pained shout, he pulled out the dagger and stumbled back. Aiden opened his palm, and a small bolt of red magic struck the Síd in the front. It crumbled to the ground, trembling and clutching at its back. Bran was at a loss. Nicki and Aiden were back on their feet and staring at the being. They looked just as lost as he felt.

Morgana strode over, her dagger out and gleaming with the silvery blood of the Sídhe. She said nothing and dropped beside the Síd. With one quick movement, Morgana thrust her blade into the neck of the Síd. It gurgled for a short while and stared up at Morgana. Her calm never faded, and Bran had to look away. He checked the trees, but all the Sídhe had been dealt with. The Síd stopped moving, and Morgana cleaned her dagger on its tunic before rising to her feet.

Six bodies were on the ground. Guilt and pity rushed through Bran, but in the end, relief that none of them were his friends won out. Morgana was kneeling beside one and searching through its bag as if this were an everyday occasion. Alex was holding Cathanáil with an odd expression on her face. Not anger or sadness, but resignation. The light orb dimmed in the air above them, and Alex turned to walk back to their camp. Bran and the others followed her. They could finish dealing with this in the morning. There was nothing they could do now.

9

Another New Life

8 00 C.E. Lyon, Burgundy

The news of the so-called New Roman Empire had put the entire city into a right state. Rumors and celebrations marked the event, though Morgana doubted most people properly understood the political ramifications. It was something that sounded exciting, even if it would not change life in the city at all. Lyon had been under the control of the Frankish rulers for centuries, ever since the assassination of King Godomar and the Kingdom of the Burgundians had been taken over.

Morgana hadn't been in the area then. She and Merlin never stayed anywhere that long, but when you were literate, you could usually learn the history that you needed. But that only convinced her that the excitement about the news was more about having an excuse to celebrate. It wasn't every day that the Pope crowned a ruler Emperor.

Still, as someone who had lived in the Roman Empire, Morgana thought they had a way to go. Improving the roads and plumbing to the Roman standard would be a good start. The dirt roads and use of chamber pots or pits would be far below the standards of the Romans. She might have been born into a world without plumbing, but she had decided centuries ago that it really should be standard.

Morgana sighed and glanced around. Their small home on a side street of the busy city gave them little privacy. The only windows faced the front as their walls were tight against the neighboring building. Merlin's small shop filled the lower level, and was stocked with cloth goods and trinkets from all across the region. There was nothing incredible in the shop, but it provided them with a decent living.

She finished sweeping the front step and waved to a neighbor who headed into the nearby butcher shop. Her nose curled at the smell, and she regretted the day that those businessmen had moved into the neighborhood. Stepping back into the shop, Morgana closed the door firmly and headed for the counter.

It was a small shop, but they kept it clean. However, keeping it clean had been easier a month ago. Merlin was behind the counter with his ledger open in front of him. He was humming as he worked, and Morgana placed the broom in the corner. Her eyes traced over the shelves that held less valuable items like rope, whetstones, and simple craft pieces. Bottles of wines and jars of perfume were stored behind Merlin. Centuries later and she was still collecting the same goods as her people so long ago. She vividly recalled the shelves in roundhouses that displayed the precious items of a family.

"Any sign of Charles and Rudolf?" Merlin asked without looking up.

"Not yet, but I'm sure they'll be by." Morgana joined him at the counter and tapped her fingers against the worn wood. "I'm not sure about those two yet."

"They're young. And they have kept the secret." Merlin closed the ledger and leaned forward to rest his chin on his hand. "We can't really ask for more than that. There is time to train them out of their bad habits and deal with their religious upbringing."

Holding back a scoff, Morgana didn't voice her thoughts there. "It's not as bad here," she said. "Things were worse back in Constantinople. The schism in the early church was awful to deal with."

Merlin hummed, but said nothing as he pushed away from the counter and turned to the back shelves. He took down a bottle of wine and poured two glasses before setting the drinks on a small table tucked into the gap between two shelves. Two small chairs stood beside the table and Merlin sank into one. Morgana cast one more look at the door before taking her seat. The shop was empty, and she expected it to remain that way.

"Any more news on Nerthus?" Morgana asked, now confident that they were alone.

"Nothing significant." Merlin shuddered and took a drink of his wine. "At least not after last time."

Morgana pressed her lips together tightly. She'd rather not think about the last time Nerthus had made her presence known. Merlin hummed in agreement with her thoughts, and for a moment, neither of them spoke.

"We should move," Morgana said suddenly. "Lyon was a fine place to live before we found Charles and Rudolf, but the situation now makes me worry about the wrong person seeing something."

"I'd hate to leave a hub of news," Merlin said slowly. Nonetheless, Morgana could see that he was seriously considering the idea. "But I think you're right. Training young mages is much easier away from others. Especially given how potentially dangerous using magic is now." He shook his head sadly. "Why couldn't Christianity have stayed a cult? Of all the small religions to survive, why did it have to be that one?"

A chuckle escaped Morgana. "Well, at least the majority of our neighbors no longer worship Old Ones. And besides, it has hardly survived in its original form." She shook her head and smiled fondly. "I remember poor Emperor Justinian desperately trying to get the church unified. Even his marriage to Theodora couldn't manage it." Then she waved her hand and dismissed the ghosts of the past. "But that's not the point. We can hardly explain ourselves if we're seen in Lyon. A farmhouse outside of the city or maybe a cabin in the woods would serve us better for now. We can come into the city from time to time to get the news. We don't need rumors to track Nerthus."

"I know you have a point," Merlin sighed. "Still, I rather like the shop."

"I'm certain that you'll have another someday. If we sell everything off and end the lease, we can get a small plot of land outside the city. There's more than enough magic now for us to care for ourselves."

"It might be difficult to buy land." Merlin wrinkled his nose. "The landowners aren't likely to part with it."

"I'm sure they can be convinced." Morgana gave her partner a knowing look. When he sighed, Morgana softened her expression. "I know you don't like it, Merlin, I do, but a small nudge to the mind can be very useful."

"I know you're right." Merlin looked towards the window and watched a man and woman walk past. "I miss the wilds. The old forests and small communities. I miss being away from people. Even moving outside of the city won't get us very far from other humans."

"It won't, but it could help." Morgana reached across the gap between them and touched his hand. "It'll be alright, Merlin."

"You like cities."

"I enjoy the perks of living in a city." Morgana shrugged, refusing to feel ashamed of it. "And you can't deny that plumbing and bathing are wonderful. I hate the lack of hygiene in this city."

"It's not that bad."

"Yes, it is. But that is not the point. Yes, I like cities, but I'm happy to leave Lyon under the current circumstances." Withdrawing her hand, Morgana weighed her next words. "And once Nerthus is dealt with, and we are confident that Charles and Rudolf can handle themselves, we can discuss what happens then. We've been together since the plague, but it wouldn't be the first time we separated."

"You would leave the Iron Soul?" Merlin sounded truly surprised.

Morgana raised an eyebrow. "Of course not. The Iron Soul will remain with me."

"Whichever one it is." Merlin was smiling now, amusement shining in his eyes. "Or will you keep them both with you?"

Pinning him with a look, Morgana picked up her glass of wine and took a long sip. Merlin's amusement only grew, and her irritation flourished. Still, she didn't snap at him. That would only amuse the old man further.

"We will figure it out." She shook her head and glanced at the doorway. The shop was still empty. "To be blunt, I'm leaning towards Charles. His presence is a great deal like Arto's and Thor's. He is bold and charismatic."

"But we don't know for sure." Merlin shook his head and became more serious. "What do you think the signs are? In the past, it seems that we knew or were able to be certain because there were no other mages around. I was fairly certain that Gofiben was the Iron Soul, despite Bran being there." Morgana suppressed a grimace at the names of their tragic students. "But this time, I'm truly not sure. The color of their magic is often different, and the personality can vary."

"I'm not sure either," Morgana admitted. "It's a feeling, I suppose. But Arto- the Iron Soul is usually a leader. They are brave, bold, loyal, and clever. Those personality traits seem to always manifest. They always seem to be strong."

Merlin hummed thoughtfully, but he didn't agree out loud. Watching him, Morgana couldn't tell what he was thinking. The Iron Soul had to be Charles. He seemed the most... well, like the Iron Soul. His presence inspired something in her: familiarity and protectiveness.

"You aren't completely wrong," Merlin said slowly. "I am also leaning toward Charles. It was only a stray thought."

"Fair enough." Morgana doubted it was that simple, but it didn't matter. They had two mages under their care to worry about. "Besides, if we teach them to smith, then the truth will surely come out."

"Ah, yes, a forge will need to be built if that is our plan." Merlin smiled fondly. "It's been too long since I worked with iron." Flexing his hands, Merlin studied them intently. "Thankfully, it is not something that you lose."

"Though iron won't be much help against Nerthus." Morgana shook her head. "There are so many strange stories about her an iron. Supposedly she locked away iron weapons. That story of her having iron locked away was to ensure that fighting didn't break out."

"And people didn't try to work in the fields while she was present."

"That too." Morgana rolled her eyes. "Perhaps that need to be the center of attention should have been a warning to us."

"All the Old Ones can become corrupted if they aren't careful." Merlin shook his head sadly. "It is a pity that Shiva is not awake. The Trishula would have been a great tool to use."

"Shiva was fighting against his corruption." Morgana did not share Merlin's compassion for Nerthus. "Lokpal made the choice to save him, and yes, it ended up working out for the best, but you know we can't expect Old Ones to always make their way back. Especially those who do not take care to purify themselves."

"You've never forgiven Shiva for being trusted with the Trishula."

"That has nothing to do with-"

The door of the shop was flung open and hit the wall with a crash. Pulling on her magic, Morgana sprang to her feet and kept her hand hidden behind the counter, but at the ready. Merlin was right beside her, but they both quickly relaxed.

Two boisterous boys came stumbling into the shop, their faces bright with excitement. Straw was clinging to Charles' tunic and pants and sticking out of his wild brown hair. His brown eyes were full of humor. Morgana's heart ached a little. There was some resemblance to Arto, enough at least that the sight of Charles was bittersweet.

Rudolf was the calmer of the two. He was smiling at Charles and suffering the slightly taller boy having an arm around his shoulder. Rudolf's dark complexion did little to hide his flush when Morgana cleared her throat and raised an eyebrow. His clothing was of higher quality as befitting a merchant's son, and she knew that they'd have trouble convincing the boy's mother to part with him.

"What trouble have you two been up to?" Merlin asked. He leaned on the counter and smiled.

"I was showing Rudolf how to brush a horse." Charles' smile widened so much that Morgana feared he'd hurt himself. "He found it frightening." Nudging his friend with his shoulder, Charles offered Rudolf a soft smile that promised he was only teasing. "But he did well once he relaxed a bit."

"Haven't you been around horses before, Rudolf?" Merlin asked with a soft smile.

"Only when they are pulling carts," Rudolf answered. "I've never ridden before or brushed one. They are… larger up close than I thought."

Charles burst into laughter. The sound filled the small shop, and Morgana found herself smiling at the brightness of it. Rudolf flushed again, but he was smiling a little.

"I'll teach you to ride," Charles promised.

"That's not necessary," Rudolf was quick to say.

"It could be a good skill to know," Merlin said gently. "Honestly, I am surprised that you haven't learned." He held up a hand before Rudolf could argue. "Though I understand that you usually ride in carriages or carts, in an emergency being able to saddle a horse properly can be vital."

Rudolf now looked thoughtful. It couldn't last long beside the force of nature that was Charles. The other young mage was rolling back and forth on his feet with barely contained excitement. Morgana braced herself for what was coming next.

"What do you think about the news?" Charles asked, eagerness in his voice. "About the Emperor?"

"Could be good," Morgana said gently. She hesitated to dim the boy's excitement. "Could be bad."

"Why could it be bad?" A pout appeared on Charles' face, and Morgana inwardly sighed.

"An empire can be a great thing, Charles, but it does not promise success. The newly conquered lands may revolt and start new wars, not to mention succession issues."

"Succession?" Charles repeated.

"Who gets to be Emperor next," Rudolf explained. He cheered up at being able to provide information. "But why would that matter?"

"The law of the land says that property must be divided up," Morgana explained. "So, this empire may be split up into smaller kingdoms depending on how many of the emperor's sons and grandsons survive."

"Morgana dislikes Salic law," Merlin chimed in. "Don't worry about succession just yet, boys."

"Why don't you like Salic law?" Rudolf asked with the innocent curiosity that only a boy could possess.

"Where I was born, women could inherit," Morgana explained. "Salic law only allows men to inherit land."

"Oh come now, Morgana," Merlin chuckled. "That's not completely true. Adjustments were made well over a century ago for daughters to inherit if there were no sons." Morgana glared at him, but Merlin did not quake. "I'll admit that it's not a perfect system, but let's be honest. Even your marriage was, in part, based on building an alliance and putting a male in charge. Our homeland was not perfect."

"How old are you?" Charles asked, looking at the pair of them. "You know so much!"

"We are quite old," Merlin said kindly. "But that's not why you came here today, is it, lads?"

"No." Charles shook his head and brought up his hands. "I still can't make any magic work, and I've been practicing-" the boy cut himself off and grimaced. "I mean."

"You are not to use your magic outside of this shop," Merlin said firmly. He hurried around the counter to approach the young pair. "Or even attempt it." He leveled his gaze upon them. "There is too much danger in people seeing you and not understanding the importance of what we do." The two boys looked nervously at each other. "The role of a mage is to serve this world and keep it safe from danger. I know that you have many questions, and Morgana and I will answer them as you grow stronger and gain control." Then Merlin reached out and placed a hand on both of their heads to reassure them he wasn't angry. "Come, let's go into the cellar. You both need practice, and there is something that Morgana and I need to speak with you about."

They nodded and rushed towards the trapdoor that led into the cellar. Rudolf stayed back to avoid Charles' wild arms as he started fighting to open the heavy door. Chuckling, Merlin turned to Morgana with a twinkle of amusement in his eyes.

"Besides, my dear Morgana, it isn't Salic law that has led to the family giving their sons minor kingdoms. There is no requirement for that. It is more of a tradition at this point. We can hope that the new emperor will look at the fate of the Merovingian kings and realize how bad an idea it is."

Having had the last word, Merlin swept to the now open trap door and followed the boys down. Glaring at his back, Morgana couldn't help the flicker of pleasure rising in her chest. He wasn't technically wrong, but the distinction was unnecessary. Charles' eager voice and Rudolf's soft, but just as interested, voice were audible from down below. Morgana took one last drink of her wine before barring the doors and windows to ensure their privacy. Then she climbed down the ladder to join the others in the cellar for magic practice.

10

Through the Woods

The solid rhythmic thumping of feet against the ground and the soft rustling of the wind through the leaves of nearby plants was soothing. Alex's mind wandered as she breathed in the sweet-tasting air. There were moments that she almost forgot where they were. The different coloration was already becoming familiar, even if it wasn't that of her homeworld, and the slow hum of magic wasn't too different from that of the Iron Realm.

But it was different enough that Alex had to remind herself that it wasn't a threat, over and over again. Rather than leaving a charge humming in her chest, it was a cool trickle of water. Refreshing, but not overpowering. She could use it, and again had that strange nagging thought that somehow this realm knew she was here to help.

Pushing aside those thoughts as they led to questions with no answers, Alex glanced around. The forest was quiet. They hadn't run into any more search parties, and she was starting to hope that they had put enough distance between them and where they entered to be safe.

"Let's stop up ahead," Morgana said. "Rest and discuss our next steps."

No one argued. Exhaustion hung over all of them, and a dull ache was trying to take hold of Alex's head from the lack of sleep. She noted a flatter area up ahead with a couple of fallen trees that could serve as seats. Speeding up, Alex headed straight for it and checked the area quickly. There was no sign of large animals or Sídhe scouts.

"Finally," Nicki groaned. "She does possess mercy!"

The dramatic cry sent chuckles through the group, and Alex managed to turn quick enough to catch a fond smile on Morgana's face. The sight of Morgana's smile, even such a small one, was a boon that Alex treasured. She glanced at Nicki and the redhead offered her a cheeky wink.

When they reached the small area, Alex checked again for anything unusual. There was a ring of rocks in the middle of the flat area, but it was overgrown and assured Alex that while there had been a camp for someone in the past, they hadn't used it in a long time. Thick and tall trees provided some shelter from the wind, but it was more exposed than what she'd considered good for staying overnight. Then again, the other campers most likely had been Sídhe, and hadn't needed to worry about being caught.

Packs were lowered to the ground with the care of people who knew that their lifeblood was contained within. Alex rolled her shoulders and stretched. Backpacking had never been her hobby, and while she'd thought she was in decent shape from jogging, she was having to walk with an adjusted center of gravity for hours on end.

"I'm exhausted," Aiden said. He slumped to the ground and leaned against the fallen tree beside Nicki, who was sitting on it. She patted his head from her perch above him and nodded in agreement.

"I understand Lance worrying about our endurance," Nicki agreed. She stretched out her legs and wiggled the toes of her boots. "I miss Emrys."

"Yeah, riding a Dragon was cool." Aiden grinned for a moment before relaxing his smile. "I hope he's doing well there."

There was a heavy moment in the camp as everyone considered their friend. Alex missed him, but memories of his pain over being unable to return home stirred in her mind. He'd been shocked and horrified to find himself on Earth, but unwilling to cause harm. Of all the beings that had ever come through to the Iron Realm, Emrys had lost the most, and yet always remained kind and helpful.

"He was happy," Alex said. She sat down on one of the logs, feeling grateful for whoever had dragged them over. "I remember... he was so sad that he couldn't return home. As bittersweet as returning to such a changed world had to be, I know it was a relief to him. He could breathe the correct air; he could fly freely in the sky once again and be the leader that he was meant to be."

"Well, it is good to know that the Dragon world is in good hands," Morgana said carefully. "Their respect for him was impressive."

"But not surprising," Nicki chimed in. "I mean, he's the only one with real knowledge of how to run an organization at this point. He knew the laws, and the lost culture. To a struggling and scattered civilization, that kind of stability probably looks really good."

"I still miss the transport service," Aiden whined, adding some levity to the situation.

"It's for the best," Morgana said firmly. "I would have hesitated to fly in the Sídhe realm." She shook her head. "Too much here, outside of the tunnels, is unfamiliar to me. I'm not comfortable drawing attention to ourselves."

Dark circles underlined Morgana's eyes, making her appear much older than usual. Every movement she made screamed exhaustion and soreness. Frowning, Alex watched the older mage take a long drink of water from her water bottle and debated how to discuss when they should stop for the night.

"It's been a quiet day," Nicki said. "No sign of any Sídhe out here."

"I hope we aren't going the wrong way," Bran said. Then he paused and tilted his head. "Then again, we don't know the right way."

Alex saw her opportunity. "We've put some distance between us and where they were searching last night. We should scout out this area and see if we can find a decent campsite. After last night, we didn't get much rest, and we still want to scry. As it is, we don't know which way we have to go."

"I'm not sure that there is a breach here." Aiden tilted his head back and looked up at the sky. "I know that it's another world, and the color is different, but things seem... calmer here, I suppose, when compared to even the Gryphon world."

"There may not be, not yet at least," Morgana said. Her tone was tight, but she didn't elaborate.

"Then I suggest we find a good spot to camp and settle in to rest up," Alex offered. "We're recovering our magic, slowly, but surely. The best thing we can do is try to scry. Hopefully, there is enough distance between us and where we came through that we can avoid any investigation."

"Hopefully," Bran agreed. A deep frown that furrowed his brow had taken over his face. "But it's still a point of concern that anyone detected it or was looking for it."

"Maybe not," Nicki said slowly. "I mean, the Sídhe have been jumping worlds for years. Would it be so shocking if they had systems in place to watch for another species doing the same?"

Everyone stopped, and Alex risked a glance at Morgana. She looked just as stunned as them, but nodded slowly.

"That is a good theory," Morgana replied carefully. "One that I had not considered. But the Sídhe would know that the only world connected to this one is the Iron Realm."

"Or the next world on the branch," Bran pointed out. "We know that there are princes, or at least there were a few years ago when Alex was taken, but we don't know what the political situation is right now. The Empire might not be united anymore: The next world could have a rival government or have people that they abandoned who are now facing the Darkness." He shrugged and gestured vaguely towards Morgana. "Or they may assume that humanity knows about them, thanks to you and Merlin, and may figure it is only a matter of time before we attack them."

"Their Riders made it back last time they came out," Nicki added. "At least for a little while. They could have reported on things like cars. Given they are still using Hounds and their version of horses, then it might not be crazy to think that our technology might have worried someone."

Morgana was overwhelmed. Her eyes were wide and shining with shock. Gesturing for the others to be quiet, Alex cleared her throat and opened her mouth. No words came out, and Nicki gave her a look. She couldn't imagine what Morgana was feeling. Merlin was gone, she was back in the realm of those who had enslaved and manipulated her as a child and now lacked the knowledge she needed despite all those years here. Alex didn't know what she was supposed to say to that but was certain that she should say something.

Still, at a loss, she stood up and moved around behind Morgana, putting a hand on her shoulder. The older mage jumped a little at the contact but quickly relaxed. Alex felt and heard Morgana take a deep breath, and the muscles beneath her hand shifted.

"You are all very correct," Morgana managed. "There are many things happening here that we lack solid information about. I think Alex is right. We need to find a good place to set up camp, maybe for a few days, and see what scrying can tell us."

"We have to start walking again, don't we?" Aiden asked sadly. He gestured to the old fire pit. "Can't we just stay here?" Morgana looked pointedly at the trees around them. "No, I guess not."

"There seems to be another ridge not far that way," Nicki offered, pointing towards where the sun was moving. "Whatever direction that is. I'm going to say west based on the sun for the sake of my sanity. We'd have some wind coverage and, hopefully, be able to hide a bit better."

They shouldered their packs and headed down a faint game trail that led in the proper direction. Alex kept looking around, trying to spot the animals that might have made such a trail. There weren't any fresh tracks, and it was wider than the trails one usually saw made by deer in Oregon. The ridge was becoming larger quickly, and Alex crossed her fingers for a moment, wishing with all her might that they could find a good campsite. They needed someplace safe to rest and scry. It was critical.

Noise in the distance made Alex look to her right sharply in alarm. Everyone's talking stopped instantly, and she glanced at Morgana. The mage's eyes were searching the forest cautiously. She could hear it more clearly now: Something large was moving through the trees.

"Packs off," Morgana whispered. "Daggers out."

There was barely time to tear off her bag and lean it against a tree before the thing came close enough to see. The creature was taller than all of them, walking on its back legs and slightly hunched forward. Alex was frozen on the spot, taking in the animal as it moved between the trees. It had dark matted fur a bit like a bison's all over its body. At the bottom of its hind legs were massive hoofs that crunched the undergrowth as it walked. Four large arms pushed branches out of the way with hands that were much like a primate's. It grasped the side of a tree, and Alex caught sight of a thumb before it pushed the trunk and made the whole tree shift. The head was long and sloped with a snout and forward-facing eyes. There was nothing in her mind to compare it to. Then it stopped and sniffed the air.

On earth, forward-facing eyes were the mark of a predator, Alex's mind unhelpfully provided. It turned towards them, nostrils flaring at the end of the long snout. The mouth opened, and the sharp-pointed teeth was all the confirmation of predator that Alex needed.

It was fast. A roar shook the air, a strange sound that rattled her bones. Instinct screamed to flee, but she'd never outrun it. A tree was knocked to the side by the creature's mass. It lowered its head and charged at them, nostrils flaring at their scents. Throwing her hand forward, Alex released a bolt of lightning, her mind easily providing the command to her magic. The stench of burnt fur hit her nose, but the thing didn't stop.

Leaping out of the way, Alex hit a tree with her arm and hissed in pain, but was able to keep moving. Magic flashed around them as everyone attacked. She turned back and pulled Cathanáil free, letting her magic flow into the blade. A stream of fire hit the creature in the chest. Flames licked all across its body as the thick fur caught fire. It screamed, the sound shaking the forest, and Aiden stumbled back, but kept his hand extended.

"Aiden!" Nicki shouted.

The creature flailed, one massive hand lashing forward and striking Aiden before he could retreat. He was flung to the side and hit a tree headfirst with a loud crack. Alex's heart stopped. Nicki screamed. Lightning arced over the metal of Cathanáil, but before she could attack, the creature collapsed to the ground. Pained whimpers and growls escaped it before fading off. Morgana stepped forward and with a swirl of silver magic doused the flames that were spreading to the plants and nearby trees while Nicki bolted for Aiden.

"Is everyone alright?" Morgana demanded. She was eying the creature with horror and fear. "It seems to be dead." Turning toward Nicki and Aiden, Morgana visibly swallowed. "Nicki, how is Aiden?"

Aiden answered her with a loud groan. A dizzying wave of relief hit Alex, and she grasped a tree with her left hand to steady herself. Nicki helped Aiden to his feet. He swayed, but didn't collapse. Lifting a hand to his head, he ignored Nicki when she tried to stop him. He lowered his hand and stared at the blood without showing either shock or horror. Aiden didn't say a thing and turned to look at the creature.

"Yikes."

"You used too much magic," Nicki scolded. She slung Aiden's arm over her shoulder and started dragging him to a fallen tree. "What were you thinking?"

"I wasn't," Aiden replied. His words were slightly slurred with exhaustion and likely a concussion, but he was at least moving in part on his own power. "It was huge and scary, and we've never fought anything like that before."

The words made everyone pause, even Nicki, and Alex almost laughed when she realized the truth of it. Aiden slumped onto the trunk of the nearest fallen tree, and Nicki knelt in front of him and proceeded to check his eyes. Bran hurried around behind Aiden and helped pull off the heavy pack Aiden hadn't managed to get off before.

"I mean, the Sídhe and Demons were mostly human-sized," Aiden continued. "The Hounds weren't bigger than us. We never had to fight a Dragon, which honestly disappoints me a little." He looked up at Nicki with glazed-over eyes. "Not that I wanted to hurt them, of course, but you know, there's something epic about the idea of fighting a Dragon."

"I know, sweetie," Nicki said gently. She had pulled a bandana out of her pocket and was holding it over the gash on Aiden's head. "There was a bit of a fight in the Gryphon world though, to help Emrys against those Dragons."

"I guess, but not the same," Aiden slurred. "And that was much more of a monster than anything we've seen before." He nodded toward the carcass and grimaced at the movement.

"True," Bran agreed. He was smiling a little and had dragged his back-pack over near Aiden, where he was digging through it. A moment later, he pulled the Chalice out and poured a little water into it. "Hey, Aiden, do me a favor and drink this."

"I'm not hurt." Aiden protested, forgetting about the blood he'd seen himself. "I mean... maybe I am."

"You are," Nicki said. "Drink from the Chalice, and then you need to rest."

"Why is it always me?"

"In this case, it was probably about the flamethrower that you hit the thing with," Bran said. He held the Chalice towards Aiden. "Come on. You look ready to topple over. You definitely have at least a concussion. Drink."

"Yeah, yeah." Aiden swayed again but was held up by Nicki's secure grip. She kept one hand on the Chalice and helped Bran guide it to his lips.

The metal flashed with magic, and Alex saw a flicker of yellow at Bran's fingertips. He caught her eyes, and she smiled. They only had to wait a moment. As Aiden lowered the Chalice from his mouth, his hands were steady, and his eyes were brighter.

A collective sigh of relief left the mages when Aiden handed the Chalice back to Bran. "Thanks, I feel better now," Aiden said. Looking up at Nicki, he offered her a soft smile. "I'm sorry for scaring you, Nicki."

"You have to stop doing that," Nicki said. "But it's okay. We should get moving. The smell of cooking meat and burnt hair are sure to attract attention."

"Do you think we should...." Aiden trailed off as he looked at the carcass. Then, curling up his nose, he shook his head and stood up. "Nope, never mind. That smells god awful." Reaching for his pack, he plastered on a wide smile. "So, to the ridge, right? Let's get moving."

Alex sheathed Cathanáil and let the familiar weight of the sword reassure her. Everyone was alright. They'd met some unfriendly wildlife, and they were okay. Exhaling slowly, she tried and failed to calm her nerves as she located her pack. Morgana helped her pull it back on, and this time, it was the older mage who squeezed her shoulder in silent support. It helped a little, but it only made Alex more determined to find a safe place for everyone to rest tonight. They all needed a good night's sleep.

11

Wanting

They got lucky with the ridge. There was a shallow cave, a bit like the first outcropping they'd camped under, but hidden by tall trees and lush plants. After checking the area over to make sure it wasn't the den of anything, they'd happily set down their packs and pulled out the supplies they needed most to get a camp set up. Aiden was moving just fine, and during the last leg of the hike, he'd been aware and free of pain.

Thus far, despite the two attacks they'd had to deal with, they had been very fortunate. Alex was unwilling to lose sight of that fact. They could breathe here, and everyone was okay despite the close calls. If luck was what would see them through, then she would be grateful and hold on tight to it.

Bending down, Alex picked up some downed branches and gathered them into her arms. The wood here was a different texture. It was softer and more pliable, with a smooth surface. Silver shades formed a gradient whenever the light hit it just right. They were beautiful, and she could hear Nicki oohing and awing a few feet away.

"When we leave, I'm going to take some of this with us," Nicki announced. "It would make such a nice art project or centerpiece."

"It will just look like painted wood," Alex pointed out. Aiden was back in camp with Morgana, setting up tents, and thus couldn't bring Nicki back to Earth. "You can make stuff on Earth look just as nice."

"But, the feel of it is different!" Nicki picked up a silver stick and swung it around, grinning at the way it glistened. "It's like a winter's day when the sun is reflecting off of the ice, except not as cold." Then Nicki straightened up, almost catching her armful of wood on the trunk of a tree. "This reminds me of that dancing princess story. The princesses went underground to a land with silver and gold trees." Nicki regarded the trees with a slight frown. "I wonder if that was based on this world at all or just imagination."

"Could be." Alex strained her memory and slowly shook her head. "But I'm pretty sure that people never made it this far."

"Maybe long ago, a human slave got out," Nicki suggested. "After all, not all the slaves stayed in the tunnels."

Or the palace, Alex silently added. She shrugged a little, unsure of what else she could say or do. "It's possible, but I doubt we'll ever know. There are lots of stories about people getting away from the Fae."

"Yeah." Nicki's energy dimmed, and she sighed loudly. "Hopefully, we'll get out."

Alex's eyes snapped over to Nicki. "We will." Stepping closer to her friend, Alex shifted the weight of the sticks in her arms. "We will get home."

Nicki swallowed, doubt flickering in her eyes for only a moment before she grinned brightly. The expression was false. The redhead turned on her heel and headed toward the camp, chatting quickly as if she and Alex were still talking pleasantly. Staring after her a moment, Alex told herself to hold on to their luck and started following. Worrying wouldn't help them. Caution was good, but they couldn't let fear make them stupid. Nicki calmed down not long after and exhaled loudly.

"Sorry," Nicki whispered, dropping her speed, so she was next to Alex. "I just had... a bad moment."

"I'm scared too. Thank you for taking the risk and coming with me."

When they returned to camp and started building a stack of wood, Alex couldn't shake the worry that Nicki's words had put in her, or, more correctly, drawn to the surface. Magic curled in her chest, flaring to life at her thoughts and emotions. Her magic rippled outward, passing through and around the trees and rocks. Everything became outlined in faint gray glittering lines. Animal life took on more vibrant purple hues, but all of it that was nearby was small. Something that was about the same size as a squirrel had a nest nearby. There were small bird animals here and there in the treetops and little amphibious creatures downstream from them. Alex didn't see any more of the massive predators and hoped that they'd dealt with the only nearby one.

Heat grew in her chest, and Alex pulled back her magic, recovering as much as she could before it dissipated. It rushed back to her, coiling in around her heart. The burn eased, but she knew that she'd used more magic than was wise. Still, Alex did not regret it in the least. It was easier to breathe now. The weight of the pack off of her shoulders helped, but the sense of emptiness around them let Alex feel... not safe exactly, but safer.

"Alex?" Morgana's voice brought her back to the present. She opened her eyes and looked around. She and Morgana were alone in the camp. Nicki had gone off somewhere, and she turned to search for her. "Nicki joined the boys in looking for food," Morgana explained gently. "I'm assuming you were checking the area?"

Alex flushed when Morgana raised the eyebrow of doom. "Yeah," she agreed. "Seemed like a good idea."

"How is your magic?"

"Fine." Alex smiled softly. "I recovered most of it."

"That is a useful ability." Morgana gestured to a log that had been dragged into the mouth of the cave when they'd first found it. "Sit down."

She didn't argue and sank onto the log. They still needed to make a fire pit for the evening. Three of the tents were up just inside the cave. Morgana started lashing together some of the longer and straighter sticks between glances at Alex.

"What are you doing?" Alex asked.

"Making a shield," Morgana replied. "It will help against the wind and hide the bright colors of the tents."

"Good plan." Alex nodded and stood, dusting herself off. "I can help with the other tents."

"Sit down." Morgana's eyes narrowed. Alex immediately sat back down. Too many of her lives knew that look. "Just rest for a moment. I can appreciate what you did. I was thinking about asking you to check." Morgana's hands moved smoothly and without hesitation in her work. "Is it harder here?"

"Not really." Alex shrugged. "In truth... the magic feels a little different, but there is energy in this world. I think..." She stopped herself, unsure if she should speak on it more.

"You think?" Morgana didn't look up from her work and adjusted the slowly forming fence against the rock of the ridge.

"We know now that the energy flows through the Iron Realm and then up through the Tree of Reality," Alex said. "So, all the energy here at one point or another was in the Iron Realm. It knows me in a way."

Morgana did stop now. Alex watched her profile and could see Morgana pressing her lips together tightly. She wanted to ask what the other mage was thinking. Then Morgana swallowed thickly, and a slight tremble in her hands and lips told Alex that she was thinking of Merlin. Imagining what Merlin would have thought of all this was impossible. A soft chuckle from Morgana surprised Alex.

"Morgana?"

"I'm fine."

Morgana turned her attention to finishing the setup of the camp while Alex tried to decide what to say. Arto was too loud in her head, his worry for his sister overruling the more cautious advice of Lokpal. Closing her eyes, Alex let the mix of voices wash over her and close her off from this strange alien world. It shouldn't have been a relief to hear them, but it was, and their whispers were a welcome distraction.

She didn't rest long. There was too much to do. Casting one more look towards Morgana, Alex turned her attention to gathering some of the larger stones scattered at the base of the ridge. Using one of the folding shovels, she dug a small fire pit and built a ring around it. Without a word from Morgana, Alex lit a small fire and welcomed the heat from the flames as it sank into her tired body.

The others returning from their food hunt prevented Alex from sitting alone with only the voices of her other-selves for company for too long. Twigs were caught in Nicki's hair, and she had a minor scrape on her arm, which would have worried Alex if Nicki hadn't been smiling. In her arms, Nicki was carrying her sweatshirt as a bundle. She knelt and opened the sweatshirt so that Alex and Morgana could see the various foodstuffs inside.

"I spotted these fruits in one of the trees," Nicki said. She laid the three fruits out in front of Morgana. "I was able to climb up and get a few, but I figured we should check them before investing too much time and energy into harvesting them."

"I know this fruit," Morgana said.

Morgana's hand trembled as she reached for it and inspected it thoughtfully. It was the shape of a pear, but slightly larger with silvery fuzzy skin. The gloss of the fuzz called to mind a toy unicorn that Alex had possessed when she was much younger. She almost laughed at the odd thought, and something must have shown on her face because Bran gave her a curious glance. Thankfully, he let it go when she shook her head.

"The fruit is safe to eat," Morgana announced. She put it down quickly as if burned. "It is... rather sweet, if I recall correctly."

"So, at least some of the food you ate came from this world," Bran said thoughtfully. "That's interesting. Did you ever see where it was grown? Was there an inside orchard or something in the tunnels?"

"I- No," Morgana answered. "I never saw anything like that, and to be honest, I was not concerned with such things then." Morgana's dark mood surrounded her like a cloak, and Alex moved closer to her, trying to offer some comfort.

"Fair enough," Aiden said quickly.

Morgana could identify most of the food as safe, and they had a dinner of fresh fruits and berries that augmented the backpacking rations nicely. Nicki discovered that the little purple berries went surprisingly well with the oatmeal-like food packet. They didn't talk loudly, but with a camp set up and fresh food, their spirits were high.

The sun sank below the horizon, and the long shadows of the trees were swallowed up by the night. Far overhead, stars appeared in the clear sky. Morgana was the first to go to bed, which didn't surprise anyone. She said her goodnights and paused long enough to touch Alex's shoulder and brush a strand of hair from her face before vanishing into the small one-person tent. Alex offered to take the first watch when Nicki yawned, and her eyes began to droop. There was no argument, and Nicki was quick to crawl into her tent. Aiden headed to bed not long after, but Bran lingered next to the fire, sitting with her in comfortable silence.

Alex watched the flames lick across the surface of the silver wood. While the silver sheen wasn't a mirror, something about it reflected the light in a way that made the fire brighter than it should be. She listened to the sounds of the forest and assured herself that they were far from anything large or anyone looking for intruders.

"What are you thinking about?" Bran asked in a low voice.

"I'm glad that fire still works the same." Alex gestured at the burning logs. "This world is a lot like home."

"Mostly, at least. I don't know if you noticed, but the hottest parts of the flames have a slight purple hint to them more than blue." Alex turned her face towards him and chuckled. It was such a Bran thing to notice.

"I can't help but notice these things," Bran said. "It's both amazing and terrifying to me." Raising a hand, he gestured up at the sky. "Look at those stars. None of them are familiar to us. This is a whole universe where what I know is questionable. Maybe some things work the same, but others don't."

"Does knowing that make it more or less scary?"

"No clue. When I find something that is the same, it reassures me." Bran shifted closer and pointed into the dark sky. "Look, at that bunch of stars, right there. I see a howling wolf."

Alex studied the stars, tilting her body closer to Bran's as she tried to see the shape. There were so many stars. Too many for her to have any sense of individual stars. Chuckling, Bran came even closer and carefully pointed out a few points of light.

"That one, follow it to that one." He moved his hand slowly, and Alex smiled. "Then, to that one. That's the nose right there."

"And you decided that it's howling."

"Of course, it's howling. What else would it be doing?"

"This world probably doesn't have wolves."

"No, but that's what explorers do. They find something familiar to comfort them."

"Did you get that from a movie?" Alex asked. She was still smiling, and her muscles ached a little with the strength of her grin.

"Probably. I couldn't tell you which one, but it's true. Stars are... fascinating. Given that we're likely in a whole different dimension or universe, knowing that there are other worlds even here is oddly comforting." He gestured at the sky again and relaxed back against the ground. "All of those are stars."

"What if they aren't, though?" Alex laid down beside him. The ground wasn't comfortable, but with the soft grass beneath them, it wasn't bad. "What if in this universe they are lost souls or some kind of great creatures that got stuck in the sky?"

Bran chuckled, the sound warm and soothing. "I'm pretty sure they aren't."

"But they could be. Despite appearances, this world could be very different from ours. Those could be tiny shoulder dragons caught in...." she had to stop and think, but Bran let her. "Caught in a giant flytrap made by an ancient civilization so they would stop eating everything."

Crackling from the fire mixed with Bran's chuckles, and the soft light made it impossible for Alex to see all the stars. She wondered just how many there would be once the fire was out for the night. Alex sighed happily as Bran stopped chuckling and closed her eyes.

"This is nice," she said happily. "I know I'm keeping watch, but I needed this."

"Glad to help then." Bran's tone shifted, and she heard him sigh. "What do you want, Alex?"

"When this is over?" Alex blinked at the question, opening her eyes in surprise.

"Yes," Bran answered. "Don't look so lost!" It was clear that he meant the words to be teasing, but the undercurrent of worry was definite.

What did she want? Alex exhaled and looked into the fire, trying to untangle the rush of thoughts that had suddenly swept in to take over. The others were so noisy, and their memories played loudly, threatening to overwhelm her own.

"I guess I want to go home and finish my degree," Alex managed. "Me going to college was important to my parents. Maybe I'll become a professor so I can stay near Morgana." Alex glanced towards Morgana's tent. "She's alone now. I can't keep her company forever, but at least I could look after her while I'm alive."

"Is that all?"

Alex shrugged again and turned her focus everywhere but him. "I haven't thought about it for a while. There's just always been something else." Alex's voice softened, and she toyed with the pastel grasses beneath them. "Right now, I want to stop the Darkness. I'll take stock of what comes next if I'm still alive."

"Don't talk like that!"

Alex turned to face Bran. The others shifted in their tents, but his sharp hiss hadn't woken them fully. The low light meant that Bran couldn't see her clearly. Some part of Alex knew she should turn it into a joke, but it wasn't something to make light of. Her stomach tightened at the notion of her death, and her palms grew sweaty.

If there had been a mirror to look into, Alex knew that the woman she saw in it would be so different from the eighteen-year-old who had first come to Ravenslake. She was an orphan now, a betrayed lover, a leader, and a warrior. She'd been none of those things. Back then, the only voice in her head had been her own. Now memories weighed her down, and echoes of the past were the soundtrack to her present.

"It's a possibility, Bran. I won't pretend otherwise." Forcing a smile, she leaned forward so more of the firelight illuminated her features. "Still, I promise that I'll do my best not to die. I don't want to, so don't worry about that. How about you?"

"Do I want to die?" he asked dumbly.

"No, what do you want? When this is all over?"

Bran hesitated. His eyes widened, and he struggled with what to say. Alex shifted closer, and his expression changed as he looked away. She stopped moving and watched him stare into the fire for a long moment.

"I'm not sure either, I suppose," he answered. Alex could hear the lie in his words but wasn't sure what he was lying about. "Finish school first and then, well, I suppose I want us all to stay together."

The last words demanded her attention. Warmth spread through her chest and limbs. Her magic spark danced with delight, and a genuine smile took over her face. Bran was smiling now, a soft and genuine smile that brightened the dark night around them.

"I know we came together out of survival and then a sense of duty, but in the time since then..." Alex thought she understood. The idea of not seeing these crazy people each day or at least frequently seemed wrong. "I hope our futures are together. For more than because there is a magical crisis."

"Merlin and Morgana always returned to each other," Alex whispered. "People are a kind of home, too, I suppose."

"Yes, I think that they are."

Bran stretched out, moving closer to Alex, and tilted his head back to look up at the stars once again. Alex followed suit and let the night air wash over her and calm the burning worry and fear that plagued her every moment. Slowly, even the voices of her past selves grew softer and quieted, allowing Alex to enjoy the peaceful night.

12

Look into the Bronze

800 C.E. Lyon, Burgundy

It wasn't the best land outside the city. The man who had sold them the small farm clearly believed that he was taking them for fools, but he had no way of knowing that in addition to having two strong young men willing to help them on the farm, they had magical abilities that would let them turn the rocky soil into something much more profitable. Still, despite the questionable nature of the land, Morgana was pleased with the deal.

Their plot was small, but they now owned it as private land. They were not beholden to a lord or a landlord. There was a small house that would suit for now, and the property had a small well with clean water. In truth, Morgana felt that the place had plenty of potential as a farm if one was willing to put in some work. Still, they'd had to sell everything in the shop and some of their possessions to afford the land, and Morgana knew there were questions as to why a shopkeeper with a decent business would switch to farming.

Merlin was enjoying the change. It was their second day here, and already, he was outlining where he wanted his new forge despite the fact it would be awhile before they could afford some iron unless the old man had some stockpiled somewhere. Morgana wouldn't put it past him. That was the sort of thing she could see him doing.

The house was a three-room cozy building, with the lower section of the wall having been made out of the local dark stone, likely stone from the farm, and the upper walls were wood and plaster. The thatch roof needed some repair, but they had spring and summer to deal with that around planting. It would be a lot of work, even with magic, but it would provide them with the privacy they needed to train the boys. But they'd gotten everything moved in good order, so there was a place for everyone to sleep and the necessary supplies of a home.

Morgana turned her attention away from the house and to the field. The remains of a fence were rotten and toppled over, and the ground was overgrown. Charles and Rudolf were hard at work clearing it. It was odd seeing Rudolf in simple clothing, but the boy needed freedom of movement more than anything right now. The boys had knocked over a young tree that had stood in the middle of the field and were sawing it apart. Sweat made their skin shine in the sun, but the slight smiles on their faces as they worked and chatted reassured Morgana that she would not have a mutiny on her hands.

She watched for a few moments before scanning the area around the farm. They were alone. In the distance, she could see some carts heading for the city, but nothing coming their direction. Closing her eyes, Morgana focused on the smell of the soil and the beat of her heart to steady herself. Then, she gently pulled on the spark of magic in her chest and let it grow and bloom into a rush of power.

Pushing the magic out, Morgana visualized the rocks just beneath the surface being pulled free. She could see them here and there, but knew that there were more rocks deeper in the soil. Silver magic sparkled in the sunlight and streamed forward to dig into the ground. Three large rocks were pulled from the earth, and Morgana flicked her fingers, directing them to the side with a thought.

The stones clanked against each other, drawing the attention of the boys. Morgana smirked, but didn't engage with them. Instead, she released another wave of magic and imagined it digging down to fetch more of the large stones. As they were pulled up, the ground shifted, and the earth was loosened. Not only would this be useful for clearing the stones, but it would help till the soil, Morgana realized with a jolt of satisfaction.

Rudolf caught Charles' attention and managed to get the other boy to help him finish with the tree. Their arms were piled with wood that they rushed over to the house. It was still green with life and would need time to dry out. Morgana watched silently as they stacked the logs against the side of the house, where the roof sloped down far enough to protect the woodpile. Then, as she expected, they came running to join her. Charles nearly lost his footing, and Morgana smiled at his enthusiasm.

"Can we help?" Charles asked.

"You may."

"So, we clear the rocks?" Charles asked. He was bouncing between his feet eagerly.

"Are you certain we should use our magic for this?" Rudolf cast a doubtful look around. "What if someone sees?"

"No one will see," Morgana assured him. "We have much more privacy here than we did inside the city."

Rudolf still didn't look convinced. Morgana couldn't blame him. The lad came from a respected, if not noble family, and life out in the countryside was proving to be messier than he'd imagined. At least Merlin had swayed his family with magic into letting him come with them. It had become a source of questions and rumors in the city, but there was a limit to what they could do there. Training mages was much more complicated than it used to be. At least both Charles and Rudolf had been fascinated with magic enough not to worry about the devil taking their souls or whatever the church taught nowadays. She dreaded the day they had to train a deeply religious boy or girl.

"We'll use the stones to repair and build," Morgana added. "And the crops will grow better without too many large rocks in the way."

"So, you'll actually be growing stuff?" Rudolf looked around uncertainly. "Do you need to?"

"It will provide us with food, a source of income, and will keep people from talking," Morgana explained. "There is enough curiosity about why your parents let you leave with us. If we aren't farming, then there will be even more rumors." She didn't add that they didn't want Rudolf's parents second-guessing themselves. "Besides, farming will give us a good way to practice your magical skills. Magic can help crops grow."

"Really?" Charles's excitement was a bright and palatable force in the air. Rudolf smirked a little at his friend's energy. "It can do that?"

"Magic is very flexible," Morgana explained patiently. "It can manage anything that you visualize, as long as you have enough magic and strength to achieve it." Schooling her features into a stern expression, Morgana stared hard at each of the boys in turn. "Remember what we taught you about what exhaustion feels like. It will not do any good if you burn yourselves out. When you start getting tired and your arms or legs hurt, then it is time to stop. Don't try to get the rocks that are more than a few feet down. They won't matter as much. We need the surface rocks cleared the most."

They nodded their understanding, but Morgana gave them each more one long look to enforce how serious she was. Excitement faded from their eyes, and their spines straightened. Determination shone in their faces, and while Morgana knew it wouldn't last after the first hour or so, she was happy to see they were taking it seriously.

"Work one at a time," she added. "One to keep watch and make sure the other doesn't overdo it. That will also leave you time to breathe. If you feel weak, sit down and meditate as I taught you."

"Yes, Morgana," they answered as one.

Morgana offered them a soft smile. They were good boys, and they really had come a long way since that first Connection on the street. Both of them brightened a little at her smile, and she turned to head back towards the house to find Merlin. She was sure that she could hear him around the back of the house. Likely, he was already working on that forge of his.

She found him where she expected; in the middle of the area he'd marked out for his forge. Morgana was relieved that he hadn't just pulled up the walls from the earth. They could have gotten away with that in the past, but today there would be too many questions. Magic was not something that she wanted to be caught using. He smiled widely as she approached and dusted off his hands. Without any prompting from her, Merlin joined Morgana at the side of the house where he could check on the boys. Morgana gave him a moment to see how they were doing and noted that his smile widened a little further.

"What do you think?" Morgana asked Merlin.

"This will work nicely for our purposes, even if it is not as comfortable."

"Depending on how long we're going to stay, we need to invest in some animals. Chickens, at the very least."

"Indeed." Merlin nodded. "But I hope the boys will master their magic soon. We haven't much time before Nerthus either comes looking for us or draws too much attention to herself."

"Have you heard anything more?" Morgana asked.

"Thankfully not. The rumors seem to blame the attacks and the razing of that village on bandits."

"Well, they would hardly blame it on a goddess that predates Christianity," Morgana scoffed. "Still, we know very little about Nerthus. She's a goddess of fertility by tradition. This seems too far west for her."

"Maybe, but she must have been asleep a long time." Merlin shook his head. "I wish I could reach one of the Norse; she seems connected to them."

"They never mentioned such a creature."

"No, they did not. But Odin might still know of her. While many of the Old Ones formed alliances to create the pantheons, others did not. I wish I could find information about her, but there's only a handful of accounts from the Romans."

"And do they offer any insight?"

"Not much. There is mention of a rather horrible cleansing ritual when the goddess left an area."

"Cleansing? In water?" Morgana asked.

"Yes, but the slaves who helped perform it were slain immediately afterward."

"So, she was bloodthirsty even before becoming corrupted? Lovely."

"We don't know for certain if that was true," Merlin pointed out gently. "You and I both know that not everything the Romans recorded was accurate."

"It was much more accurate than the so-called histories of this era," Morgana growled. "I understand your caution, Merlin, but I'm inclined to give credit to the source. That sounds like something an Old One would do. Having a ritual with water... it fits."

"It does." Merlin sighed loudly. "I know." He rubbed his eyes, weariness in his posture. "I should investigate."

"You aren't enough to defeat her."

"No, just to spy. If we can find a pattern to her attacks or a weakness, that will help. If she is fully corrupted, then I dare not fight her alone."

Looking at the boys, Morgana found Charles levitating a rock with his earthy green magic while Rudolf cheered him on. The display should have made her smile, but it didn't. These two were learning, but it was slow. They weren't ready to take on Nerthus. She and Merlin had faced down corrupted Old Ones before, but she hesitated to go without them. Magic had chosen two more mages, and their power was growing. That meant something. Two more mages was a clear sign that they needed the help. The world was bending under the strain of Nerthus' actions and needed the mages to fix it.

They needed to be careful. They needed to be ready before confronting her. But Morgana couldn't help but feel guilty for the people that would be harmed in the meantime. Nerthus had decided to have some fun, and unless she went back to sleep, they were the only ones that could stop her.

"Let's go inside," Morgana said softly. "The boys will be fine. This is good practice for their control."

"It might be faster to do it by hand."

"It might, but they need the training." Morgana nodded towards the house. "I'll scry and see if I can find anything."

"That's a good idea. But only if you're sure."

His worry was warming, but it changed nothing. She cast her eyes over at the boys and headed for the house. Soft laughter was coming from them, and Morgana was certain that they'd already found a way to make it into a game. That was just as well. Merlin followed behind her, staying close as they entered the small house.

The front room contained a large stone fireplace that would serve as a source of heat and their cooking area. A table with four chairs sat in the center of the room, and shelves along the walls were already filled with items they'd purchased in the city. A small trap door that led to the cellar that Merlin had carved out two days ago was mostly hidden under a faded rug.

Morgana ignored the unfamiliar smells here and the odd way that the glass of the window distorted the light. These were minor details that she would grow used to. Instead, Morgana went to a shelf and found a wooden box. Merlin closed the door and sat down at the table while she retrieved the large cloth bag inside. Morgana took a seat across from him and pulled the ancient bronze disk from the bag. The polished surface shimmered in the light coming through the window. Merlin gave her an expectant look and settled back in his chair.

She hesitated. Morgana realized with a flush of irritation and embarrassment that she was nervous. After all the centuries, not much scared her, but Merlin's report about what Nerthus had been like before becoming corrupted frightened her. Still... that was no excuse for stalling. Closing her eyes, Morgana focused on slowing her breathing and returning her body to a more normal state of rest. Merlin said nothing, giving her the time to center herself. Her magic flared to life in her chest, and Morgana tightened her grip on the bronze disk, letting the magic flow into the object.

"Show me Nerthus," she said out loud, commanding her magic. "Show me where she is."

Opening her eyes, Morgana smiled as her magic rippled over the surface of the disk. The old bronze gleamed, and colors began to swirl and appear on the surface. Merlin shifted in his seat, but her partner stayed silent. Heat churned in Morgana's chest, warning her that she didn't have long. Her demonstration for the boys had taken too much magic.

Then she saw her, Nerthus, standing in the center of a small village beside a stone well. The figure was tall with wide hips and a long veil hiding her features. A faint glow surrounded her, assuring Morgana that this was the Old One she was looking for. Bare feet touched the cobbled stones and vines were breaking up through the surface to curl around her ankles. Dressed in a pale simple gown with a belt around her waist and a garland of flowers draped around her neck and hanging across her arms, she stood out as something different.

The humans around her were on their knees, their heads turned down and silent. One young man, roughly the age of the boys, walked towards her in a daze. Nerthus raised her hands towards the young man. He sped up, almost tripping over his feet. A bad feeling rocked in Morgana's stomach. The crowd was too silent, too still. This was a Christian country. They shouldn't have been so... enthralled. Vines broke through the soil, tangling around the young man's limbs and lifting him into the air. He didn't struggle and kept gazing with pure adoration at Nerthus.

Morgana leaned closer to the mirror. Nerthus didn't move from her spot. The vines curled higher around her legs, vanishing under the hem of her gown. But the vines around the boy twisted, bringing him closer to her. She raised a hand, and the vines dug into the boy's flesh. Morgana gasped. Skin was pulled away, and a scream escaped the boy, echoing in her mind as his mouth dropped open in shock. Dropping the disk, Morgana closed her eyes and tried to dispel the terrible image of that young man being flayed alive while the villagers did nothing. She heard Merlin call her name, but it barely registered. All she could see was the face of Charles on that boy as he let an Old One rip him apart.

13

Disjointed Visions

Visions were Bran's cup of tea. His first magical experience had been a flash of the future that had saved him and his mother in a car crash, and he'd received several warnings during his tenure as a mage. The problem was understanding the visions. Their only warning of Arthur's betrayal had been a vision where Bran was stabbed in the back. Direct, but not helpful if you can't see the face of the person who stabbed you.

Sometimes they were useful. He'd had dreams of the Sídhe tunnels, of the creation of the Iron Soul, or at least of its creation in a way that he could understand. Over the years there had been many flashes of insight that had helped him stay alive. Sometimes in a battle, he thought he knew what an opponent would do before they moved. Sometimes the sense of déjà vu would be so strong that it almost knocked him over.

The strongest visions had been of his former life, of the Bran he had been long ago that had led them to the Chalice. Those visions haunted him. In his dreams, he thought he might remember being that man, but was never sure. Emotions teased him when he woke up from such dreams, and he was never sure what was a true vision and what was just a figment of his imagination. Only when he scryed did he have any certainty.

Bran exhaled slowly. He needed to calm his mind and turn off his random thoughts, but it wasn't easy. A sense of dread had crept up on him overnight. He couldn't put his finger on the source. Talking with Alex had been fantastic last night, but keeping watch had left him tired, and the dreams had... He shoved the thoughts away.

The ground beneath him was cold: he could feel the chill even through his folded sleeping bag and tarp. He was vaguely aware of the others watching him and Alex. It had been decided that only he and Alex would scry while the others stood guard. Sometimes this took a long time. Alex sat down only inches in front of him, her knees almost touching his from her place on her folded up sleeping bag.

"Ready?" Alex almost sounded shy.

Smiling, Bran extended his hands and hoped that he looked calm. Alex's lips shifted, but it wasn't a full smile. Her eyes shone with worry, though he didn't see any doubt in them. That was enough for him. Bran knew that he should be worried that it was enough, but he didn't have time for that. Not right now.

Alex took his hands. Her fingers were warm against his, and he exhaled as he relaxed. The calluses on Alex's hands were familiar and more developed than his own. Inhaling slowly, Bran closed his eyes and turned his attention inward. Meditation didn't come easily these days. His magic fluttered to life, a warm yellow spark that filled his gut and rushed to fill his chest. For a moment, he basked in the power, in the confidence it instilled in him.

Then Alex's magic hummed against his hands. He smelled the sharp scent of ozone and was reminded of his purpose. Holding back a sigh, Bran pushed his magic through his arms and into his hands. His magic slipped away. It flowed through his limbs into Alex, leaving him behind in a rush to reach the Iron Soul. Before the last traces faded from his fingertips, Bran could feel the magic change. The smoothness of his energy changed to the sharp sting of Alex's. Like lightning, raw electricity, it was always ready and alert. His magic didn't fight the change at all.

It welcomed it, as if it was returning to where it was supposed to be. Bran couldn't dismiss that thought. His chest tightened at what had been merely a stray thought, but now led him to a scary path. Should he read more into that? Should he dismiss it?

He was never sure when it came to Alex. Everything got... fuzzy, around her. His instincts weren't as sharp. He couldn't put things together like he normally could, and she disrupted him. There was a part of himself he'd made peace with years ago that she made him question. It was hard to understand, and he didn't have all the information. Bran knew he wasn't as objective when dealing with her as he needed to be. His heartbeat a little faster at the unfamiliar direction of his thoughts. Licking his lips, Bran swallowed and told himself to focus on the magic, on finding what they needed.

"Bran?" Aiden called. "You okay, man?"

"Fine," he answered. "I'm fine." Bran kept his eyes closed and tried to focus on the flow of magic to Alex. But she needed more than his magic: She needed his concentration. "Just give me a second."

"Focus, man," Aiden said. His tone was teasing, but Bran heard the note of worry. "Keep in mind that this world won't recharge you as fast. Don't waste your magic."

The warning was well made. Aiden was right; this was different from usual. He couldn't rely on his innate connection to the world around him. Keeping his eyes closed, Bran inhaled slowly and squeezed Alex's hands. She returned the gesture, sending a flurry of emotions racing through him that this was not the time to deal with. They needed to find the source of the Darkness.

His magic shifted, the warmth vanishing. Panic hit Bran. He was pulled before he could do anything, his connection tightened and stretched, becoming taunt and fragile. His panic faded a little, but fear for how little control he had took its place. His feet tingled with pressure; he was standing rather than sitting now. Light burned against his closed eyes, and Bran opened them slowly, scared of what he was about to find.

It was the hall, the grand white hall that he'd seen before. Bran blinked at the sudden brightness and groaned as the pain in his eyes eased. Looking around, he couldn't shake the feeling that it was brighter than before. Then his eyes landed on the figure on the far side of the room. They were shorter than him, with long, loose blonde hair, and wearing jeans and a metal crown. The sight of it made his stomach tighten with dread.

"Alex?" he croaked.

The figure did not answer, did not turn. His magic fluttered. The air thrummmed against his skin, hot and heavy like a humid day before a storm. He could smell lightning in the air. Around Alex's still figure, light churned and warped, dancing around her and illuminating the crown. His magic tightened. The tether snapped. Bran's stomach swooped as he was pulled, thrown, and dropped through empty air.

Colors and images flashed past him, too quick for Bran to see anything clearly. His stomach lifted and fell as if he were riding on a roller coaster. Snapping his eyes closed, Bran's hands grasped at the empty air. He'd lost Alex somehow. He needed to find Alex. He needed Alex.

His body slammed to a stop. Bran was on his feet once again, though he hesitated to open his eyes. Smells of ash and decay made his nose wrinkle, and his feet were sinking a little into the ground he was standing on. Bran didn't want to open his eyes. Illness had settled into his stomach, and he knew that what he saw when he opened his eyes would only make it worse. Nonetheless, he braced himself, took a deep breath of foul and stale air, and opened his eyes.

The sky was swirling, and debris floated aimlessly against the dark purple. He'd expected something worse; a pitch-black world or one on fire. But as the dunes of ash and small bits of exposed ruin sank in, Bran realized that this was worse somehow. There was nothing fast and brutal here. This had been slow and absolute.

"It's here." Alex's voice echoed around him. It didn't sound right: It was like she was speaking in time with other people. She wasn't in front of him. "The source is here. This is where it enters the Tree of Reality."

He looked around but did not see her. Alex wasn't nearby. Turning around, he searched the dead landscape. Calling her name did nothing. His voice simply rolled across the dead world without any answer. Frowning, he looked up once again. There was a long rip where the Darkness met the sky. It wasn't as clear here thanks to the dark color of the sky and the debris, but it was there. A gaping hole that had consumed much of the visible sky. How were they going to deal with this?

"Alex?" He called again. "Do you think we can fix this? It's huge. It'll take... more magic than I think we have."

"It must be healed." Her voice was wrong again, but it sounded closer now. "I have to stop this."

A hand fell on his shoulder. Bran could only turn enough to see it, but not the person it was attached to. The familiar shape of Alex's hand reassured him. He knew the nails that she kept short and simple, but still painted with a clear topcoat. The callus on her thumb from working in the forge was barely visible, and a small scar on her middle knuckle that he'd never learned the story behind were familiar. She was silent behind him, and his eyes moved back to the sky. There was nothing left to save here, but it was an open wound infecting the rest of the Tree of Reality.

"It doesn't have to flow along the connections between worlds," he said out loud. His voice was haunting in the dead landscape. "It reaches everywhere."

"Yes," Alex agreed. The echoing quality of her voice was fading. "It has to be stopped."

Magic rippled across his skin, so strong and blunt that Bran couldn't help but gasp. It felt like dropping into a hot tub or the first moments of a hot shower. Pleasant, but he hadn't been expecting it. He opened his mouth to ask Alex what was happening, but no sound came out. The magic weighed down his shoulders. It was warm, comforting, and gently pulling him under. With a flicker of alarm, Bran was suddenly aware that the source might not be Alex.

But he was falling again. There was no control. The dead world was fading away, the last image of it the vivid purples and blacks of the sky and the swirling debris scattered across it. He drifted. In his chest, his magic was washing back and forth like a swinging pail of water. Then it stopped. His magic settled all at once, and he was aware of the solid ground beneath him. Bran was once again sitting cross-legged with the sweet smell of the strange Sídhe-ruled world around him.

Opening his eyes, Bran gasped for air and repeatedly blinked to clear his senses. Someone was holding his shoulder. They squeezed gently, reassuringly, and his heart rate eased. His magic pulsed weakly, and he released his hold on it. The thin tether that had been keeping him connected to his body faded into the spark, which promptly dimmed. It wasn't painful exactly, but he had definitely been nearing his limit. Giving his head a small shake, Bran tried to burn the last details of what he'd seen into his memory. They had seen the world where the Darkness was worst again, but that wasn't really helpful. It hadn't told him anything about what to expect or how far away they were from that world.

Disappointment welled up in Bran. Had he done something wrong? His thoughts had been scattered before starting, and maybe that had affected what he'd seen. He was preparing to apologize as he looked up at Alex, only for the words to vanish.

Alex's gray eyes were sharp and bright, like polished iron catching the light of the sun, and determination colored her features. Bran could only blink and fight down the illness still clinging to his gut. Alex did not seem to have been affected the same way. He glanced over at his shoulder and found Aiden holding onto him.

"You okay, Bran?" Aiden asked. Bran nodded, not trusting his voice just yet. "Alex?"

"I'm fine," Alex said. "We're close, but it is two worlds away. We need to make another jump, tomorrow if possible and then jump again."

She frowned thoughtfully, and Bran was suddenly sharply aware that Alex had seen something different than him. Again, he tried to speak, but exhaustion weighed him down. His chest burned hot in brutal warning that he was at the edge. They had the Chalice, but it was best not to risk it and use the magic without true need. Inhaling slowly, he let the cool evening air ease the heat. When had it become evening? He looked around in alarm and confusion.

"There's a branch off of the next world," Alex continued. "I was able to see it in the Tree of Reality. It's... I don't think it has survived at all, but it is the other branch where the Darkness came through. I caught... glimpses, I guess, but I'm still not sure what they did to cause it."

"Do you think it is important?" Morgana asked.

"I'm sure it is." Alex shuddered. "The sky... it's horrible, Morgana. When I look at it, I can see faint hints of magic being eaten away as it spreads and spreads. Whatever they did... it created small holes through-out the upper branches of the Tree of Reality. The Darkness has been seeping through them ever since."

Bran hadn't seen that. He swallowed. It wasn't clear why, but maybe magic didn't feel they both needed to see that. But he'd seen the sky. Not like Alex had, but he'd seen it. Then again, he didn't have her ability to see magic and read energy. Only Alex could do that. But he had seen something. There was something that he'd seen that Alex hadn't. He squeezed Alex's hand, grateful that they were still connected. She stopped speaking with Morgana and turned towards him for a moment, and smiled. It wasn't enough to completely ease his fear, but it helped. Her hair was slipping out of her braid, long blonde strands framing her face and making that soft smile seem like a work of art. She was messy and tired, with no crown in sight.

What was that crown? This was the second time he'd seen it. A sense of foreboding was churning in his gut. A certainty that he wasn't going to like what the vision meant, but he had no idea how to even begin understanding his vision. Like Arthur's betrayal, it would probably only make sense when it was too late.

14

Jump to Action

Absolute calm and certainty that they were on the right path was a rare commodity in the lives of humans, and likely all sentient beings, but Alex had it. Her magic was strong and flowing smoothly, like a river, through her chest. The way forward had been made clear to her. They needed to move to the next world, and then one more jump would take them to the end of the branch. No human had ever traveled so far! It made her little adventure in the tunnels look like a spring holiday on the coast.

She almost smiled as the last of the camp was packed up. Her heavy backpack was sitting by her feet, waiting for her to pull it on, and Cathanáil's familiar weight rested against her hip opposite Mjǫllnir. The Iron Pendant around her neck seemed heavier today than it had yesterday, but Alex wasn't worried about it. Flickers of her dark gray magic danced just under the surface of the metal. It was hers, in the same way that Cathanáil and Mjǫllnir were. The way that the Iron Trishula back on Earth was hers, and the Iron Chalice at the top of Bran's pack was hers.

Strange to imagine now that she could have ever thought the Sword could belong to Arthur. How could she have not known the instant she touched it? Then again, it had felt right in her hand when Cyrridven had thrown it to her, hadn't it? That night was a blur with a few very clear details. She shifted her hand and touched the Sword while the others got organized.

Bran was moving slowly. Hesitation hung around him and colored his every move. Every so often, he would glance her way, but had yet to explain. She met his gaze, only for Bran to drop his eyes. He shook his head a little and grabbed his pack. With Aiden's help, he hoisted it on and secured the straps. Morgana came over and helped Alex with her own pack, and Alex was distracted, helping Morgana with hers. When there was time to take a breath, she'd talk to him.

They were ready. The others looked at her, and Alex pulled Cathanáil out of the sheath secured to her belt. She gave Nicki a soft smile, once again, very grateful for her friend's amazing work on the magical item. Hopefully, when this was all over, they could turn Nicki loose with materials and time to see what she could come up with. Then again, Arthur was dead at last, and if the Darkness was stopped, fewer creatures would try to come to Earth. Eventually, the level of magic would drop again. Alex dismissed her thoughts. That was a good thing.

The still morning air seemed to know what she was about to do. Colors blurred slightly, and the faint hint of mist made the area around Alex seem to quiver with anticipation. Cathanáil sliced through the air, and the fabric of this world was cut open. She stopped the swing of the blade, unwilling to do more damage than was absolutely necessary. The last thing they needed was her leaving wounds in the Tree of Reality that would make it easier for things to go wrong.

She took a breath, letting the sweet air of this world fill her lungs and held it in as the others formed a line behind her. They all grabbed hands tightly. Stepping into the tear, the tidal wave of magic that swept her forward did not surprise Alex. A glittering tunnel of magic surrounded her. It wasn't rough or painful. They were following the natural flow of magic this time, and it made the ride much smoother. In the corner of her eye, Alex caught sight of stonework and doorways, but they were gone as fast as they appeared. An idea formed in her mind, but there was no time for it to fully manifest before her feet hit solid ground. Stumbling forward, she gasped as the weight of her bag shifted and quickly sought to right her center of gravity as she released her grip on the mage behind her.

Alex sniffed the air. There was a dusty, almost musty note to it that made her nose curl as Alex held back a sneeze. That smell did not inspire confidence. Her eyes rose to the sky, and relief washed over her at the sight of the violet tinted dim sky. It wasn't Earth, but it wasn't the stormy sky of the final world. Alex felt herself smile. Her confidence and certainty were not misplaced so far.

Turning back to the portal, Alex watched the others come stumbling through. Morgana barely stayed on her feet and looked around nervously. They were in a forested area, but had come through at the top of a hill in an open patch. From its height, Alex could see that the forest seemed to cover several hilltops and spread up the sides of a nearby chain of mountains. They were worn-down mountains, reminding her of the old Appalachian Mountains that as a child she hadn't been impressed with upon comparison to the familiar Rockies of the west.

The forest looked very similar to the last one. The shape of the leaves was wider and longer, more like those of tropical trees on Earth than the thinner leaves on the last world. There was a hint of green in the trunks here, though the color was still very silver. Alex walked to a nearby tree with a thick trunk and branches heavy with leaves. Touching the trunk, she rubbed her thumb over the smooth outer bark. It was almost soft to the touch.

"Everyone alright?" Alex asked, shaking her head and turning back to the others.

"That was easier this time," Aiden said. He was a little hunched over but appeared fine. "Not as bumpy, but still, the speed is like being on a roller coaster."

Nicki nodded and said nothing. Alex noted that she was a little green and frowned. The journey had felt pretty smooth to her. She glanced around again, trying to take in the sounds of this forest and listening for potential threats. The wind was rattling the leaves, which were louder than she was used to, hitting each other with hard smacks. She thought she heard something moving to her right but didn't see anything in the shadows of the trees.

In the distance was something much more interesting to them all. Silver spires were visible and reached into the sky over a scattering of rooftops that they could barely see over the tree line. It was a city—a real city on an alien world. Alex's heart jumped despite her knowing that the Sídhe were not friendly, and they couldn't go see it.

"Okay, I feel better about the idea that we are actually in another world now," Nicki said. A nervous giggle escaped her. "Walking through a forest just doesn't give that vibe."

"Even when the trees are silver?" Aiden asked dryly.

"Shockingly, no."

Now it was Alex's turn to laugh. Morgana shook her head at them, but she didn't hide the small smile that curled her lips. Levity was a grand thing. Turning her attention back to the opening they had made in the world, Alex rolled her shoulders as much as her pack allowed and raised Cathanáil. Heat flared in her chest, but her magic responded to her call.

Lightning arced over the blade of the Sword before leaping into the air to knit the portal back together.

That done, Alex sheathed Cathanáil and scanned the horizon, forcing herself to pay attention to more than just the city. If she'd had a phone, she would have taken some reference shots, but that wasn't possible. It was a pity they hadn't thought to pick up a battery-powered digital camera. She turned to find Bran scribbling in his notebook once again and smiled.

"Okay, what do we think?" Alex asked. "Camp until we can make the last jump, or find a more isolated area to recover?" Her fingers itched to open the final portal, but Alex knew that her magic was too low for that. "The valley below doesn't look too bad."

"We need to rest for at least a few hours," Morgana warned. "I know that the magic of Cathanáil helps you open the portals, but we shouldn't push ourselves to exhaustion given that we don't know what's waiting in the next world."

"So we're only staying for a few hours?" Bran asked. He sounded a little disappointed.

"The Darkness didn't originate here," Alex replied. She shrugged, even though she understood his curiosity. "And I'd rather not cross the locals."

"Morgana, do you think this or the last world was where you lived?" Nicki asked. "Or were you raised between worlds in the tunnel? How did the tunnels even work?"

"I'm not sure," Morgana admitted. "I... I always imagined them as being between the worlds, but since we started this mission, I've been rethinking that." Morgana paused and looked towards the city with a frown. "This world is very similar to the last. The glimpses of the Sídhe world I grew up on that I had were very limited. The interior of the palace was very closed off from the outside, the same as the tunnels, and I was kept rather isolated as you can imagine."

Alex could imagine a lot. She didn't like anything that she did. The Queen wouldn't have kept Morgana in a cell or anything so obvious. Alex didn't doubt that Morgana was well fed, well dressed, and technically cared for, but Arto's memories of how tightly Morgana had clung to her loved ones told her a lot. Scáthbás had been emotionally manipulative and abusive to Arthur, even after birthing him. She knew the Queen had been just as damaging to Morgana, if in different ways. It was an unsettling thought. Alex stepped closer to Morgana and caught her hand, giving it a squeeze. Her mentor raised an eyebrow, but Alex could see the gratitude shining in Morgana's eyes.

A snap in the trees to their left made them all tense and turn towards the noise. Shifting her left leg back, Alex adjusted her body and reached for Cathanáil before second-guessing herself. Raising her hands, she gestured to the others in what she hoped was a clear "relax" signal. The shape became clearer rapidly. It was moving towards them, not sneaking, and not trying to be quiet.

It came out of the trees, carrying a spear and staring at Nicki, who was closest to it. The Síd was a small creature, slighter and shorter than those Alex had seen on Earth. Large violet eyes glared suspiciously at them. They sniffed the air, and Alex blinked at the odd behavior. She'd never seen any Síd on Earth do that. Next to her, Morgana was in a solid and protective stance. Alex didn't have to look over to know that Morgana was glaring at the creature.

"Identify yourself," Morgana barked. Her cold hand gripped Alex's arm, and Nicki's warm hand was quick to join it. She saw the dark green of Bran's jacket in the corner of her eye. "I will not ask again."

"You are the stranger." The Síd crept a little closer and reached for them with its right hand, only to quickly pull it back. The movement let Alex see the sword hanging on the Síd's belt under the cloak. "What are you?"

"Human," Nicki answered. Morgana made a warning sound, but Nicki continued regardless. "Of the Iron Realm."

The Síd's eyes widened, and its mouth dropped open in shock. There was a moment that stretched out into minutes before the Síd recovered. It checked them over with a sharp gaze as Alex tried to identify the gender. A loose tunic and pants made it difficult for Alex to gauge the physical build, and the features were effeminate like most Sídhe she'd seen over the years. Unlike most, the white hair of this Síd was cut short, almost a pixie cut which exposed its pointed ears and slender neck. The height made Alex think it could be a young one, but she wasn't sure. Sharp and elegant features were common amongst the Sídhe and made it difficult for her to pinpoint age.

"You can't be human. All the humans died out centuries ago. And the princes have no new tunnels." It bared its teeth at them. "We would have heard."

"We are human," Morgana said. Her voice left no room for argument, and the mage's presence seemed to unfold and fill the surrounding space. "We opened our own path here."

"Why?"

"Something threatens the entire Tree of Reality," Alex answered.

"Tree of Reality?" Confusion darkened the Síd's face, and it eyed her suspiciously. "What are you talking about?"

Alex felt foolish. "That doesn't matter, but there is a force threatening this world and ours. We've come to stop it before it can do more damage."

"Alex," Morgana hissed in warning. "Don't. We have no idea what this thing will do with that information."

It was Aiden who cleared his throat next and spoke. "I am sorry if we startled you," he said kindly. Aiden ignored Morgana starting to talk. "We mean you no harm. If you're willing, please go on your way and forget that you ever saw us."

The Síd raised an eyebrow. Its dubious expression was so much like Morgana's that Alex almost burst into giggles. She'd never say it, but the idea that Morgana had picked up the behavior from Queen Scáthbás was both funny and terrifying. Vague memories of Merlin saying something similar echoed in her mind. He was braver than Alex if he'd truly voiced that thought.

"We don't want any trouble," Alex said carefully. "We aren't staying. We promise."

"Alexandra." Morgana's anxious voice made Alex tense.

The Síd was uneasy until a noise in the trees behind them made the creature shift back, its posture relaxing slightly. Alex braced herself as three more Sídhe came stomping into the clearing. Judging from the swords and spears they were carrying, they'd heard at least part of the conversation. Alex kept her hands away from Cathanáil's hilt and tried to look friendly. She didn't smile, aware that baring her teeth might not be taken as a friendly gesture in this world.

"We don't want to fight," Alex repeated.

"That one does," one of the newly arrived Sídhe said, gesturing towards Morgana. This one was taller than the first with very short white hair and a dark gray scar across its face. "She's hostile."

"A bit," Alex sighed. "Morgana, stand down."

"Alexandra."

"Let's not start a fight," Alex whispered. "Our magic is drained."

Anger and worry radiated off of the older mage, and the Sídhe took a nervous step back. Holding back a groan, Alex wished desperately that Merlin was there, only to be rewarded with a wave of grief from both her own heart and her other-selves. Thankfully they were quiet, allowing her to focus on the Sídhe. Bran and Aiden were staying put and watching the proceedings and listening with alert expressions.

"That one speaks of things that Eirwen does," the first Síd said. It pointed right at Alex. "Spoke of a danger in the Tree." They glanced towards the other Sídhe, and Alex bit her lower lip nervously. "Come with us."

"No," Morgana scoffed.

"You will come with us," the Síd repeated. "Eirwen will want to see you. He'll be the judge of your reasons for being here." Their lips twisted unpleasantly. "Besides, you are too close to our base for us to let you roam free."

More Sídhe had come out of the trees while they were talking. There were seven of them now, and they were surrounded. Spears had been lowered, but the threat was still present. Morgana growled softly, but Alex touched her arm once again.

"Alright," Alex said. "We won't fight you. Please, take us to see this Eirwen. We'll go from there."

"Alex?" Nicki asked.

"They haven't attacked us," Alex pointed out. "Let's not start hurting them if we don't have to," she added in a whisper.

Alex was the first to start walking when their Sídhe escort gestured them forward. Morgana stayed glued to her side and grasping her hand. The others were close behind, and Alex knew that she could expect a lot of grabby hands if a conversation started again. Glancing around at the Sídhe, Alex tried to decide how much trouble they were in. Her magic was a weak little flame in her chest, and she didn't trust it not to sputter out when she needed it. Crossing between worlds was exhausting, and it would have been much better if she could have taken a nap first.

But the magic had dropped them here, right in the path of this patrol. Maybe she was running on too much faith, but it seemed like the answer. At least for the moment, it was better to go with them rather than exhaust themselves and have more Sídhe after them. She glanced over at Morgana, who looked no happier.

"What is your name?" Alex asked the Síd who had found them and seemed to be the leader. "I'm Alex."

"Jarven," the Síd answered shortly. "Just stay close. This is contested territory."

"Contested?" Morgana repeated, brow furrowing.

"Yes. Prince Arston currently rules the capital city," another Síd said. This one was looking fearfully into the trees around them. They were heading away from the city now, into a deep valley thick with silver trees. "His patrols-"

"Adravin," Jarven barked. "Enough."

"Are you rebels?" Alex asked. The word was heavy on her tongue, and something like hope bloomed in her chest only for guilt to take hold.

Jarven scowled over their shoulder and ordered everyone to hurry. But the word was out there, and something in the air had changed. Someone grabbed onto her shoulder. It was a small shift, but it was there. Jarven shivered and glanced back at Alex once again, this time with softer and more curious eyes as if they had felt it too.

"Did you really think that every Sídhe was happy with the slavery?" Jarven asked. "That all of us approved of the warfare and the genocide?" The Síd's violet eyes were narrowed and angry. "There is a rebellion.

There has always been a rebellion. For thousands of years, Sídhe have struggled against the Princes."

"Thousands of years," Nicki repeated. "Yikes." Alex wasn't surprised that she'd been the one to grab her for translating purposes. "Even now?"

"Even now." Jarven shook their head. "No more questions. If you mean what you say and are friendly, then follow us and cause no trouble."

Alex eyed Morgana, but some of the fight had left her mentor. She was staring at Jarven with wide, shocked eyes that betrayed her doubt. The hand against Alex's was trembling ever so slightly. Squeezing it in response, Alex took in a long, slow breath to calm her own racing heart. This was important. This is why they'd arrived on that hill. Alex had to have faith that it was for a good reason. She had to trust in her magic.

15

Fallen Idol

801 C.E. West bank of the Saône River, Burgundy

It always ended in smoke and fire. The Old Ones, when corrupted and cornered, always called upon that primal human fear of fire to try and force the mages back. But the mages always pressed on. They did not falter, even when an entire village was burning, and smoke stung their eyes and ash-covered their tongues and throat.

The last hints of snow and frost had faded from the land, but now ash was choking the fresh plants trying to spring up. Morgana coughed and blinked her eyes, trying to see properly around the burning village. Her fingertips glowed with her silver magic, and she waved her right hand, imagining the smoke being pushed away. Silver sparks swirled in the air, and the smoke cleared enough for her to see the bodies lying in the street.

This was worse than the last villages. There had been survivors there—traumatized survivors who didn't understand what had happened beyond destruction. Nobles were on the lookout for bold bandits trying to sack villages, and rumors told of a rogue group of Vikings that had been cut off from the river they came into the empire through. Morgana knew that they were all wrong. This wasn't bandits or Vikings: It was a petty would-be-Goddess.

They weren't far from Lyon. Nerthus had inched closer and closer all fall and winter. The Saône River was less than fifty feet from Morgana, and one of the burning docks collapsed into the waters with a loud splash. She could see people fleeing, running away from the river in the false belief that their torment had come from there. The ringing bell of the local church echoed in Morgana's head, though it had stopped its warning call.

Rudolf was bleeding from a head wound. He was on his knees, dazed and confused with Charles trying to pull him to his feet. Both had taken the brunt of a blast of magic, but thankfully Nerthus wasn't focusing on them. Instead, she was staring Morgana down.

Nerthus had shaped her form to be beautiful by the local standards. High cheekbones, shapely hips, long golden hair, and too large blue eyes were meant to enthrall, meant to mark her as something more than human. A faint glow of power surrounded her, but there was no sign of the dark marks Morgana usually associated with a corrupted Old One. The so-called goddess was dressed in a white shift that was stained with mud and splattered with blood. The oozing remains of human entrails covered her right hand and arm. Still, Nerthus was smiling serenely.

"The Grand Mages have come to see me. It is an honor." Nerthus inclined her head to them, the smile never fading. Morgana flinched as those blue eyes settled on her. They were swirling with madness, a familiar desperation, and entitlement. It was too similar to her memories of her foster mother. "Though you have been most disrespectful." Nerthus raised her blood-covered hand and gestured to her face. "I am without my veil. I fear you must die. None who see my face are permitted to live."

"Nerthus," Merlin said firmly. His fingers were white-knuckled around his wooden staff. "This has gone on long enough. Return to the waters."

"I shall," Nerthus assured him with a smile. "It is my custom to always return to the waters. I am cleaned by my servants, and then they die. As you must die already, you should fill that role. I will permit you to cleanse me and return me to the waters."

"That's not enough, Merlin," Morgana hissed. "She's too far gone, and she doesn't care."

Morgana respected the power of the Iron Trishula, but it had saved Shiva because he was fighting. Nerthus wasn't. Even if they could have gotten Shiva here, instinct told her that even the Iron Trishula wouldn't work. Merlin, however, wasn't looking at Nerthus with disdain. Instead, he was calm and seemed interested. If she hadn't known her partner so well, she'd fear that he was under whatever spell this Old One could weave.

"Lady Nerthus, surely there is no reason for you to continue this... celebration."

Nerthus laughed. "Are you appealing to me to have affection for humans?"

"Not precisely, my lady." Merlin shook his head but never took his eyes off of her. "These people have committed no crime. Coming to their villages, entrancing them, and then killing them does no good."

"They have forgotten me," Nerthus snarled. "I never asked for much, Merlin. Celebration in my name when I arrived and a few sacrifices before I slept. It was fair." Nerthus' fingers curled into fists, and her mouth twisted into a sneer, breaking the spell of beauty that she projected. "I did not ask to be born into this world, to be torn at by this world."

That answered that question. Nerthus was one of the Old Ones who had been made in the Iron Realm. Morgana wished she could destroy every Old One that thought reproducing in a world where you weren't welcome was a good idea. All they were doing was setting up their children for a lifetime of agony. Her eyes moved back to the boys, checking on them again. They were both on their feet and, thankfully, staying back.

"I know," Merlin said kindly. "None of us asked for this. I am a child of rape that magic allowed to grow and be born so I could protect this world. I never asked for it. Morgana never asked for her burden, and no mage asks for their magic."

"I don't care."

Nerthus barely twitched her hand, but it was enough that Morgana shouted a warning. Vines burst out of the ground, and Merlin barely twisted away before being ensnared. He swung the iron sword he carried to cut them off while his bright green magic flared around his left hand. The ground quaked. In the distance, Morgana heard the screams of the last people fleeing the village. She hoped they were all out safely.

The sun was marching towards the horizon, but the flames around them cast a hellish glow. Nerthus' vines were coiled and ready, writhing in the air like grasping hands. Taking a step towards the boys, Morgana pulled on more of her magic and smiled as the silver glow around her hands intensified.

"Do not raise that sword to me," Nerthus scoffed. "All iron is banned in my presence!"

"I was hoping to ask you about that," Merlin said calmly, as if he wasn't facing down a dangerous beast. "You aren't a Sídhe, so iron doesn't really harm you. Why the ban then? Was it originally symbolic of you banning warfare around you, or..." Merlin smirked now, his eyes glittering. "Were you symbolically banishing the reminders that you did not belong here?"

He was an idiot to bring that up in front of an Old One. The vines lashed forward, trying to grab them, but the ground shuddered beneath them, and slabs of stone jolted up from the trod-down street to crush the vines. Nerthus screamed in rage, and Merlin's green magic seeped into the ground beneath her. The Old One sank as the terrain gave way below her.

Knowing there were only moments before Nerthus freed herself, Morgana released her magic. Silver bolts shot through the air like arrows. They collided with the Old One's chest, tearing through the flesh and clothing. Nerthus shrieked, but her body rippled, and the holes were patched up as quickly as they had been made. The Old One shimmered and, in a blur of twisting colors, was a few feet away from where she had been. It was almost impressive to Morgana.

"How?" Rudolf gasped behind her. "How did she do that?"

"She's not a real physical thing," Morgana reminded him. "She's a mass of light. Nerthus can look like whatever she wants."

"So, what do we do?" Rudolf asked, his voice small and scared. "If we can't hurt her-"

"We can hurt her," Morgana growled. "Use your magic and keep wounding her. She can't go on forever. The more damage you do, the weaker she gets."

It was a poor explanation, but they were short on time. They should never have brought the boys here. Morgana's stomach flipped in her gut as Nerthus rolled her shoulders and tossed her golden hair back lazily. Morgana could only hope that her dismissal of the pain she'd been in moments before was a front.

"And to think, you're the mages that everyone fears," Nerthus scoffed. "I was expecting more of a challenge."

"Is that why you've been moving towards our home?" Merlin asked.

Nerthus shrugged and inspected her gore covered hand. A smile tugged at her lips at the sight. The glow of the flames made the blood gleam. This brought back memories of another Old One who had embraced destruction. Morgana stepped in front of the boys, chest tightening with the bad memories all of this called forth. She would not lose them like they lost Gofiben and Bran.

"Stay back," she hissed.

"But we're here to help," Charles replied. She didn't have to turn to look at him. Morgana could imagine the angry and defiant expression on his face. "She can't keep doing this! Vikings are bad enough; we don't need another force rampaging the country."

They'd be lucky if people believed a Viking group had made it this far south. Morgana could only hope that they would. She didn't say that to the boys though, and stayed in front of them. Frustration poured off both of them.

"Wait for an opening," Morgana cautioned softly. That was as much permission as she could bring herself to give them.

Power radiated off of Nerthus as a pale light that twisted and distorted the area around her. She wasn't attacking. She was watching them closely. Another building collapsed with a grinding and a crash. Merlin's magic spun around his free hand as the standoff continued. Nerthus was smiling serenely, as if the collapsing village around her was entertaining. Perhaps it was.

Morgana's magic coiled tightly in her chest, reacting to her worry and anxiety. Something had to happen. They couldn't just-

Nerthus moved first. A wave of golden light blasted towards Merlin. He slammed his staff in front of him, and a wall of green magic solidified to protect him. Confident that her partner could defend himself, Morgana unleashed the pent-up magic in a flurry of silver bolts. Flexing the fingers of her right hand, she summoned the remaining magic into a whip and lashed it at the Old One. The bolts tore into Nerthus, drawing a scream from the being, and Morgana crashed the whip across her side, tearing into the nebulous form Nerthus was holding.

A wave of energy crashed into Morgana. Her chest ached as a sharp shock traveled through her body. Purple and pale blue bolts of magic shot past her and struck Nerthus. Vines with a green glow entangled the Old One's feet before a slab of rock jolted from the ground and hit her back. With a cry of fury, Nerthus blasted it all away. The air shuddered, and thunder rolled through the village. A wild glaze had taken over Nerthus' eyes.

"I'll kill all of you!"

Morgana gasped, her body shaking. The air shimmered all around them, and not from the smoke. Nerthus' eyes turned white, and the solid form of her body began to fade, becoming ghostly. Power surged around her, the wind picked up, and the smoke thickened. Merlin's shield began to falter, and Morgana could see the old man struggling. Throwing up her hands, Morgana created a silver dome around her and the boys.

"Morgana, what do we do?"

"Hold onto your magic until I drop the shield," Morgana ordered. "If we're lucky, she'll tear herself apart!"

Unlikely, but Morgana could hope. She could be optimistic. But the power waves didn't stop coming. They battered against her magic, and Morgana grit her teeth. A slow burn was taking hold in her chest and spreading through her muscles. Nerthus' face was indistinct now, glowing with power and lacking a solid appearance. Morgana wasn't sure if that was good or bad.

Merlin's shield cracked. Nerthus moved towards him, her body retaking some of its human appearance. Dark marks were all over Nerthus' skin, like bruises. Dropping her shield, Morgana tried to muster more magic for another attack, but only gasped at the pain. Lights danced in her eyes, and Morgana slumped to her knees. The voices of the boys were distant as she shook her head and tried to regain her senses.

Nerthus was turning towards her. Rudolf jumped ahead of her and held out his hand. Purple magic shot forth, but the Old One dodged the attack easily with a laugh. She was stronger than Morgana had feared. The dark marks on Nerthus' skin were spreading. The Old One wasn't trying to hide what was happening to her anymore.

Suddenly water burst out of the river, sweeping up and over the nearest charred buildings. Morgana twisted around to look, her body tensing with shock and hope. Cyrridven was on the surface of the water, her bronze skin dull in the distorted light of the smoke-filled sky, but her body glowing with power. Her eyes were bright with anger, and the glowing droplets of her circlet illuminated the scowl on her face. In her hands was Cathanáil, the blade gleaming with promise.

Relief washed over Morgana as the water flooded across the surface of the village, already muddy with dirt and ash. Another building collapsed with a groan. She could smell the mud now as the earth pulled in the water. Dizziness struck her, but Morgana stayed on her knees as water hit her hands and flowed around her body. It was cold and dirty, but even that did nothing to dim her joy at the sight of their ally.

"She came," Merlin groaned gratefully. He was alive, at least. "I wasn't sure she heard me."

Morgana didn't blame him for his surprise. Cyrridven slept deep and well in the waters of the world. Sometimes, you could reach her, and sometimes you couldn't. Her eyes were locked on Cathanáil. How long had it been since she had seen her brother's sword?

"Cyrridven," Nerthus purred as Cyrridven turned toward her. "You aren't truly here to help the pathetic mages, are you, dear?"

Cyrridven didn't answer. Morgana was too far away to see the expression of their ally, but Nerthus fell silent and drew back a few feet. Waves crashed out of the river, splashing over more buildings and rolling around their battlefield, cutting them off from the rest of the world. Then Cyrridven lifted Cathanáil and threw it through the air towards Nerthus. Horror filled Morgana, but she couldn't move.

Charles reached up and caught the golden hilt. Dizzying relief hit Morgana and she could only smile. They'd been right about which boy was the Iron Soul, but now was not the time to be congratulating themselves. Nerthus screamed, and energy rolled off her body. The temperature rose and there was a hiss of steam as the water vaporized. Morgana shouted a warning to the boys, but they were already drawing back.

Nerthus lunged forward, her body elongating unnaturally and reaching toward Rudolf. Talons ripped at Rudolf, and he dropped to his knees, clutching at one arm. Charles swung the Sword. Nerthus tried and failed to twist away. Rudolf grabbed her ankle and sparks of his purple magic dug into the Old One's flesh. Morgana tried to move, but she was too weak. The blade struck Nerthus' chest. There was no burst of blood, but the Old One's form rippled and shifted. A snarl ripped from Nerthus' throat. Golden sparks rose into the air like embers off a fire from Nerthus' body.

Cathanáil flashed, the metal lighting up with a pale green glow as Arto's magic mixed with Charles'. Eyes widening, Morgana could only watch as Nerthus' body flickered. More magic poured out of Charles' hands and danced across Cathanáil. The boy's face was contorted with pain, but he stayed in position, keeping the Sword in Nerthus' chest. Rudolf climbed to his feet and planted himself behind Charles, keeping the other on his feet against the waves of pressure rolling off Nerthus.

Water swirled around Nerthus' feet and turned to ice, locking her in place when she tried to pull away.

There was no explosion of light. There were no final screams or threats. Nerthus' body flickered and then was gone, leaving wisps of light in her wake that quickly vanished. Cathanáil glowed brighter for a moment, but then even that light faded. Charles collapsed on the ground beside Rudolf without a sound. That finally gave Morgana the strength to move. She threw herself forward and stumbled to her feet.

Her knees ached as they once again hit the ground. She was burning and shivering all at once. A splash of water and more hissing as the fires were extinguished wasn't enough to make her look up. Charles was breathing. Rudolf sighed in relief and slumped back, resting his forehead against his knee. Morgana could see the bruises already forming on the young man's arm and the scrapes through the torn fabric of his clothing, but he was alive. A soft groan escaped Charles as his eyes fluttered open.

"Did it work?" he asked in a gravelly voice.

"Yes, it worked." Morgana smiled down at him. "You were able to keep her in place and injure her gravely. She's gone."

Sighs of relief escaped both boys, and they lay back in the mud. Their clothing was already ruined, and Morgana didn't have the heart to scold them. Breathing hurt. She'd used too much magic, but sitting on the ground was already helping, and a glance around assured her that the fires were out. No doubt, they had Cyrridven to thank for that.

Charles released Cathanáil, and the Sword hit the ground with a soft thunk. Morgana stared at it and found herself smiling. She made no move to touch it despite the desire to. Her body was too heavy, and Morgana settled for resting her hand on Charles' ankle. Rudolf laughed at something that Charles said that Morgana had missed, and she inhaled slowly.

Merlin was at their side a short time later. He was moving slowly, but seemed uninjured. His hand touched her shoulder for a moment before he knelt down with the help of his walking stick. Merlin picked up Cathanáil with a soft smile and inspected the blade. It looked as new as the day Morgana had watched Arto make it. Her eyes met his, and Merlin offered her a small smile before he turned towards the river. Words rose into Morgana's mouth, but she held them back.

Cyrridven was waiting by the shore, a soft smile on her face. Merlin bowed his head as he approached, and she held her arms out to him. Lowering her eyes, Morgana swallowed back a wave of jealousy and focused on the boys. Let Merlin have the support of Cyrridven; she'd focus on their students who had managed to overcome an Old One. Pride and affection filled her chest, driving away the fear and guilt that had plagued her for so long. She'd make sure to tell them that as soon as she had the strength to speak.

16

Rebellion

They followed a twisting path down the hill that curled around trees and large stones. It wasn't really wide enough for them to walk two by two, but the Sídhe insisted and kept a close eye on them all. Alex was able to keep hold of Morgana and Nicki's hands and hoped the boys were staying close behind them. Under other circumstances, she might have asked if the translation spell was still working, but it took all of her concentration to keep her balance on the sloping path, and the Sídhe were not talkative.

Jarven was the group's lead, their spear hitting the ground like a walking staff with each step. Around them, the forest was dense and oddly quiet. The leaves were too large and heavy to rustle in the wind easily, and Alex didn't hear any animals moving in the underbrush over the crunching of their feet.

The forest was beautiful. The silvery trees here were even thicker and taller, giving her the impression they were older. Her mind wandered as she looked around, despite the Sídhe escort. Alex knew it was silly not to stay focused on them, but part of her hoped that being calm would help keep their captors from getting twitchy with those spears. As it was, she could feel Morgana's magic stirring beneath the surface of her skin as it was slowly renewed.

Deeper and deeper into the valley they went, and the darkness around them grew. Layers of tree branches full of large leaves blocked out the already dim and small sun. Nicki released Alex's hand, either so she could better keep her balance, or finally giving up on the Sídhe providing any conversation. Alex's eyes adjusted to the low light, and she could only hope that it didn't get any darker. Her only comfort was that the Sídhe were slowing down too. They were low light creatures, not creatures of the night, no matter how much they might occasionally resemble vampires.

They passed guards at a checkpoint that Alex didn't see until they were on top of it, thanks to the dense foliage around it. The two guards on the ground were startled by the mages but stood back when Jarven waved them away. A pair of archers in nearby trees leaned out of their hiding places for a better look, and Alex could feel their gaze on her back.

"Is this a Sherwood Forest thing?" Nicki whispered.

"Don't know," Alex replied.

The steep side of the valley was made of dark rock, and small piles of fallen stone were visible around the trees. Hidden in the shadows was a narrow cave entrance and another checkpoint. For better or worse, they were at the rebel base. Nerves fluttered in Alex's stomach, and she briefly considered refusing to go in. Caves hadn't bothered her in the past, but here, surrounded by Sídhe, it reminded her too much of the tunnel she'd been taken into. Morgana squeezed her hand.

"In here," Jarven said. Their voice was a shock after so much silence. "Be warned: If you try anything, we and the rest of our people will not hesitate to strike you down." Narrowed violet eyes backed up the promise.

"Understood," Alex answered for the group. Her mouth was almost too dry. "We want to talk."

This tunnel was dark and cramped. Cold air encircled them, and Alex was grateful that they had so many layers on. Columns of stone had been formed where the water dripped, reassuring her that erosion and deposits were still forces of nature in this world. There was no light except for the lanterns hung on small pegs. They were far apart, and it was still nearly too dark for humans, though the Sídhe had no trouble.

After a slow slope down, the tunnel opened into an enormous cavern with lanterns strung on cables overhead. It was at least three stories high, with rooms carved out of the stone overhead, and ladders and bridges linking levels in a chaotic mess. Sídhe were moving around, seeing to tasks, and carrying items. Many stopped and looked at them, their eyes widening, but none approached. Alex saw adults and children peering their way and more guards taking up defensive positions.

"Be respectful to Eirwen," Jarven ordered. "He's the one who will decide your fate."

The statement was meant to be ominous, but it was so cliché that Alex had to bite the inside of her mouth to keep from giggling. They'd stumbled into a new genre all of a sudden. Well, not really. Rebellions against corrupt rulers were a common element in fantasy, but she hadn't been expecting this. Jarven narrowed their eyes at them, but said nothing more before they were led to the very back of the cave.

The room was large, with a worn table in the middle made from the silvery wood of the trees. Rough shelves lined the sides of the room and were filled with scrolls and what looked like oddly bound books. Alex took it in with a glance as best she could. A few lanterns provided a little light here and there, but the whole of the room was too dim for her to see it in detail. Everyone gathered close to Alex, either holding her hand or touching some part of her.

"Morgana, the former Queen Scáthbás' favorite," an unseen speaker said.

"You know me?" Morgana demanded.

"Yes, we know of you."

The speaker stepped out of the shadows. It was a hunched over Sid, far older than any that Alex had ever seen before. His pale skin wasn't wrinkled as much as a human's would have been, but there were small markings all across his face. He wore a finely made blue tunic and a black cloak and matching gloves. Alex risked a glance at Morgana, but she showed no signs of recognition.

"I'm curious as to what my reputation here is." Morgana's tone was as dry as a desert.

The Síd chuckled. "Scáthbás ranted and screamed for days after you chose to side with the mages. Many would still consider you the greatest traitor in Sídhe history, but I am not so dramatic. Regardless of what she tried to make you, Morgana, you were always part human."

"And you are?" Morgana demanded. Her grip on Alex's hand was clammy, but she showed no other signs of distress.

"I am Eirwen." He bowed a little. "You would not know me. I was a low-ranking member of the court, but I was there the day that you were brought to meet Scáthbás. She plunged the hall into darkness, and your magic created a light." He shook his head and moved to a seat at the table. Without waiting for Morgana to say anything, Eirwen sat down and sighed. "I wasn't part of the rebellion then, but something about that day... your fear of the dark and Scáthbás' cooing manipulation of you after you revealed your magic. It left a bad taste in my mouth."

"Convenient," Morgana said. She raised a doubtful eyebrow. "I never heard of any rebellion."

"You wouldn't have. You were being groomed by the Queen, and Scáthbás was vicious towards any rebels she found."

"And here you are now, still hiding away."

"The sealing of the Iron Realm changed the political landscape for some time. In the aftermath, with Scáthbás suddenly gone and her advanced guard lost in the Iron Realm, the rebellion made many strides. It was during that period that I joined." He sighed again and slumped back in the chair. "I am the last rebel leader of that generation, I fear. Those were good days. For a few centuries, the rebellion held almost two worlds in the Empire."

"What happened?" Nicki asked. She was gripping Alex's left hand painfully tight.

"The princes warred amongst themselves for what was left," Eirwen said. "They still do, until reports of the Darkness came. Rumor has it that Scáthbás was aware of it and that it drove her rise to power. Some believe that those before her knew as well and that the fear of it is the foundation of the Empire, but I cannot say for sure. Knowledge of it was buried, hidden even from those who seized power." Eirwen shook his head. "While the princes did not make true peace, the threat of being destroyed if they could not extend the Empire was enough to change the balance of power."

"So, the Sídhe population knows what is coming?" Bran asked.

"No. The Darkness remains a secret. It has destroyed an entire continent in this world, and I dare not even speculate as to the condition of the homeworld. The princes unified against the threat and used the information to leverage support from powerful figures who might have otherwise supported us. Others were swayed by greed for new resources and slaves. We haven't exposed it out of fear that self-preservation instincts would only make everything worse." Eirwen looked to Morgana. "We have been trying to find a way to stop it; to save our worlds and make the invasion of the Iron Realm unnecessary, but we have had limited success."

Alex nodded in understanding. That made sense based on what she remembered from the tunnels. The soldiers hadn't been afraid. They'd been excited. She remembered references to the princes, but there hadn't been anything absolute. Slaves and proof that the tunnels worked had likely been step one of a full invasion. The uncertainty about how the population would react on the part of both the princes and the rebellion was understandable.

"You all hold hands," Eirwen observed. The subject change surprised Alex. "Is this some human custom that I have forgotten?"

"I have an item that is helping us communicate with you," Alex said. "We don't speak the same language."

Eirwen's expression changed from curious to amused. A small chuckle escaped him, and he nodded. "I see. Similar items have been used in this realm for years, though they are rarer now."

"Really?" Nicki's eager voice made several of the nearby Sídhe grimace.

"That would explain some things," Morgana said. "But how did you make such things?" Her eyes were narrowed suspiciously, and several of the Sídhe shifted into defensive positions.

"There is some magic at our command, as you should recall." Eirwen was meeting Morgana's glare with a calm gaze.

"Of course," Morgana said. "If this isn't the native homeworld, then every Sídhe here is a transplant. You aggravate this world, all of you, at all times." She narrowed her eyes. "No wonder there was magic here.

Even if only a few of you could control it, this world must constantly be generating it."

No, it wasn't that simple. Alex was aware of the energy flowing through the ground. It was struggling. There was magic, yes, but it was weaker than it should have been. Magic on Earth was a defense system with mages as the white blood cells. Here, the immune system was cannibalizing itself to keep the planet alive. Alex's stomach turned.

"Yes and no," Eirwen replied. "I'm afraid that my knowledge is too limited to answer your question, but something was done during the first crossings and early invasions that made this world a bit more comfortable to us. And it is within the same branch. Your Iron Realm, from my understanding, shares some similarities with other worlds, but it stands alone. It is not part of any branch. But that isn't what you're here to discuss. I imagine you are not willing to evacuate the Sídhe to Earth?"

"No," Morgana answered. Eirwen flinched at the tone.

"We need to get to the homeworld," Alex said, trying to draw the conversation back to something useful. "That's where the Darkness first emerged, and it's the place where we need to stop it." She glanced around the room, noting the guards once again. "I hope you understand that we are not your enemies."

There was a moment of silence that was so thick with tension, Alex was tempted to swing Cathanáil a few times as a joke. Of course, that was a joke that relied on an English phrase, and she doubted the pendent would manage that translation before the guards attacked. Eirwen was staring at Morgana thoughtfully, and she was glaring in return. Jarven shifted to Eirwen's right, their hand tightening around their spear.

"We have no reason or desire to hurt you," Alex added. "Please just show us the way out of the cave, and we'll be on our way. We didn't attack your scouting party."

"Yes, that surprises me," Eirwen said. His eyes swung to Alex, and Morgana nearly growled. "But I am grateful."

"So, we all go our separate ways?" Alex tried again. Calculation shone in Eirwen's eyes, and Alex could feel Morgana getting ready to attack. The glint of the lantern light off the tips of the spears caught Alex's eyes. "What do you want?" Alex asked before anyone could start a scuffle.

"It could benefit you as well," Eirwen replied. He relaxed his shoulders and folded his hands in front of him. It was such a human mannerism that Alex was thrown for a moment. "There is information at the palace that we need—troop movements and where some of our fellow rebels are being kept prisoner. We've considered making a move on the palace before, but none of us have any magic. You do."

"And why do you think this would benefit us?" Alex asked carefully. She was grateful that the others were letting her negotiate.

"If you're going to the homeworld, wouldn't you be better served having some information about the source of the Darkness first?"

"Do you know something?" Morgana demanded. "We are worried about the survival of everything! Your kind lives a long time; you'll easily live to see everything die."

"Is that really true?" Nicki asked. She was faintly flushed, and her eyes were wide. "How was he there when you were a kid, Morgana? That was three thousand years ago! And time seems to move normally, I mean, doesn't it?"

Alex thought it had to. Morgana had gone into the tunnels as a child and, after she'd been fused with a Changeling, had still been the same age. At least... she thought so, but that wasn't something she remembered from Arto. He'd only been a small child then. Everything that young, from all of her lives, was fuzzy.

"Sídhe can live a very long time," Morgana reminded Alex softly. "Remember, you killed the very Síd that nursed me as a child when you were taken into the tunnels. A generation to them is a very different thing."

"They don't live that long on Earth," Alex said. "Frea is long gone. Do you think that could be a difference in how time moves here?" Her stomach tightened, and her mind spun as she realized what that might mean for them if it was true.

"No, that is part of how Earth affects them. Their natural lifespans of thousands of years are cut to two centuries at the most. It's one of the reasons... well, they struggle on Earth for many reasons."

"How are there not more of them?" Nicki whispered. "I mean, thousands of years, how come the whole planet isn't a giant city?"

"Our reproduction is slower than yours," Eirwen said calmly, as if they hadn't been frantically whispering. "Morgana is correct: There is a chance that I might live to see the Darkness consume this world as well." He stood up, keeping his hands where they could see them. "I understand your desire to keep moving, but the world has survived this long; will a few days make such a difference? If you can help us be in a stronger position when you stop the Darkness, then perhaps we can stop the more imperialistic aspects of the empire. The soldiers who have attacked the Iron Realm in recent years are following orders and craving slaves like they had long ago. If you really want to protect the Iron Realm, then helping us get that information is important. And who knows, the records of the first crossing and potentially Scáthbás' research could help you."

Scáthbás had claimed that she wanted to save her people. Alex wasn't sure if she believed that. The late Queen had been a master of manipulation, and Alex was certain that with her dying breath, she wouldn't have stopped trying. It didn't really matter. Scáthbás had been Queen and had followed a path of conquest and enslavement.

Had there ever been moments when Scáthbás had considered another way? Had she ever considered allying with the mages of the Iron Realm, or had she considered them too weak and primitive when she took the throne? Alex's knowledge of the timeline was foggy, but she was certain that the Sídhe had been raiding the people of Bronze Age England for a long time even before Merlin and Morgana had been born. Scáthbás hadn't been the first ruler of the Empire, and she hadn't started the conquest. She had only pushed harder than those before her.

It was a history that Alex doubted she'd ever get to know. Wondering did no good, but for a moment, Alex couldn't help but try to imagine a world where Scáthbás had put a stop to human enslavement and sought to work with Merlin. How different might everything have been if she hadn't determined that adding Earth to her Empire was the best way forward?

The voices were loud in response to that thought, nearly drowning out her awareness of where they were. Around her neck, the heavy iron pendant seemed to hum in response to her distress. Shaking her head, Alex pulled herself out of thoughts of what if. It would do no good now. This was the world as it was, and she had to find a way to save it.

Eirwen was waiting for an answer. Morgana hadn't taken her eyes off of him but had stayed silent. Alex looked down at her mentor and wondered if she wanted to know what Morgana was thinking right now. Nicki, Bran, and Aiden were watching her, waiting for her to speak for the group.

"If we say no, are we prisoners?"

"No," Eirwen replied. He gestured at the guards, and they shifted back. "I will simply insist that you be escorted far from here before using more magic, lest you lead the army right to us." He paused, and his violet eyes glittered. "But that palace is the very same that Scáthbás ruled from. The archives have been preserved for all these years. If there is an answer to what started all this, then your best chance for finding it is there."

Morgana remained silent. Was she in shock at the confirmation that the city they'd seen was the one she'd grown up in? Alex licked her dry lips and swallowed, wishing she had some water. What was the right decision here? Press on to a dead world with only the fragments granted by visions to guide them, or try to gather information? Leave the Sídhe to sort themselves out, or give support to a faction that didn't hold with slavery? Should they focus on this, or worry about sealing up the hole in this world, or leave it alone with the assumption that the Darkness would stop once they fixed the original entry point? And all that was if they were telling the truth.

The voices were torn. Strangely, out of all of them, it was Arto's voice that was suddenly the clearest. His eagerness, his hope, and his sorrow pushed through the clouds of fear and doubt, piercing into Alex's consciousness like a sunbeam.

"Help them."

17

The Capital

Nicki was torn. On the one hand, going to a magical world and helping the rebels against cruel overlords was something right out of dreams she'd had as a child. It rolled together *Star Wars* and *Lord of the Rings* and made her giddy. But the more serious part of her was worried. The part of her that had always been a little freaked out about magic being real and coming with so many strings attached. The part of her that remembered looking down at her best friend, her damn near brother, in a coma in a hospital bed was sharply aware of how bad things could go.

They didn't know if these Sídhe were telling the truth. They were hiding out in the woods, which seemed to lend credibility to them being the rebels, but it wasn't proof. And the promise of records that could answer some of their questions and maybe prepare them for facing the origin point of the Darkness seemed too good to be true. But on the other hand, they lived so long that maybe that event had only been four or five generations ago. There could be records, or at least everything that Scáthbás knew. Nicki didn't know what to think, and it was driving her crazy!

Jarven and five other Sídhe had come with them from the cave. Their names had been given in a rush, and Nicki wasn't sure who was who. There was one more of them than their group so Nicki figured the Sídhe weren't trying to be intimidating. Her mind kept reviewing the simple plan for getting into the palace, and trying to ignore the fear gathering in her gut. Without her pack, she felt naked and unprepared, but she was also grateful for the absence of the weight as they climbed a hill on their way to the city.

Nicki had a bad feeling about this. All of it. She understood what Alex wanted to do, but they should cut their losses and go to the next world. That was where the Darkness had broken through. That was where they needed to be. Her feet kept moving as she followed their escort through the jungle. Pushing aside some of the large, heavy leaves, Nicki reached blindly for Aiden's hand with her left one. Her friend caught on and took her hand, giving it a firm squeeze. He came forward, ignoring the narrowness of the trail to walk beside her.

"You okay?" Bran asked from behind them. "Nicki?"

"I've got a bad feeling." She swallowed and shook her head. "Not sure what it is."

"The whole situation," Bran suggested. "I don't like this either, but... well, I caught a glimpse of that world. There's nothing there to give any guidance if we can't easily close the hole. I get why Alex is eager for some real data."

"Was it bad?" Aiden asked. "She hasn't said much."

"It... It's hard to describe, honestly. Visually, it was disturbing to see a place so empty and torn apart, but there's more to it than that." Bran shuddered, and Nicki's stomach rolled. "I'm not explaining it well. Let's just stay together through this, and we'll be fine. Alex won't do anything too risky. If this doesn't yield anything, we can talk to her about another plan."

Imperfect, but fair. Nicki hated it, but kept her mouth shut. Pushing Alex right now when she didn't have any helpful ideas to offer wouldn't do any good. The blonde might be trying to put on a calm face, but the way she got spacy told Nicki that the voices were loud right now, and she didn't need even more opinions being thrown at her.

Her thoughts were distracted when they reached the top of the hill, and the city once more was in her sights. Eyes widening, Nicki took in the city below with a smile. It was large and filled a long valley with the palace perched high above the rest on top of a hill. Three walls encircled different areas of the city, echoing a rather medieval design to Nicki. She could see gatehouses where roads lead into the city, and the low light of the sun glittered off golden armors below.

Inside the walls, the buildings varied in size, but most appeared to be two to four stories high, with flat rooftops. She could just make out figures moving around the rooftops, and in a few places, bridges connected rooftops over roads. There was no grid system, and instead, the city streets curved and turned around blocks of buildings. It was busy, and even from their place in the hills, Nicki could hear the hum of life.

"It's impressive," Alex said. "Morgana, do you remember-"

"I never left the palace," Morgana answered flatly. "Never saw anything beyond those walls. I know nothing of the city." The words carried no small amount of bitterness.

Nicki wondered if Scáthbás had been worried about something happening to Morgana, like her being captured by a rival, or if she'd been trying to protect her from abuse by other Sídhe, who didn't know she was under the Queen's protection. Or had she been trying to make sure that Morgana saw the Sídhe as divine and perfect figures? Going into a city with the noise, waste, and general messiness of life would have ruined that illusion.

She glanced at Morgana. The older mage was watching the city with sharp green eyes that burned with... anger? Resentment? Nicki wasn't sure, and swallowed. This was feeling more and more like a bad idea with Morgana here. How could they expect her to be rational right now? She was going to ask how Morgana was when Alex stepped closer to the older mage and whispered something. Some of the tension left Morgana when she looked at Alex. Nicki decided to stay out of it.

"So, we're going in there?" Aiden asked. A Sídhe looked at him in confusion. Sighing loudly, he stretched out and gripped Alex's shoulder, earning him an unimpressed look from the Iron Soul. "So, we have to go into the city?"

"Yes," the Síd answered. Their eyes jumped to Alex and then back to Aiden. "The sun is setting soon, so it will be a little darker."

Nicki looked into the sky. It was odd to look right at the sun, but she could. It was about half the size she was used to and a pale violet color. She searched her memory for information on star colors, but all her brain could think was how pretty it was.

"There aren't any violet stars in our universe," Bran said from beside her. "At least none that we've discovered. Blue stars are the hottest, and red are the coldest. There's no violet in that spectrum."

"Guess that's one of the differences then." Nicki wiped some sweat off her brow. "Hopefully, that's all."

She was distracted from learning more about stars from one of her nerdy companions by movement from the Sídhe. They had opened their packs and were pulling out cloaks. Nicki felt twenty degrees hotter at the mere sight of them. She was sure that it hadn't been this hot before. Maybe the stress of being found by Sídhe had distracted her.

"Cloaks won't hide us," Alex said doubtfully. "Not really." She gestured at her head. "We don't have horns, and a whole group trying to hide their faces will draw attention."

Nicki was so glad that someone had said it. Sure, it worked in the movies and in some books, but most of the population weren't wearing anything over their hair and horns. They'd stand out. Plus, they might die from the heat.

"You should use magic then," Jarven suggested. They tilted their head and examined them all thoughtfully. "You are correct that it will be difficult to hide you."

"Are there any less guarded areas we can go in?" Alex pressed. "Or a time that isn't as busy?"

"This is the lowest level of guards," Jarven replied. "There are even more at night, and you aren't seeing well as it is."

"That's true," Alex agreed. A soft sigh escaped her as they all waited for her decision. "Magic it is then. We've kept people from seeing fights in the past; this shouldn't be too hard."

"I'll take care of it," Morgana announced. She was staring hard at the Sídhe escort. "I have the most experience."

"Alright, then." Alex looked back towards the gate. "Are there patrols inside? How much do we need to worry once we're inside the city?"

"There are side roads that we can take."

The cloak was more cumbersome than it looked, and the fabric settled uncomfortably on Nicki's head. It didn't come forward as much as cloaks on Earth, due to most Sídhe having horns. She wasn't sure how much it would help, but so far, she hadn't seen any sign of red hair anywhere. Nor brown hair like the boys and Morgana had. It seemed like the stories of the Fae liking dark hair might have some basis in reality. Everyone liked what they didn't have.

Their group moved towards the gate slowly. Nicki lowered her gaze, hoping that would help the hood cover more of her face and hair. Soft silver light shone from Morgana's hands, and the surrounding air rippled. A soft sigh of relief left Nicki and she walked a little faster. Two of the Sídhe moved normally, hoods down and talking as if everything were normal while the guards watched them. Jarven and the other Sídhe were staying closer to Morgana. Nicki wondered if their faces were known.

Nothing happened. They walked through the gate without anyone stopping them. Staying silent, Nicki tried to keep her head down, but couldn't resist a glance up every few steps. Now that they were inside, Nicki could see signs of technology. There were small carts running through the streets along rails, what appeared to be gas lights on some buildings, and she could hear a voice over what seemed to be a loudspeaker system. Not modern to her definition, but not medieval either. Weird.

Staying together, they moved up one of the gently sloping streets. The buildings were made of a shimmering stone material with wooden sections. There were small windows here and there, but they were uncommon compared to Earth. Nicki wanted to ask. The anthropology student burned with the question of why they didn't use windows, but she held it in. This mission was going to kill her in multiple ways.

Her eyes adjusted to the dying light as they went. Further and further into the city, Nicki's awe wore off more and more. There were holes in the road, waste along the streets, and the buildings showed signs of decay. Several had been gutted, and there was no sign of repairs. She looked towards the walls, noticing missing sections on the top further from the gates. Whether they were in a bad part of town or things were really run down in general, Nicki wasn't sure.

Morgana's magic glittered around them as they climbed the hill towards the palace. No one bothered them, but Nicki's whole body was tight with restrained energy. A massive wall blocked their way to the palace. Jarven directed them into a small alley only a block or so away from the castle without a word. Nicki's eyes traced the wall, and she wondered what the plan was now. She hoped the Sídhe weren't assuming that they could fly.

"What now?" Bran asked Alex.

She turned to Jarven and repeated the question. A series of musical words that meant nothing to Nicki was the answer. Alex nodded, and Morgana, who was still holding her hand, grumbled but didn't argue. Nicki glanced at the boys. Bran just shrugged, and Aiden rolled his eyes.

"We're going in when the guard is being changed," Alex explained moments later. "We all might need to use magic to be on the safe side." She gave Morgana a worried look. "According to Jarven, there are fewer guards inside. The current ruler keeps most of them patrolling the city and surrounding areas."

Nicki didn't need the translator to know that Morgana wasn't comfortable with this, and Jarven noticed. Tension weighed down on Alex's shoulders, but she was desperately trying not to show it. Regret was probably setting in. But Nicki nodded that she understood, and a few minutes later, after letting Morgana catch her breath, they were back out in the streets.

Summoning her magic, Nicki watched the blue aura dance around her fingertips. The spark in her chest was bright. She could feel the light and warmth from it, but it was smaller than it would have been on Earth. It was a sobering reminder that they had to be careful. Speeding up her steps, Nicki pushed the magic around their group, willing them to vanish from the sight of outsiders. A ripple of dark gray reassured her that Alex was hiding them too.

"Bran, Aiden," Alex whispered. "Let us do the magic; you stay fresh just in case."

In the gateway, the guards were moving in practiced rows. The guards who had been on watch were organizing themselves on one side while the fresh guards came in from the other. Nearby citizens were moving away from the gateway quickly, some looking over their shoulders nervously.

There was little space between the guards. All of them were dressed in the familiar golden armor of the Riders and carried golden weapons; some spears, but mostly swords. Their horns were long and curled out of their foreheads, with golden decorations wrapped around them. Nicki did note, however, that their gauntlets were not as impressive as those she'd seen on Riders. They were made of some sort of animal hide with golden accents, but were not the plate gauntlets she'd seen on Earth.

There was no time for her to wonder about such things. Jarven hissed something to Alex, and the group surged forward as one line of guards walked out of the gateway and down the main road. From their place along the wall, they twisted through the opening and hurried beyond the gate. Nicki held her breath, pleading with her magic to keep the cloak up, to keep them safe. Around them, the air shimmered, and the scent of ozone hit her nose. Alex's magic. Hopefully, that was a good sign.

Nicki's eyes dropped to Mjǫllnir on Alex's hip and then to Cathanáil on the opposite side. They had the Iron Artifacts; the Chalice was with Bran in his daypack, and they all had iron weapons that the rebels hadn't even tried to take. They'd be fine. Yet the bad feeling lingered.

The courtyard was massive, with towers rising high above it on all sides. But even here the stone was crumbling, and one set of staircases leading to the upper walls had collapsed. Morgana hummed at the sight, but said nothing as they hurried across the courtyard. The Sídhe were moving faster now, eagerness in their every step. Jarven was leading them towards an archway with a heavy door that was off to their right, leading into the palace, but not the front entrance.

"Here," Alex said after Jarven spoke. The translation was unnecessary, but the sound of a human voice and English words calmed Nicki's nerves a little.

The door opened with only a soft slide of wood against stone. One of the Sid leaned forward and then headed inside before gesturing to them to follow. Alex led the way for the mages, with Morgana staying right beside her. Nicki looked back one more time as her chest burned with exhaustion from the cloaking spell. No one had noticed them yet, and she slowly released her hold on the magic.

They were in a corridor that was dimly lit, but they wasted no time in moving forward. Behind her, one of the Síd slid the door shut with barely any noise. Jarven led them straight ahead, past two doorways on either side of them to an intersection that stretched in all directions further than Nicki's eyes could see in the low light.

High curved ceilings loomed over them. The architecture was similar enough to what Nicki imagined a castle was like to be familiar, but the stone shimmered in an unnatural way. The path before them was dim with only low light from gold wrought chandeliers to help them see. Jarven turned to her fellow rebels, speaking in low tones that made Alex and Morgana frown. Nicki gripped Bran's hand, pressing closer to the others and put her free hand on Alex's shoulder.

"Okay, we're in," Alex said. She was panting a little, but still standing straight and tall. "That took a lot of magic, so we need to try and avoid any interior guards we can. Which way?"

"The library is that way," Jarven replied. They pointed down the corridor straight ahead of the way they had come. "But we need to be careful. A report from a sympathetic servant said that part of the palace in that area has collapsed." Jarven glanced at Morgana, but the Grand Mage said nothing. "Keep your cloaks up."

"Wait," one of the Síd said. Nicki thought their name was Barit. "We're in the palace?"

"Yes," Jarven replied. Impatience shined in their eyes. "We haven't much time."

"But, we're IN the PALACE." Nicki could see a bad idea being born in their eyes. "We have a chance to kill Prince Welven!"

"No," Alex hissed.

For an instant, something like hope that this wouldn't be a disaster tried to bloom in Nicki's chest. For a split second, she had some hope that Jarven could regain control. Her hand slipped off of Alex's shoulder when the other mage took a step forward, and she couldn't understand the next words. Nicki summoned her magic, prepared to make it translate for her before a spark of pain warned her not to try. While she caught her breath, she watched Barit's face and tried to understand the Síd's expression. But then that hope was dashed when Barit and two other Sídhe took off running down the hall to the left and into the darkness. Nicki released her magic and let loose a soft "fuck." And honestly, that word really fell short.

18

New Life in the Lowlands

1 536 C.E. Antwerp, Flanders

Peace always settled awkwardly on Morgana's shoulders. She'd lived at peace more than she'd lived at war, but Morgana could never completely trust it. Long periods of peace where she kept her head down and waited for the next bit of trouble tended to blur together in her mind. Morgana's magically enhanced memory could remember so many details about Arto and his war against the Sídhe, about Thor, and the other battles she'd lived through. But if you had asked her details about the times the world was at peace and the places she'd lived, Morgana would struggle to answer questions.

This new life would be no different. Time had forced her from Strasbourg a few years ago, when her lack of aging threatened to draw attention. She had drifted through the Rhineland, Italy, and France with Merlin for a few years before heading north. He had gone west to Spain. Michel was living a peaceful life, though Morgana knew Puck was a frequent visitor to their old shop. She tried not to think about it too often. Michel was an adult and had earned the right to his choices. If he wanted her opinion on everything, he would have sold off the shop and moved to Flanders with her.

But then again, Morgana was grateful that he hadn't. Too many of her memories revolved around that man as a baby, a toddler, her precious student, and as her son. If she saw him today face to face, she knew that there would be gray in his hair. He'd likely look older than her now. Watching Airril grow old had been hard enough; watching that happen to Michel might be even worse. Children were different. They always were.

Shaking her head, Morgana returned her attention to sweeping the floor of the small house she was renting. It had three rooms, providing privacy for Morgana, space for cooking, and room for her to work. The house was a recent construction, and thus far proved to be better insulated than the old shop in Strasbourg.

The house was growing darker as the sun dropped in the sky outside. Nostalgia for the old roundhouses rolled through Morgana. They'd always been darker than modern homes. There hadn't been any windows, only the door and the hole for the smoke. During the day, light had entered the center of the houses, but the furthest edges of the houses had never been bright. This twilight was familiar, even comforting to Morgana.

Movement drew Morgana's attention, and she turned around to check on the other occupant of the house. A young boy, roughly eight years old, was seated at the kitchen table, quietly reading the book Morgana had left him with. His legs were swinging thoughtlessly as he worked his way through one page after another. Realizing that the boy was still reading, Morgana paused in her cleaning and hurried over to light the candles on the table so he didn't strain his eyes.

If Merlin asked, it was for legal reasons that she'd taken the child in. Women with children were a legal family unit without a male head of the household in the lowlands. That was rare in Europe, and Morgana enjoyed being able to live her life without Merlin pretending to be her husband. Or worse, having to be married to a mortal. She hadn't done that often, but sometimes it was necessary for a few years at a time.

At least Merlin had never abused his power when they'd acted as a married couple. She couldn't say the same for every husband. There was a reason that Airril would always be her favorite. The necessity of the façade bothered her. It was an itch beneath her skin that she couldn't get rid of. It was a constant temptation to use her magic to change the mind of lawmakers. But she knew better. Morgana was an outsider even when she lived in the middle of society. She was too old, too long-lived, and too jaded. Her place was not trying to shape the world.

Antwerp was a good sort of place for her. The city was rapidly growing, with new businesses forming every day, artists arriving, and traders coming in. No one noticed the arrival of a new woman who had come to work in the textile industry. The rapid change in the area provided opportunities, and Morgana had to admit that she was suffering from a touch of optimism.

Trying not to linger on her thoughts, Morgana set the broom to the side and walked over to the table to check on her foster son. Lieven's precious brown curls were tangled, but the boy didn't notice and kept running his left hand through his hair. Morgana knew she should stop the bad habit, but she only smiled and watched him fondly. His soft brown eyes were sweeping across the page of the book with interest. Morgana knew he was mostly looking at the pictures, but he would grow into the stories.

"Are you enjoying it?" Morgana asked.

"It's interesting," Lieven said. "Thank you."

"Are you understanding any of it?"

"Some." A sheepish smile took over the boy's face. He pointed to a few of the words. "I understand this part, but not..." He gestured at the rest.

"I'll read some to you tonight," Morgana offered. "And remember what I said about context clues. They can help you with the words you don't know yet."

The book was one of the recently published Dutch histories, and likely too advanced for him. Morgana tried to remember how Michel had progressed with his reading, but she'd had Merlin to help her then. They'd been able to spend more time reading one on one with him. The boy didn't need mathematics books yet, and books on language would only confuse him. Maybe some pamphlets would be better, as long as the subject material was appropriate. At least things beyond bibles and prayer books were being mass printed now.

She watched Lieven for a few minutes. He mouthed the words as he read them, his finger moving slowly along the lines. Morgana had glanced through the book when she'd purchased it, but hadn't read much of the contents thus far. Most of the books she owned and still had with her were in German or in Latin. She'd managed the switch to Dutch without too many problems, but the language was different enough in written form to confuse Morgana more than she liked. That wouldn't last long. If there was one thing she knew, it was how to adapt.

Morgana finished sweeping the main room and opened the door to the street long enough to push the dirt out. Lieven was still enthralled by the woodcarvings in the book, giving her time to cut up a few onions and toss them, some stew meat and a few other scraps into a pot for dinner. There was a rhythm to this new life of hers, and Morgana was enjoying it.

With the house clean, her spinning done for the day, and dinner started, Morgana puttered around the house for a few minutes in search of something to keep her busy. Her hands were cramping from the earlier work, and she gently massaged the fingers of her left hand. The soft turn of another page reassured her that Lieven was staying out of trouble. Morgana doubted that he would be this easy to keep busy and happy in the future.

Her eyes moved to an unfinished letter sitting at her place at the main table. A small inkwell was beside it, closed, but ready for whenever she resumed her writing. The quill she'd made with a pigeon feather was showing signs of wear, and she briefly considered buying one of the metal-tipped wooden pens that were being sold in the city. Morgana dismissed the idea quickly. It wasn't worth it when you could find a feather and fashion a quill at home.

The unfinished letter taunted her, and Morgana leaned on the back of the chair to read over what she had so far. It was a reply to a message Michel had sent nearly a month ago. She wasn't sure how much she should write about Lieven to Michel. She didn't want him to think that she'd replaced him. Michel was dear to her. He was the first Iron Soul that she'd raised from a babe and the only one who had ever rivaled Arto in her heart. But... he would be gone sooner or later. Morgana knew herself well enough to know that she'd kept Michel at a greater distance than she'd kept Arto. Back then, she hadn't known that she would live for thousands of years. Back then, she'd allowed herself to care more deeply.

Then again, Michel had taken in a child himself recently. He might understand her needing someone in her life more than she was giving him credit for. A soft sigh escaped Morgana, and she stepped forward to rest her hand on Lieven's head. The boy stopped his reading and looked up at her with wide eyes.

Playing with his hair, Morgana offered Lieven a soft but real smile. Europe seemed to have an endless supply of war orphans, and he was one of them. When she'd found him six months ago she hadn't been planning on taking him in, but learning of the Flemish laws regarding women with children had changed her mind. Picking up that there was nothing wrong, Lieven turned his attention back to his book. Given what the boy had been through, she considered herself lucky that he was so at ease with her. Morgana wasn't sure what it was that made him comfortable with her. Maybe she was more maternal than she thought, or "cupboard love" was more powerful than she'd given it credit for.

Lieven would need a better education than she could give him at home. Her spinning and weaving provided a good income. Even with her magic weak, she had enough power to ensure that their life was stable and safe. Michel had inherited a shop from her and Merlin. He was a merchant of comfortable means and had a better-than-average education. Lieven wasn't a mage and wouldn't have magic to help him along. She'd need to arrange an apprenticeship soon.

Morgana wasn't anything noteworthy in Flanders. She was a new arrival, though independent, with some money to her name. Studying the boy, Morgana tried to imagine what trade would suit him. If Merlin was here, he would instantly suggest smithing, but Flanders enjoyed a strong art culture. Painting, sculpture, or woodworking all commanded respect.

Woodworking was valuable beyond art, she considered thoughtfully. If he didn't have great artistic talent, then he could still be a carpenter and enjoy a solid career. And he was fascinated with the woodcarvings featured in the book, so it might not be difficult to convince him. She would focus on his reading, writing, and math for now at home, but Morgana knew she couldn't leave the rest for long.

A knock on the door brought Morgana sharply out of her thoughts. Lieven glanced up, but the threat of an unexpected visitor didn't put him on edge like it did Morgana. Narrowing her eyes, Morgana brushed off her dress and walked to the door. It was nothing. There was no reason for her to be worried. She was tense today. That was all it was. The door swung open, and Morgana blinked in surprise.

"Merlin," she greeted.

Her counterpart was smiling widely at her, a bag slung over his shoulder and his walking stick in his right hand. Dust covered his tunic, and she had a bad feeling that he'd walked here. It had been less than two years since she'd seen him, but his curls seemed a little grayer now. Or that might just be more dust in his hair.

"Hello, Morgana." He stepped closer, giving her a moment to pull away before he kissed her cheek. "You look well."

"And you look filthy."

"Ah, yes." Merlin looked down at himself. His smile faded for a moment, but only for a moment. "Sorry about that. Normally, I'd have tried to clean up a bit."

Shaking her head, Morgana decided it didn't matter and stepped to the side so that the other mage could enter the house. Merlin nodded to her but didn't step inside right away. He dusted off his tunic and cloak with his free hand. Huffing softly, Morgana reached out and took the walking stick so he could use his second hand. She supposed she should be grateful that he was trying to tidy himself up, given that she had just swept.

What was he doing here? Usually it took more than a couple of years for him to feel the need to track her down. Merlin stepped inside, and Morgana shut the door with a firm thud while Merlin looked around the main room with open curiosity. Lieven had looked up from his book, but he didn't smile at Merlin.

"A child?" Merlin raised an eyebrow at her. Their native language rolled easily off his tongue. His eyes were bright. "Michel recently took in one of his own. But I'm a bit surprised that you followed his example."

"It made sense," Morgana replied, allowing herself to slip into the old language. "When did you see Michel?"

"Last month. I just came from Strasbourg. It was on my way east."

"I see., How was Spain?"

"Pleasant enough. I think you might like it. The Spanish are rather forward-thinking regarding the education of women. They also still follow the Roman way and ensure that women inherit property."

Morgana nodded. She'd heard as much, but for now, she was happy in the lowlands. "Noted," she replied. "But I'm doing well here for now. What brings you east? No trouble, I hope?"

"Nothing like that." Merlin unbuckled his cloak and hung over the back of a nearby chair. "I'm wandering at the moment."

He didn't offer any more information, and Morgana didn't pry. They had been settled in one place for many years when they'd been raising Michel. Merlin, Arto, and herself had been travelers for years, and Merlin had been a wanderer before she and Arto had joined him. Sometimes the man needed to stretch his legs and see the world.

"I am sorry that I didn't send warning of a visit," Merlin offered.

"That's alright," Morgana assured him. If it wasn't trouble, then she wasn't going to put the effort into being cross. "How is Michel?"

Merlin's smile faded a touch, and he hesitated. "He's well," he assured her. "It was strange to see him face to face again." Morgana understood. It was the same reason she'd contented herself with letters over the last few years rather than visiting. "His ward, Jakob, is a very sweet young boy. You'd like him. He reminded me of Michel at that age." A wistful expression settled on Merlin's face. "The old neighbors have moved away, so I was able to stay for a few days without anyone noticing me."

"Let's sit down," Morgana said. Then she switched to Dutch and smiled at her foster son. "Lieven," Morgana called. "Please give us the table, dear."

The boy nodded and grabbed his book. Leaving the table, he moved over to the fireplace and sat on the floor by the hearth. Her ease with Merlin seemed to have been all the assurance he needed. Or speaking in a language he didn't know meant he lost interest quickly.

He barely looked up from the book, and Morgana reconsidered woodworking. If the boy was this fascinated by the written word, then perhaps she should consider other options. A good secretary could make excellent money in a major trading city.

"Have a seat, Merlin," Morgana ordered in their language.

Merlin chuckled, but obeyed and slumped into one of the chairs. Morgana turned away and went to the cabinets to retrieve some wine. Grabbing a bottle and two glasses, Morgana returned to the table and poured them each a drink.

"Thank you, Morgana." Merlin took a long drink from his glass. "Ah, that was just what I needed. Strange how one can forget the dust and dryness of the road."

"It's better than the rain and snow."

"True." A shudder shook Merlin's body. "So very true. I have too many memories of freezing, despite our gifts. But enough of that; how are you, Morgana? Truly?"

"I am well, Merlin," she promised. "I've settled into the city, and I'm supporting myself without any issues."

"How long do you plan on remaining here?" Merlin asked.

"A few years. I have Lieven to worry about." Sitting down in her chair, Morgana sipped her wine with a soft smile. "I was considering his education before you arrived. And the city is busy enough that if I don't draw attention to myself, I shouldn't have too much trouble for a while."

"Good, I'm glad to hear that." Merlin leaned back in his seat.

Morgana glanced towards Lieven and found the boy watching them carefully, despite his face being turned down. She smirked at the sly little boy. He needed to work on his technique, but the effort wasn't in vain.

"Lieven, this is an old friend of mine," Morgana explained. Casting her eyes back to Merlin, she asked, "How long are you staying?"

"That depends on you, honestly. I haven't anywhere I need to be."

"You should stay a couple of weeks then," Morgana offered carefully. "That'll give you time to rest before you head to wherever you are going. You can share my room."

Merlin nodded, and Lieven went back to his book. At least the boy was too young to be wondering about his foster mother sharing her bed with a strange man. Morgana was already considering what relation to say Merlin was in case she was asked. Merlin watched Lieven silently, giving her time to process her thoughts. She wondered if he was thinking of Michel's Jakob, and wished that she could have seen the boy. It was bittersweet to imagine Michel as a parent.

"What are you reading, Lieven?" Merlin asked. He spoke slowly, the Dutch words uneasy on his tongue. Merlin slid out of his chair and sat on the floor beside the boy. "Ah, interesting. It is marvelous that so much is available in Dutch. I'm afraid that I am not well versed in your language. Perhaps you can help me during my visit."

Morgana rested her chin on her hand and fought back a smile. Lieven didn't look happy, but curiosity was winning out. It was annoying how easily Merlin understood children. Morgana shoved down the flare of jealousy that shimmered in her chest. He wasn't staying. She knew what he was like when he was in a wandering frame of mind. Content with that knowledge and happy to see him despite herself, Morgana hummed a little as she stood up to check on the stew.

19

The Archive

The library/archive was not what Alex had expected. After the books and scrolls on the shelves of the rebel base, she had expected more of the same. The shelves closest to the main door did have paper-like books and manuscripts on them, but everything beyond that was wooden boxes with words indicating what was inside them, carefully fitted on the shelves. Further from the door, the shelves shifted from wood to stone and metal, and more of the boxes themselves were metal.

Despite knowing that they likely had little time, Alex couldn't help but turn slowly to take it all in. The high ceiling was almost impossible for her to see because of the low light. Small lamps were fitted along the stone walls above the shelves. They weren't candles, but the glow they produced was much softer than any electric lights Alex had ever seen.

"We haven't got much time now," Jarven growled. Anger radiated off them. "Those fools will draw the attention of the guards."

"But they won't know where we are," Alex pointed out nervously.

Jarven gave her a dubious look that made her feel like she'd said something idiotic. "The guards will probably kill my soldiers..." Sorrow flickered over Jarven's face, but immediately vanished. "And the guards will release the Hounds. They will track our scents so regardless, we have little time."

Alex's throat tightened, and she nodded. It had been a long time since she'd last seen a trained Sídhe hunting Hound, and she was in no hurry to fight the wickedly fast things again. Had that group of rebels been planning this on the way up, or had they really been this stupid? Alex's ears were strained as she tried to hear what was happening outside the library. There were only three of them. Maybe they'd get through undetected, but Jarven didn't seem to think so.

"What we need is over here," Jarven said. They pointed at the shelves with paper materials and then gestured further into the library. "Records of the first crossing will be further back."

Jarven and the last Síd started pulling papers and books off shelves, putting some into their packs and dropping the rest on the floor. Alex stared at them before it sank in that they weren't going to help her and the others search. Morgana raised an eyebrow at Alex. She turned on her heel to head for the back. Alex hurried after her, with the others right behind her.

"Any idea what we are looking for?" Alex asked Morgana.

"No."

That answer echoed against the stone. Suddenly, the air was a lot harder to breathe. Alex looked up at the shelves. There was a pattern of numbers that was likely a date on many of the boxes, but she didn't know what she was looking for.

"Let's use magic," Nicki suggested. She looked at Bran and Aiden. "You two are fresh. We've found things before with magic."

Alex was dizzy with relief at the suggestion and nodded. Usually, she'd prefer to find it without everyone getting exhausted, but it was their best option. The boys didn't argue and turned to face each other. They joined hands and closed their eyes. Magic rippled over Alex's skin, and she eagerly pulled it in. Nerves twisted in her gut, and Alex ran her teeth over her lower lip and tapped her foot.

There was weight in the air here. Alex didn't know if there was something special about the room to protect it, but she was willing to believe that. There was a scent similar to a bookstore, but it was mild thanks to how little of the library seemed to actually include paper. Her eyes moved around the room as Bran and Aiden worked on their spell and took in the row of desks between two sets of shelves. Cabinets next to the desks had paper, binding materials, and other supplies, but on one of the desks was a set of engraving tools and sheets of metal. Scribes were apparently still a thing in this world. Alex wondered how they were using metal like this and hadn't figured out a printing press.

That thought was dismissed as silly and human-centric immediately, though Alex suspected that when they got back home Nicki was going to over analyze everything they saw here. Even now, her fellow mage was looking at the nearby shelves with desperate interest. Sadly, they did not have the time to indulge in innocent curiosity.

A light appeared between the boys, a shining orb that shimmered with magic flaring off of it. Alex stepped closer but kept herself from reaching out for it. Beside her, Nicki visibly relaxed as the boys opened their eyes and grinned at their success.

"Well done," Morgana said. "As long as it-"

The light suddenly burst to life and flew past them all and further into the darkness. Alex didn't wait. She lunged forward and took off running after the light with the others behind her. It wasn't going too fast. She only had to jog after the initial burst, and Alex wondered how much urgency the boys had pushed into their magic. The guiding light in Paris hadn't been this fast.

Following the light, Alex and the others turned a corner. Around her the shelves loomed ominously, and there were fewer and fewer lanterns. Back here, it was dark, and the scent of decay had taken a firm hold. But the light did not stop, and they had to keep going around a turn to the left and even further back. The shelves were stone now, and carved into columns that supported the room. Alex swallowed. That hinted that this was the older part of the archives.

A gate and heavy golden fence blocked their path, appearing out of the darkness, and the light went on without them. Morgana's silver magic flashed, and the gate was blasted open in a wave of dazzling light. Alex opened her mouth to comment before common sense stopped her. The metal clattered against the stone floor, and the sound echoed around them.

"They already knew there were intruders," Morgana said sharply, but there was a hint of embarrassment in her voice. Taking a slow breath, Morgana walked forward to follow the light. "Come along."

She followed Morgana without a word. The library was silent again after the ringing crash, and Alex could only hope that was a good thing. Speeding up to a run so she could catch up with the light, Alex and the others found themselves in a very dark section, with a deep metallic tang filling their noses. The light moved to one set of shelves that were set into a pillar and then vanished. Blackness surrounded them at the light's sudden absence.

"I got it," Alex said. Her voice was too loud in the silence.

Calling on her magic, Alex easily formed a gray orb in her hand and tossed it into the air. It did as she imagined and hung above them, casting a warm pale glow all around them. She went to the bookshelf and inspected the boxes closest to where the light had vanished. There was a faint layer of dust on them, but Alex suspected that if this place had been more exposed, there would be more.

Pulling off a box that she could reach, Alex huffed at the weight of it. Bran was immediately beside her, helping to support the box and keeping her from tipping over. Aiden came over to help a moment later, and they lowered the box to the ground. The lid slid on rather than being hinged in place, and thankfully, it wasn't locked. The scraping sound of metal against metal sent an icy shiver down Alex's spine, but she got the box open.

Thin sheets of metal were tied together, with narrow characters covering them. The lettering had been engraved into the metal and filled in with gold to create a clear contrast. Alex ran her fingertips over the material while she wondered what metal it was. Then again, the gold only looked like gold to her. It vanished in the Iron Realm once it wasn't touching a living thing from this world.

Their supplies didn't do that. Alex frowned and wondered at the reason. When they'd crossed over, she hadn't even considered worrying about that. Maybe that was based more on the magic of the Iron Gates rather than on any natural aspect of the Sídhe materials. Shaking her head, Alex dismissed the thoughts. It was interesting, but they had more important things to be concerned with.

"Metal," Nicki chuckled. She was leaning over the box, and Aiden moved out of the way to let her get closer. "Makes sense when you think about the lifespans of the Sídhe. Paper doesn't last that long. Records that are that old in our world were sealed away or made of stone. It's just funny to think that the Sídhe have to do things like that within their own lifespans." Her tone was soft, almost awed, and Alex gave her a moment to bask in the discovery.

"Where should we start?" Alex asked.

"Well, they look labeled," Nicki said slowly. "Honestly, I'm worried that the light didn't direct us to one box because they are all about that subject." Nicki ran her finger over the nearest box and inspected the dust. "So, we need to focus on finding what is most valuable to us. If they have any kind of similarity to our way of thinking, then maybe a final report drawn from all the combined research...."

"Nicki, here," Alex pulled the translating necklace over her head, nearly tangling it in her hair, and thrust it towards Nicki. "You use it: I think you'll best know what to look at."

Nicki's eyes widened, but she grinned and snatched the pendant from Alex's hand. Her eyes were bright and greedy. Alex almost pulled her hand back to remind Nicki that they had a mission, but it was too late. Nicki already had the necklace around her neck and was moving off to inspect the label plates.

"I really hope this is a well-organized library," Bran sighed. He rubbed his eyes. "I'm afraid that Nicki is right." Bran studied the shelves. "Should we try again, narrow the focus?"

Alex wasn't sure. Nicki was already digging through the box that Alex had opened. Aiden was pulling down another box with Morgana's help. Bran rushed over to lend a hand, and Nicki didn't even look up. There wasn't space for four people to handle a box, so Alex stayed where she was. The noise of the others and the movement of the metal sheets as Nicki "flipped" through them was the only noise. Given that she knew a group of Sídhe had gone rushing off to murder a prince, she was uneasy at the quiet.

Alex sat down on the floor, facing the entrance of this library section. She felt lighter without the heavy iron pendant around her neck, but she was highly aware of its absence. In her chest, her magic flickered to life. She'd used a lot of her reserves in helping cloak their group coming inside, and recovery was slow here. Inhaling and exhaling slowly, Alex let her worry drift away and focused on the soft but steady pulse of energy beneath her.

It was so similar to what she knew from Earth. So similar to what she'd used in the Dragon world. Energy with a hint of the flavor of the world it was passing through. Flexing her fingers, she reached for it. Her skin chilled as every nerve came alive, and her awareness shifted. There was a moment of dizziness, almost as if she was going to drop off to sleep before the blackness of her eyelids lit up with lines of color.

Nicki's bright blue presence was behind her, along with the red and yellow outlines of Aiden and Bran. Morgana's silver was a burning flare by the dark shelves. Further away in the library, she sensed Jarven and the other Síd. They were moving frantically. Even further were dark golden shapes that were coming closer and closer.

Alex pulled at the line of energy beneath her. It sparked at her touch, burning brighter than before. Energy washed over her skin, and she soaked it up. Her chest grew hot, warming as more and more energy shifted into magic that she could use. Raising a hand, Alex opened her palm and gathered power there. A soft sound from Morgana assured Alex that it was working.

"Alex?" Morgana asked.

"Preparing," Alex answered.

She watched the others pull down two more boxes without turning around. Energy rippled over her skin in small waves of warmth that contrasted with the cold stone she was sitting on. Minutes ticked past. Nicki made a happy noise behind her and metal scratched against metal. Aware of the beating of her heart, Alex breathed slowly and pulled on more and more magic to prepare.

The shapes in the distance were moving. The dark gold shapes would be on them soon. Alex opened her eyes and swallowed. Dark gray magic hovered in the air as an orb beside her. Alex's limbs sang with renewed power, and she slowly smiled. A triumphant cry from Nicki made her smile, but she didn't turn around. Jarven and the other came running into view, both of them carrying stuffed packs. Nicki stepped closer to Alex and placed a hand on the back of her neck, putting bare skin to skin.

"Hounds have been loosed!" Jarven snapped. "The others must have been found! We have to go now!"

"I think I've got what we want," Nicki said. "This box seems to have the final report! It isn't everything, but it should be the summary of what they learned about the death of the homeworld."

That did sound promising. Alex hoped it was enough. Climbing to her feet, Alex rolled her shoulders, but didn't dislodge Nicki's hand. Calm had settled over her. The voices were soft and low, leaving her mind clear and sharp.

"Is there another way out of the library?" Alex asked after snagging Nicki's hand.

"No," Jarven answered. "To protect everything inside, there is only one entrance and no windows."

"Then let's get as close to the door as we can," Alex said calmly. "The less distance we have to fight our way out of, the better."

"Can't you use your magic?" the other rebel demanded. They were eying the gray orb curiously.

"It isn't unlimited," Alex answered. Her body was humming with the energy she'd been able to collect, but a fight would exhaust that quickly. "We need to stay calm and move."

Jarven nodded, disappointment shining in their eyes, but Alex dismissed it. There was no water to make a water tunnel, and even if there had been, that was a trick Alex was not going to try on another world. When the Sídhe turned away, Nicki fumbled with the Iron Pendant and pushed it back into Alex's hand.

"Let's not confuse things," Nicki hissed. Then she wrapped her now free hands around the box.

"Do you need help?" Aiden asked, as Alex pulled the chain back over her head. "That's got to be heavy. It took three people to get it down safely."

"I can carry it, just watch my back."

With that, they started speed walking towards the front of the library with Alex's light orb and magic orb staying near her. Long spaces between shelves were barely illuminated, and Alex released some of the magic she'd gathered. Her senses spread out around her, but she ordered them to focus on the path ahead. The dark gold shapes were in the library, blocking their way.

"Six Sídhe are by the door," Alex said. She kept her voice low but spoke so that everyone could hear her. "With four Hounds."

A collective inhale. The slide of metal being pulled from sheaths and soft orders from Morgana for Nicki to get behind her followed in quick succession. Drawing Cathanáil, Alex and the others crept towards the front of the massive room. The light that she and the other mages needed was a beacon to the guards. A shout alerted all of them, and as they came around a sharp corner made by the shelves, Alex threw her left hand forward and released a bolt of lightning into the rallying guards.

There was a crash as one was thrown to the ground. A horn was sounded, and in the distance, a bell rang. Alex only saw a flicker of panic from one of the guards as they turned towards the door before silver magic shot past her, and Jarven leapt forward with a battle cry. The

Hounds lurched forward with howls, and she raised Cathanáil, pushing magic into the blade, readying for battle.

20

Battle for an Exit

Slamming the blade into the side of the Hound, Alex tightened her jaw. The squishy, wet sound that filled her ears despite the noise all around her made her stomach turn. Silver blood gushed out from the wound as she ripped Cathanáil back before it could become stuck. The Hound twisted to snap at her, slowed by the injury, but still fighting. Kicking her leg forward, Alex ignored the yelp and thrust her sword into its neck. This time it collapsed and stayed down.

'*Well done!*' Thor boomed.

The others were less excited, but their nervous titters kept her from staring at the corpse. This wasn't a dog, not really. It was a creature bred to attack and kill. Still, it was harder when they didn't just vanish. Silver blood splattered from the battle made the floor slick, but Alex turned to check on the others.

Morgana had one hand extended, and a silvery shield was holding back a pair of Sídhe guards. One slammed a sword against the shield, and it rippled. Jarven and the other rebel were going toe to toe with another guard. A long cut on Jarven's face was dripping blood. Bran and Aiden were standing defensively in front of Nicki with their iron daggers drawn. Magic glittered around their free hands, but they weren't throwing it forward. The mages were on the defense.

But with Cathanáil, Alex had greater reach than she would have had with a dagger. Another Hound came tearing at her, and she swung Cathanáil down to catch it in the head. Teeth barely scraped her leg, but the creature was already dying. She tugged her leg away and ignored the sound of her jeans ripping as she thrust Cathanáil down into the creature's side to be sure. A wet noise filled her ears.

More blood spilled onto the stone. It was silver. There was no red blood. Alex would keep it that way. A guard turned to face her, its sword catching the light. Her body moved without Alex commanding it. Cathanáil swung up, knocking the sword off its path, and the guard staggered. It almost slipped in the blood. Her body was off balance, but Alex shifted the weight of Cathanáil to help center herself. Bran came into view and thrust his dagger forward into the Síd's unguarded neck. Disgust and shock filled his face before he pulled his dagger free and stumbled back.

The guard hit the ground with a thud. In a rush of pale hair and golden armor, another came at Alex from her left side. She couldn't move Cathanáil fast enough to defend herself, but the Sword hummed at her alarm. Pulling on the magic stored in the gray orb, Alex pushed it at the Sid. Lightning flashed through the air, jumping off the blade of Cathanáil and striking down the guard. There was a gasp beside Alex, but she didn't turn to check.

Much of the orb was gone, but Cathanáil glowed with renewed magic, and tiny arcs danced along the sharp blade. The stench of burning hair and flesh made her nose curl, and Alex focused on another guard. More were coming, and in the distance there was howling and bells chiming. She focused on that sound. It pulled her away from the assault on her senses. Swinging Cathanáil to the right, she dented the armor of a Síd that was physically beating on Morgana's shield. The armor didn't crack, but the hit knocked the Síd to the side and it tumbled over a Hound.

Jarven was on it immediately, slamming a golden sword into the guard's head. The guard's limbs twitched until they drew the blade out as the Hound recovered from the impact and snarled at them. A flare of red magic hit the creature, knocking it into the legs of another guard, sending that guard tumbling.

There wasn't time to focus on that. Another guard was moving towards Alex, but this one held a long spear. Alex had only a moment to be grateful that the Sídhe didn't have bows and arrows. Why, she didn't know, but if there had been archers at the ready, they would have already lost. The guard thrust the spear towards her. A wave of yellow swept it up and threw it into a bookshelf.

The shelf fell backward, starting a chain reaction of collapsing wood and metal. Clattering and crashes echoed through the room, startling everyone present. The last Hound flinched and looked towards the noise, giving Aiden an opening to kick its head and then stab its neck. Brutal and efficient. Alex's stomach tightened again.

Only two guards were left, and they had just realized it. One turned to run, only for Jarven's remaining rebel to close in and slash its neck from behind with a wicked-looking dagger. The last dropped its sword, looking to Jarven hopefully, but there was no mercy. Before Alex could say anything, before her conscience could catch up, Jarven stepped forward and drove their sword into the side of the guard where the armor joined together. It grasped at them, opening its mouth, but only gurgling before Jarven dropped it to the ground to finish dying.

Gasping in air, Alex was suddenly aware of the ache in her muscles and the rapid beat of her heart. She looked at the others, checking them for injury. Bran and Aiden wore uneasy expressions, and silver blood was splattered across their shirts.

'I'm sorry, Bran,' Gofiben whispered. 'He has always been a gentle soul.'

'They are your enemies,' Thor reminded them both firmly. 'And in truth, you are seeking to protect their world as well as the Iron Realm.'

Thor was right, but that never meant it was easy. Self-defense was one thing, but they had broken in here with the rebels. It wasn't something Alex had fully considered when she'd agreed to help. She looked towards the box Nicki held and desperately hoped that it had something of use to them.

"Everyone okay?" Alex asked. Her voice cracked a little, and she swallowed.

"We're not hurt," Aiden answered. Then he shuddered and shook his head. That seemed to help as he straightened up, and his expression cleared. "Nicki?"

"I'm fine. I have the box. We should go."

Jarven and their remaining ally didn't argue. It occurred to Alex to confirm their name. They had all been introduced before leaving the rebel base, but she couldn't remember. So much had been happening all at once. Though when Jarven gestured for them to follow, Alex decided it didn't matter. Following the others around the corpses, she kept Cathanáil drawn and ready.

The hallways beyond the library seemed even darker than they had been when they'd come here. There were no windows, so the setting sun shouldn't have impacted it, and yet, Alex was certain that it was harder to see and colder. Jarven eyed the empty corridor suspiciously. It was risky, but Alex closed her eyes and inhaled slowly.

Wisps of magic hung in the air. They were fading away fast, but she quickly drew on them. Silver, red, yellow, and gray all swept towards her. There was more as well, flickers of energy around them that Alex called to. Deep below them, the energy of the Tree of Reality pulsed, and Alex gently tugged on some of that power. She didn't dare take much, not when every instinct warned her that the energy was all that was keeping the Darkness already consuming this world from total victory. Alex had seen all too clearly with her own eyes, or through the eyes of her other selves, that magic helped counteract the Darkness.

The magic gathered in her left hand, warming the skin and sending some pleasant tingles up her arm. Alex drew some of it into her body, letting it soothe the dull aches taking hold. Then she pushed the rest out into the world, ordering it to spread and show her the surrounding area. Keeping her breathing even and measured, Alex slowly searched the immediate corridors around the library.

"Alex, can you see more guards?" Bran asked urgently.

"Give her a second," Nicki said.

"What are you doing?" Jarven asked, and Alex remembered that they wouldn't understand what the others were saying.

"I'm using magic to check the area," Alex answered sharply.

Spilling through the air, the magic crawled across the walls and over her friends, making the world shimmer as Alex closed her eyes. This feeling would never be familiar. It would never be comfortable. It was too... too many different things, but Alex's senses shifted and traveled beyond her. Down the way they had come were dark gold shapes moving fast towards them. They were all over the place, above and below them, to the right and to the left. No matter which way they went, there would be trouble.

Recalling as much magic as she could, Alex swayed until Bran grabbed her arm. The world spun, and a faint burn in her chest warned her to be careful. Everyone was looking at her, even Jarven, though the Síd's expression was one of discomfort. Her skin was hot despite the chill in the library. Keeping her eyes closed for a moment, Alex allowed herself to recover, but she knew that the dark gold shapes were coming closer.

"More guards are coming from that direction." Alex pointed to the right. "They're all over, but that way is the least guarded."

Jarven nodded, their unease apparent. With a glance back at the mages, they gestured to their remaining soldier and headed to the right. Morgana stomped after them, distrust radiating off of her, but there was no arguing. Alex switched Cathanáil to her left hand long enough for her to wipe her sweaty right hand on her jeans.

Walking down the dark hallways, Alex kept the light orb low and close to them. It was brighter than Jarven wanted, but the strange electric or gas or plasma torches along the wall did not provide enough light for humans. She glanced at Morgana and wondered if it had been brighter three thousand years ago because of the human slaves. Alex didn't ask.

Their footsteps were muffled in the corridor outside the library thanks to their boot soles and the long blue carpet that ran down the center. It was new, and Alex had a bad feeling about what it meant for where they were going. Morgana was looking around curiously with a pensive expression on her face. Alex opened her mouth, but stopped the question. This wasn't the time to talk. The sound of bells and shouts were faintly echoing towards them.

Then the corridor opened, and Alex knew that coming this way had been a mistake. They were in a massive hall, having entered on one side. It was filled with carved pillars and statues of Sídhe that towered over Alex, which supported the arched ceiling. Streamers of faded blue crisscrossed above their heads. Light was provided by standing candelabras and re-flected off polished gold that covered almost every surface, including the floor. Alex looked down at the seam where the pale stone they were walking on met the golden tile, and noted that the gold here was badly worn away.

The centerpiece of the room was a golden throne on a raised dais. Like the floor, the gold showed obvious signs of wear, and the blue cloth draped over one arm was fraying slightly at the edges. Despite that, it was an impressive sight to see, and the great space loomed over them like the nave of a cathedral.

A hush had taken hold of the room, as impossible as it was. Morgana was frozen in place. Around Alex, the room seemed to echo with distant voices. In the dim light, it was cold and alien, housing a quality that Alex couldn't put her finger on, but that made her want to run. The air was still around Morgana, as if afraid to disturb her.

"This," Morgana said. Her voice echoed around them. "Is the throne room."

"Morgana." Alex stepped forward. Her feet were heavy. Magic was shimmering around Morgana, wild and untamed. It didn't belong there. It shouldn't be this strong, not here, not away from the Iron Realm. Then again, Morgana was part Sídhe. She'd been made, in part, from their magic. "Morgana," she tried again. "Calm down. We need to keep moving. The guards won't be far behind."

"This is where I first used magic," Morgana explained as if she didn't hear Alex. "Where I first met her."

"I understand." Alex touched Morgana's shoulder. Magic tingled across her skin, and she gently pulled it into her body rather than losing it. "Morgana, we have to go. Please, sister." The last word slipped out: Arto was too loud, too worried for her to stop it, but it did the trick.

"Art-" Morgana turned; her green eyes wide. Then she caught sight of Alex and swallowed. "Alex... yes, you're right. I'm sorry."

Forcing a smile, Alex nodded and squeezed Morgana's shoulder. Her mouth was dry. Arto's worry was overwhelming. At least, Alex told herself that it was Arto's worry. Michel, Thor, and Gofiben were whispering supportive words as if Morgana could hear them.

"Let's keep moving," Alex added. The words of encouragement from her other selves threatened to come spilling out, but there was no time for that. "Jarven, how do we get out from here?"

But Jarven was looking around the room with sharp eyes. They were looking for something, and Alex's stomach turned over with dread. Something moved on the far side of the room, but there wasn't enough light for Alex to see what it was. Her left fingers twitched, and her magic sparked to life.

Two Sídhe stepped closer, and Alex recognized them at once despite the layer of silver blood that stained their armor. One was injured and leaning on the other, who was moving them towards Jarven. The second Síd looked mostly intact, though there were long cuts on their face that glittered with dried silver blood.

"You idiots are still alive," Jarven growled. They strode towards them but slowly reached out to touch their shoulders, revealing their relief. "What of the others?"

"Dead." The injured one answered with grave finality.

"Did you at least kill the prince?" Jarven asked.

"No, but General Donnawrig is dead."

Jarven made a sound of pleasure that echoed too loudly in the room. They turned their gaze to the rest of the room, searching for an exit that they could use.

"It was still foolish, Dubhstal," Jarven scolded. "But we need to leave before-"

A horn blare and rush of footfalls on the far side of the room was all the warning they received. Opposite them on the other end of the hall was another opening, and more light spilled into the space as rows of armored Sídhe marched into the throne room.

Tension filled the room like smoke from a fire. Whatever positivity their rebel friends had been enjoying at the reunion was smashed as a large group of Sídhe entered the room. None of the rebels or the guards spoke, but in the center of the group was a figure that absolutely stood out. Jarven and the others held their weapons tighter and glared at the figure, telling her who it was.

Alex didn't know what she had been expecting from a Sídhe prince. She'd seen one, or rather thought she'd seen one, in the tunnels all those years ago, but so much had been happening that she hadn't committed the being to memory. This figure was tall and regal, dripping with golden ornaments and fine blue material. Their horns curled out of their head, and golden chains wove between them to create an ornate spider web effect from which additional jewels hung.

A sword hung at their side, its golden hilt glinting in the light of her orb. The being gave them a haughty expression, clearly unimpressed with the disturbance at the palace. Guards stood around the figure, dressed in the familiar golden armor with weapons at the ready. Unlike the Riders, all of them carried round shields made of the silvery wood and braced with strips of engraved gold. Silvery Hounds snarled beside them, just waiting to be loosed.

Alex wasn't impressed by any of it. Not the gold, not the jewels, not the Prince's utter lack of concern. Frustration that this was how the prince lived while the realm was already falling apart to the Darkness roared in her chest. Alex's mouth was dry, and a reasonable part of her, likely Gofiben, suggested telling the prince of their mission. If the Darkness could be stopped, then that was better for everyone.

But Morgana made the decision for her. With a low and raw snarl, a sound Alex had never heard from her mentor, Morgana launched a volley of silver bolts. The magic was nearly wild, sparks spinning in all different directions like fireworks. On instinct, Alex called for the fragments of power before they could be lost. The bolts hit one of the Hounds, and the guards raised their shields.

Everything happened at once. The rebels pushed forward, Jarven thrusting their spear at the head of the closest guard. Hounds lunged forward with fierce growls, and chaos took hold. Flashes of red and yellow slipped past the rebels to strike guards. Alex drew Cathanáil from its sheath, but hung back and considered calling a retreat. Bells were ringing in the distance, no doubt summoning more guards and soldiers. They had come for information, not for a brawl.

She glanced towards Nicki. The redhead was clutching the metal box against her chest, and blue magic was circling her hands. Nicki hadn't attacked yet. Maybe it was best if they withdrew. But Morgana's magic was flashing wildly around the room. Bolts of silver were raining down on the guards, forcing them to raise their shields high and expose their bodies to the rebels.

The injured rebel fell, a sword breaking through their armor. The body hit the floor and did not vanish. Dubhstal shrieked with rage, striking a guard with their sword over and over in a flurry born of fear and fury. Alex opened her mouth to call for her fellow mages to stop. They were using too much magic. They still needed to get out of here.

"Aillil!" someone shouted.

The guards moved, blocking the view of the prince and telling Alex exactly who Aillil was. She finally moved when a Hound twisted around the side of a rebel and attacked her. Instinct born of many attacks forced Alex's hand to move. Cathanáil thrust into the creature's neck, cutting through muscle and scraping off the bone. The Hound slumped, its weight making the Sword heavy. With a twist of her wrist and a hard pull of her arm, she freed Cathanáil and made her decision.

"Fall back!" Alex called. "We can't fight them all!"

The rebels ignored her, but Bran and Aiden, who had moved forward, immediately retreated. One guard reached for Bran only for him to slash it across the face with his iron dagger. It screamed and dropped its sword, bringing the free hand up to its face while the flesh sizzled. Pushing magic into Cathanáil, Alex took comfort from the steady hum of the Sword's power and brought it up to swing at a guard that lunged for Bran. Another fight it was.

21

Old Bronze Disk

1 540 C.E. Antwerp, Flanders

The polished bronze disk in Morgana's hand flickered with magic, but no images appeared. Small sparks of silver danced just below the surface of the well-worn metal, betraying both its prolonged use and the amount of magic that had been poured into it over the years. It wasn't iron and didn't cling to the magic to the same extent, but Morgana would have been lying if she said that there was no power in the metal.

Her hands had polished the disk down over the centuries. It was smaller than it had been when she'd first received it. Small scrapes here and there disrupted the otherwise smooth surface, but for an item that was so old and that had been with her so long, Morgana knew it was in good condition.

The mirror had been a gift from Queen Scáthbás. Morgana had carried it to the Iron Realm from the Sídhe lands the night she had been merged with her Changeling self. Hidden beneath her dress, none of the humans had found it, and she had guarded it over the years. Its origin had never been revealed to her, and Morgana now believed that it had been from the Iron Realm, taken to the Queen, and potentially enchanted. But it was an artifact of her past that remained a mystery.

She stared into the surface, waiting for something, for anything to appear. Her magic rippled across the metal, shifting the rich earthy golden tone to silver and then back. Had she been as poetic as Merlin, Morgana would have found it beautiful, but right now, she took it as a sign of her weakened magic.

Things were quiet. There was magic in the air, but it was fading more and more with each passing day. Morgana knew it was a good sign. There was always a little magic in the world. It was natural, given the number of creatures from other worlds that lived in the Iron Realm, but the Iron Realm wasn't on the defensive. Still...

Morgana sighed and shook her head. She was looking for trouble. The scrying mirror had revealed nothing. There were no visions, no warnings, and no clues of where to go next. Right now was a time to rest and wait for the next crisis. Of course, she wouldn't stop her weekly ritual of scrying. The last thing they needed was for her to miss a critical clue and give their next enemy more time to prepare.

Still, there was nothing now. She had done her duty and checked. There was nothing magic needed her to know. Morgana hadn't even caught a glimpse of Merlin. Last time she'd seen him in the mirror, the old fool had been fishing on a sunny riverbank. Nothing had been amiss, and he'd seemed very relaxed. That had been nine months ago.

Merlin's last message had been three months ago, and he'd warned her that he was going further east, so she shouldn't expect frequent messages. According to Michel's letter around that time, Merlin had come to see him and Jakob before leaving the city with next to nothing. Morgana didn't know what the old man was up to and told herself that she didn't care.

Tapping the edge of the bronze disk against the table, Morgana contained a sigh. She was restless. It was time to admit that. Normally it took longer than this, but that was the truth of the matter. So much had gone unresolved, in her opinion. Puck had caused a great deal of trouble, both to the Sídhe and to humans, and then had slunk off like the rat he was.

There was no fight where Puck was destroyed. There was no clash of the mages against the army of Sídhe he'd rallied. Instead, he'd come to them for help because he'd finally realized that he was in over his head. Sensible, but it didn't provide her with closure. It didn't eliminate a potential threat. Maybe Puck had truly learned better, but Morgana wasn't convinced.

The door opened before Morgana could seethe and worry further. Lieven all but stumbled in, his lanky body off balance thanks to his latest growth spurt. The boy never seemed to know where his feet were now. Morgana looked up and grimaced as he knocked his hip against the table by the door. He twisted quickly and grabbed the edges before anything could fall off. Not that there was anything fragile on it. She had some herbs wrapped in linens and completed skeins of thread ready for market on it. Still, she appreciated his instinct.

"Are you hurt?" Morgana asked, in lieu of a proper greeting.

"No." Lieven's voice cracked the tiniest bit, and he turned red.

Morgana hid a smile behind her hand. Her poor boy was just at the beginning of the most awkward time in his life. Lieven had grown, as all children did, and now glowed with health. The malnourished and frightened boy she'd taken in was transformed. She wasn't sure exactly how old he was, but she estimated him to be about twelve now. His love of books had faded slightly as the novelty of reading wore off, but he was still proving himself a clever lad even if he didn't know where his feet were anymore.

His interest in woodworking was one thing that had not changed. As he'd grown taller, he'd become more and more fascinated with the elaborate wooden altarpieces at the Cathedral and the art he saw in her books. Morgana's prediction for his future as a woodworker from years ago was well on its way to coming true. Even if he never became a master artist in his own right, Morgana was reassured at the knowledge that he would be able to make a living. Morgana couldn't help but be proud of him. Lieven had adapted to every change and challenge she put to him.

At this rate, he wouldn't be home much longer. It was only a matter of time before Master Arnoud took him on full time. The apprenticeship contract had already been drafted and was being reviewed by one of the local guilds. Morgana knew that life would be harder for the boy. Master Arnoud was fair, but the life of an apprentice was difficult. They slept and ate when their masters said they could.

Learning of all this had been uncomfortable for Morgana. She'd been isolated from it with Michel, as they'd been training him in magic and in how to run the shop. They hadn't needed to worry about arranging for him to be an apprentice. Morgana vaguely remembered Michel talking about the lives of some of his friends as apprentices, but she hadn't really listened. They had been mundane humans, and her concern had been Michel.

Still, it wasn't as if she'd never see Lieven. Master Arnoud took Sunday rest seriously. If the boys had local families, they went to see them after church, so she'd have Lieven at least once a week. The woodworker was a good man, and his wife was the sort of pragmatic and responsible woman that Morgana could handle overseeing her foster son's care.

"Morgana?" Lieven sat down at the table. "What are you doing?"

"Oh, I was just..." Morgana trailed off. Four years together, and Lieven still had no knowledge of magic. She was determined to keep it that way. "I was still looking at something." Shaking her head, she found herself running her thumb over the edge of the bronze disk once again. "It was given to me long ago," Morgana said softly. "I suppose I was just remembering."

"What does it do?"

"It is a mirror." Morgana shifted her hand so that her reflection showed. It was not as clear as the reflections created by modern worked metal, but it was still good. Besides, they couldn't afford the fancier kind of mirror. "Made of bronze. This was how mirrors used to be made. They would cast a piece of bronze and polish it."

"That sounds like a lot of work." Lieven tilted his head in consideration and curiosity.

"It was. Bronze is more difficult to work with than most other metals. You can't reheat it and reshape it like you can iron."

Lieven nodded. He wasn't training with a blacksmith, but the boy had seen enough smiths at work to have a vague idea what she was talking about. Morgana smiled wistfully. It was odd, talking about the way that the world used to be. She hadn't heard of bronze working in a long time. Some methods might still be in use for gold, but not bronze. It was a metal of the past.

"Who gave it to you?" Lieven asked. "Was it Uncle Michel?"

Morgana froze at the question, and even Lieven's innocent question about dear Michel didn't calm her. She brushed her finger over the metal once again and considered her answer. Then she gave up, telling herself she was overthinking it. Lieven was a child; of course, he would be curious.

"No, it wasn't Michel," she answered. "It was someone I knew a long time ago."

Something in her tone must have betrayed her because Lieven shifted uneasily in his chair. "Why do you still have it if you don't like them?"

"It's not that-" Morgana stopped herself and sighed. It wasn't that simple, but Lieven was so young. Maybe not to most, but he was to her. He wouldn't understand. "I didn't like them," she admitted. "But... they were important to me before we started hating each other."

The soft and sweet words that Queen Scáthbás used to coo to Morgana echoed in her ears. Her foster mother's promises and affection had been like water to her as a child. Morgana had grown up in fear of the Sídhe even as she near worshiped them for what she saw as their great power and perfection. Morgana had been a child from the backward and poisonous Iron Realm, and yet Scáthbás had adored her anyway.

It had been twisted and cruel. She had been taken from her family, from her mother, who loved her desperately, only to be returned as an enemy of her homeland years later. Morgana remembered it so clearly, even after so long. Her mother's hug when she'd woken in their roundhouse after being merged with her Changeling counterpart had been so warm and comforting. At the time, she'd felt guilt, but now Morgana knew it had been the first chink in her armor.

"Morgana?" Lieven called. "Morgana, are you alright?"

"I was just thinking." Morgana forced herself to look at the boy. "I'm alright."

"I'm sorry I asked about the mirror," Lieven apologized.

"No, I don't want you to be afraid to ask me things. You know that." Morgana gave him a smile and then nodded towards the back of the house. "Now, be a good lad and refill the water jars for me."

Lieven gave her a thoughtful look, but he didn't argue. Morgana watched him as he went to fetch the bucket, trying to look casual. Yet the mirror was still clutched in her hand. Four years and she'd finally slipped up and allowed Lieven to get close to magic. Giving the boy another smile, Morgana waved him out the door and sighed as soon as the door closed.

Why had she kept the mirror? Morgana looked down at it. Even after siding with Merlin, she'd never thrown it away. For centuries, Morgana had held onto it and used it as a scrying tool to the benefit of the Iron Realm. It had never occurred to her to have an artisan make her a new mirror, or at least melt this one down to reshape it.

No, this was the mirror that had been hidden beneath the scratchy human clothing she'd been put into that night. This was the mirror that she'd reported to Queen Scáthbás with when she was young and foolish. Changing a little through the years, being worn down, and scratched up as time marched on. A bit like herself, perhaps.

Morgana tilted the mirror and studied her reflection. She did not look as young as she once had, but her hair was still rich and dark. There were some faint lines around her eyes, but they were few. The bronze was imperfect as a mirror, but it was enough. Morgana was an old woman in the body of a woman in the prime of life.

Morgana smiled and shook her head. It was a good thing that Merlin wasn't here. He would laugh at how dramatic she was being. If in all of these years, he'd never worried about the mirror despite knowing that she'd used it to keep in touch with the Sídhe, then there was no reason for her to be overthinking it so much.

Rising to her feet, Morgana rolled her stiff shoulders and took a deep breath. Some of the tension drained from her body as she stretched her arms. A faint heat in her muscles and a soft ache nearly made her laugh. There were times that she could travel thousands of miles in minutes, but now, with the world at peace, the act of scrying drained her magic. It was a strange world.

Putting those thoughts away, Morgana went to her room and returned the mirror to the soft cloth string bag she kept it in. She turned her attention to her work, determined to manage something productive this afternoon. When Lieven returned, she was hard at work at her spinning wheel, with thoughts of the mirror, the Queen and Merlin safely tucked away. The past was the past, and Morgana would not allow it to have power over her.

22

Mage of Destruction

Cathanáil collided with the golden armor of the closest guard. It staggered to the side, and Bran thrust his dagger into its neck. Silver blood sparkled in the corner of Alex's eyes as she turned her attention to the next one. The brutality washed over Alex like water. There was no time for remorse or guilt now. Targets were closing in around them, swords and spears ready.

Releasing a burst of magic, Alex shouted, and the closest three Sídhe were sent flying back. There were gasps of shock and a barked order to attack from the prince. The three staggered to their feet, but their places at the front had already been taken by others. She swung at the next target, a Síd with a broken left horn. Its violet eyes met hers as it brought up its shield, but it was too late. Cathanáil hit the shield at the edge, knocking it to the side, and Alex thrust the sword forward towards the weak point of the underarm. The plates of gold offered no protection there.

A soft intake of breath was the only sound the creature made. Something moved behind her, and she felt Bran shift, his magic brushing against hers. She dismissed that threat and pulled Cathanáil free. Another Síd thrust a spear at her. A wall of blue magic stopped it, and the point of the spear shattered. Silver bolts blasted through the air, striking down another two Sídhe.

Her heart raced, her body was hot with aches, and sweat stuck her hair to her neck. Alex didn't stop. Cathanáil flashed through the air, slicing across the neck of another Síd. More blood. There was no smell of iron. Silver, not red. That knowledge, that observation, was on repeat in her head. It was a mantra. Alex didn't know if she was the source, or it was one of her other-selves. It didn't matter.

A Síd fell to the combined attack of Bran and Aiden. Yellow magic held it fast while Aiden delivered the killing blow. Blue magic washed out from Nicki in waves, pushing back their attackers as Alex and the others slowly moved back. Morgana was a wild beast on the far end of the line, dagger in her right hand and silver magic flaring off her left. More and more of the guards were moving towards her. More and more were falling as her dagger found its mark or her whip ripped through bodies. Several corpses near the feet of the eldest mage were torn in large pieces, their silver blood splattered across the floor.

It would haunt her. That small thought echoed in Alex's head, and not even Gottfried's soft voice, the voice of a loving father, could stop it. Another Síd attacked her. Alex sent a bolt of lightning through Cathanáil. The smell of burning hair made her nose wrinkle as the Síd fell to the ground. Noise was echoing in her ears, an irregular drumbeat that took her too long to realize was coming from behind them.

Crashing metal against stone grew louder and louder. Reinforcements, someone shouted in her head, but she couldn't tell which one it was. Everyone was shouting warnings and advice, meaning that none of it was helpful.

Alex thrust Cathanáil into the side of the nearest guard, sliding the sword through the joint in the armor. The guard cried out, trying to twist away, but only making Cathanáil slice deeper. Pulling out the sword with a grunt, Alex ignored the soft dying cries of the being as it slumped to the floor. Another guard was on her. More kept showing up during the fight. They were being swarmed. She didn't stop to count.

Shouts came from behind them. Alex twisted around to avoid a blow and released a wave of magic. Dark gray sparks flashed through the air, throwing back the nearest guards. Spinning around, she searched for the new threat as her magic fluttered in time with her heart.

Lines of Sídhe swarmed them from behind. They were in glittering armor, but red bands were wrapped around their forearms and horns. Some of the armor was engraved with unfamiliar emblems. At the back of the lines was a Síd dressed in a mixture of an elaborate robe and golden armor pieces. A circlet was on their head, and golden decorations with large gemstones weighed down their horns.

"For Prince Torniall!" Came a shout from the troops.

The new soldiers, dozens of them, rushed toward their counterparts. Their entire focus seemed to be on the guards in gold and the prince behind them. Alex had only a moment to bask in the shocked fear on the prince's face before the weight of the situation they were in hit her. She slammed Cathanáil's sharp blade against the extended arm of a Sid guard. They screamed and dropped. Silver blood, no smell of iron.

Alex kept pushing towards the others, slicing Cathanáil at every Sídhe who came too close. Sometimes it hit metal and sometimes flesh. Alex didn't stop to check on her targets. All of her focus was on the other mages as Sídhe clashed around her. She reached Nicki first, exhaling in relief as she checked her friend over with a sharp look for injuries.

"What is happening?!" Nicki demanded.

Nicki's eyes were wide, and she seemed just as confused as Alex. The new Sídhe charged towards the prince and the guards. Some looked their way and stopped in their tracks as soon as they noticed the humans. But even that wasn't enough to stop the crash of battle as the two waves met.

"I think it's another prince's army!" Alex shouted. She moved closer to Nicki, whose left arm was still wrapped around the box and her right hand holding her iron dagger. "It's hard to make it all out!"

"We need to get out!" Nicki insisted. She was struggling to hold onto the heavy box and Alex saw blue magic rippling across its surface. "Try to get the rebels' attention!"

Alex nodded and shouted to Jarven, who had just cut down another guard with a fluid swing of their sword. One of the new soldiers, distinguished only by the red of its cloak, surged past Alex. Hesitation colored Jarven's face for only a moment before they attacked that one. Alex nearly screamed. They were a tiny group with dozens of soldiers packing around them.

"Fall back!" Alex shouted again. "Mages, move!"

Aiden grabbed Morgana's arm, nearly getting slashed with her dagger for his trouble before the older mage realized what was happening. Alex gestured for them to hurry to her and Nicki. A soldier broke off, caught sight of them, and charged. The one lone soldier was no match for the burst of blue magic Nicki sent its way that crashed into the golden armor and staggered it. Alex swung Cathanáil at its head and grimaced upon contact. She didn't look at the being as it fell to the ground, but her stomach still turned.

This had been a mistake. Getting involved, as well intentioned as it had been, was a mistake. She could only hope that what Nicki had found would be helpful enough to make it worth it. For now, the most important thing was getting her family out before they were truly caught between the feuding princes.

Pulling Mjǫllnir free of the leather loop it hung on, Alex huffed at the strain it put on her left arm. Mjǫllnir's weight was heavy and solid in her hand. Alex's left hand was weaker than her right, but she had the strength to lift the Hammer over her head. Magic flashed through her body, and the Hammer hummed to life. She was a little stronger now, but knew it wouldn't last.

Alex swung the Hammer with all the might of her left arm into a charging Síd. Metal hit metal with a crash, and the Síd hit the floor, gasping for air against the collapsed shape of its armor. Glancing around frantically, Alex swung at the legs of the guard that was running past her. It went down in a crash of metal against stone. Backing away from the fight, Alex moved towards her fellow mages with Nicki beside her.

Flashes of light illuminated the hall as they reflected off the gleaming armors and pools of silver blood. Above them, Alex's light orb was still humming with power, but none of the Sídhe were paying it any mind. She ignored it, letting it slowly dim and letting the light of the room's wall torches and the lights carried by the troops be her guide.

Morgana was surrounded. Alex's eyes widened as she found her. Aiden and Bran were attacking the flanks of Síd guards who had swooped in around them. Morgana's light whip circled around her, slicing through armor after armor like a hot knife in butter. The mage had made herself too big a threat to ignore.

Another Síd hit the ground. Glee sparked in Morgana's eyes. Alex stopped moving. More were coming in. The princes were shouting at each other and their armies, but Alex ignored them. Morgana's eyes were strange. The crisp green was dull despite her energy, despite her awareness of every Sídhe around her.

'Morgana!' Arto cried.

Alex heard herself shout with him. Other voices echoed with worry and with fear. More magic flashed around Morgana, pushing the Síd-he back and taking others down. One soldier pushed forward, only to scream as its body turned to ash. Magic shook the air.

Morgana's scream echoed over all the other noise. The hall shuddered, and the walls trembled. Everything stopped. Alex quivered. Magic was spilling out, churning around them, and banishing the sweet taste of the air. Now it was bitter. All across Alex's arms, hairs stood on end, and her jaw tightened in fear and against a wave of illness.

Silver light was radiating off Morgana. Her eyes were distant and glazed over. The horde around her was shoved back. Most scurried away while Bran and Aiden gaped in shock. One soldier did not run. It clamored to its feet and grabbed a spear off the ground. Alex leapt forward, slamming Mjǫllnir against the back of its head. It dropped with a crack. Another was rushing towards Morgana, sword drawn, and terror in its eyes. Alex met it before it reached Morgana, using its distraction to swing Cathanáil at its face.

Her arms burned. Magic and wielding both of her weapons was taking its toll. Muscles spasmed, but she had to keep moving. Mjǫllnir collided with the chest of a guard. Magic flashed, and the guard was thrown back. Cathanáil was sinking in her right hand; Alex was no longer strong enough to hold it up.

She looked back at Morgana. The silver magic was pulsing in waves, pushing away the guards. For a moment, Alex wasn't sure what was happening, but then she heard the sound of stone grinding against stone. A crack overhead was the only warning given. Everything stopped. The guards and soldiers halted their assault. Alex's gaze turned up.

A section of carved buttress hit the tile floor with a thunderous crash, crushing a Sídhe that didn't run fast enough. There was a split second of silence save for the echo of the crash against the stone walls. Then the rest of the roof shuddered.

Stones rained down from the ceiling. Sídhe scattered, shouting in terror or barking orders. The crash was deafening. The sound rang off the walls, and the screams became distant but haunting. Alex had just enough presence of mind to return Mjǫllnir to its hoop on her hip before turning to Morgana. She dared not release her grip on Cathanáil.

"Morgana!" Alex reached for Morgana before thinking better of it.

The ground quaked beneath them as another wave of stones hit the floor. Alex found herself looking over just in time to see the first prince crushed by a partially carved boulder. Aiden and Bran screamed for them to move, that they needed to run, and Alex pulled herself back to the present. Morgana was still beside her, staring beyond the falling rocks and the dying Sídhe at the throne. It was barely visible in the dark room, but the gold glittered in the low light.

"Morgana, please," Alex begged. There was too much noise. It was clattering, clanging, and demanding attention all at once. It was in her head as the voices fought to be heard and all around her as the guards, soldiers, and rebels clashed and battled. "Morgana!" Reaching towards the older mage, Alex released a wave of magic to force the nearby attackers back. Her chest sparked, her muscles tightening and turning hot with warning. "Morgana! Sister, we need to go!"

The word sister worked again. Morgana stopped and glanced back at Alex. The burning rage in her eyes softened a little. It was enough. Alex grabbed her hand, feeling Morgana's magic burn hot against her palm. "Let's go! Please, we need to go!" Even shouting, Alex could barely be heard. "We don't have enough magic to fight them all! This isn't why we are here!"

Morgana stirred. She let Alex pull her away from the screaming army, away from the collapsing roof and certain death. The pillars were swaying as they ran. Overhead, the grinding of stone promised that more deadly rain was coming. Whatever Morgana had done was spreading through the entire building.

Alex pushed her body forward. Her muscles and lungs were aching. She could see Aiden, Bran, and Nicki ahead of them, but had no idea where the rebels were. Screams echoed off the stones only to be drowned out by crashes seconds later. Dust filled the air; it was hard to see and harder to breathe.

Alex's eyes burned, but they had to keep moving. Her grip on Morgana's hand didn't falter. She couldn't let go of Morgana's hand. More rocks came crashing down. The ground quaked at each impact. There might be a level being torn in two below them. Alex pushed her legs harder. Sídhe were running now. No one was attacking them.

Looking back, Alex searched for the throne, and she found it glittering in the darkness before a pillar fell and crushed the metal. For an instant, the world slowed, and she could see the opening in the roof. Stars were visible in the sky above through the cloud of billowing dust. More sections collapsed, ripping the hole open like a stretching wound.

Turning her attention forward, Alex followed Bran around a crumbling column. Rocks were coming down from the walls in small landslides. Nicki threw one hand over her head, and a wave of blue magic swept a deluge of rocks away from them. Ahead of them was a massive doorway. It was still holding, the archway shaking but keeping one section of the wall upright. There was shouting and screaming beyond the door, but a hint of sweetness in the air beckoned to Alex.

The roar behind them was all she could hear. Morgana's tight grip on her hand and the burn of her muscles was all Alex could feel. Fear and desperation had slipped away, driven back by raw survival instinct that refused to give into panic. Bran and Aiden crossed the threshold first, turning to look over their shoulders. Nicki was through, and then Alex and Morgana.

They were in a courtyard. Soldiers and guards were fleeing with no regard for them. Slowing down, Alex had only a moment to inhale desperately before Aiden pointed to their right and Bran nodded. She didn't know what they had noticed, but followed them eagerly when they resumed running.

More crashing behind them. A strange musty smell all around them and dust in the air. Alex noted all of it, but didn't stop running. The outer walls were crumbling at the force of the shaking ground, leaving them half sized ruins. Boulders were colliding with the outer walls as the palace fell. Alex didn't look back.

Aiden and Bran had found a destroyed section of wall that was climbable which looked towards the woods. Bran clamored onto the rocks, flinching as a massive stone rolled down from the palace and struck the wall. It stayed stable under him, and he gripped his daypack protectively. A sigh of relief escaped Alex. He still had the Iron Chalice. Bran caught her eyes and managed a small smile before offering a hand to Nicki. She didn't release her grip on the box, but let Bran help her up the wall with Aiden shifting protectively behind her.

Alex finally released Morgana's hand and followed the others up the wall. Rocks slid beneath her feet, but she made the climb. When she reached the top, Alex looked into the dark forest and then towards the city below. There were alarm bells ringing and buildings on fire. It only occurred to her now that the bells hadn't been an alarm for them, but the invading army.

"We need to keep moving," Bran croaked. His face was covered in dust. "I can't- my chest is burning. I can't use any more magic."

Nodding, Alex climbed to the other side of the wall before realizing that Morgana wasn't with them. She turned around and found Morgana watching the palace collapse. Despite knowing better, Alex stared at it as well. Torches and moonlight lit it enough for Alex to see a swaying tower topple over in a rain of stone over the gutted ruin of the main hall. Alex did not move. She couldn't speak, and instead listened to the ring of stone against stone as the palace where Morgana had grown up came crashing down.

23

Question of Magic and Morgana

Morgana was asleep against the trunk of a tree, her body only moving the tiniest bit as she breathed. Alex was sitting nearby, Cathanáil drawn and resting across her lap as she stared at the exhausted form of her mentor and former sister. There was no sign from Morgana that she knew she was being watched or that she was uncomfortable.

After reaching the forest, Morgana hadn't made it far before her magical attack on the palace had caught up with her. Raw fear had led to Alex using the Iron Chalice on her before she completely collapsed, just to make sure that they didn't lose her to a coma. But that had taken the last strength that Alex possessed. No sooner had Morgana fallen asleep than Alex's legs had given out, and she'd found herself in her current spot.

Bran and Aiden had gathered up a bit of wood as they stumbled their way through the forest and had set a small fire that was barely illuminating the area they had found themselves in. The heat was just enough to warm Alex's aching legs and ease some of the bitter pain that had taken hold of her. Everything hurt, and exhaustion weighed on her shoulders like an overloaded backpack.

But she couldn't sleep. Exhaustion clung to her, but her mind was busy and alive with information and worry. Nicki was asleep a few feet away, cradling the box from the library and using a sweatshirt over it as a pillow. Once the fire died down, Alex doubted she'd be able to sacrifice her sweatshirt for comfort like that. Bran and Aiden were still awake and speaking in low voices. Aiden's head kept nodding, and Alex was sure that he'd be asleep soon as well.

When was the last time that they'd slept? Everything had happened so fast after they met the rebels. Alex swallowed and looked in the direction they had come. A faint glow was visible over the tops of the trees from the burning city, and pillars of smoke cast shadows over the large moon. The chaos caused by them and the army was enough to shake that poor city to the ground. Still, Sídhe or not, Alex hoped the citizens were alright.

She sighed out loud at her thought. Morgana might scoff at it, but Alex suspected that Morgana would understand. On the surface, she hated all Sídhe, but she and Merlin had adopted a live and let live attitude on Earth. Sure, on one hand, it was because trying to hunt all the Sídhe down would have likely started another war with all the Fae creatures uniting. But Alex liked to believe that compassion had played a role as well. Especially given how allowing the creatures to exist on Earth had affected the magic of the Iron Realm.

Merlin and Morgana had been excellent teachers regarding using magic, but Alex had some of her own theories about what magic was. If nothing else, jumping through worlds and being aware of the pulse of energy in each of them had reassured her it was a great deal more universal. Her thoughts and ideas on what magic was and how it worked swirled in her head like water; there, but hard to catch. Every time she thought she had it figured out, something happened, or a new thought appeared that reshaped her conclusions.

Magic was power. It was energy, a mostly unknown form of energy, but energy nonetheless. She hadn't been the best at physics, but Alex was comfortable with that conclusion. Her gift was controlling energy, pulling magic together, and using it. She could sense it, taste it on the air, and even turn other forms of energy into magic at her command.

It was all connected. Her power told Alex that. The extent of that connection was unknown, and it was why she hesitated to pull on the energy around her. How easily could she break something? How easily could she rob a living thing of the energy it needed to keep its heart beating? Magic was energy, and she didn't know where that line was. So, she stayed as safe as she could.

Mages could use magic, some of the Sídhe could use it, and most Demons could use enough to hide their true forms on Earth. She'd known from her earliest days as a mage that magic wasn't only used by humans, but she'd never managed to pin it down. Alex hadn't seen much magic used in their trip thus far, so it wasn't common anywhere.

Magic was produced in larger amounts when something from another world came through not just as a defense system, but as a balancing act. It was extra energy trying to cope with a push against the natural laws, the new matter brought into the universe that Earth was a part of while also making sure that the natural laws didn't fall apart.

Yet, it also connects all the worlds. It flowed from the trunk of the Tree of Reality out into the branches, providing nourishment, connection, and protection. Worlds stored that power, living off it in some regards and releasing it when under threat. Alex was beginning to doubt that Earth itself had ever generated the magic she used. It flavored it, maybe, tailored the energy for the use of mages.

But why? That was the question. If beings moving between worlds forced worlds to spend their energy protecting their natural order, then why were the worlds even linked to begin with? Had it been an accident? Why risk such a thing?

But then again, maybe they had to be connected. Maybe worlds needed a connection to that light in the trunk that produced the energy that flowed through the tree. She hadn't seen all the worlds personally, but Alex knew in her gut that all had life, or at least had had life in the past, before the Darkness.

Sighing again, she dropped her head back against the tree trunk with a soft thump. It didn't hurt, but the sensation was grounding. The smell of the forest was wrong. There was too much of a sugary scent, a bit like a candy coating, and not enough earthy scents. She tapped her fingers against the smooth blade of Cathanáil. There was no sign of silver blood on the blade thanks to her wiping it off on the large leaves of a tree as they reached the forest, but Alex reminded herself that it was far from sanitary.

Memories of the piled-up bodies and the blood came rushing back. Alex's jaw tingled and tightened with the threat of her getting physically ill. Closing her eyes, Alex imagined the faces of her brothers instead. They were hazy. Panic hit her and pushed away her horror at the carnage she'd just witnessed. How could her memories of her brothers already be hazy? It hadn't been that long. And yet it had been. The images that formed in her mind weren't bad, but there were details missing. She remembered the shapes of their faces, the color of their eyes and hair, and the shapes of their noses, but small things were missing. Enough that she knew something was off. Now she felt sick for a completely different reason.

"You okay?" Bran called.

She looked up sharply, her right hand moving to grip Cathanáil's hilt. It was only Bran, walking towards her slowly and looking apologetic as soon as he understood that he had startled her. Alex nodded to him in response to the question. She was physically fine, and the trauma that would likely follow the battle at the palace was avoidable for now.

"Aiden's asleep," Bran whispered. He sank to the ground beside her with a groan. "God, everything hurts."

"I know." Alex chuckled softly and closed her eyes for a moment. "Me too."

"But we're alive."

"Yeah. I just hope that what we got was worth it."

"Me too," Alex answered.

Silence surrounded them, and Alex closed her eyes again. The burning in her chest slowly receded. In the air was thin magic that reached for her. It wanted to help. She wondered what Morgana would say about that. A small chuckle escaped her. That was something she wasn't going to try to explain anytime soon.

"Alex?"

"Nothing."

Alex opened her eyes and stared up at the stars. They were unfamiliar and hard to see because of the brightness of the moon. Thanks to it, the world was almost as bright as it was during the day. It wasn't as bright as a full moon back home, but there wasn't as much light to reflect, so that didn't surprise her.

"Are you sure?"

"I'm just thinking." Alex hesitated. She didn't look at him but could feel faint warmth radiating off Bran's body. "I'm sorry for getting us into that. Nothing went according to plan."

"I wouldn't say that. We're alright, and our magic guided us to the most important information."

"We hope, at least." Alex licked her lips, suddenly very thirsty and wishing they had more supplies. She was hungry, and cold. "Still… it was ugly in there. I'm sorry that I agreed to help them."

"Hard to say what would have happened if we hadn't agreed to help," Bran reminded her. "And we understand. I get wanting to leave this world in better shape when we leave. If there's too much chaos and death, then an invasion could follow anyway."

Another sigh followed by a groan escaped Alex. "Not sure our efforts will prevent that."

"We did all we could."

Raising an eyebrow, Alex turned to look at Bran. His shape was dark and indistinct. She heard him chuckle.

"I can't see you," Bran said. "But I can imagine the eyebrow you're giving me."

And she could hear his smile. The levity allowed her to inhale deeply, and she leaned her head back again. A shiver raced through her body, and she wondered if waiting until dawn was really a good idea. But her chest ached at the very idea of using more magic. She was dangerously exhausted, and the last thing they needed was someone falling into a coma. They might have the Iron Chalice, but Alex didn't know how long it would take to charge up enough to be of use.

"I can hear you thinking," Bran said gently. "Penny for your thoughts?"

"They're messy," Alex warned. "And all over the place. Probably cost you at least a dollar to get them all."

"Sorry, I left my wallet at home. Didn't see the need for it. And I didn't want to have to replace everything when we got home if something happened to it."

"It's a good thing you trust Avani, Lance, and Jenny, then."

"Jenny's dad pays for her credit cards."

"Fair enough."

Alex smiled at the memory of her friends. She wondered what they were doing now. Was it night back on Earth, or morning? How did they occupy their days right now? Jenny was probably turning into the 'mom friend' due to her worry and trying to make sure that Lance and Avani were okay. Robin was keeping an eye on them. Alex was certain of that. Puck, no matter the name or shape they wore, was one of the most compassionate and loyal beings they had ever met, even if Merlin and Morgana hadn't seen it that way.

Looking towards Morgana, Alex strained her eyes to confirm that the woman hadn't moved. The fire was dying down to embers, and clouds were drifting across the moon. She was still breathing and seemed calm enough. The last thing they needed was Morgana having nightmares. It was growing darker as clouds covered the moon overhead, and Alex eyed their small fire wearily. Sooner or later, she'd have to get up and move. At least the forested area they were in had a lot of downed branches they could use, but that would still mean moving, and that idea just sounded awful.

"She seems okay, despite how much magic she used," Bran said gently. "She just needs rest."

"I hope so." Alex shook her head and closed her eyes again. "I still wish that things hadn't escalated like that."

"I think... I think she still has a lot of issues with the Sídhe," Bran said slowly. "And I don't blame her. Not at all. I just wish that she hadn't lost control like that."

Alex said nothing in Morgana's defense. There was no denying it. Morgana had lost control. Understandable, of course, like Bran had said, but still... Morgana had always been the controlled one. So many memories of hers were of Morgana being cautious, Morgana being serious and careful with her magic.

"She scared me there for a moment," Alex admitted. Opening her eyes, she studied Morgana's sleeping form. "I don't think I've ever seen her like that. I've seen her hurt and angry and scared and ashamed." Those were all true, but now that Alex was thinking about it, there were a few distant memories of Morgana where she'd been lost. Glastonbury Tor, when Arto's blood spell had revealed her loyalty to the Sídhe and a strange, vague memory of Morgana asking Merlin not to take them. "It's been a long time since something has hurt her like seeing that throne did."

"What do we do now? Do we try to find the rebels again?"

"Our packs are there," Alex answered. "All of our gear and food. I hesitate to jump into the last world without that stuff." She couldn't help but think of the iron and Galahad in the bag. "We might need it."

"True, and we helped." Bran shrugged a little. "The prince is dead. I think, at least."

"Yeah, the prince that lived in the palace was killed. Not sure about the other one, but they're down a good chunk of warriors if they survived."

"What even is our life?" Bran groaned. "Really, Alex?"

"I don't know." A soft laugh escaped Alex at his tone. It was a bit whiny, but didn't cross the line. "I really, really don't know. Maybe if I had a pen and paper, I could make you a chart, but I don't completely understand how we got here."

With a bit of levity having been achieved, Alex turned so that she could use the tree to leverage herself up. Her legs trembled at the weight of her body, but they held. Exhaling slowly, Alex rolled her shoulders and carefully stretched her arms. Once she was confident that she knew how to move her limbs again, Alex sheathed Cathanáil and extended a hand to Bran.

"Think you can give me a hand finding more wood before we completely lose the fire?"

With a soft huff, Bran nodded in agreement and gripped Alex's hand. Thankfully, he used the tree to help him climb up because Alex knew the moment that he pulled on her hand that offering to pull him up had been a horrible mistake. Hopefully, it was the only one they'd made. Alex had the feeling that come morning, they would know for sure. Those rebels better have left Galahad alone.

24

The Next Scene is Set

1 998 C.E. Philadelphia, United States

Lemon hadn't been a smell that Morgana ever expected to like. She hadn't grown up with a scent like that, and it wasn't the most pleasing smell that she'd ever encountered. But it was clean. Association was a powerful thing, and her kitchen smelled of lemon over a bleach base. Clean; really clean, the sort of clean that even five hundred years ago she'd never have imagined.

The modern age was glorious in how clean things could get, and as a medical practitioner, she approved. Her colleagues would never understand her obsession with the smell of cleaning supplies. Maybe it would fade someday, but things had improved so much, even in the last forty years. It was remarkable.

Humming softly, Morgana picked up the mug and poured in the hot water. Damn Merlin for getting her started on tea. Why had the old fool moved home for a bit and picked up the habit? At least it was easier to find good tea in the United States now than it had been when the old man had introduced her to it forty years ago. She'd held off on trying it a long time, but now it had its hooks into her.

Morgana took her mug out of the kitchen and sat down at the small, round, wooden dining table that only she ever used. Having company over had never been Morgana's idea of a good time. She set the tea to the side and picked up the soft cloth bag waiting in the center of the table. The red color had faded, despite her making this bag less than a decade ago. It was one more thing that would need to be replaced. So few things had survived the ages, and those that had usually had magic to thank for it.

A familiar bronze disk slipped out of the bag and into Morgana's waiting hand. The polished metal gleamed in the white electrical light of the chandelier that hung over her dining room table. She put her elbow on the table and focused her attention on the smooth surface. In her chest, magic flared to life. It was a weak spark, but it was there.

The mirror shimmered, the polished bronze surface glittering with light. Morgana straightened up in her chair, her eyes widening in surprise, and her brightly painted lips opening as she released a shaky exhale. This was a strong reaction, stronger than any she'd seen in several centuries. Leaning forward, Morgana let more of her magic flow into the ancient bronze deck.

It didn't take much. The magic seeped into the metal and swirled to form images, creating sharp colors that allowed Morgana to clearly see a green city sign. It was the sort that dotted the interstate and highway system all across the United States. The words were painted in white, and the contrast made it easy to read, even through the medium of her mirror.

"Ravenslake," Morgana said softly. The word hung in the air, and Morgana smiled. "Sounds mysterious."

There was no time to dwell on the name of the town as the image rippled and shifted. Colors twisted into new shapes. There were brick buildings built to look old, but much newer than the style suggested to Morgana's eyes. Grassy areas surrounded them, and a more modern building caught her eye. There were flower boxes alongside sidewalks and young people in their late teens and twenties walking with bags and backpacks. Likely a college, she decided.

Images flashed across the bronze surface faster now. She saw a lake, a hillside with a dark tunnel leading into it and familiar silver Hounds. Her heart jumped at the sight of the Hound. They didn't exist on Earth. Either none had survived the war, or they'd quickly died out. That meant-

It changed again. Now she saw an office. There was a calendar on the desk, partially covered, but she could see the first three numbers of the year. 201. That was years away. A nameplate on the desk had the name Morgana Cornwall, and Morgana could have laughed. That name was a bit on the nose, but she was growing tired of being Morgana Johnson.

Pain flared through her body. Morgana gasped in surprise at the sudden sting. Pulling her magic back roughly, her legs twitched, and vertigo swept through her body. For an instant, her vision flashed with small lights, and she was floating, unaware of where she was. Her brain was aching, even as the images replayed themselves and tried to make sense.

Slowly, the world returned to what it should be. Morgana's head still ached, and the lights were still dancing in her eyes. Her stomach was churning, and her jaw was tight. It had been a long time since she used so much magic at one time, and she'd lost herself in the vision. Rubbing her eyes, Morgana gently set the mirror down on the table. There was a telltale burn in her chest from using so much magic, and she was grateful that she'd stopped when she did, despite her curiosity. Exhaling slowly, Morgana let her hand drop from her face and closed her eyes. She focused on her breathing and let her body relax.

Morgana didn't leave the table for a long time. There was a pen and paper off to the side, something she kept for messages and shopping lists, but Morgana hadn't imagined she'd need it for anything magical. She pulled it over and jotted down all the details she could remember before they completely faded. The name of the town was sharp and vibrant in her brain, as were a few other useful details. Ravenslake wasn't a familiar name, and she hoped that would make it easier to find. Once that was done, she returned the old mirror to the soft bag and pulled the drawstrings to close it.

Standing slowly, Morgana made sure that her feet were stable beneath her before she picked up her tea and moved away from the table. She left the mirror there and headed into the living room. Her rotary phone was on the end table by the sofa. Compared to the television and the computer tucked back in her spare room, it was already an antique. Given she was looking at a change of scenery, the old thing would most certainly be replaced. Taking a long sip of her tea, Morgana sank onto her sofa and was all but swallowed by the soft cushions. Morgana closed her eyes for a long moment, letting the hot mug warm her chilled hands.

There was no rush. The calendar showed that there was plenty of time for her to sort out her affairs and make arrangements, but Morgana was almost eager to start. Energy hummed beneath her skin in a way that it hadn't for some time. It would be hard work to deal with her estate and establish a new identity. With so little magic at their disposal and so many legal hoops to jump through in the modern world, Morgana and Merlin always had to be precise.

Yet, such a strong and clear vision from the mirror meant that something big was coming. This would be another great chapter in her life. Most likely, the Iron Soul would be reborn, and Morgana could meet the new incarnation. Her fingers tightened around the mug as emotions fought for dominance.

"You'd think after centuries of this, I'd be used to it by now." Her words lingered in the empty room, and Morgana sighed. "And now I'm talking to myself."

That made up her mind. Morgana turned and set the mug of tea on the side table next to the phone. She didn't need to look up the phone number. The click and whirl of the rotary phone was a welcome sound to Morgana. It was real and modern, far removed from anything she associated with the ancient war. According to her vision, that might soon change. Morgana wasn't sure yet how things might look. It had been three thousand years. Had the Sídhe changed? Were they still using horses, or had their technology advanced? The human slaves would have long since died off, so maybe there had been radical social change. The last few centuries had shown her just how fast things could transform.

"Hello?" the sound of Merlin's voice pulled Morgana back to the present.

"Hello, Merlin."

She couldn't stop a smile from forming on her face. It was good to hear his voice. How many times in the past would the burden of living have been easier if they'd had phones? There were many wondrous inventions that had amazed her in the past few centuries, but the telephone had to be amongst her favorites.

"Morgana," Merlin's voice greeted with a hint of surprise, but also a clear note of happiness. "Lovely to hear from you, my dear."

"How are you?" Morgana asked. Her vision hadn't indicated anything so urgent that she felt the need to be rude.

"I am well. Though, I must confess that Boston is becoming a bit dull for my tastes. I've been considering moving on and doing something new. And yourself? I hope that this call finds you well."

"I am well," Morgana assured him. She even allowed a hint of fondness to color her voice. "Life is pleasant enough. My work and volunteering keep me busy." Morgana hesitated for only a moment before deciding that the best way to break the news of her vision was to simply tell him. "I had an abnormal bit of luck with the mirror this evening."

"Oh? How much abnormal luck?"

"I have a very clear idea of where we need to go," Morgana said. "Though it seems there is time. The vision didn't provide me with an exact date, but I saw enough of a calendar to know that we have years before the trouble starts. Over a decade, in fact."

"That is unusual," Merlin agreed. "But I won't complain. I suspect that you're thinking of moving."

"You'd be correct." Morgana cast her eyes around her comfortable living room. It was a small apartment, suitable for one person, and she'd been living here for well over a decade. "In fact, I have a career in mind."

"Oh?"

"We're looking for a place called Ravenslake. I believe we will find a college there. In the vision, I was looking at a desk that I presume belonged to me. The desk of one Professor Morgana Cornwall."

"It has a certain ring to it," Merlin chuckled. "Any idea on the subject?"

"No." Morgana hadn't thought to inspect the bookcase of the office, but the calendar had been far more interesting. "I have time to decide."

"Any sign of me?"

"None; perhaps I go solo on this?"

"Certainly not. If it is serious enough for magic to show you so many clear details, then I can only assume that the event will be major." His tone was teasing, but it reminded Morgana of the Hounds she'd seen and the glimpse of a tunnel. Holding back a shiver, she took a deep breath. "Morgana?" Merlin asked through the phone. "What's wrong?"

"I saw a tunnel and Hounds."

"I see." Merlin's sigh was loud through the phone. "Well, we knew that someday the Iron Gates would fail completely. In truth, the magic has lasted far longer than I originally expected. Except for that nasty business in the Norse lands."

"Let's not speak of that." Morgana shivered at the memory of the corrupted and twisted Sídhe that had pushed through the magic. "At least they never tried that again."

"I am often grateful for that." Merlin hummed thoughtfully on the other end of the line, and Morgana simply listened to the sound. "I'd like to move soon, if I'm honest. If the Sídhe are going to be an issue again, then establishing a base well in advance would be for the best. I haven't had space for a forge in centuries. I fear that I might be rusty, so regaining my skills would be an early goal. Then reinforcing residences."

"Isn't your current one reinforced?" Morgana asked.

Her eyes moved to the windowsills of her living room, where thin iron rods had been mounted. A horseshoe hung over the front door. They wouldn't stop a Fae that came looking for trouble, but it was usually enough to make them hesitate.

"There is iron in the portals, but if we find ourselves dealing with true Sídhe, then I want more than what I have," Merlin said honestly. "Were there any clues as to what they might be after?"

"I saw the Hound and the tunnel. Nothing more of them. But that doesn't lead me to believe that the Sídhe have changed their ways. We need to be ready for the worst."

"I see." Merlin's sigh filled her living room, even through the phone. "I wish that was not the case, but we will be ready. Were there any hints as to the identity of the Iron Soul? Any sign that they will be there?"

"Nothing certain," Morgana admitted. "But it is a college town, or at least that was the impression I got. That will bring many young people through town. If we position ourselves properly, we'll have the chance to see hundreds, if not thousands, of new faces each year."

"Yes, that will make it easier to find the Iron Soul." Merlin chuckled softly. "It's strange to imagine what it will be like. The world has changed so much since the last time we worked with an Iron Soul. And it is dramatically different from the last time the Sídhe opened a tunnel."

"You're not wrong."

That was putting it lightly. Morgana tried to imagine for a moment what it might be like when they found the next Iron Soul. She hoped an incarnation would be there. If the Sídhe were returning, then they might need them. The view towards magic had changed drastically over the centuries. Long ago, they had been celebrated as great protectors and heroes. Then everything had changed, and magic became something hidden and feared. For a time, you could get away with magic in small amounts as long as you didn't draw attention to yourself. They'd always been good at navigating that.

"How do you think modern mages will react?" Morgana asked.

"I suspect that will depend on their reading habits." Merlin sounded far too amused. "Or viewing habits. A lot of popular culture is much kinder towards magic than it used to be."

"I suppose so." Morgana exhaled and let the silence stretch out between them. "So... how soon do you think you'll move?"

"There are some matters that I need to attend to," Merlin replied. "And of course, we need to identify where this Ravenslake is. But I think

I can manage it within a year. As you say, it will be easier to manage whatever is coming if we know the area."

Morgana didn't ask what profession he was considering. She knew that Merlin would join her at the university. They'd need to research that. Neither of them had any experience with the modern university system, though Merlin had been at a university before. That had been over two hundred years ago and in Spain. Regardless of how quickly they transitioned and built a new place for themselves in this Ravenslake, it promised to at least bring some new experiences.

25

Back to the Rebels

In the end, they didn't have to rely on magic to find their way back to the rebel camp or try to remember where it was. When morning came and everyone was awake, they dragged their sore and hungry bodies off in search of food. A couple of hours of wandering through the forest and letting Morgana confirm what berries and fruits were familiar later, a small scouting party found them. Eirwen was the only Sídhe even remotely happy to see them when they were brought back to the cavern that served as the rebel base. Alex was too tired, sore, and hungry to care. They were brought to the main library and seated around the table while Eirwen ordered for food and water to be brought to them.

There was an energy in the cave that Alex couldn't read. Tension or anticipation, anger or grief, she wasn't sure. Sídhe, it seemed, were less emotive than humans. They had emotions, of course, but either as an aspect of culture or a difference in facial muscles, they didn't project as much as a human might have. Alex couldn't read the reactions of those around them who took up guarding positions in the war room.

"Are any of you injured?" Eirwen asked. He took a seat opposite Alex at the table. It left a lot of space between him and the mages. None of the other Sídhe took a seat.

"No," Alex answered. She shifted her right hand so Morgana could easily touch it. "We had some minor injuries, but we've tended to them." Eirwen nodded, his gaze sweeping over them. "Is our gear safe?" Alex asked. She ignored a plate of cut fruit and kept her gaze focused on Eirwen.

"Yes," Eirwen answered. He seemed surprised by the question, but quickly schooled his face back to a neutral expression. "I suppose after a night in the forest without a guide, you would be worried about such things." Gesturing to a nearby rebel, he said, "Bring the mage's gear in here."

"Was it searched?" Morgana asked.

Morgana was leaning back in her chair, not touching any of the food and giving Eirwen a sharp look. Her left hand was touching Alex's forearm so that she benefited from the translating magic. It probably wasn't helping anything, but Alex was honestly relieved to see Morgana acting a bit more normal. Out of the corner of her eye to her left, Alex saw Aiden roll his eyes and reach for some of the food. That said, he kept his right hand touching Nicki's arm, to Alex's immediate left.

"No," Eirwen answered. He showed no sign of discomfort. "There was a discussion about that, but it was decided that it was too likely there was iron in your packs."

"You would be correct on that," Alex replied. She almost smiled, thinking of the iron stored at the bottom of her pack. "We tried to bring a bit of anything we might need."

"Please," Eirwen gestured to the packs that had been brought in. "Check for yourselves."

Morgana stood first, releasing Alex and going to the packs. Alex turned to watch Morgana level a glare at one of the guards, who quickly moved further away from their gear. Bran stood up and moved to his pack, shifting some things around and putting the Iron Chalice back on the top. Then, with a huff, he hoisted it up and placed it beside his chair. With deliberate movements, he picked up half of a fruit and bit into it.

Following their example, Alex quickly went to her pack and opened it up. Nothing looked like it had been moved, which was just as well given the amount of iron in her bag. Galahad was near the top, and Alex ran her fingers over the small stuffed body. With a grunt, she picked her bag up and moved it to her chair. Before Nicki could get up, Alex brought her bag over while Bran moved Aiden's.

"Thank you for keeping our supplies safe," Alex said politely. "We appreciate your help."

"Then perhaps you will repay us by answering some questions?"

Morgana gave Alex a warning look that she didn't need. If this being had been a part of the court, then they were used to playing whatever part was necessary. Alex may not have been raised in such an environment herself, but she knew to be careful without Morgana telling her so. Her fingers slipped into the top of her bag and found Galahad.

"Reports are incomplete at this time," Eirwen said. Their tone was calm and measured. Alex was grateful for his self-control. "What we know for certain is that the palace has been destroyed. A force was seen advancing on the capital city soon after you left."

"That fits," Alex replied. Exhaustion hung over her, and her fingers dug into Galahad's soft sides. "I don't remember the name of the prince that attacked. Everything happened so fast. We were in the throne room with Jarven and the others. Jarven had a bunch of materials from the library, and we were trying to escape when that invading force came in."

"Do you know if Jarven survived?" Eirwen asked. "What happened to the materials she secured?"

That answered the question of Jarven's gender, Alex thought with a sigh. "I don't know. When the fighting started between the prince's guards and the attacking force, I called for a retreat. There were so many of them." She shook her head. "I lost sight of Jarven in the battle, but I can say for certain that the prince who was in control of the city is dead."

That announcement got murmurs from the Sídhe, who had stayed to listen. Eirwen nodded thoughtfully and was watching her with careful eyes. Alex was tempted to use magic to see what he was thinking. Were they suspicious of them? Did they blame them for what had happened?

"Do you know what brought the palace down?" Eirwen asked.

And there was the question. Alex straightened up in her seat. "Magic. During the battle, I guess one too many of the support pillars got hit. It started a chain reaction." That was an answer; it highlighted why magic was dangerous and didn't direct potential anger at any one of them. "I know you lost agents in that collapse. I'm sorry for their loss."

Eirwen showed no grief. Maybe they were used to it. This was a rebellion, after all. His eyes turned towards Nicki, who still had the box in her lap. "Did you find what you need?"

"We haven't looked at the documents yet," Alex answered. "There have been more immediate concerns."

"I suppose so." Eirwen folded his hands in front of him. "Despite the loss of life, it seems this was a victory for us. One prince dead and potentially another as well, and likely each of them lost their advanced guards."

Eirwen's face showed no happiness, but Alex relaxed a little at the words and tone. At least they recognized that something significant had changed. Alex hoped they hadn't unleashed too much chaos. The point of helping had been to offer stability when the Darkness was defeated.

On the other hand, bringing down the palace was certainly a show of strength.

"I must speak with our scouts. We need more information and to identify the nobles still alive. A scramble for power is likely." Eirwen stood and nodded to one of the guards. Morgana tensed, and Eirwen almost flinched at her reaction. "Please grant me use of the war room."

The guards stepped closer. Alex jumped to her feet, and the two nearest to her started reaching for swords on their belts before second-guessing the action. Her fellow mages were on their feet in seconds, and silver magic flashed around Morgana's hands.

"Hold," Alex ordered sharply. "Eirwen?"

"Forgive us, I only meant for them to show you to a safe place to wait," Eirwen nodded deeply, and his violet eyes were shimmering with worry.

"Alright," Alex said. That sounded reasonable on the surface.

She reached down and picked up her pack. It was heavy, but she hoisted it up with some help from Morgana. Her eyes never left the nearest Síd guard, and when her pack was on, she casually rested her right hand on the hilt of Cathanáil. The weight of her pack made it hard to look nonchalant, but it was worth the attempt.

"Lead the way," Alex said. She hoped it appeared friendly, or at least non-threatening. Then again, she still had her hand resting on Cathanáil's hilt. "Please."

The guards moved ahead of them, three leaving the room to guide them back into the large main area. Fewer Sídhe were in open view now, and Alex wondered if they were sleeping. She had no idea what time it was anymore. The few Sídhe that she saw gazed at them curiously, only to turn away the moment she glanced towards them.

When they made it to a small side room that had been carved from the hillside, Alex both grimaced and sighed in relief. It was small for all five of them, but seemed to be private. The stone, while smoothed down, lacked the refined finish of the Sídhe tunnels. There was a padded surface that looked like a cross between a daybed and a sofa, and a couple of simple chairs that had been made from the local silvery wood. Between all of them was a short table that was between the height of a dining table and a coffee table. The guards slipped past them and closed the wooden door with a solid thunk.

For a moment, none of them said anything. The faint hum of the Sídhe moving around outside was the only sound, and it was muffled by the door. Alex wasn't sure if the small space with only one way in or out felt secure and safe or like a trap. Judging from the expressions on the faces of the others, she wasn't the only one unsure of that. Nicki set the box on the table with a loud crash and shrugged off her pack with a grateful sigh.

"Do you think we're prisoners?" Aiden asked with a heavy frown.

"I doubt it," Morgana replied. "We have our gear, and they know we have magic. It's not worth it for them to keep us contained." She studied the doorway and shook her head. "But that doesn't mean that they won't try to point us at something. Jarven may have seemed surprised by half of the team running off, but they might have had orders from Eirwen to do so in order to put us in the prince's path."

"That's a dark idea," Nicki said. She was already opening the box.

"It's the Sídhe." Morgana raised an eyebrow. "And they are at war. We are nothing to them."

Alex handed the Iron Pendant over to Nicki without a word. Of all of them, except maybe Morgana, Nicki had the best background to review a historical report. Morgana was obviously the best option, but she was already pacing like a caged animal. Tension swirled around the mage, and if she hadn't been low on magic, Alex was certain that Morgana would not have control over her powers right now. She could only be grateful that Morgana had kept it together in the war room.

'She's never had to go back before,' Arto said. It was obvious, but his voice dripped with guilty worry. 'Both Morgana and Merlin were hybrids, but it was easier for Merlin. He never believed in them. They meant nothing to him beyond enemies.'

That might not have been true. Maybe once upon a time, Merlin had struggled with the truth of his parentage, but he had never revealed such a conflict to any of her lives. His reliable determination and optimism had always been a guide to them. Cuthbert scoffed at her sentimental thoughts, but said nothing.

'Morgana loved Scáthbás, no matter what she may say,' Arto added sadly. 'It took time, and a great deal of human love for her to understand that what the Queen showed her was not genuine affection.'

Scáthbás had been a terrible parent. Arthur proved that a thousand times over, and Alex held back a shiver as certain uncomfortable memories replayed. She'd never understand how Scáthbás thought, how she felt, and maybe she never would. Maybe there was something too alien about the Sídhe ruler for Alex to understand. She just wished that it didn't have to hurt Morgana, even after three thousand years.

Glancing at Nicki, Alex found her friend eagerly reading the first set of plates and moving her lips as she went. The temptation to demand Nicki read out loud tore at Alex, but she held back. Rushing things would not help. Honestly, she should consider herself lucky that the Iron Pendant worked with the written word at all. When she'd made it, Alex had been thinking of spoken languages. It seemed her subconscious had been smarter than she was.

Thor laughed at that thought, and amusement rippled through her mind as a welcome relief. Alex sighed and leaned against the wall. The voices were almost pleasant. They were a link to the Iron Realm and their history there. When they had been quiet, Alex had missed them a little. What caused them to fade in and out, she did not know, but feared the answer lay in her emotions or her need for guidance.

With no reason to keep standing, Alex asked Bran to help her take off her pack. She set it against one of the chairs and sank into it with a groan. The muscles of her legs were tight and sore. Alex wasn't sure if it was from too much use or too little. It had been a strange week. The others took seats and opened their packs to pull out snacks. Even Morgana gave up her pacing and slumped onto the daybed.

"Hungry, Alex?" Bran asked. He held out a wrapped snack bar.

"Not right now." Alex managed a smile. "We should have grabbed the fruit."

Morgana raised an eyebrow, but said nothing. Alex didn't think she had the energy, judging from how Morgana was sprawled on the padded surface. If she didn't topple over, they'd be okay, but there wasn't enough space for anyone to really relax. Aiden had pulled out a sleeping roll and filled most of the floor space with it.

"The report is thankfully laid out in a pretty logical way," Nicki said suddenly. Her voice broke the silence and pulled Alex roughly from her thoughts. "I'm afraid that it doesn't go too much into the history of the flight from the homeworld, but it covers it vaguely." Nicki waved her hand as if dismissing this. "Oddly, things are phrased, as much as the Pendant can translate at least, almost as if this was information pulled from legends. A large group of Sídhe were brought to this world to conquer it and establish a colony. It was likely an arc project. They tried to make sure that something of their culture and their people survived. According to this, there were three separate arrival groups. All of them were at least 10,000 in number. They didn't just bring weapons and supplies for a war, but major culture heirlooms. There is a list of pieces of artwork, not something that you bring if you're only going to war."

Alex's mouth tasted of ashes, and bile burned her throat. How much had those first Sídhe known? Did they know the truth, but hide it from their descendants to avoid a panic? Was this first mission and the desire to keep things a secret the root of the Manifest Destiny ideology that seemed to have such a tight grip on the Sídhe culture? Alex rubbed her forehead and held back a groan of frustration.

"What got Scáthbás interested in this?" Morgana asked as she rose from her resting place. Now it was her turn to lean over Nicki in a vain attempt to see the text.

"There isn't anything about that, I'm afraid." Nicki tucked a strand of hair behind her ear. "But soon after she took over, she commissioned a full review of the oldest records. It seems that information about the Darkness and a grave threat was found in the records."

"And who knows when that breach that destroyed the continent started," Aiden offered. "That might have been what made her curious. Hell, maybe she was a librarian who found something and put it together, and that was what drove her to take power."

Morgana frowned, and something flickered in her eyes. Alex stayed silent. Old memories of small things that Morgana had said over the years to her and her other lives echoed. Scáthbás had been a twisted being, obsessive, but... Alex believed that part of her obsession really had been to protect the Sídhe. That was what had driven a wedge between her and Arthur. That and her years of abuse. A shiver raced through her body.

"I suppose that is possible," Morgana said slowly. Some of the anger had faded from her voice, but she was still taut like a string ready to snap. "There are so many questions." A loud sigh escaped her. "I doubt we'll ever have the answers we want."

"There are a few theories in this," Nicki offered. "This is a summary, so there are mentions of evidence, more like bullet points, but the full documents aren't here. One suggests the arc theory I mentioned and points out that contact with the homeworld was cut off over eight thousand years ago. If this was written three thousand years ago, then that would be almost eleven thousand years ago."

"That's not that many generations," Bran said with a frown. "Not with how long they live."

"No, it isn't," Morgana agreed. "But it is a few. It could have easily been great-grandparents who came over. Then again, we don't know for sure if they always lived this long. It could be the result of living in this world."

"A fair point," Alex said. "Just think about Emrys."

"True." Bran was glowering at the plate, a furrow between his eyes. "But does this actually help us? That was the point of this, trying to get information that could help us."

"I haven't read all of it yet! Give me some time." With that, Nicki went back to reading, making small noises here and there.

Alex turned and reached into her bag and pulled out Galahad. She hugged the stuffed animal tight against her chest and inhaled the familiar, slightly musty scent that lingered in the old plush fur. Nicki's fingers were moving across the metal tablet in front of her, and she was about to fall out of her seat. Aiden was stretched out on his sleeping roll, about to fall asleep, and Bran was shifting on the padded seat so Morgana could lay down again. There was nothing to do now but wait and hope that either Eirwen or Nicki learned something useful.

26

Sound and Silence

Time had little meaning to Alex. She drifted in and out of consciousness despite the uncomfortable position she was sitting in. The chair's wooden back lacked cushioning or neck support, but a night in the woods with no sleeping roll or blankets had already done a number on her. When they made it back home, she was going to spend a week in bed and guilt Jenny into bringing her food.

Morgana had fallen asleep, and eventually Bran had moved off the sofa and followed Aiden's example. His sleeping bag was between Aiden and the doorway, and he was softly snoring. If the door opened, he'd have an unpleasant awakening. Alex's fingers shifted over Galahad's fur, drawing comfort from the stuffed animal. She was too tired to even be embarrassed by that.

Alex's head started to slump. Twisting in the seat, she propped her head on her fist, resting her elbow on the arm of the chair. She eyed the space next to Morgana and seriously considered going over to her and nudging the older mage against the wall. Maybe two people could fit, and she and Morgana had snuggled plenty of times when she was Arto.

Nicki almost seemed happy. She'd given up on the chair and was sitting on the floor with her sweatshirt serving as a cushion. At some point she'd pulled off her boots, and Alex didn't have the heart to point out that if something happened that might be a problem. From time to time, she heard someone move outside the heavy wooden door, but they never lingered. There were only the soft snores of Aiden and the slide of the metal plates as Nicki examined them.

Quiet was good. Quiet was safe. Probably. Alex still found herself looking towards the door every time she woke from her doze. No noise meant that soldiers were not marching towards them, that weapons weren't clashing, and magic wasn't bringing down an ancient structure. Her eyes slid closed, and the sight of the first great stones smashing the tile replayed. The memory of the noise, the destruction, was enough to jar her wide awake for a short time before the process restarted.

Looking around the room, Alex examined the small torches along the walls that provided light. They were similar to the lights in the city, making Alex wonder if the cave was wired with electricity, gas, or something completely unknown to her. Or was it some kind of magic? Did this world have low-level magic at all times that the people used in their day to day lives?

A knock on the door, a real solid knock rather than soft movement outside, made Alex jump in her seat. Morgana made a sound in her sleep but didn't wake. Nicki had been pulled from her reading and was blinking at her surroundings as if she'd forgotten where she was. Alex stood and managed not to sway the instant she was upright.

"Wha..." Aiden's voice was thick with sleep, but Bran was already sitting up and moving away from the door. "Alex?" Aiden asked as she stepped over him.

"Someone's at the door," she answered.

Alex didn't have to push him to wake up. As soon as she moved past him, Aiden stood up with a sigh. Another knock on the door made Alex pause as she realized that she didn't have the Iron Pendant.

"Nicki, we're going to need you for translating," Alex said.

That got the redhead moving. She grumbled a lot, but leveraged herself onto her knees with the help of the table and stumbled to her feet. Nicki looked at her boots thoughtfully, but the person outside knocked again. This time, Morgana woke up and snapped into a seated position with wide eyes. Lunging forward, Nicki grabbed Alex's left hand as Alex opened the door.

The Síd in the doorway was shorter than Eirwen and Jarven, with softer features than Alex was expecting. Pale white hair was piled on their head, with small braids keeping it in place. Immediately, Alex got the impression that they were very young compared to the others. Of course, in human terms, the being could still easily eclipse all of them by centuries.

"Hello," Alex greeted. Again, she wasn't sure if she should smile. "Does Eirwen need to see us again?"

"The talisman is very impressive," the Síd said carefully. Their eyes kept jumping between them as if they were afraid.

"Thank you," Alex replied. Keeping her hand wrapped tight around Nicki's, she nodded to the young Síd and wished she knew a way to put the creature at ease. "I only wish that I'd made more of them."

"You made it?" the Síd's eyes widened. "Really?"

"Uh, yes."

Morgana had crept up beside them. Her eyes were narrowed on the Síd, and she touched Alex's shoulder. The boys were watching from the side of the room and didn't seem to feel the need to interject themselves, which Alex was grateful for. The space around the door was already crowded with the three of them and their Síd visitor.

"The old amulets only work for one person at a time, even if they are touching, and I don't believe that they could translate the written word." The Síd paused. "They were easier to make, though. All the Riders have them and anyone who works in the direct tunnel connections."

"That makes sense," Alex agreed. She tried to remember if she'd seen amulets like what the Síd was describing when the Síd in the tunnels died, but wasn't sure. Then again, if it was magic, then maybe it wouldn't survive. "I'm just grateful that we can communicate with you."

"Yes, that is good." The Síd cleared their throat. "My apologies, I didn't mean to talk about your magic like that. The old magical items have always been of interest to me." There was no blush on their pale cheeks, but Alex still got the impression that the Síd was embarrassed. "Uh, Eirwen wanted to be sure that you have what you need. Are you thirsty or hungry? Most of the food we have should be safe for human consumption."

"Some food would be nice, thank you."

"Is there anything else you require?"

"No, it's a bit small of a room for the five of us, but we're managing. Please be sure to knock before entering. So that you don't hit anyone who might be on the floor."

"Of course." The Síd's eyes dropped to Alex's sword. It wasn't politeness that would keep them from entering, Alex recognized. Fair enough: she didn't exactly trust them either.

A rush of noise beyond the doorway made their visitor jump. Alex tilted her head and peered around them as the Síd spun around. There was a mess of Sídhe dressed in armor and plain clothing gathering in the center of the cave. Alex couldn't see anything clearly, and their voices were a din of questions and shouts that even the Iron Pendant couldn't make sense of.

"I apologize," the Síd said quickly as it turned back to them. "Please excuse me."

They weren't given much choice. The Síd grabbed the handle of the door and pulled it quickly, forcing Alex and Nicki to shift back. Displeasure rolled off of Morgana, but she leaned forward and pressed her ear to the door as it shut while still keeping a hold of Alex.

"I can't make anything out," Morgana said. "But something happened."

"Maybe one of the people who went with us made it back," Aiden suggested. "Or a scout came with a report."

"Either of those might be bad for us," Morgana replied. Her exhaustion had vanished, replaced with her familiar sharp focus. "Pack your things up and get ready to move."

Nicki took that as her cue to let go of them. She hurried back to her chair and picked up her boots. An expression of distaste crossed Nicki's features, but she pulled the boots back on and laced them up while Alex returned Galahad to the top of her pack.

"Nicki, are you having any luck with the report?" Alex asked, glancing over as Nicki started to pack the plates back into the box. "Anything helpful."

"Well..." Nicki hesitated. "There's one section, a part that paraphrases a section of an even older report or record. Probably the original documents this was made from. I'm not sure if the pendant can't translate or if I just hate what it seems to say."

"Why?" Aiden asked. He was pulling on his sweatshirt and tying his coat around his waist. "What does it say?"

"It said 'laser gun' or something really close to that," Nicki answered.

They all stared at her, and Nicki nodded before a soft chuckle with a hysterical note to it escaped her. "It's not clear, but it seems to point to this all being an experiment. The Sídhe found this world, the one closest to them, but wanted to know more. They built some kind of device so they could investigate and..." She gestured around vaguely.

"They ripped a hole in the Tree of Reality," Morgana sighed. Rubbing her temples, the mage looked three thousand years old and done with it all. "That fits, I suppose. The Darkness isn't an evil force: You were right, Alex, it's a catastrophe that's the result of an accident. It's matter or something else completely from outside this universe that's incompatible. It's what happens when worlds collide within the Tree of Reality on a much larger and destructive scale."

"Yeah." Alex didn't like being right, but she rallied. "Plus side, it confirms that the source of this is where we think it is. There is probably only the one entry point. After the Darkness started pouring in, I doubt the Sídhe did another test. It also means that the source is near the world like it appeared to be in my vision. We can reach it. We don't have to try and float out into the nothing between worlds."

"I guess that's good news," Aiden said slowly. "Nothing else?"

"I haven't gotten through everything," Nicki reminded him. "And honestly, given what Alex has described from her visions, it's not like we'll find the original lab and laser gun on the Sídhe homeworld. It's gonna come down to magic no matter what else is in the report."

Alex wasn't sure what she'd been hoping for. This confirmed some things for her, but it didn't give her anything else. She sighed and rubbed the back of her neck.

"Well, that's something, I guess," she said. "Not sure it was worth the trip to the palace..."

"We know that if we fix the first hole, things will improve," Bran offered. "We suspected, but knowing that this was caused by the Sídhe, even by accident, means that it isn't going to happen again naturally down the road."

"Answers are rare," Morgana added. "They aren't wasted." She was lifting her pack onto the padded surface to pull on, and Aiden rushed over to help her. "Though I wonder about the drop in technology. If we assume that the Iron Pendant is providing Nicki with the best answer possible, then where did that technology go? They still use swords after all, and they don't have the excuse of their primary foes being deathly weak to the material."

"Maybe it was about material?" Aiden offered. When Morgana looked at him, he shrugged, which was an achievement with his pack on. "I mean, does iron exist here? I'm unclear on that. There's a good amount of it in our realm, but probably not here. Their technology might have been based on something that they couldn't get here. The first settlers might have included researchers and scientists, but maybe something happened to them, leaving the others without a way to rebuild or repair technology they brought."

"Good point," Bran agreed. "After all, all of us know how to use a cell phone, but other than Aiden, none of us would be able to build one, even if we were given all the parts we needed."

"I might," Nicki insisted.

"Sure, Nicki." Aiden stepped closer to her and patted her on the shoulder. "I'm sure you could."

Her answering expression made Alex smile. There were dark circles under Nicki's eyes from lack of sleep, and her red hair was a mess. If it had been anyone but Aiden, Alex would have worried that they were about to be attacked. As it was, Nicki simply glared at him and huffed in annoyance.

"If things go bad, what is the next step?" Bran asked softly. The noise outside had lessened slightly, but it was still louder than before the return of whoever had come to the cavern. "What direction do we head?"

"Bran, we don't know the area well enough to even say that," Aiden pointed out. "Other than going right, left, or straight out of the cave."

"Straight," Morgana said firmly. "But if it comes to that, try to keep a magical shield up. You saw the defensive positions they hold."

"Let's not talk about this," Alex hissed. She nodded towards the door. "We need to stay calm, and hopefully, they'll stay calm too."

They lingered in the room, everything packed and with shoes on, but not talking about anything in particular. Nicki told them a bit more about the report as they perched awkwardly around the room on the furniture with their packs either on or at their feet. Alex barely registered any of the details that Nicki listed off. Nothing seemed important, and she kept thinking about her visions. She'd seen the dead world herself. What had she been hoping to find? There was a persistent sense that there was a missing piece to the puzzle.

"What do you think is going on out there?" Bran asked. He was staring at the door.

"I don't know," Morgana said. "Hopefully, we aren't being thrown under the bus."

"Morgana, be positive," Alex replied.

"When did you start channeling Merlin?" Morgana asked. She almost smiled before a faint hint of surprise crossed her face. Then grief filled her eyes. "We have to be careful."

She'd kicked a puppy. That was the only way to explain how she felt. Nicki grimaced, and Aiden stood up and inched towards the door.

He was leaning forward to press his ear on it when a solid knock rang through the room. Aiden froze and looked back at them. Nicki ripped the Iron Pendant over her neck and thrust it towards Alex. With fumbling fingers and cursing herself for not taking it earlier, Alex slipped the Iron Pendant over her head.

"Open the door," she told Aiden.

He hurried to comply, and Alex was glad to see that it swung open with no trouble. No one had tried to lock them in. It was a different Síd standing in the doorway this time. There was no sign of the younger one. This one had stern features and longer curving horns. Small bands that looked like leather were wrapped around the base of the horns, a decoration that Alex hadn't seen before, and it was wearing similarly thick bands around their forearms. There was a sword on their hip, and they were dressed in simple, but effective looking armor.

"Eirwen wishes to speak with all of you. Immediately."

Alex relayed the message to her fellow mages. Their escort didn't turn away. Instead, it took a few steps back, keeping their eyes locked on their small group as everyone made sure they had their packs. Beyond the doorway were two more armed guards. It was intimidating, but they hadn't sent a guard for everyone. They still outnumbered them if foul intentions were what Eirwen had in mind.

The first escort Síd finally turned its back to them to lead the way. The other two flanked them on either side. Keeping her shoulders relaxed, Alex set a slow pace that prevented the Sídhe from hurrying them along. As they stepped into the main cavern, Alex noted many Sídhe were still gathered around and were standing on the pathways overhead, peering down at them. Eirwen stood in the center of the room, and beside him, battered and bruised, was one of the Sídhe that had run off to kill the Prince.

27

The Final Home

Modern Day Ravenslake, United States

Ravenslake was both precisely what Morgana expected and not at all what she was expecting. The main street was an odd mix of hundred-year-old buildings and new facades. There was neon everywhere on a small stretch of Central that bummed up against classic sandstone constructions. More shops than were possibly needed filled the lower levels, and the upper levels were a mix of condos for professionals and cheap apartments for students.

A few big box stores were near the campus which competed for the business of the college kids. The town lived and breathed its land grant college, but also boasted of the beauty of the area hiking trails and their namesake lake in tourist brochures. Upon arriving, the name of the lake had confused Morgana. Apparently, it was Ravens Lake, while the town was the one-word Ravenslake. The locals laughed it off, and she had quickly accepted it as a local quirk.

There were many of those, and she'd need to learn them all. Despite being a college town with young people constantly coming and going like the tides of the ocean only a few hours away, the town was cautious towards adults that moved in. It wasn't that small of a town. By modern standards, it was barely a city, but it easily had twenty times the population of the entire region she'd grown up in at the time of her birth. Yet, on every shopping trip, she got the sense that people knew each other.

The jury was still out as to if she'd like that or not. Hopefully, the locals would accept her and Merlin and move on before anything magical began to occur. She did like the campus. It wasn't Cambridge or Bologna or Siena. It lacked the weight of history that those much older universities were rich with, but there was an energy there nonetheless even if Morgana wasn't completely sold on the wild mixture of architectural styles employed by the university. Morgana knew she'd warm up to it.

What she did like was the house. She'd been staying in a hotel for the past three weeks while she finalized the paperwork. Property purchasing was another aspect of the modern world that had become much more complicated. It was a side effect of there being so many more people, so many more laws and complexities to deal with. When she was born, you had a roundhouse, and the village knew who it belonged to. That was enough.

Not that she'd made things any easier. There had been photos online, and she'd been able to communicate with the local realtor, but Morgana hadn't made up her mind until she'd arrived and seen the house with her own eyes. Then she'd had questions. The Victorian-style house was lovely and Morgana had gone over everything several times. At this point, the realtor was likely grateful to get away from her.

A meager stack of boxes filled only one corner of the living room. The privacy of a home out of town would be a benefit whenever magic became stronger, but it reinforced to Morgana how little she had. Rather than move the furniture across the country, she'd donated it and packed up the little that mattered. There were framed sketches of her various late adoptive children and one of Airril that Merlin had never seen.

Packages with new pots and pans and plates covered the surface of the new dining table that stood off the kitchen. They'd need to be washed. It was one more item on the list she was making in her head. A glance out the window told Morgana that it was getting late in the day. Her body was aching from the bending down and scrubbing that she'd been doing all day. Despite all the work done, she wasn't happy with the amount of chores still waiting for her.

Leaning against the counter, Morgana eyed the boxed-up plates and pots while she debated with herself what the next step was. If she got the kitchen in order, then she could run out and buy more than microwave food. A knock on the door distracted Morgana, and she looked towards the front of the house in surprise. She wasn't expecting any company, and the movers had been here for only a short time the other day, not long enough to draw attention to her. Morgana hadn't showered today, and her long dark braid was a mess.

She was considering ignoring it when the knocking started again. This time it was to the rhythm of an old blues song. Morgana's lips quirked into a smile, and she headed to the front door, opening it without further delay. Merlin was standing on her doorstep with two plastic bags in hand. A very appetizing spicy smell was coming from those bags, and Morgana's stomach grumbled. The sound clearly amused Merlin, and Morgana didn't bother to scold him for his widening smile.

"Special delivery." Merlin held up the bags. He grinned at her and stepped inside before she invited him in. His footsteps echoed slightly on the hardwood floor, and he hummed softly as he looked around.

"I like it," Merlin said. "It needs a fresh coat of paint on the exterior, but I must say that the Victorian style suits you."

"I'm not sure how to take that, but I'm happy with it." She paused and looked around. "It is a bit more space than I was originally planning on. If we weren't expecting trouble, I might consider fostering children."

"Trouble may not start for some time." Merlin smiled encouragingly. "I wouldn't write off the possibility just yet."

Morgana didn't bother arguing, but she knew she wouldn't. As much as she'd enjoyed giving children a safe home over the years, this was not the time and place to risk it. Her vision pointed to years in the future, but that didn't mean that they wouldn't encounter Fae or Old Ones in the meantime. And in the age of the internet, she had no desire to have someone without magic that close.

Merlin headed into the dining room and set the bags down on the table with no prompting. "I wasn't sure if you'd get the kitchen in order today or not and decided to make sure that you ate something." Merlin started unpacking several to-go boxes. Morgana didn't recognize the name of the restaurant but recognized the first dish as sweet and sour chicken. "I doubt you ate lunch."

She hadn't, and didn't bother confirming that for Merlin. Instead, she went into the kitchen and retrieved two bottles of water from the pack she'd purchased yesterday. The glasses hadn't been unpacked yet, so this would have to do. Merlin took the offered bottle with a smile and a nod.

"How is the unpacking coming?"

"Slower than it should," Morgana admitted. "I've got my bedroom largely sorted, and my office is mostly ready. It's a bit bare now." She took a box of almond chicken, and one of the plastic forks Merlin had been wise enough to get. "There's another room. I'm not sure what I'll do with it. I suppose going ahead and making a spare bedroom makes sense, just in case."

"Fair enough. My home is smaller than this, but my belongings don't go far filling it up. It's funny. When mortals imagine immortals, they usually think that we'd be hoarders."

"Nothing lasts forever; you learn to focus on keeping what actually matters." Morgana shrugged. "Let them believe what they want."

"Well, there are a few old things I still have." Merlin laughed. "Would you believe I brought that old telescope of mine?"

Raising an eyebrow, Morgana held back a laugh. "Are you serious? The old brass one? That thing is ancient. You'll never actually take it outside, and you know it."

"I know, I know. It's just such a lovely piece of history."

"Then I may steal it from you for a lesson."

"My dear Morgana, you have but to ask," Merlin replied breezily.

She knew she wouldn't. Morgana was already outlining her plans for the next year and couldn't imagine a class where bringing in an antique telescope would be helpful to the students. This was college, not second-grade show and tell.

"How is your planning going?" Morgana asked.

"Not bad. I'm going to stick close to the material that my predecessor used. By all accounts, he was an excellent professor before his early retirement." Merlin smiled at the mention of the early retirement.

"Yes, yes, that was well done," she said. "Clearing the way for us with those windfalls. Very nice, but you can let it go now."

"You never let me savor my victories. Given the low amount of magic I had to work with, I thought I did very well."

"You did." Morgana nodded her agreement and rewarded her partner with a smile. "We have new jobs in the place that we are supposed to be with no fuss. I've been in contact with the department head. They've been welcoming and don't think anything is strange."

They talked about nothing important over dinner. Merlin had already been visiting some of the local stores and sights. The old man was already scouting the area around the lake. Morgana had to admit that having time to learn the lay of the land was a nice luxury.

"You're going to make me go hiking, aren't you?" Morgana asked dryly.

"We used to hike all the time."

"For travel! Before we had the luxury of cars, airplanes, trains, and horses!" Giving Merlin a withering look, she patted her mouth with a paper napkin to clean up the last of the sauce. "Not for fun."

"I find it soothing. Just us and the sounds of nature." Merlin's smile was almost wistful. "And as beautiful as the northeast is in the autumn, I'm excited about having mountains and a forest in my backyard."

His energy was too much. Morgana shook her head fondly and started to clean up in an attempt to hide her amusement. Merlin stood and helped gather up the remains of dinner. Refolding two of the boxes, Morgana noted that there would be enough for a quick breakfast in the morning. That bought her more time to get the kitchen in order. Merlin followed her into the kitchen and leaned against the counter while she put the boxes in the mostly empty fridge.

"Thank you for bringing dinner," Morgana said, realizing that she'd never thanked him.

"Of course. We've been so busy that I haven't had the chance to see you."

"It's not like we were separated for long this time. We visited each other frequently. Thanks to trains."

"It's not the same." Merlin was almost whining. Then he perked up and laughed. "I just realized that this is the first time since the war that we've lived in the same town and haven't lived together."

Morgana quirked her head but realized that he was right. "Yes, well, I no longer have to live under standards that make me pretend that we're married."

"Very true." He rubbed his hands together. "Is there anything I can do to help?"

"If you're offering, I think I've got a little more work in me."

"Then what can I do?"

"Wash the dishes." Morgana pointed at the boxes of pots and pans, hoping her glee that someone else would wash them was hidden. "Please," she added for good measure.

"You didn't move much, did you?" Merlin asked. He cast his eyes around the room thoughtfully and leaned so he could see out into the living room.

"I didn't see the point, Ambrose." Morgana shrugged and cut through the tape on the nearest box. "Moving this much was a chore." When he chuckled, Morgana gave him a stern look. "How much have you unpacked?"

"I'm almost done, actually." Merlin joined her at the counter and carefully lifted out the packing foam and paper that padded the plates. "I need plenty of things, of course, but overall I'm happy. Construction workers are scheduled to start on my workshop next week. They should be done within a couple of weeks."

"That's good, given that you have a curriculum to work on."

"I'm confident that I'll manage." Merlin paused and seemed to consider something. "Though... I am concerned that my lack of experience will show too easily. The hiring committee believes that we both have been professors before."

"You've been a teacher before."

"That wasn't the same. The expectations today are very different."

"You'll figure it out. We haven't enough magic to shift memories too often. But I'm confident you'll manage." Raising an eyebrow at him, Morgana couldn't help but smirk a little.

"I'm flattered, my dear Morgana." He gave her a wink and took the first stack of simple white plates over to the sink. "Your confidence is all that I need."

"Silly old man," Morgana grumbled.

Even so, she felt lighter as she unpacked the pans. Merlin hummed loudly enough that she heard him over the splashing of the water and the soft clinking of the plates. She hurried to the bathroom after realizing that she'd forgotten to get a drying rack and brought one of the new blue towels out to serve as a drying surface. They moved around each other easily as Morgana walked around the kitchen and added to her shopping list.

This was easy. For a new house, it was already becoming familiar and comfortable. Morgana found herself smiling softly as she returned to the living room and opened the next box. It contained old books that she hadn't been willing to part with and a few little odds and ends from the last centuries. A framed photo of her with some of her hospital colleagues gave Morgana pause. In an instant, her good mood fled, and she questioned herself as to why she'd packed the photograph. Who she had been two months ago was legally dead and gone. Shaking her head, Morgana focused on the sound of Merlin moving in her new kitchen and the bang of a pot against the side of the sink.

This was where she was now. Morgana Cornwall was her name, and she was a newly arrived professor at Ravenslake University. It didn't have to feel right tonight or even tomorrow. There was time. There was time for this to become home, and for her new life and profession to become comfortable. She studied the photograph, allowing herself a moment to grieve for the life she'd abandoned before putting the photograph face down on the coffee table. This was her home and her life now, for as long as magic needed it to be. She had time. Morgana kept working and focused on Merlin's humming. If nothing else, he was with her, and that meant that she was home.

28

Down with the Rebellion

Keeping her shoulders relaxed, Alex nodded in greeting to Eirwen. She couldn't help but glance at the gathered Sídhe. Her mind raced with questions, and she quickly turned her attention back to Eirwen. Morgana moved closer to her and placed a hand on Alex's shoulder, likely for both the use of the translation magic and support. Nicki, Aiden, and Bran crowded in close. They didn't grab onto Alex, but she suspected they were touching Morgana.

"You wanted to see us," Alex said calmly. "Is there news from the capital?" She fought not to stare at the Síd who had returned. Dread rolled in her gut, thick and cold like slush. "I see you survived."

"No thanks to you," the Síd said. It was fidgeting more than Alex had ever seen a Síd do. Their voice lacked the bite that Alex imagined they wanted it to have. "Jarven is dead now, thanks to your actions."

Alex narrowed her eyes. That was vague. Morgana's hand squeezed her shoulder in warning. Something about the Síd's words was off in tone. She hesitated to call them out on it, unsure if that was a quirk of language that the Iron Pendant couldn't convey, but suspicion gnawed at her.

"Things didn't go according to plan," Alex agreed. "But we weren't the ones who deviated from the plan to start with." She weighed the next words carefully, but the low mumbling of the onlookers and the closeness of armed guards made up her mind. "You and the others leaving the group alerted the guards. That's when the plan faltered. The guards found us in the archives soon after."

Eirwen's expression was calm and neutral. He might as well have been a statue for all he revealed to her. Sharp, violet eyes swept across their small group, and Morgana's hand on her shoulder tightened painfully. The others huddled close, all of them tense and ready for trouble. The Síd beside Eirwen straightened up and narrowed their eyes.

"How dare you lie, you iron filth!"

"Peace, Gilford," Eirwen snapped. "Your story and theirs are rather different."

"Eirwen, the mages destroyed the palace," Gilford insisted. They turned to face Eirwen before looking around at the assembled Sídhe. "They sought to destroy everyone once they got what they wanted. Jarven and the others... It was the mages' fault. I don't know what they told you, but that is what I know."

"Our magic did destroy the palace," Alex admitted. "But that was an accident in battle. It is why we try to avoid using our magic too often. There are consequences, and if we are pressed, then it is easy for things to get out of control."

"Gilford had a rather different report," Eirwen replied. He gave nothing away. "Specifically, regarding your actions with Jarven."

A low growl escaped Morgana, and Alex's stomach tightened. If Morgana lost control here, as she had at the palace, it could be a disaster for everyone. There was movement behind her, but Alex kept her focus on the Sídhe in front of her. She had to leave calming Morgana down to the others. As it was, Alex could smell the tang of ozone in the air as her magic flowed down her arms and filled her chest.

"Jarven went with us to the library after some of the group decided to use the opportunity to go after the Prince," Alex explained. It was a struggle to keep her voice even. "Jarven kept to the plan and led us to the library. We got what we needed, and they had a pack with documents. The group that went after the Prince raised an alarm and troops found us. After fighting our way out of the library, we headed for the Great Halls." Alex nodded at Gilford. "That's where we met some of the others, but not all of them. Another Prince arrived with their force, and in the battle, the palace was destroyed. There was a lot of chaos, but I'll remind you we have our box. We went to the library."

Gilford took a step back. Pleasure at the fear finally sparking to life in their eyes filled Alex's chest. It was petty, but she didn't care. It had been an exhausting and cold night because this idiot and a few others hadn't been willing to stick to the plan.

"Our magic let us sneak in with no trouble," Alex continued. "We had no reason to deviate from the plan."

Whispers broke out. Eirwen still gave nothing away, but the guards were keeping their distance. Morgana's grip had eased a little, and the tension in the room had rolled back. Her words had struck a chord. Not necessarily a good one, but she was confident that a few of the Sídhe had realized the truth.

"Gilford?" Eirwen called.

"It wasn't like that," the Síd insisted, but it was weak. They were looking beyond Alex and her fellow mages. Towards the entrance, she realized with a twist in her gut.

"Something is wrong," Alex muttered.

There was a sound of assent behind her. At least she wasn't crazy, but there was no time to mull it over. Shouting behind them put Alex on the alert. Her hand went to Cathanáil, and she drew the Sword.

"Soldiers!" Came a cry from the front of the cavern behind Alex. She didn't turn, but heard the collective gasp of alarm. "They're heading right for us! At least fifty, all armed for battle!"

"How?" someone screamed.

"I'm sorry, Eirwen," Gilford cried. They sounded sorry, but this was still happening. "Just surrender, everyone. Surrender, and they won't hurt you!"

Alex ignored them after that. Soldiers were closing in, and the un-armored Sídhe were falling to their knees or running further into the cavern. She had no idea if there was another exit, and now wasn't the time to find out. Her pack was weighing her down, and she dared not try to run. Alex raised Cathanáil and light glittered off the smooth metal blade.

"Gilford, how could you do this?" Eirwen asked.

If an answer came, it was lost in the rush of noise. The Sídhe were scattering around the cavern, running towards hiding places or weapons. Out of the corner of her eye, Alex saw the guards of the rebel camp mustering near the side of the cave. One of the Síd was barking orders to them and pointing around the large open cavern.

"We need to move," Morgana hissed into her ear. "We're all too tired for another confrontation."

The truth of those words hit Alex like a punch to the gut. She almost doubled over as her concern for the rebels was eclipsed by worry for her friends. Nodding, Alex swallowed down any sense of guilt and turned to look at the others. Bran didn't wait for a suggestion and gestured for them to follow him towards the main entrance. It wasn't ideal, but no one seemed interested in stopping them. Their packs were too heavy for a run, but they hurried in the direction that most were fleeing. A few guards were marching near them, giving them sideways looks, and a few

Sídhe were running out ahead of them. Likely, they were hoping to get out and avoid the troops like Bran was.

The scout had given no clear details about how close the soldiers were. Alex entertained a hope that they were still far enough off that she and the others could move away, but when they reached the cave entrance, Alex could already hear the sounds of battle. Shouting and dying groans echoed off the stone of the hillside.

There was no time to care about that. Alex viciously shoved down the part of herself that was worried for the rebels, both for their lives and what it meant that the soldiers had found them. Gilford had been captured and made some kind of deal. That much was clear, and there was nothing she could do to change that.

"Move!" Nicki yelled. "Keep moving. We don't have enough magic to fight them."

Beneath Alex's feet, the world was humming with magic. She could feel it, stronger than before, but she didn't know what it meant. On her back, the iron at the bottom shifted just enough to threaten her balance. Alex grabbed a tree to keep herself steady. Soldiers were pushing through the underbrush only a few feet away. Violet eyes widened as they caught sight of her.

"Shit!" Bran snapped. "Daggers out."

"Be careful with your magic," Morgana added. "We haven't had much time to rest!"

The soldiers rushed them, turning their attention away from the rebels trying to hold their lookout points. It bought the rebels time to muster their forces, and Alex hoped it would be enough. Swinging Cathanáil at the nearest soldier, Alex reached for her magic and the power in the surrounding air. It hummed, thrumming in response to the danger, her fear. This world was suddenly on the edge of a knife and knew it. Beneath her feet, the pulse of the world's magic quickened in time with her own. Vertigo hit her, but Alex did not fall despite her knees quivering. Magic surged up her body, pushing, urging, and begging for help.

She didn't understand. Cathanáil crashed into a Sídhe blade and the golden metal bent at the force of the blow. Her arms quivered, but Alex pushed forward with all her strength, shoving her opponent back. They stumbled, dropping their sword arm, and Alex thrust Cathanáil forward. The Síd dodged back.

The others were staying close to her. Without using their magic, they were limited to only their daggers, and the packs restricted their mobility. Alex's heart raced, beating loudly in her ears. This was bad. This was bad. Magic curled in her chest. She could feel it growing in power. Beneath her feet, the pulse of energy was getting stronger.

Energy rippled through Alex's limbs. Minor shocks of pain slowed her down. There was no warning burn as she carefully pulled on her magic. Cathanáil was heavy in her right hand, but Alex brought her left hand to Mjǫllnir. It slipped out of the loop on her belt easily, and the handle fit perfectly in her hand.

Yellow sparks shoved a Sídhe back. A red fireball exploded further back in the line of soldiers. Alex almost smiled. They weren't as helpless as she feared. The Hammer was oddly light in her hand. Magic hummed in her fingertips, strengthening her tired limb, and Alex had no time to worry about using too much power. She slammed the Hammer against the shaft of a spear as it was thrust towards her. It shattered, and the sharp spear point fell to the ground. Before the Síd could recover or pull another weapon, Alex thrust Cathanáil forward into their upper chest. The blade cut through the lighter leather-like armor over the upper chest with some resistance.

The angle was all wrong. It was too high, and Alex couldn't free Cathanáil easily. Releasing the hilt, she let the body fall back and brought her right hand to Mjǫllnir's handle. Swinging as hard as she could, Alex crashed the Hammer's wide end into the next Síd. Lightning flashed off the iron, and the Síd flew back. Silver bolts sailed past Alex, striking two Sídhe. Lunging forward, Alex grasped the hilt of Cathanáil again and pulled up. Her shoulder protested the movement, and she had to fight the weight of her pack on the shoulder strap.

The Sword thankfully came free, sliding out of the corpse as Alex tried not to look at it. Dead violet eyes that were rapidly growing pale stared into the sky. Alex retreated towards the others. Their line shifted back. Alex's pack bumped into someone. The show of magic seemed to finally be making the soldiers hesitate.

Spikes of ice burst from the ground in a wave formation, slicing through three of the Sídhe at the front of the line. Blue magic shimmered in the air, and Alex tugged on the sparks, drawing the magic towards her. It tingled up her arms, making her a little stronger. More soldiers were pushing forward, cutting brutally through thick ferns.

Lifting Mjǫllnir, Alex inhaled slowly and scanned the front line of soldiers. They were armed with spears, putting more distance between them and the mages. Caution filled their eyes, but there were still too many of them for a full retreat. It would be too easy for the soldiers to spear them from behind. Anger grew in her chest. She'd been trying to help, trying to ease the strain on this world before moving on, but these Princes-

Lightning shook the air. Thunder crashed around them, but Alex didn't flinch back. It struck the Sídhe line, dancing from soldier to soldier. Screams filled the air, taking the place of the thunder in Alex's ringing ears. Bodies crumbled one by one. Further back, the line of soldiers was hesitating. Alex's eyes checked their numbers. There were more than she'd thought at first. At least thirty more were in view, pushing their way through the forest two by two, and the trees could be hiding more.

In the corner of her eye, she saw rebel Sídhe running from the mouth of the cave behind the defenses. They were scrambling up the hill. Silently, she wished them luck. There were more soldiers coming, rallying as Sídhe in more elaborate armor barked orders. The rebels were raining arrows and spears down upon them, having reclaimed a defensive position, but the soldiers were still focused on them. Gilford must have warned them they'd likely be here. This was their chance to kill the mages and strike back at the rebels.

How had it gone so wrong? The hope had been to improve the rebellion's chances and now... Alex wasn't sure. But it was too late now. Alex screamed in frustration, slamming Mjǫllnir against the chest plate of the nearest Síd. It shattered, and a dagger was thrust forward by Bran. Silver blood splattered across the front of her t-shirt. They were too close. It was suffocating. It was asking for one of them to be stabbed in return.

"Everyone have their gear?" Alex yelled. It was a stupid question. They didn't have time to stop. "We need to go!"

"Go?"

"Portal!"

Swinging Mjǫllnir around wildly, Alex shoved her magic roughly into the metal. Electricity arced off the Hammer and into the soldier line. She backed up, trying to hurry, but fearful of losing her footing. A wave of silver magic struck the soldiers, knocking them back. Morgana stepped up beside her, hands extended, and silver sparks swirling around her fingertips. Their eyes met for a moment.

"Whatever you're planning, do it quickly," Morgana barked. "I'm still weakened."

There was no time for Alex to focus like she had when bringing them here. Soldiers kept coming. The others couldn't pull on the ambient magic like she could. Alex turned away from the soldiers and raised Cathanáil. The other mages shifted to give her room, joining Morgana as the front line of defense. Her lungs burned. It was hard to breathe, but Alex inhaled slowly. The sounds of fighting and shouting washed over her, but Alex closed her eyes.

The image of the dead world came to her easily. It was a familiar and haunting sight. So many dreams and visions had burned it into her mind. Magic flared in Alex's chest, burning hot and flashing down her right arm to Cathanáil. The hilt thrummed in her hand. Alex pushed her magic into the blade, and her lips moved as she held the image of the dead Sídhe homeworld and whispered for her magic to take them there.

Opening her eyes, Alex sliced Cathanáil through the empty space before her. The air rippled, and the light of the dim sun twisted, creating dark ribbons of color that tangled around each other. The portal shifted, opening wider and wider. For a moment, there was only black beyond it, only pitch darkness, and Alex feared that she'd failed, but then the hazy dark dunes of ash came into view. It was all out of focus, but their destination was in front of her. Alex shouted for the others to follow, and before fear could take hold, threw herself forward.

29

The Last Grand Mage

The scent of decay hit Alex first as she tumbled to the ground. So sharp was the contrast from the air she'd just been breathing that she gasped, inhaling the ash and tasting death on her tongue. The air was thin and cold compared to the world she'd just fled. It left her dizzy as she stumbled forward. Blinking, Alex took in the dunes of ash and the violet sky. Her eyes closed as fire shook her limbs and battered her chest.

The pain centered her; it pulled her back to what was happening and forced back the vertigo. Pulling back on her magic, Alex gathered as much as she could manage and forced herself to her feet. She almost slipped in the ash and released her death grip on Cathanáil and Mjǫllnir. As she turned back to the portal, guilt, worry, and relief washed over Alex, leaving her cold and confused.

The portal was shimmering, already collapsing. She peered at it as her mind tried to understand what was happening. Nicki fell through, her right foot just beyond the portal, and she frantically scrambled away. Bran and Aiden were right behind her, Bran coming out moments before Aiden and jumping over Nicki to avoid stepping on her. Aiden swayed to the right, blinking and gasping for air that he wasn't going to find.

Nicki made it to her feet and hauled Aiden away from the portal. Lines of ash already covered her face, having stuck to her sweat and made her look too pale in the dim light of the world's sun. Images were distorted beyond the portal, but Alex could see one final shape moving for the opening. Her heart was pounding, and a headache was forming between her eyes. Ignoring the weight of her pack, Alex reached for Cathanáil, digging it out of the ash. Mjǫllnir's hum was weak when Alex snatched it up and climbed to her feet.

"Morgana!" Alex yelled. Alex didn't know if Morgana could hear her. "Morgana! Hurry, the portal is already closing! I don't know why!"

Adrenaline was taking hold as Alex watched the figure move. The Sídhe were indistinct, but their disappearance hadn't stopped them. The portal was quivering along the edges, the air and light twisting rapidly in a way that made Alex nervous. But the shape reached the portal and fell through. Morgana hit the ground. Dark ash was thrown into the air, twisting around the fallen form like smoke. Red blood spilled from an ugly wound in Morgana's gut as she lifted herself off the ground. Long dark hair was falling out of its braid and framed a pale face. Alex's eyes widened, but she didn't move. Morgana's arm gave out, and she crashed face-first back into the ground. Behind her, the portal closed without even a whisper or final shimmer.

Dropping to her knees, Alex dropped her weapons and gathered Morgana close with shaking hands and desperate strength. Morgana was still breathing, but only just. Alex struggled for a moment to get Morgana's pack off, but managed it. That would help Morgana breathe. It would ease the strain on her body. The others had seen her fall. They'd be coming with the Iron Chalice. That thought repeated in Alex's head over and over as she looked at the ugly wound. Her left fingers dug into Morgana's shoulder, and Alex adjusted Morgana's shirt to cover more of the wound, trying to put pressure on it. Morgana hissed in pain at the action, drawing Alex's attention back to her face. Morgana was smiling. It was a soft, sad sort of smile that did nothing to mask her pain.

"It's okay," Morgana said. Her voice was barely more than a whisper. She swallowed, as if thirsty.

Alex remembered that. Her gut ached with the phantom pain of when Arthur had stabbed her. Thirst. She remembered that so clearly. And cold. She gathered Morgana closer. Around them, the wind threw ash into the air and chilled their skin. Alex's chest throbbed when she attempted to pull on magic to warm Morgana up or start the healing process.

"The others are coming," Alex promised. "Hold on, please," she begged. "We have the Chalice. Just stay calm and we'll-"

"I'm sorry." Finality rang in the words. A cold weight dropped in Alex's gut.

"Please don't leave me." Alex's throat was closing up; it was a struggle to say the words. "Please, sister, don't leave me."

Morgana's mouth moved, but there was no sound. Already, her gaze was growing distant. Alex pulled at her magic, only to be rewarded with a burning ache. Grimacing in pain, she hissed and tried again with the same result. She was teetering at the edge, exhaustion weighing her down and not enough magic around them to refresh her body.

"Please," Alex tried again. "Hold on." She pulled Morgana closer, ignoring the red blood smearing across her shirt and jacket. The scent of iron invaded her nose. Sharp and metallic. Familiar and yet wrong. Alex licked her too dry lips and pulled frantically on her magic. There was no hum of power, no flare of energy, only a growing burn that worsened with her attempts. "Please, Merlin's gone. You can't go too. You can't. Please, please don't."

Tears were rolling down her cheeks now, spilling forth without Alex having any way to hold them back. Morgana's eyes turned to Alex's face, and for a moment, they sharpened back to awareness. The old mage tried to raise her hand, but it just trembled. Alex adjusted her grip, keeping Morgana steady with her left arm and shoulder, and took Morgana's hand with her right one.

"I'm here," Alex said. "I'm here. Stay with me."

"Tired." Morgana's voice was weak. "Tired, Alex."

"Don't talk like that."

"Not enough magic." Morgana's eyes widened, fear suddenly entering them. "Alex, not enough…"

Morgana trailed off, her eyes turning wild and dazed. Her lips moved, and she struggled. The fog that had taken her was lifting, but terror and worry were taking its place. Alex tightened her grip on Morgana, trying to keep her still.

"Easy, easy," Alex said. "Bran is getting the Chalice, just hold on."

"Alex, I can't get the Chalice to glow." Bran's voice was low and desperate. "I have no- my magic is too low."

Alex blinked at him. Those were words, but they made no sense. Bran was kneeling next to them now, the Chalice in hand, but it was dull. Nicki knelt and reached out to touch the Chalice, closing her eyes in concentration. There was a faint glimmer of something in the metal, but no true glow of magic. They shared a look of fear. Bran shook himself and brought the Iron Chalice forward. The water inside the Chalice caught the low light of the world, glinting with a reflection of the violet sky.

Morgana swallowed. Water splashed over her cheek and rolled down into her dark hair. A few gray hairs were visible along the nape of Morgana's neck that Alex hadn't noticed before. Alex waited, watching and waiting, but the dull color of the Iron Chalice and the lack of any reaction made fear coil in her chest.

"We're too weak," Nicki whispered. She reached for Morgana, but pulled her hand back. "Alex, I'm sorry."

Sorry? The word clanged around in Alex's head. She tried to summon her magic. Bran helped Morgana take another sip, but the older mage's eyes were staring into the sky. The voices in Alex's head were a mess of panicked cries. They crashed over her, agitating the already choppy waters of her emotions. Alex looked at the Chalice. There was magic swirling in the metal, trying to come forth. With a weak and clumsy hand, Alex reached out to touch it. The magic gathered to her finger, like one of those electrical globes she'd played with as a child.

It wasn't enough. The realization sank in Alex's gut, resting like the broken remains of the Iron Chain on her chest. She couldn't breathe. Bran, Aiden, and Nicki were all huddled close, staring at Morgana. Their hands came up to touch the Chalice. Magic sputtered and flickered. It wasn't enough. It glittered in the metal, but there wasn't enough.

'I'm sorry,' Gofiben said, his voice cutting through the others. 'I was young-'

The Iron Chalice needed magic they didn't have. Tears slipped from Alex's eyes. She curled around Morgana, holding her tight. The world was still beneath her. Alex couldn't feel even a faint pulse of magic, no flicker of power.

"Merlin," Morgana whispered. "Merlin...."

Old memories trickled to the front of Alex's head. Merlin and Morgana. Together. Always together. Even when they split up to lead different lives for a time, they were always connected. And now, one half of that equation was gone, wiped out by the Light. Her grip tightened on Morgana. She made herself look down at Morgana's pale face. Alex pressed against the wound with her right hand, but could feel blood seeping out.

"He can wait," Alex whispered. "Please, stay with me."

Alex shifted her hand to brush strands of dark hair from Morgana's face and tried to smile, but tears were taking over. Now red smears of blood decorated Morgana's features. The old woman turned her head and looked at Alex. Then Morgana smiled softly. Her eyes were glazing over. Alex wasn't sure who Morgana was seeing, if it was her or Arto or someone else completely.

"Goodbye," Morgana whispered.

Then Morgana stilled, released by that word. There was an exhale, and the tight, pained posture of her body relaxed, cut free from the agony of dying. The old mage's sharp intelligence, her determination, her rage, and her grief all faded. Merlin had been taken in a violent moment she couldn't prevent, and now Morgana had slipped away.

Alex screamed. The sound exploded across the empty landscape. There was no one to witness it except the three human mages huddled close together. None of them made a sound. Tears rolled down cheeks and hit the dead ground, gifting it with the first moisture it had seen in millennia. Emotions echoed through the fast-moving air, adding to the storm growing around them.

Thunder cracked through the air. The ground shuddered. Nicki grabbed Aiden's arm, who gripped Bran's shoulder. The blood on Alex's hands burned her skin. She smelled a hint of magic in the air only for it all to fade in moments. The rumbling stopped, and Alex lowered her eyes back to Morgana. Her chest burned with brutal pain. Breathing was difficult, and her limbs were weighed down. In grief, she'd summoned the magic she'd been unable to use to help Morgana. The sharp, bitter cold of that didn't stop the painful burn.

Alex sat there in the dust and ash. She didn't rise. Didn't let go of Morgana. Somehow, she looked up from Morgana's face again. Alex's eyes found one of the dark ash dunes and watched the ripple of the ash as the wind blew across it. Before her was a black desert, devoid of life. It was fitting.

"It's not fair," Nicki whispered. "Why did she have to die here? On the Sídhe homeworld?"

No one answered her. No one had an answer. Alex had not moved. She was still holding Morgana's still form. Her body shook and trembled as Alex held back her sobs. She didn't look at the others. Alex wasn't ready to see their expressions. Their grief, their pity, their fear, and their worry for her.

Morgana had been her sister. Morgana had been her mentor and, in a few lifetimes, her mother. Memories were battering her like the winds of a storm assaulted ships that failed to secure their sails. Morgana hadn't been there in every life, but her presence, her love, had left a mark on the Iron Soul. They all felt this. All of Alex felt this loss. Perhaps even more than the loss of Merlin.

One last scream ripped through the silence. Alex raised her eyes toward the sky. Debris swirled in the thin atmosphere and overhead, the dark pulsing wound of the Darkness loomed and threatened them with an even darker fate. Morgana was gone, and they were at the place Alex had seen so many times in her dreams.

This was the ultimate destiny of the Iron Soul. This was the climax of Alex's story, the climax of all the stories her soul had ever been a part of. And the Grand Mages had not survived long enough to see the final act unfold. They wouldn't have liked the coming ending.

"Alex?" Bran was beside her, his hand on Alex's shoulder. "I think... Why don't you let me take Morgana? We can at least wrap her-" Bran choked on his words and closed his eyes. They were red and the tear tracks on his cheeks were lined with ash that had stuck to the moisture. "You don't have to hold her."

Alex said nothing, but somehow, she nodded. Bran shifted in front of her and gently eased Morgana from her arms. With slow movements, he laid her in the ash. Nicki was beside him a moment later, dragging Morgana's pack and pulling off the sleeping roll. They rolled it out and unzipped it. The understanding of what they were about to do finally sank in.

Alex's fingers reached out to touch the triskelion necklace that hung from Morgana's neck. Alex gently ran her thumb over the worn silver. Her memory stirred at the sight of it, and she remembered the pin that Morgana wore long ago. Airril had given it to her. Was it in storage somewhere or long gone? She remembered Merlin's pin and forging it to the Iron Urn.

They didn't have the Iron Urn. It was at Morgana's house, Merlin's old house, waiting for the Winter Solstice. They were going to take him to the burial place of the great leaders of his people with Morgana. But Morgana was gone now, too.

"Alex?" Nicki called. "Can we move her?"

Releasing her grip on the necklace, Alex leaned back, and Aiden and Bran lifted Morgana off the ground and put her in the sleeping bag. It was a poor makeshift body bag, leaving Morgana's too pale face exposed. Nicki reached down, and with a trembling hand, closed Morgana's eyes. With the wound and most of the blood hidden, Morgana almost looked like she was sleeping.

Alex's stomach turned. She needed to say something. Opening her mouth, Alex tried to form words, but her mouth was too dry. Ash landed on her lips and flew into her mouth, adding to the taste of death. Closing her mouth and her eyes, Alex tried to think, but it was all white noise and literary quotes that kept playing through her mind. They offered no ideas, no words of comfort, and no guidance. She needed Morgana for that.

Her hands grasped at nothing. Ash slipped through her fingers. Swallowing, Alex looked around until her eyes found the Iron Sword and the Iron Hammer. They were still here. Without bothering to get up, Alex crawled to where she'd let them fall when trying to help Morgana. Her right hand found the golden hilt of Cathanáil, and her left the handle Mjǫllnir. They hummed against her skin. It was weak, but there was still some magic in them. Too little, too late. Morgana was dead.

30

Return of the Sídhe

Modern Day Ravenslake, United States

Samhain. Morgana hated Samhain. The knowledge that her magic was weaker grated at her, and even in times of peace, she felt too vulnerable. But it was worse than the other seasonal change days because of the culture around it. Other holidays had come and gone over the years, but Samhain had transformed in ways that Morgana never knew what to make of. There were enough of the traditions she'd known as a young mage to be familiar, yet applied in ways that confused her.

It was one of the few holidays where modern people strayed a little too close to the truth of the world. In her experience there were no ghosts, but there were other worlds, and on this day the veil between them became too thin. Earth was too vulnerable, and its people were too at risk. Her fingers clenched at the empty air. She wished that she could have brought a jack-o'-lantern with her. That was probably overkill, but her office and her home each had several of the homemade talismans. At least many homes did as well. That would offer some protection to the mundanes, who were so unaware of the danger they were in.

Morgana strode across campus, the heels of her boots clicking against the cement of the sidewalk. Her eyes swept across her surroundings, and her ears were straining for the sounds of danger. Old instincts were reemerging quickly, despite the decades of peace that she had enjoyed. It seemed that no matter how long it was between conflicts, Morgana always remained a battle-ready mage. She could only be grateful for that.

Approaching one of the lampposts, Morgana debated which way she should go now. The campus was thankfully empty. People were either still at parties or driving home. The sharp chill in the air would discourage students from walking across campus. While too many would drive drunk, right now, she was thankful that there weren't too many tempting targets out.

Halloween had to fall on a Friday night this year, as if she and Merlin didn't have enough to worry about. Their students were being foolish, and the sounds of the parties on Greek Row were audible even in the center of campus. That was not making her task any easier. The blend of music from the different houses was horrible, and the creepy sounds that at least one party was playing kept distracting her. How had the police not been called yet?

A howl cut through the night, and Morgana stopped. Her back straightened, and even beneath her coat, she could feel her hairs standing on end. Hounds. Of course, it would be Hounds. A brand-new tunnel could be dangerous. It was better to send Hounds through first and see if they returned with their bodies intact. If they were lucky, it would only be Hounds, and the Riders would wait a little longer. She slipped her right hand into the pocket of her black overcoat and found the iron dagger she'd placed there. The weight was familiar and comforting.

Fear bubbled up in her chest. Morgana hated it. She didn't fear Hounds. She didn't fear the Sídhe. Except part of her did. She had felt the Sídhe break through. It had been a jolt of cold and pain. Her magic had surged despite today being a seasonal day. Their magic should be weaker as the world's energy shifted, but the sudden arrival of the Sídhe had brought a fresh wave of magic. It wasn't as much power as she would have tomorrow or the next day, but Morgana knew that she'd need the boost.

The Sídhe were back. Her heart raced as the words echoed in her mind. They had returned, and creatures of their world were in Ravenslake. Morgana swallowed and shook her head. This was not the time for a breakdown. If her hands were trembling, Morgana would say that it was the cold. Merlin would have the sense not to question that explanation.

Minutes ticked by as she walked. Merlin was checking the other side of campus. If they both kept to their paths, they'd been meeting up soon enough. The weight of her cell phone was comforting in her pocket. The ability to reach out and connect with her partner so easily was welcome. It didn't even drain her magic.

Another howl drew her attention. It echoed off the brick buildings, but Morgana's eyes narrowed in the direction it had come from. Walking faster, she glared into the darkness beyond the street lamps. Where were the Hounds? She sped up her pace, not quite jogging yet, but ready to sprint if she found something.

Were the Hounds tracking the new mages? She'd been afraid of that, and hoped that they'd come after her and Merlin first. Morgana's mind spun, reviewing all the details she knew of the four young mages. Her and Merlin's research ensured that they both knew the children's class schedules, the basics of their lives before school, and their dorm assignments. But it was Halloween, and the children had posted online that they were attending parties. Stupid.

Another howl, this one closer. She couldn't tell how many there were. A group of staggering, laughing students were hurrying up the sidewalk and passed her without incident. Morgana glanced their way and dismissed them. None of them were the children she was most concerned about. Nicole, Brandon, and Aiden had all gone to the same party. Those three were staying together, making her job easier, but Alexandra had gone to another party.

And what of the young man she'd caught glimpses of when scrying? Who was he, and what was his part in all this? Morgana feared that there might be a fifth mage in town, but her scrying hadn't revealed that with any certainty. In the distance, Morgana thought she heard shouting, and not the drunken revel sort. Her eyes searched for any movement. It was difficult to pinpoint where the sound was coming from.

Then she saw it. One Hound, sniffing at the air in the shadow of the Carlson Building. Rushing towards it, Morgana ignored the ache forming in her chest. She had to bury her emotional reaction. This was not the time for it. That repeated over and over in her head. Suddenly the Hound tensed. It whirled around; the eyes flashing in the light of the lampposts.

Morgana froze. Her breath caught. It was a Hound all right. Its translucent fur stretched over narrow ribs that were visible below its skin. The pointed ears were turned towards her. It snarled, revealing sharp teeth. Her emotions stormed in her chest. It had been so long since she had seen these creatures. Even as a child, they had frightened her with their long, sharp teeth and brutal natures. She'd been raised to respect and worship the Sídhe, but their Hounds had been another matter. That small child part of her retreated in horror at the sight of them.

The Hound lunged. It smelled her magic. It knew that she was a target. Instinct took over. Morgana threw her right hand forward. Her mind summoned the image of her magical bolts, thanks to years of practice. Below her skin, her magic was wild and hot. It tugged her in multiple directions. She was unfocused, but it was still enough. Silver bolts jumped off her fingertips and blasted through the air.

The first wave ripped through the Hound, knocking it back and tearing its flesh apart. Its eyes met hers. There was pain there. Morgana couldn't even be satisfied with that. The Hound's suffering offered her nothing. Releasing another wave of bolts, Morgana made sure that the magic destroyed the creature. It collapsed into a pile of dust.

Exhaling slowly, Morgana closed her eyes for a moment and shuddered. Complicated emotions swirled together like dyes in water. Opening her eyes, she stared at the pile of dust. It was blowing away, and by morning it would be gone with the wind or mixed with snow. Even after all this time, it never ceased to amaze her how the beings of other worlds vanished upon their deaths. She was grateful for that. It made her job easier, but the sight of it was unsettling.

More shouting, followed by a howl, drew her attention back to the present. Shaking herself, Morgana spun around and searched for the source of the noise. It was further down the walkway. Morgana ran. The dark shape of the Kittell Building was just visible in the low light of the campus lampposts. It grew larger with each passing moment. Morgana saw running shapes. They seemed human. Ahead of her, the sounds of the Hounds were growing louder, with their snarls echoing off the brick building. Her heart raced, and her throat tightened. Human instinct told her to run, to get away from the threat, but years of battle kept her running forward.

She saw the sleek silvery bodies of the Hounds first. They were moving between pools of light too quickly for her to count, but there were at least two. They were slinking in the shadows and stalking prey. Anger replaced fear at the sight of them. Rage burned in her blood, and the spark of magic in her chest exploded into a fierce flame, ready to smite them all.

But the Hounds didn't notice her, and Morgana found the target of their attention.

It was the four young mages, all dressed up in costumes and huddling near the building. Despite going to different parties, they'd all found each other during Samhain. Morgana allowed herself only a split second of surprise before turning all of her focus on the Hounds. Her magic flashed to life at her command. A whip of silver light formed from sparks of her magic, and Morgana lashed it forward. The Hounds whirled on her, turning their attention to her, and she glared at them.

Stepping into the light of the lamppost, Morgana embraced the warmth of the magical sparks dancing around her hand. Despite the circumstances, it was good to feel the full weight of her magic once again even if it was weaker today. She heard the children gasp and realized that in the lamppost's light, they could see she was their rescuer. This wasn't how she'd wanted to bring them into magic, but it would have to do. At least they wouldn't be able to deny it. She spared them a quick glance and was satisfied to see that none of them had pulled their phones out. Good, that showed some basic common sense. Run from danger, don't record it.

"Stay back," she ordered them.

So far, none of them had done anything stupid. She'd have to hope that they'd continue to be smart. Killing the Hounds would be simple enough if no one got in her way. The first Hound leapt at her, and she easily visualized what she wanted to happen. Her magical whip lashed at the attacking Hound, but the second Hound was trying to flank her. Morgana's magic tingled down her arms as she moved to attack that one as well, but the ground rumbled beneath her feet. She almost smiled.

Under the second Hound, the dirt and grass came to life, grabbing the Hound and pulling it down. The snapping of bones was loud in the chilly night, and Morgana allowed herself a tiny smirk. But she kept her attention on the other Hound. Her magic entangled it, sending it crashing to the ground with a thud.

Merlin stepped up beside her and didn't say a word as he drew his iron dagger. They quickly finished killing both Hounds with the iron to conserve their magic. It was a long time until sunrise. Morgana's ears were listening for the sounds of any additional Hounds. The night seemed quiet save for the distant sounds of too loud music, but even that was thankfully dying off.

Morgana glanced at Merlin, and their eyes met. A dozen thoughts and ideas were communicated in mere moments. She could see his concern for her and knew that he wouldn't believe whatever bluster she tried to wear. Defeat and resignation flickered in his eyes, but he said nothing. They would talk tomorrow, about many things, and she would ignore his attempts to convince her to open up about her emotions.

Now it was time for the children. Morgana inhaled slowly to steady herself. The sight of the Hounds had affected her more than she liked. Unlike the Sídhe, who continued on Earth in the form of the Fae and who had tried to break through to Earth in the Norselands, it truly had been three-thousand years since she had seen a Sídhe Hound.

Whether he sensed her mood or simply wished to take over, Merlin was the one who stepped closer to the children. Their eyes locked on him, and Morgana scanned them all. There were no signs of injury, and for that, she was grateful. Things were already complicated enough without needing to heal anyone.

How all four had found each other, Morgana did not know. She knew all of their names, knew their histories, and more of their personal preferences than a teacher should. Morgana took them in, one by one, watching the fear fade a little from their features, replaced by confusion.

Nicole's eyes were wide and eager, while her best friend, Aiden, was a bit more cautious. Brandon was watching Merlin and her with thoughtful eyes, already trying to sort it out for himself. Alexandra still seemed shocked by the turn of events.

This was the first time that Morgana had been so close to them. There weren't other students around and no desks separated them. Excitement shimmered in her veins. What she and Merlin had been waiting in Ravenslake for was finally beginning. A new chapter in their story, and four new mages to aid them.

"No injuries," Merlin said. She could hear a soft smile in his voice. At least he was calm for the sake of the children. "That is good, but we cannot linger. There may be more."

Merlin turned to her and nodded before gesturing for the children to follow them. They hesitated for only a moment, showing some more good sense. Morgana hoped they would hold on to that. They would need it in the coming battle. The Sídhe had returned, and these four college freshmen were now a part of a dangerous and ancient war.

They moved quickly, all of them eager to be out of the cold and in a more secure location. Morgana listened for the sounds of more Hounds with dread. If there were more, then they were an obvious target. Morgana took a protective position over the small group while Merlin guided them towards the Hamilton building. It seemed that her office would be the site of the induction of their new little mages. Morgana wondered how they would take it. She wondered what the future had in store for them and hoped for their sakes that it wouldn't be too horrible. But that was out of her hands.

31

Darkness Creeping In

Numbness pervaded every limb. A dense fog had rolled into Alex's mind, and the only thing to break through the haze was the horrible realization that Morgana was dead. Every time that hit her, Alex's body trembled, and the thick fog returned with extra strength, driving her back into dark numbness. She preferred it to the stinging pain that came with Morgana's death. The numbness masked the ache of her swollen eyes and her brutalized throat.

Alex knew the others were worried. She could feel the weight of their eyes on her and occasionally heard a soft whisper between them. The wind stole most of the noises her friends were making and stung her cheeks with bits of ash. Still, Alex didn't move. Someone had shifted Morgana's dead body from her arms and laid her out as if she was sleeping. Ash was settling on the pack Alex had wrestled off Morgana like a dusting of gray snow.

Her own pack weighed her down. The heavy weight of the iron pulled on her shoulders, but she still did not move. The voices were quiet. All of them were either too shocked or too lost in grief to say anything. Even Cuthbert was quiet. Maybe he was capable of respect. Alex closed her eyes and inhaled slowly. It did not help. Another breath didn't help.

Grief was ebbing, but fear and guilt were roaring in to take its place like the ocean tides in a storm.

The Iron Chalice had failed. For the first time, it had failed them. Merlin had died too quickly, and it could not raise the dead despite the stories and myths that surrounded it. But Morgana, she'd been sure they could save if her mentor held on long enough for them to get it out. Yet it had failed. The Chalice had always needed a bit of magic to get going; a jump start to summon the power that Gofiben had granted it.

They had no magic. For the first time in years, Alex's chest was empty. That spark in her gut was low, a dying ember in a chilly night that wouldn't save anyone. There'd been nothing to give the Chalice, and thus the Iron Chalice could give them nothing in return. Alex didn't know if the others had realized that. If they understood what it meant. If there was no magic here, there was no way back. She had brought them to a dead world where there was no hope of survival once their supplies ran out.

Dunes of ash dotted the landscape. There were a few places where the ruins of buildings were barely visible, but they were cruel reminders. Alex tried to think of a plan. Magic had guided them here. She'd seen this place in her dreams. This was where she was supposed to be. It wasn't possible that all of it only brought them here to die. She couldn't accept that.

Something had been pushing them here, towards this moment, and Alex knew it. That force, whatever it was, whatever intelligence lay behind it, hadn't gone to all this trouble for them to die. She remembered too vividly how the dying worlds had welcomed her. Alex had always been taught that the other worlds would reject them, and while it wasn't comfortable exactly, she had felt the magic of worlds that were not her own trying to help her. Maybe it was because all the power flowed through the Iron Realm first. Maybe it knew her. That hope was enough to convince her that this wasn't the end.

There was a way forward. There had to be. Still, her hands trembled, and she didn't stand. Her head and heart battered at each other, neither winning the struggle for what she did next. Alex closed her eyes. The wind tugged at her hair. Ash clung to her cheeks, where her tears had moistened her skin. She breathed slowly. The scent of decay surrounded her. She could taste the years of death that ravaged this world on her tongue. The ash around them had once been buildings, been plants, and once been living beings. Now it was dust.

"Ashes to ashes," Alex whispered. Her tongue was heavy, forming the words. The funeral prayer had it right. The poems she'd read had it right. "Dust to dust."

Without opening her eyes, Alex reached down and dug her fingers into the ground. Only the first inch or so had any give. After that, it was hard and firm, packed down over who knows how long. The records they'd found gave clues, but again, that assumed that time moved equally between the worlds once there wasn't a strong connection any longer. Alex wasn't sure. It had been a long time since the Sídhe first found their way to the last world. How many had been left behind? How many had watched the world slowly fall apart?

Sympathy rose in her chest. Alex hated it. Morgana was dead because of the Sídhe. Her life had come full circle with them stealing her life as a child and now her life for good. Merlin would have called it a tragedy. He wouldn't have been wrong, but waste seemed a better word. All the knowledge and experience that Morgana had possessed was gone. Three thousand years of languages, history, and culture, snuffed out.

The voices were silent now. If it was respect, shock, or maybe that her magic was too low for their echoes, Alex didn't know. There was nothing in her head except an empty ache. The fog was comforting. It was cool. It twisted around her, cutting her off from everything else. It was almost a relief. She could fall into that. She could embrace that... except for the others. They were shifting behind her.

It took effort to move. The numbness lingered. It held her down, pinning her to the ashy ground. Her jeans were covered in black and gray, the blue color already lost below the knee. She was joining the ashes. Fascination filled her, and Alex watched, entranced, as the wind formed a tiny dune in front of her. Reaching out, she touched the delicate curve, only for it to collapse. Alex shook her head. The fog was growing thick, and the others were moving.

Her parents were dead. She'd given up her brothers to save them, and Morgana and Merlin had fallen. But she wasn't alone. Not yet, no matter what the fog made her feel. The others were behind her. They were watching; they were waiting and worrying. As bad as this was, as thick and cold as this grief was, there was still more to lose. She could still lose them. She could still lose herself.

An icy hand gripped Alex's heart at the thought. The voices stirred but did not speak. Breathing came easier for a moment. It wasn't good. Clarity settled, and Alex closed her eyes. A tear, one last tear, escaped her eyes, and her mouth burned at how dry it was, how parched she felt. That was it. She would lose one more thing before this was over. Certainty found its hold. She knew it like she knew when reading a novel how the final climax was going to unfold. The setup had long been established, and there was only one thing she was willing to lose now, and it was not the war.

Gathering her strength, Alex shifted her body so she could see what the others were up to. She seethed at the weakness of her muscles. Another wave of grief and anger began to build but failed to fully manifest. There was only exhaustion. It wouldn't help her. She remembered this from when her parents died. Somehow this was worse, and that conjured guilt. If she had possessed enough magic, Alex would have rebuilt the defenses she had once created against grief. But Morgana wouldn't approve of that. Alex needed her grief, her anger, and everything else she could pull on to help her now. And the task was still at hand.

Somehow, she turned around. Her legs were shaking at the effort, and Alex hadn't moved her knees more than a few inches off the ground. Her fingertips were coated in ash, and the grains filled the gaps between her fingers.

Breathe in. Breathe out. It hurt. The ache in her chest was impossible to ignore. Was it from crying, or was the air too thin here? Then again, the fact that they were breathing on a planet that had no vegetation and not much of an atmosphere left reinforced Alex's certainty that something had brought them here. They didn't have magic to help them, so something else was keeping them alive. Swallowing, Alex inhaled slowly again and pulled on the memories of Morgana's meditation lessons. Just keep breathing. That was the first step. There was one thing left to lose. She had to make sure that more wasn't lost.

The fog was rolling back. The cold was sinking in, reaching for her, but Alex couldn't fall into that dark. Not yet, at least. Later... maybe later.

The others had set up three of the small tents. They were staying up despite the wind, and guidelines had been tied to stakes buried deep into the ground to help keep them steady. It was a good idea. Alex's mind was slow to realize that. They would need shelter. Nicki and Aiden hadn't noticed that she was looking their way and were debating about something. Morgana's pack was between them, and both looked extremely uneasy. Alex wondered briefly when they had moved the pack.

She should care about what the problem was. Alex swallowed and inhaled slowly. Already, she was going nose blind to the ashy air, and the taste of it had long since coated her tongue. Her limbs were weak.

"Alex?" Bran called gently, so very gently that it was a rush of heat against the cold. "Are you-" he cut himself off. "I'm so sorry."

Bran, Nicki, and Aiden were watching her. Maybe they were waiting for her to fall apart again. Maybe they were trying to find the right words to say or a good time to offer her a hug. She wouldn't take it. That would make her cry again. There was no magic to lock up the pain with, so Alex would have to deal the old fashion way: pushing through.

"We need a pyre," Alex said. She turned her gaze back to Morgana's corpse. The woman had never been so still in three thousand years of existence.

"Alex, we have only a small amount of wood," Nicki replied gently. "There isn't enough and our magic... it isn't coming back."

"I know." Alex shook her head, trying to clear it. "But you can burn Morgana's supplies: her sleeping bag, her tent, her clothes."

"I think most of that is probably fire retardant," Aiden pointed out.

"We can't leave her here, and we can't-" Alex cut herself off. She didn't know how to finish that sentence. "We aren't burying her on the Sídhe homeworld. She'd want her ashes taken to Stonehenge with Merlin's."

They were supposed to take Merlin's ashes to Stonehenge. Morgana had planned that for the next winter solstice. The cold crept up her spine. Alex couldn't stop it, but did her best to ignore it. Given their relationship, she was probably the closest to a next of kin that the pair had. If-when they got back to Ravenslake, there would be so many things to sort out. That brought a new tide of grief in, and Alex had no defenses. Shivering, she swallowed and brought a hand up to rub her eyes. Thankfully, she caught sight of the ash on her hands before she did and quickly lowered it again.

The others were slowly moving to do as she had said. They didn't have the supplies to stay here long. Alex had to get moving. She had to figure this out. After making sure that she had Cathanáil in its sheath and Mjǫllnir on her hip, Alex wiped her filthy hands off on the sides of her jeans. It didn't all come off. Blood had dried with ash stuck in it to her hands. Water might get her clean, but they didn't have much. That would be a poor use of it. There wasn't too much left on her hands. Alex decided she could live with it.

She looked into the sky. The rip in the world was apparent here. Dark violet sky met pitch black in a jagged line. Around the edge, the sky seemed to shudder and bend like a cloth in the wind. Deep in the black spot, Alex could see only faint hints of purple as it churned and caught tiny flickers of light from the dying world below.

Standing so close to an open wound in the world stole Alex's breath. It was massive, a storm overhead that she could almost reach out and touch. A droplet of Darkness fell from the opening and hit the dead ground less than a mile away. Faint memories of a similar sight in a blue sky flitted across her mind. Earth had faced this before. The Iron Soul had stopped it then. They had protected Earth then.

It was growing darker than it had been when they arrived. The distant sun of this world was still burning. The Darkness hadn't swallowed the star. Alex licked her lips, tasting the salt of her tears and ash on them. The Darkness was destructive, but it was following magic rather than spreading across the whole of the space of this universe. That was something, at least. If they failed, then maybe only Earth would be destroyed.

Now she felt sick on top of everything else. Her heart started racing, and black spots flickered at the edges of her vision. Alex closed her eyes and dropped her chin. Looking at the sky wouldn't help her. The answer wasn't above.

Taking off her pack, Alex groaned gratefully at the sudden relief from its weight. But she didn't have time to stretch out to ease her aching muscles. Digging into her bag, Alex inhaled sharply when her fingers touched the soft, plush fabric of Galahad. New tears sprang to her eyes. The world went fuzzy, and she pulled out the stuffed animal. One moment. She gave herself one moment more to hug the stuffed dog tightly to her chest. It hurt. A sob gathered in her mouth, but Alex clenched her teeth and pressed her lips together to hold it in. One moment. One inhale and then she tucked Galahad under her arm, not willing to discard him in the ash. Already, some of the dried-up blood and ash had smeared onto his golden fur.

She dug deeper, pushing aside her spare clothing and her rations. Lance had taught them how to fit a lot into these packs, and she was grateful. It was funny to think about that now, how important that lesson might end up being. At the bottom of the bag, Alex found what she was looking for. Her fingertips brushed against the first half of the broken Iron Chain. Magic sparked up her arm, and Alex closed her eyes in relief.

This world's magic was exhausted. This world's magic was all but gone, but they had brought some with them. She had iron. She had the Iron Chain. She had Mjǫllnir and Cathanáil, the Chalice, and the Pendant. The Iron Soul had their real weapon, and they weren't done yet. Alex swallowed and tightened her fingers around the iron. Her chaotic, messy thoughts were aligning. Old dreams, Bran's visions, and a sense of what the climax was supposed to be were coming together. She could see it. There was one thing left to lose. And one thing left to make.

32

Final Forge

The iron bars hit the ashy ground with a thud as Alex dumped them out. She eyed the dull gray bars with curiosity, but nothing happened. Theoretically, the beings of this world had been weak to iron, but iron against what was left of their world did nothing. That was probably a good thing. Alex touched one of the iron bars and concentrated. The magic reached up to her, a soft and reassuring pulse of power. It steadied her.

If only they'd had time to try this before. Anger choked Alex as the memory of Morgana's death replayed in vivid color in her head. The bright red blood was too intense. If she'd been thinking, Alex could have pulled the magic out of the iron to charge the Iron Chalice. If she'd been more aware-

"Alex!" a call from Aiden drew Alex out of her thoughts.

She turned to find Aiden, Nicki, and Bran walking across the dark desert to her. At some point, the others had moved off, and she'd lost sight of them. Alex knew from her visions that there were many ruins in the area and small sections that were less exposed than others. There was no sign of Morgana's body, and she could only assume that they'd had some luck finding a better spot.

"We have things set up," Bran offered. His Adam's apple bobbed, and he struggled for a moment. "We wanted something a little protected from the wind," he explained. He gestured at a large dune in the distance. Alex thought she saw a hint of stonework poking out from the ash. "The fire will need all the help it can get."

"We used some of the lighter fluid," Aiden offered. "I mean..." He looked nervously at the sky. "We can't stay here long." He glanced at the tents that were gently swaying in the breeze. "Actually, it might not be a bad place to move the tents to."

"Let's not," Bran said. "The smell...." He trailed off and looked green at the thought.

He wasn't wrong. With the pyre not being all wood, they couldn't count on the smell of wood smoke drowning out the scent of burning hair, flesh, and clothing. Alex shifted the iron to her pack and hoisted it onto her back. She'd need the iron for her plan.

"We may not have a choice about how long we're here," Nicki added. Her eyes were boring into Alex. "Please tell me you have a plan, Alex. There's no water here, and our magic isn't coming back."

"There's some magic in the iron and the artifacts," Alex said. Her voice croaked a little, still raw from the abuse she'd put it through when sobbing and screaming. "I have a plan."

They waited for her to share. Alex opened her mouth and tried to find the right words. The idea was there, glittering in her mind, bright and strong, but there were no words. How could she explain what needed to happen? And if anything went wrong, then they would be stuck here to die of thirst or maybe exposure, depending on how cold it got at night.

"I have a plan," she repeated. Her voice was weaker than she wanted it to be, but fear was coiling around her heart. Alex knew she had the right idea, but it did... It scared her. "I don't know how to explain it. Just trust me."

"Alex." Bran reached for her. Realization was slowly dawning on his face. Fear, worry, hope, and guilt flashed through his eyes and swirled together, making them darker than normal. "Are you...?"

"I'm not okay," Alex admitted. There was no point in lying about it. "But we have to get through this."

Bran wanted to say something; that much was clear from his expression. Alex frowned and studied him. What did he know that she didn't? What had he seen that she hadn't? She didn't ask. The words wouldn't come out, and Bran didn't share. Alex suspected what he had seen, but didn't dwell on it. What was coming, what she was about to do, didn't need dwelling on.

They guided her away from their origin point and around one of the dark dunes. Alex smiled in surprise when, on the other side, she found a collapsed roof that now formed a slightly slanted stone floor. The ash dune was built up against what remained of the upper floor wall of either the same building or the next building over. It created a small protected area that would be much better for what Alex had in mind. She put her pack on the ground with a heavy thud. The iron at the bottom rang against the stone.

Near the wall was Morgana's pyre. It was almost an insult to call it a pyre, but Alex had to give the others credit for trying. Morgana's body had been wrapped up in her spare clothing, with the sleeping bag discarded to the side. Her face was covered, and despite the mismatched colors of the clothing, there was some dignity to it. The little wood that they had was stacked around Morgana to help keep the flames going, and the sharp smell of gas reminded Alex that some of the emergency lighter fluid had been used.

Some rocks, which looked like building stones, likely from the end of the crumbling wall, had been placed at the very bottom to allow airflow. That would help feed whatever flames they got going. It would also help protect the coals and give Alex access to them. Old memories of primitive forges flowed across her mind. Arto hadn't even used a true forge to make Cathanáil. She could work with this.

"Thank you," Alex managed when she finally turned her attention back to the others. "For doing this."

She didn't ask who had taken on the horrible job of wrapping Morgana up. That was cruel, and it should have been her. Alex's hands tightened at her sides. The wind howled beyond the small protected area, and she struggled with what to say. Aiden had produced a lighter from one of the packs and held it out to her with a solemn nod. She swallowed and accepted it with a nod of her own. The four remaining mages gathered around the pyre.

"We should say something," Nicki suggested. She was rubbing her hands on the sides of her jeans. "Don't you think?"

"Yeah," Alex agreed. Her throat was tight. The others were waiting for her to start, but she had no clue how to begin. The silence stretched on.

"Farewell, Morgana," Bran said gently. "You were a great mage and a good teacher. Thank you for helping us get this far."

"Thank you for supporting us," Aiden added. "For being understanding of the pressures we faced as students, and as mages, and helping us navigate that."

"Thank you for taking on the burden of being pragmatic," Nicki said. "For watching over all of us and never shrinking away from the hard decisions."

The others went silent. All of those things were true. But they were also such a small part of what had made Morgana who she was. Fresh tears gathered in Alex's eyes, and she knew there was no stopping them. The voices were returning, soft and broken. Arto and Mikael were the clearest, but there were others blending together. It was becoming difficult to pick out individuals.

"Thank you for being a wonderful sister," Alex forced out. Her mouth was too dry, and the tears were rolling down her cheeks. "For choosing me, choosing us over and over again even when it was hard. Thank you for being a good mother, for protecting me and loving me even when you knew that you'd lose me. Thank you for being a good friend and believing in me when I didn't believe in myself."

Soft sobs and cries from the others filled Alex's ears, helping to drown out her own. Alex shivered and stepped forward to light the wicks that had been created out of fabric and lighter fluid. The small flame at the tip of the lighter glowed with power. This was it. Alex's hand trembled as she held the flame to the first wick. It caught easily, and she moved to the next one and the next.

The flames began to consume. They held no love for the precious being wrapped in the scraps her students could manage. Stepping back, Alex watched as the fire slowly spread. It was having trouble with some of the materials, but it was catching. Already, heat was rolling off the pyre and warming Alex's sore limbs. Alex tried not to enjoy the warmth.

Besides, she had work to do. Alex took a deep breath and closed her eyes for a moment. She reached for the magic of this world, but it didn't react to her. Most of the energy, what little there was running through the ground, was being drawn towards the Darkness. A pitiful defense. But now that she was calmer, Alex was aware of a small amount of magic in the air. It swirled around them, and Alex almost smiled.

They were alive. She was alive. Tears pricked at her eyes. Alex swallowed. Grief and fear twisted in her chest. Her hands trembled. She didn't have the magic to send out into the world, but somehow the ribbon of energy still glowed faintly to her. It wove through the ground beneath her feet before reaching into the sky, towards the Darkness.

Opening her eyes, Alex stared into the Darkness. Flickers of light danced at the edges where the sky collapsed into the void. It shimmered with dying colors. With her eyes open, she couldn't see the line of magic. It was there, though, flowing into this world and holding back the Darkness. But it wasn't enough. Alex had seen the evidence of that. The Tree was dying. It was only a matter of time. Already, it had reached the Iron Realm, the trunk of the Tree of Reality.

And that white hall... that was the roots. Magic, the energy that connected the worlds, originated there. It flowed through Earth, but it came from there. Weight settled on Alex's shoulders, heavier than the pack had ever been and impossible to take off. She reached for her bag and started unloading the iron bars onto the ground. While unloading the iron from Morgana's pack, Alex found a cloth bag with something solid inside it. Alex knew what it was at once and slipped it into the large pocket of her hoodie, unwilling to part with it.

"Alex?" Bran called. "What are you-"

"I need you to unload any of the iron that you have in your packs. I put magic into all of it. There wasn't time to use them with the Chalice." Alex hated saying that out loud. In truth, there might have been, but in her panicked state, she hadn't thought of them. "But I can use that magic now."

"Is it enough to stop the Darkness?" Nicki asked. She didn't sound convinced.

"I have a plan," Alex repeated. "I need the iron."

Ozone tickled her nose. It shouldn't be possible. Alex was out of magic, and there was no power to draw on here, but she could smell it.

A storm was coming. The voices were soft, encouraging words washing in and out of her awareness like the tide. They formed a gentle rhythm now. It was a song building towards the final chords.

There was one thing left to lose. One last thing that Alex was willing to part with.

She threw the first of the iron bars into the fire. The magic in the pieces of iron exploded in a rush of heat and flames. Surprised shrieks from the others drew a chuckle from Alex. Flames licked at the material of the clothing. It was far from the pyre that Morgana deserved, but it was what they could manage. A flicker of guilt sparked in Alex's chest as she considered her next course of action. The iron was still dark gray amongst the flames, but it would change soon.

It would be both a poor forge and a poor pyre. Disrespectful, perhaps, but Morgana would have understood. In fact, her pragmatic mentor likely would have nodded in approval. Mjǫllnir was heavy on Alex's hip. She remembered realizing as Thor that the tool was magical. It had served her well as a weapon; it had broken the Iron Chain, and had proven useful as a tool when she'd made the Iron Pendant. Now, it would serve as her tool once again.

If she did this right, then all the Artifacts that she'd brought here would serve a purpose. All of them would aid her. Only the Iron Trishula was missing. It would have been useful, but Alex was still glad that she'd left it with Shiva. The Iron Pendant was heavy around her neck. Alex's stomach turned. She had a plan. She knew what she had to make, but nervous flutters were taking the place of grief.

"Alex?" Bran called. He set his pack beside her and started to unload the iron he'd been carrying. "Are you okay? What do you need?"

"I'll be fine." She frowned at the bags. "I need something I can use as tongs."

"Uh... okay." Bran was uncertain. She couldn't blame him. "I think Nicki packed some basic tools in her bag."

That made sense, Alex decided. They hadn't discussed that, but bringing the iron wouldn't have been as effective if they didn't have any tools. Bran moved off, speaking to the others, but Alex didn't listen to what they were saying. It didn't matter. Her eyes traced Morgana's wrapped form as flames engulfed it. Welcoming the heat, Alex's fingers itched to work. The image of what she needed was clear in her mind.

The way had to be opened. Cathanáil wasn't strong enough on its own. The Iron Pendant was heavy around her neck, and the pieces of the Iron Chain were waiting. Mjǫllnir's magic hummed, and the scent of ozone grew stronger. All of them carried the power of the Iron Soul. Her power, her magic, her will at one time or another. In one form or another.

The tongs Bran brought her were old and a simple shape, no doubt taken from Merlin's workshop, but they were exactly what Alex needed. Bran also set the small hammer down. Alex didn't need that. An anvil was the next issue. She eyed the wall, searching for another loose stone. Aiden followed her gaze and rushed over, gesturing for Nicki to follow. Bran lingered beside her.

"Alex... uh, what are you making?" he asked.

"I need a way to pull magic from other worlds," Alex offered. "I have it in my head. It'll be okay. I promise."

"But-"

"Here you go! We found an anvil!" Aiden shouted. He and Nicki were wrestling one of the stone blocks out of the wall. Dark ash poured onto the ground as it came out, but it wasn't enough to disrupt the dune. "Where do you need it, Alex?"

"Close to the pyre," she answered.

That should have been obvious, but she could understand their hesitation. The heat was growing, and the fire was raging. Sparks of magic were granting the flames small bursts of color. Like fireworks on the 4th of July, Alex decided, but with far more purpose.

With a thud, the stone was set near the pyre by Aiden, who immediately retreated from the heat. Alex reached up and let her hair loose before binding it up in a tight braid. Sweat was already gathering on her face from the heat. She pulled off her long-sleeved shirt, leaving her in a t-shirt, grabbed the tongs and pulled Mjǫllnir free from her hip. Coals were falling to the stone ground, visible between the rocks that held up the rough pyre.

Heat rolled off the pyre, much more than Alex would have expected under normal circumstances. The fabric was burning, and the smell of scorching hair hit Alex's nose. She didn't gag. That was good. If the heat kept building, then Morgana's body would burn away to ash.

The Iron Chain was heavy in her hand. The hints of magic in it reacted to her touch, reaching for her, and Alex ran a finger over one of the links. The accidental Iron Artifact was about to finally have a true purpose. More magic exploded in the fire as one of the iron ingots began to melt. Alex's skin warmed, and hints of magic danced over her bare arms.

Closing her eyes, Alex called to the released magic. There were bright sparks of yellow, red, and blue amongst the flickering flames. The magic of her friends glowed to her eyes and rushed towards her. At the first touch against her skin, the ache in Alex began to heal as magic rushed to fill the void. Power licked at her insides, offering promises to her that it would all be alright. Another bar burst, and silver magic spilled out.

Morgana's power rushed to Alex at her call, gathering in her hand and her chest. The next bar released green sparks, and tears stung Alex's eyes. She didn't open them. They would do no good, and Alex pulled on the magic. It was harder here. The world sought desperately to absorb the magic itself, like parched ground in a rainstorm. A dark-gray orb formed in her left hand, glowing with energy. Mjǫllnir burst to life in her right hand, arcs of lightning flashing over the metal.

"Alex? What are you doing?" Nicki demanded. "If there's magic in the iron, then shouldn't we-"

"It's okay," Alex answered. Her voice was calm. It was as if someone else was speaking. She opened her eyes. "I have a plan. Don't worry. I'll get you home."

Bran tensed in the corner of her eye. He opened his mouth as realization brightened his eyes. So he did know. He had seen something. Aiden touched Bran's shoulder. His expression was stern and thoughtful, more so than any Alex had ever seen on him. Letting go of the dark gray orb, Alex allowed it to hover in the air beside her, holding the magic and waiting.

"Let her do what she needs to do," Aiden said.

"Cathanáil still has power," Alex offered. "I just need to finish this. Then I can get you home."

This was a poor forge, but magic and determination pulsed in Alex's veins. The first links of the Chain went into the fire, resting on a small bed of coals on one of the stones. The voices were blurring together. Alex couldn't tell anyone apart anymore. Cuthbert's sarcasm and disdain for anyone who wasn't white was gone. Michel's grieving for Morgana had faded into the shared voice. Only a hint of Arto remained. The voice carried a suggestion of his tone and syntax, but it wouldn't last.

The weight was growing. Ozone filled her nose and the air. Magic radiated off the pyre. Alex called to it, gathering it tighter and tighter into her hand. Using her foot, she pushed the anvil closer to the fire, ignoring the sting of the heat and ignoring the worried calls from her friends. They wouldn't interrupt her. Alex knew that.

Using the tongs, she pulled out the first red hot link. Alex slammed Mjǫllnir against the metal. The rock was a poor anvil with a few small grooves. It didn't matter. The magic was what was important, and power was flowing from Mjǫllnir into the metal. The link crunched and flattened down. Alex pulled out another link and repeated the process, pushing the pieces of iron together with heat, strength, and magic. With mechanical motions, she repeated the process over and over until the chain was a dark gray slab of metal.

Back into the pyre, it went. Smoke caressed Alex's face, and sweat trickled down her forehead, both stinging her eyes. Her bare hands ached. Small burns were already forming. She didn't care. Her eyes were fixed on the iron as it heated. Another bar melted, glowing red in the fire and releasing a rush of dark gray sparks. The flames grew.

Alex didn't stop. Couldn't stop. Bran tried to call to her once or twice. Nicki came up and touched her shoulder, but Alex shrugged her off. They moved away from the smoke, but not far. Alex didn't stop to see what they were up to. It grew darker. The distant star of this world moved off. Cold cloaked Alex's back as night took hold while heat consumed her front.

The pyre shifted, the middle collapsing as Morgana's body crumbled. There was crying behind Alex. Her eyes burned, and tears slipped down her cheeks, but she pulled the iron forth again and hammered it against the anvil. It was thin and long now. Lightning jumped from Mjǫllnir into the metal with each strike.

"Alex." Bran was beside her again. "Stop and rest. We moved the tents. We have food."

"I have the fire now," Alex replied. It hadn't been that long, but her voice was already rough from the smoke and disuse.

"What are you making?"

She didn't answer him. The words were too scary. She was making a bridge. She was making a link between all the worlds. She was making the last Iron Artifact. The Iron Hammer nearly fell from her hands.

"The way home."

Bran shifted. Alex didn't look up at him. An ember landed on her bare arm, burning her skin. Hissing in pain, Alex didn't stop working. The voices were a soft song now. Even Arto had faded into the others. It was soothing. Comforting and promising her it wouldn't hurt.

"Alex?"

The name sounded strange in the air. Shaking her head, Alex blinked and put the iron back into the fire. The flames were dying down, and bright coals glittered against the ash like stars in the night. Mjǫllnir thrummed against her hand. Cathanáil's weight was comforting on her back.

"I'll need the Chalice," Alex said. "Put some water in it."

"Uh, sure." Bran stumbled back. "There's no... right, you have magic."

She pulled the iron out of the fire as Bran set the Chalice down near her feet. Water rippled across the top. Alex set the iron down on the stone using the tongs and reached down to touch the rim of the Iron Chalice. Pushing some of the gathered magic into the Iron Chalice, Alex called its power forth. A soft glow was her answer, and she smiled.

There was no horn on this stone anvil, no easy way to turn the iron, but Alex had magic. It bloomed in her chest, and the dark orb shimmered. Reaching for it, Alex closed her eyes and grasped the orb of magic. It was warm. The cold on her back vanished. The orb disappeared in a surge of sparks, the dark gray magic swirling around her left hand.

She picked up the tongs, one last time and raised the piece of iron in the air in front of her. Without releasing Mjǫllnir, Alex pushed the magic into the metal. Magic answered. Dark gray magic washed over the rapidly cooling iron. Alex closed her eyes. Morgana's words from years ago, her lessons from many lifetimes on controlling her magic, replayed.

Magic shifted the iron, pulling the two far ends together. Alex didn't have to open her eyes. Through the tongs, she could feel the vibrations as the metal twisted and pulled itself so the two ends could meet. When she opened her eyes, a rough metal ring was clasped in the tongs. It wasn't enough. Alex finally returned Mjǫllnir to her hip. She grasped the hot metal in her right hand.

Gasps from the others went unnoticed. Her skin burned and blistered, but the magic ran free, digging into the metal. Alex dropped the tongs, and her left hand moved to her neck. Seven spikes rose from the ring of iron, reaching towards the sky. One for each branch of the Tree of Reality off Earth.

Someone was yelling. The chain around Alex's neck snapped, and the Iron Pendant rested in her palm. Turning the Crown, Alex pressed the last piece into the metal ring. The iron triskelion glowed hot, pulsing with magic. Alex's left hand burned. The triskelion welded itself into the Iron Crown.

Dropping to her knees, Alex wretched her right hand off the Iron Crown. Skin tore and cracked, blisters formed, and the others shouted. Alex felt nothing. Hands were reaching for her, trying to stop her, trying to pull her away from the pyre. Magic rolled off Alex, pushing them back with great waves of pressure. The pyre's flames surged.

Her hand found the Iron Chalice. The Iron Crown still glowed hot in her hands. Without a word, she poured the water over the Iron Crown. It hissed, and the metal darkened. Her blistered hands healed. She dropped the Iron Chalice and stood.

"Alex, don't!"

Alex ignored Bran. Softly, the voice, now one voice, called to her. Memories flitted through her mind. This was it. This was what she had to do. The Iron Crown was heavy in her hands, the weight of the iron solid against her palms despite the soft warmth of the magic radiating from it. That certainty was now reality. The voice beckoned with no false promises. Alex lifted the Iron Crown and set it in place on her head.

Only one more loss to suffer.

33

Imbolc

Modern Day Ravenslake, United States

The Rider collapsed into the snow, silver blood gushing out across the muddy slush that their fight had created. Morgana inhaled slowly, seeking to calm her racing heart as the Rider's body and armor dissolved. Its horse was long gone, destroyed by a powerful bolt of silver magic. She had only a moment to catch her breath before she swung around as another Rider surged towards her.

Violet eyes met hers. The Síd raised its golden sword overhead and swung it down. Morgana leapt out of the way and threw up her left hand. Silver sparks exploded forth, ripping through the side of the steed. It staggered to the side, and the Rider jumped down. The horse turned to golden dust before it even hit the ground. The Rider stumbled, but stayed on its feet. Morgana didn't wait to let it attack. Her silver whip ripped through the air, slashing through the armor.

It didn't fall right away. The golden armor cracked and dissolved. The Rider's eyes widened as it debated fight or flight. Her magic was weaker than normal, but Morgana was confident. The weight of her iron dagger on her belt was reassuring, but Morgana did not draw it. Instead, she snapped the whip again, this time striking flesh. The Rider didn't scream as its body turned to dust. It reached towards her to no end. Soon it was just another pile of dust mixing with the slush and snow beside the road.

Morgana kept her hands up and ready. Magic tingled under the skin. It was weaker than normal, the seasonal day was taking its toll on her, but her magic was there and ready. Straining her ears, Morgana listened to the world around her. The sound of traffic was picking up. People were up and on their way to work now. Winter seasonal days were the worst. Their nights were long, and people were awake through far too much of them. She'd already erased two people's memories tonight and was worried about home surveillance systems.

No new Riders appeared. She was already at the edge of town, having chased this pair down. Looking towards the east, Morgana studied the horizon and tried to judge how long they had before sunrise. Not long, but she had to keep moving. She couldn't rest yet. The Sídhe had sent their Riders out in force, and Morgana didn't want to know how many missing persons there would be in the morning. Morgana wiped a layer of sweat off of her brow and turned to make her way back to her car. A gust of wind made her shiver, and she pulled out her phone. There were no new messages from Merlin.

It would be dawn soon. Then she could go home and sleep. Exhaustion hung around her neck like a noose as she climbed into the warm car. She'd left it running, and the heat was welcome. Fighting in the snow was always unpleasant. Moving and adrenaline kept you warm during the fight, but cold crept in quickly.

She rubbed her hands together and eyed the road, trying to decide where to go next. After hours of canvassing the town, Morgana was tired, and her brain didn't want to function. The ring of her phone distracted her from the question, and she pulled it out. A quick look told her it was Ambrose Yates calling, and she immediately connected the call.

"Morgana," Merlin greeted. His tone was cautious and nervous. She sat up straight in her car, her heart tightening in her chest. That voice never meant anything good. "I... I found Alex's car and evidence of a fight. There's no sign of her."

"What?" The word escaped Morgana. "Are you sure?"

"Yes, it is her vehicle. It has her student parking pass inside."

Morgana didn't know what to say. Rationally, she knew what this meant. Her exhaustion cleared, and she mustered the presence of mind to demand his location. Merlin gave it without argument, and Morgana left the call on while she pulled onto the road. Ravenslake wasn't a large town, and after her years living here, Morgana knew all the roads well. Traffic was still light, and she paid no mind to the speed limit until she found Merlin's SUV pulled over near Alex's car.

"What happened?" She demanded as she leapt out.

"There are signs of a fight," Merlin answered. "Morgana, I'm sorry, but it appears she was taken."

Morgana struggled to rein in the emotions sparking in her chest. Her eyes traced over the area. Red blood was splattered in the snow amongst smears of mud where there'd been a struggle. Someone had fallen and been dragged away by their assailants. Judging from the tracks, at least one person had been removed by humans on a gurney.

"She could be in the hospital," Morgana said.

"No. I called the hospital," Merlin answered. "I wasn't able to get much information, but the woman brought into the hospital didn't match Alex's description. That was hours ago."

So that someone was alive, but it wasn't Alex. Swallowing, Morgana couldn't stop the waves of worry and guilt battering against her. If Merlin was right- and she knew he was - then Alex was likely underground.

"We need to find her. We know the general location of where the tunnel likely is."

"Morgana-"

"Let's go. We'll take your car."

Merlin hadn't locked the doors, and Morgana climbed into the passenger side. They'd sort out vehicles later. Her partner hurried after her and took his position behind the wheel.

"Morgana," he tried again.

"Just drive," Morgana said. She slammed the door of the SUV shut and glared at Merlin. "We know the general area of the tunnel. We might be able to catch up."

"Morgana, there is no reason for Alex to have been out this early. I told you that the woman was brought in hours ago. She must have been taken closer to sunset rather than-"

"Merlin, get us there. I'm going either way. It's better for us both to go."

Tension filled the air between them, building like a thunderstorm, but Merlin did not argue further. Of the two of them, he was the better winter driver and had them out of Ravenslake in good order. Morgana watched the sides of the road, noting every tree and searching for any sign of Alex.

Snow was trampled off the road near town, and branches were scattered, having been snapped off the leafless winter trees. Morgana didn't have to alert Merlin; he saw the signs as well. They pulled over slowly, Merlin cautious on the ice, but Morgana was almost vibrating. She opened the door and stepped out into the snow. It had drifted in the ditch higher than her boots. She didn't care and immediately began moving towards the slope of the hill where she could see tracks from horses.

"This way."

"Morgana!"

She summoned an orb of light and started to climb, refusing to allow Merlin or the snow to slow her down. Morgana's eyelids were heavy and dizziness was creeping up on her, but she didn't stop. Her hammering heart urged her on. They had to try: they had to find the Sídhe tunnel and try to save Alex and any children that the Sídhe had taken. There was little hope. Morgana knew that deep down but refused to listen to the doubts creeping over her.

How long had it been since something went right? Since an evening went according to plan? Before the Sídhe had returned, Morgana had known what to expect and been in control of the situation around her. To think she'd been almost bored with her peaceful life of teaching classes and grading papers. Morgana had thought that she remembered what this was like, what living with the threat of the Sídhe had been like, but somehow this was worse than her memories.

There were more consequences now. Secrecy was vital in modern times, while in the first war, they'd been heroes whose great deeds had been celebrated. It made everything harder. They had to sneak around, lie, and worry about the moment that the wrong person saw a Sídhe and put a video up online. She hated the constant worry. It was a distraction and one more thing that Morgana couldn't control.

The light orb hung in front of Morgana, moving with her as she and Merlin scaled the hill. Rocks and roots jutted out from the rough path. The Sídhe Riders hadn't bothered with following a game trail or anything so sensible. They'd come through, seen the city below, and charged down the hill, trampling the vegetation and muddying the snow as they went. The hoof prints of the Sídhe steeds offered a track for her and Merlin to follow. Most headed towards the city, but some were following a path up the hill.

On their return, they'd used some of the animal trails, and the deeper tracks told Morgana that the horses had been carrying heavier loads. They'd tried so hard to find the Riders and stop them, but it was clear that they had failed. They had captives. Morgana had been lucky to escape the horrible slave system, and they had new stock to restart it. If she hadn't been a mage... if the Queen hadn't needed her to spy on Arto...

Morgana couldn't change that. It was dark, and the shadows of the trees provided too many hiding places for the Hounds, but she sped up anyway. Alex was missing. She should have called their students throughout the night to check in with them. Morgana had assumed that they'd be home safe and sound. Apparently, Alex hadn't been.

Stupid girl. Morgana urged her legs to go faster. The magic in her veins pulsed weakly. Damn the seasonal days, damn her magic for being weaker, and damn Alex for forgetting about the seasonal day. They'd explained it over and over. Halloween should have been a sharp enough lesson to ensure Alex didn't leave her dorm room. Why had she been out? Stupid girl! But Morgana kept climbing the hill.

"It's unlikely that we'll find her," Merlin said. He was panting around his words. He was voicing what she already knew, as if that would change her course of action. "Morgana-"

"Hush, the sun hasn't risen. The Sídhe might not have taken her into the tunnels yet." Morgana's chest tightened painfully. She didn't want to think about Alex, about any of her young students in the tunnels. Morgana didn't want to think of anyone being taken there. Memories bombarded her. Memories that she'd once cherished that had rotted with time and understanding of the truth, mocked her. "We at least have to check, Merlin," Morgana insisted. "We can't just write her off."

Her partner didn't argue. Morgana could guess what was going through Merlin's mind and didn't want to dwell on it. It was strange, though. She was the one holding out some hope, despite knowing better. If the Sídhe had captured some humans, they would have quickly taken them underground. After thousands of years of no human slaves, she was certain that the Sídhe were eager. And to think that she'd entertained a tiny spark of hope that maybe they had changed. She was a stupid girl too.

"I suppose we do need to find this tunnel," Merlin said carefully. "The exact location, not just the general area."

"Yes." Morgana swallowed. Her mouth was dry. She was too thirsty and hungry to keep going, but somehow kept putting one foot in front of the other. There hadn't been time to stop and get supplies for this hike. They'd jumped in Merlin's SUV and gotten as close as they could to the area Morgana had scryed for the Sídhe. No supplies, no extra iron, and no plan. "Stupid," Morgana grumbled.

Merlin didn't reply if he heard her. There was nothing he could say that would help. Morgana grabbed at a nearby tree, leveraging herself over a rocky section of the hillside. Deep tracks in the snow and snorts drew her attention. A horse was nearby. She gestured to the tracks with a large movement. Merlin glanced over and nodded.

They slowed down despite the urgency of the situation. Those tracks led back up the hill. Riders could be nearby. They couldn't afford to be flanked now. The light orb gave them away as it was. Around them, the forest was loud with the natural sounds of the rustling leaves and animals stirring as sunrise approached. A yawn tried to escape Morgana, and she clenched her teeth together. One all-nighter was nothing. Their students, their actual college students, did it all the time. But it was still winter, and the sun was only just beginning to rise. It had been a long night, and Morgana's fear did nothing to ease her exhaustion and aches.

A crack of wood up ahead made Morgana pause. She pulled on her magic and shared a look with Merlin. He shifted into the shadows of the trees with green magic swirling around his feet. All sounds of his footfalls or the vegetation shifting vanished. He wouldn't be able to hold it long. Morgana pushed forward, following the noise and readying herself for battle. They had to keep moving, whatever it was needed to be killed off fast.

It was a Síd. Rage roared in her veins at the sight of it. The Rider was dismounted and struggling to get its horse up the steep hill. Judging from the slush and mud around the horse's hoofs, they'd been at this awhile. There was no sign of a prisoner. Had it gone out and come back once or twice already? The Sídhe beast tossed its head, and the pale hair caught the dim light of the moon. Even if she hadn't known what the creature was, Morgana knew that she'd never have mistaken it for an earthly horse. Its master's golden armor and horns only reinforced that.

Morgana's light orb reflected off the gold armor, scattering light around them on the trunks of trees and rocky hillside. The Rider spun to face her. Its violet eyes widened in surprise as Merlin stepped out of the shadows to its left. Morgana didn't have time to wonder if the Rider was surprised that it was her and Merlin, or simply that a pair of humans had flanked them. Magic flared to life in her hand. The Rider reached for its golden sword. A green bolt ripped through the armor, sending the Síd to its knees. Morgana thrust her dagger into its neck. Silver blood splattered across her hand. It faded away seconds later when the Rider's body crumbled. The horse reared and began to run, but Morgana made quick work of the creature with another bolt of magic.

There was no time for relief. The sun was creeping ever closer to the horizon, and a faint glow was slowly appearing. Morgana moved, pushing herself to go faster than before. Thoughts of caution faded from her mind. Soon it wouldn't matter. All the Sídhe had to be going underground. With the dawn, the mages would become stronger, and the bright light would put the Sídhe at a disadvantage.

Every step took too long. Slowly, it was sinking in that Alex had to be gone. The Sídhe wouldn't have kept the prisoners on the surface. They would have taken them down the moment they made it back to the entrance. Morgana remembered the nights when new children were brought to the nursery she was raised in. They'd arrived throughout the night, being tossed in while they sobbed and screamed. The nurses had bundled them up in new clothing and put them into beds while guards stood outside and prevented escapes.

Fear and grief had always echoed in that room. Was it still the same room? The old main tunnel might still be in part intact. Morgana trembled. Alex was too old for the nursery. There was no point in trying to 'train and educate' someone of her age. And if they knew she was a mage, if she'd fought back at all or they found the iron dagger on her, then they'd know she was dangerous.

The sound of cheering made Morgana gasp. The voices weren't Sídhe. They were too young, rang too pure, and their joy sent a shiver through her body. The sun was rising, and hope flared in Morgana's chest. She and Merlin were running. The steepness of the hill was unnoticed. Her lungs burned, but Morgana didn't care.

Cheering. Grateful sobs that resonated with relief. She heard them. They didn't seem real. Morgana looked towards Merlin. His eyes were wide and eager. So he heard it too. It wasn't just in her head. The sounds guided them further up the hill and to the left. They found a small game trail, and Morgana sped up. She tripped on a rock but caught herself on a tree before hitting the ground.

"Morgana?"

"I'm fine. We have to find-"

"I know." Merlin's voice now echoed with hope and urgency. "We might..." He didn't finish the thought.

Then they reached it. A flatter area of ground with a hole in the hillside with dying plants around it. The entrance to the tunnel was dark and foreboding, but the sight before it was miraculous. Children were running out, cheering and laughing. They ranged in age from barely in school to teenagers. The youngest boy was crying and clasping a baby against his chest. One young girl still had marks from being bound on her wrist. Stunned eyes were the norm, even as they laughed in relief and celebrated.

But Morgana's eyes went to the figure in the center of it all. The one who had yet to move away from the tunnel. It was Alex in golden Sídhe armor that was falling to dust. Alex's hand moved, and she caught some of the dust from the armor, her eyes dazed and exhausted. Morgana smiled. She heard Merlin laugh out loud in amazement.

Alex had gotten out herself. More than that, she'd brought out other prisoners. Never before had Morgana witnessed such a thing. Warm sunlight spilled across the small, flattened patch of earth as the sun crept higher in the sky. The darkness of night was fading into a bright pinkish shade with hints of gold.

Morgana stared, just stared, at the scene before her. Her mind raced. She should move. She should help Alex. There was blood on the girl's leg, and it was clear the Sídhe had attacked her. It was clear that Alex was exhausted and traumatized, but Morgana still stared.

A mage had not only gotten out but saved a group of children in the process. Heart in her throat, Morgana struggled to breathe. Alex's eyes met hers. They were dazed, almost glassy. Then Alex crumbled, a strange groan leaving the young woman's body.

Morgana lunged forward. She didn't think about it. Alex was falling. The girl showed signs of a beating, had open bloody wounds, and was staggering. Still, an air of victory hung around her, and there was still a faint smile on her lips even as she collapsed. Alex hit her knees, and Morgana flinched in sympathy. Reaching out, Morgana caught Alex's shoulder and held her steady.

"Alex," she called. Morgana struggled with what to say for a moment. Too many emotions were billowing in her chest. Merlin appeared at her side and draped his coat over Alex's shoulders. Morgana paid him no notice as he went to check the entrance of the tunnel. "Welcome back," Morgana managed. The girl hadn't looked at her yet. Morgana tightened her grip on Alex's shoulder as she watched the last of the girl's strength give out. "Happy Imbolc." As soon as the words left Morgana, Alex's eyes slipped closed, and Morgana cradled her close. "I knew you could do it." Morgana closed her eyes and breathed, welcoming the gentle waves of relief and pride that washed over her, happier than she had felt in a long time.

34

She That Wears the Crown

Visions weren't Nicki's area, but she trusted her gut and trusted Bran. Terror filled his eyes as Alex lowered the newly forged Iron Crown onto her head, and fear flared to life in her chest. Nicki had already been horrified when Alex grabbed the hot Crown, had been unsettled by the single-minded determination that Alex put into it, and worried by Alex's unwillingness to answer questions. Now terror took the place of all of that.

Something extraordinary was happening, something that would change everything. Nicki could feel it in the air. And it frightened her as much as it excited her. She'd wondered what being present when history unfolded felt like. If people knew at the time that something important was happening before them. Nicki had hoped to one day experience such a moment for herself and find out. Now she was.

Without thinking, she grabbed Aiden's hand and held on. The Iron Crown flashed brightly, dispelling the gloom around them. The dark metal glowed with power, making the spikes of the Crown appear taller, like glittering towers reaching into the sky. A wave of energy rolled off Alex, striking Nicki in the chest. Gasping, she took a step back as her skin warmed and tingled. Beneath them, the ground rumbled.

Heat exploded off the pyre as the flames jumped. What had been a low fire was now a burning inferno. Smoke and ozone filled the air. The swirling black smoke created shadows against the stone wall as it danced in the light of the Iron Crown. Overhead, the sky rumbled. Nicki didn't look up; her eyes were fixed on Alex.

The Iron Crown glowed with a low, dark light, creating a halo around Alex as she drew Cathanáil in one smooth motion. The Iron Sword glowed in Alex's hand, and hints of lightning jumped off of Alex's skin and were running along the blade. Wisps of long blonde hair were falling loose around Alex's face. Hints of blood still lingered on her hand. The sudden wind was pulling more hair and making it blow around Alex. She was beautiful.

Alex didn't look at them. Alex's eyes dropped to Cathanáil, and she raised it into the air with one hand. With a graceful, sharp movement, Alex sliced the sword through the empty air. Alex's gray eyes turned a solid, glowing dark gray color with no visible iris or pupil. Aiden tightened his grip on Nicki's hand. Nicki wanted to move, wanted to speak, but she couldn't.

The empty air shimmered and unfolded in fractals of color. Sparks of magic and light spun in the air like tiny fireworks before swirling together to create a circular portal with light pouring out of it. Despite her confusion and no small amount of fear, Nicki was curious and leaned forward. This was different from the other portals. Her feet were still too heavy to move, but she caught a glimpse of what the portal linked to. Beyond the portal was a white stone hall. She heard a pained gasp from Bran and knew he'd seen it, too.

Streams of light poured through the portal, flowing like water to Alex's outstretched free arm. The rush of magic danced around Alex's fingertips and washed up Alex's body, caressing her face. Alex lowered her chin, and Nicki couldn't make out her friend's expression. Aiden pulled Nicki back, and Bran joined them in huddling away from the portal. Bran grabbed her free hand, and a soft sob escaped him. Nicki didn't ask. She didn't dare take her eyes off Alex. Not now. Still, Bran's shuddering breaths echoed in her ears.

Alex turned her face up, and the light of the Iron Crown and the portal illuminated her features. As her eyes opened, Nicki could see that the solid glow had faded, but dark gray eyes stared through the portal without trepidation. Her features were relaxed, expressionless. Droplets of sweat and tears had left tracks down her face, carving paths through the layer of ash coated on Alex's skin. She didn't react when her long hair brushed across her face. She didn't sputter and put it behind her ear. Alex's facial muscles were neutral, revealing nothing of what she was thinking. Over the past few years, Nicki had seen Alex happy, grieving, and everything in between. This was nothing.

Magic danced around Alex, gathering in her free hand and swirling around her. The glow of Cathanáil was growing stronger. On her hip, Mjǫllnir sparked with light, and arcs of lightning flowed over the metal. The Iron Chalice on its side at her feet was glowing once more. The bright light overwhelmed the hellish glow of the pyre, which was finally dying down once again.

Then the color of the light shifted, turning a deep dark gray like the color of iron, and the scent of ozone tickled Nicki's nose. It was getting stronger, overwhelming everything. If she hadn't known the source of Alex's magic, she would have searched the sky. Along her arms and the back of her neck, Nicki's hair stood on end. Her stomach turned, whether from nervousness or excitement, she wasn't sure.

The magic rushed into the air, twisting around itself to form a pillar and lighting up the dark sky. Around them, the wind picked up, and ash flew into the air. Alex didn't move. The dark gray magic swept into the hole where the Darkness was dripping through. At first, it vanished. More magic, more light, kept spilling through the portal. Alex held her position. All of it flowed to Alex, who moved with graceful motions, almost like a dancer. The magic darkened to Alex's dark gray and circled into the sky.

Not a dancer, Nicki decided as the sky brightened at the volume of magic being thrown into it. A conductor of light. A conductor of magic. Lightning flashed across the sky with no clouds. Nicki breathed in, realizing suddenly that the dull ache she'd been bearing since they arrived here was fading. Magic was returning to her. She envied Alex's ability to see ambient magic and wondered how bright this dead world suddenly was to Alex's eyes.

A grin took hold of her face. The magic was pushing at the Darkness, lighting up the rip. Warm gray blurred with the inky blackness. Lightning flashed at the meeting point, brilliant white against the strange backdrop. Nicki squinted, wishing she could better see, and found herself leaning forward again. Bran's grip kept her from going too far, and Aiden pulled her back. Aiden made a small sound but didn't manage words.

More magic surged to Alex. Her left hand barely moved as she directed the energy into the sky. Nicki followed it with wide eyes. Slowly, the rip in the sky, the hole in reality, shuddered and began to shrink. Nicki sucked in a surprised and eager breath. She squeezed the boys' hands and trembled. More light lit up the world around them. The portal grew in size, and Alex pulled more energy through. As it reached her, it swirled around Alex as it changed color before leaping off her fingertips and spinning into the sky.

It kept coming. Nicki's skin was warm with energy. The burn was gone, replaced by a low ember of power that she knew would burst to life if she called. But she didn't. Nicki didn't move. The chill of the night was fading away. Beneath her feet, the ground hummed. Nicki's eyes rose to the rip in the sky once more. Her heart raced, and her throat constricted in a mix of terror and glee.

A storm brewed. The ash scent in the air was long gone. Now ozone was all she could smell. Lightning arced across the sky, illuminating the night and destroying chunks of debris. A weight settled on Nicki's shoulders and chest. Aiden and Bran's grips tightened, and Nicki knew she wasn't alone in feeling it. Pressure built, and Nicki watched as merely a bystander.

Blackness churned. Darkness spilled forth through the narrow opening. Like a wound being cleared of pus or an enemy army making one last desperate charge before defeat. Alex didn't react at all. More magic, more bright glittering energy, surged out of the portal and spun around her, taking on a darker hue before being pushed towards the opening. Alex's dark gray magic collided with the Darkness in a fresh wave of power and conflict. Sparks flew, and the sky rumbled.

Then it was gone. The gaping hole was pulled shut with bright lines of magic highlighting where it had been. They faded quickly, leaving the dark sky and debris hanging overhead. Lightning flashed and danced over where the gap had been, and the natural color of the night sky beyond faded into view as the last remnants were burned away in the final bursts of magic.

Rumbling echoed across the dark, ashy plain, but it was the only sound. The wind tugged at Alex's hair, but it was growing weaker. Nicki's exhale was too loud, and she grimaced, afraid of disturbing the peace.

The light from the portal dimmed, and Alex lowered her hand and the Iron Sword.

Magic rained down from the sky. Everything that was left from the effort glistened like falling stars and faded away into the night sky. But now, Nicki thought she could see real stars. They were faint, but there were points of light beyond the debris field. Aiden squeezed her hand again. Nicki looked up at him. The pyre was almost out, but there was still enough light that she could see the smile on his face.

Nicki looked at Bran. He was watching Alex. Her own fear was fading, but Bran's was brighter than ever. Nicki opened her mouth to ask, but her tongue was too dry. Her lips were already chapped from the wind, ash, and cold and cracked when she tried to move them. The warmth of Alex's power was fading, allowing the chill of the night to take hold once more. The scent of ozone and the rumbling in the sky were fading, returning the world to what it had been like before with one major exception.

They could leave now. With so much magic in this world through whatever the hell Alex had done, they could be back home tonight. At least, the rational part of Nicki thought so, but... something was wrong.

Magic spun around the Iron Chalice and lifted it off the ground. The magic poured inside, and Alex extended her free hand to pluck the artifact from the air. She didn't address them at all as she studied the Chalice for a moment. The Iron Chalice glowed in Alex's hand, the metal shimmering with magic. Nicki swallowed. She had no idea how long it had been since Morgana had fallen, but they hadn't slept. It had only been a few hours and now....

Liquid spilled from the goblet, hitting the barren ground without a sound. Nicki had only a moment to marvel that it had been empty before. Alex had used conjured fire and water and used telekinesis all in quick succession. Nicki's eyes followed the droplets of water, marveling at how they caught the light of the flowing magic. They dampened the ash, falling beside the other patches of moisture from when Alex had "tempered" the Iron Crown. She couldn't see any change, but the smell of the air was already shifting. Nicki doubted herself for a moment, doubted what she thought she smelled, but a sweet scent was overwhelming the smell of death.

Nicki almost missed it. A dark-gray glow shimmered across the surface of the ground. Its color was too close to that of the ash for it to be obvious, but it was there. A small stream of iron-gray rose out of the ground, forming a large bulb that opened seconds later to reveal a brilliant purple flower with lines of white and blue on its petals. The glow and the magic spread, more flowers grew forth from the ashes. It kept spreading. This time, Alex didn't need to refill the Chalice. The glow rolled across the landscape and more plants sprang forth from the remnants of the old world.

A happy squeal escaped Nicki. Around her feet, flowers were blooming, and a few ferns with silver leaves were expanding in size. Bran shifted away from her as a sapling pushed up between them. Grinning, Nicki backed away and released Aiden's hand so she could spin around. Beyond them, the ground was shimmering, and plant life was rapidly taking hold. It wasn't everywhere. There were plenty of empty patches and spaces between plants, but the difference was startling.

The only light now was the steadily glowing Iron Crown on Alex's head and the portal. Nicki turned back to Alex as the rolling magic reached the end of what she could see with that light. Alex's attention was not on them, and instead, the silent woman had turned towards the pyre.

"Alex," Bran called softly.

She didn't answer him. Bran's expression shifted towards defeat. Nicki gripped his arm and frowned, trying to unravel what he knew. She glanced at Aiden, but he only shrugged, confirming his own confusion. Bran gently brushed off her hand and moved a few feet away to his pack. A flash of dark gray magic drew Nicki's attention back to Alex.

Ash swirled up from the burned-out pyre, gathering in a mass before Alex. Her dark gray eyes regarded it calmly, and Nicki gasped softly as she realized that the ashes were likely those of Morgana. Her good mood faded immediately. Nicki's eyes fell to a nearby flower, and she wondered what Morgana would have thought of it.

"Here," Bran said. His voice was weak and strained. In his hand was a canteen. "I emptied it out." Bran wasn't looking at Alex. His eyes were fixed on one of the flowers at his feet.

Her confusion chewed at Nicki. Her eyes darted back and forth between Alex and Bran as she tried to understand what she was missing. Bran had been scared, but now he was resigned. And Alex remained terribly silent. The soft glow of the Iron Crown surrounded Alex, bathing her in soft light. With the Iron Chalice in her left hand, Cathanáil in her right, and Mjǫllnir on her hip, she looked like an image off one of Bran's tarot cards. A distant and beautiful figure that held a meaning Nicki couldn't comprehend. She wasn't a threat, but there was no sign of happiness or victory on Alex's face. That finally sank in.

Nicki swallowed thickly as a terrible idea took hold. Alex wasn't acting like Alex. She should have made some remark to celebrate the closing of the gap and the stopping of the Darkness, but there had been nothing. Even the grief and shock of Morgana's death didn't explain her silence. Licking her lips, Nicki tasted the ash from the world and the salt of her tears on her skin. Tear tracks on Alex's face glimmered in the light as the mage nodded her head, and Morgana's ashes filled the large canteen.

"What now?" Aiden asked. "Should we..." he gestured at the portal. "Uh..."

"Come with me," Alex said. Except there was something wrong with the voice. It was deeper. It sounded a lot like Alex, but it echoed. As if multiple voices had been blended together with Alex's as the primary one.

Alex handed the canteen to Bran, who clutched it against his chest, but still didn't look at Alex. He capped the canteen and said nothing as Alex stepped past him. Nicki watched him swallow. He knew. Bran could answer the questions brewing in her mind, but she couldn't ask. The moment Nicki asked, it would become real. Bran must have felt her gaze because he looked up. Tears were slipping from his eyes. He said nothing and stumbled to his backpack. Without a word, he pulled out a couple of items and shoved them into the pockets of his coat. Then he went to Alex's pack and zipped it up before hoisting it onto his back.

Nicki retrieved her pack and helped Aiden pull his on. Aiden's smile had faded, and Nicki could see his suspicions taking root. That made what she feared more likely to be true. In the distance, Nicki heard the tents flapping in the wind. No one made any move to retrieve them. It didn't matter. The task was done. They could go home now, but it wasn't Earth waiting on the other side of the portal.

Alex was waiting for them by the portal, her silhouette dark against the bright white behind her. Nicki hesitated, and Aiden took her hand. Bran was holding the canteen tight in his left hand. His right hand was toying with the dog tags around his neck. Nicki took a deep breath and cast one last look at the smoldering coals of the pyre before moving towards Alex. As if sensing her, Alex stepped through the portal into the strange white hall beyond. There was nothing else for them to do but to follow.

35

The White Hall

Bran would never forget the first lie he told. Not a childish lie that they teach you is wrong and gets you scolded by your mother, but a proper lie. The sort of lie that forces you to grit your teeth and makes you sick as you shove a part of yourself deep down. The sort of lie that you know is going to linger inside of you for a long time.

He'd been eleven, and at a silly school dance, the sort that they really shouldn't have in middle schools because it makes everything horrible for at least two weeks on either side of the event. Todd had confessed to the group that he'd kissed Laura Tyler under the bleachers, and suddenly it was clear that he'd missed a memo. When had girls stopped having cooties? He replied with an 'ew' automatically and covered it up with a correction that he'd rather kiss Susan Bellows when he received odd looks. The first big lie.

Trying to understand sexual attraction hadn't gotten easier, and trying to understand why he didn't feel it had been hell. He sort of understood romantic attraction, but never to the level of his classmates and peers. It was an elephant in the room that everyone else could see, touch, hear, and smell. They all described it a little differently, but all of them understood it. The straight guys, straight girls, gays, the bis, and lesbians all were united in understanding what it meant to want someone. Bran didn't. He liked people from time to time, but there were never the dreams and fantasies that everyone else was familiar with. He was broken. At least he'd thought that for a long time, and the only positive side had been that most advertising had no power over him. Lies became familiar, but they never stopped burning his tongue.

Thank God for the internet. Thank magic that he lived in an era where you could discover your word. When you could be reassured that you weren't alone in being separated from what seemed like the most universal human experience. College had been a fresh slate. He'd been honest and learned to be comfortable with his truth. Magic had brought new lies, but none as bitter and harsh, nothing he couldn't live with.

But Bran had forgotten something important that he'd learned when he'd turned to the internet. It was a spectrum. Sometimes, you could meet someone that you liked so much the wires that had never been connected could jump a spark, and you started... feeling things. So, Bran had reverted. He hadn't reverted all the way to lying, but it was just as bad. He buried a new and surprising part of himself, shoved it deep down so that it didn't cause him trouble.

Now that lie made him sick. Things unsaid burned on his tongue. His stomach turned, and already regret was filling in every crack as they formed. Somehow, he followed what remained of Alex through the portal. It would do no good to stay in this world. Even with the spark of life it had been given, real recovery would take time. That was the truth, and no lie he could tell himself would change that or what had happened to Alex. What he had been unable to prevent despite the warnings.

Around him, the portal was warm. Magic flowed across his skin and charged the spark of power that dwelt inside of him. They weren't holding hands. They weren't holding onto anything. Flashes of worlds they'd been to and a few they hadn't rushed past them in between stretches of darkness and splashes of color.

Then the portal opened. He stumbled through and exhaled. The White Hall was exactly as Bran had seen it in the vision, and yet it was somehow brighter, and the glow of the stone was stronger. Behind him, he heard Nicki and Aiden gasp as they stepped through the portal. He'd seen it before, and Alex up ahead of him in the Iron Crown was too familiar a sight. Jeans and a long gray shirt. Her hair was falling out of the braid and would soon hang loose, like in his vision.

He didn't stare at the grandeur around them. This place was a link point between the source of magic, the energy that gave life to the Tree of Reality, and everything else, and he hated it. Bran hated the subtle glow of whatever it was made of. Hated the magical energy that thrummed all around him. Most of all, he hated the way the Iron Soul moved too easily here. Alex's body flowed as if all weights had been removed, all chains and shackles cut away. Bran hated all of it. His eyes narrowed on the Iron Crown.

"Where are we?" Aiden asked. He stepped up beside Bran, their shoulders brushing briefly.

"The heart of the trunk," the Iron Soul answered. They turned to face the others. Their hair finally finished falling free, framing Alex's face with long dirty blonde hair. "From here, the magic of the Tree of Reality can be controlled and sent to the branches. With the source of the Darkness cut off, I can ensure that the worlds recover."

And that was it. Wrapped up in a nice little bow. The Iron Soul was looking at them, watching them, and Alex... He didn't see her in those eyes anymore. Bran shrugged off Alex's pack and swung it to the front before letting it hit the ground with a thunk. It toppled over, and poor little Galahad rolled out of the unzipped top. The Iron Soul looked down at the stuffed toy with no reaction to it being on the floor.

"Did she know?" Bran demanded. He took a step forward, his toes kicking the side of the bag. Rage burned and tears stung. "Did Alex know what was going to happen if she put that Crown on her head? That-"

"Yes, she knew." The Iron Soul watched him with those distant eyes that were familiar and alien. "She was the last thing she was willing to lose."

"Oh," Nicki breathed. Her voice quivered, and Bran knew without turning around that his friend was crying. "That's why..." Nicki's voice gave out. Bran didn't turn around. If he saw Nicki crying, then the weak tears escaping him now would turn to a deluge. "I was hoping..."

Nicki had been hoping she was wrong. Bran understood that feeling. When Alex had started working with the iron, he'd been terrified that his vision was coming to pass, but had been equally afraid of stopping her. The vision had worried him, but he hadn't really understood it until it was too late. The truth had become all too clear when the Iron Soul had summoned forth all that magic and achieved their goal without breaking a sweat.

Bran's hands were shaking, and the Iron Soul looked at the three of them, each in turn, with their gaze holding on him a moment longer than the others. Or maybe it just felt that way. Tears were escaping his eyes and rolling down his cheeks despite his attempts to hold them back.

"Then you're the Iron Soul?" Bran asked. The words stung to say out loud, but the weight lessened with verbalizing his fear. Swallowing a rush of bile, Bran glared at the being before him. "The merging of them all." A weak, maybe hysterical chuckle escaped him. His hands were trembling, and he tightened his grip on the canteen serving as a makeshift urn in an attempt to regain control. "The final destination."

"It is time for you to return to the Iron Realm," the Iron Soul said. "Your mission is complete."

They lifted Cathanáil into the air. They didn't answer the question. Maybe they didn't see the point. Bran finally realized that the portal to the Sídhe homeworld was gone. He hadn't noticed it close. The air shook. Something like thunder echoed in the strange hall, but Bran kept his gaze on the Iron Soul. A new portal formed where Cathanáil had cut the air.

Nicki and Aiden stopped in front of the portal and looked back at him. The magic swirled and twisted around itself along the edge. Bran didn't focus on what was beyond it. The shapes were blurred, but he was pretty sure that it was Earth. The colors looked right.

"I'll be right behind you," Bran promised. His voice echoed in the hall.

Nicki's eyes saw too much. Pity shown in her eyes. He hated it and wanted to correct that. But it would only be another lie. Bran didn't speak. Nicki and Aiden turned to the Iron Soul. He waited for them to say something. Nicki covered her mouth with one hand and cast her eyes down.

"Can you turn back?" Aiden asked.

"I am what I am." The words echoed around them. "This was the final destination."

That almost set Bran off again, but Aiden was calmer. "That force... that intelligence we thought was guiding us, was it always you?"

"It was. I forged myself and brought myself here. The Tree must survive."

There was no way to respond to that. Bran wondered if Alex had really understood. He didn't want the answer. The Iron Soul said that she knew, but he couldn't fathom it. Had Alex been hiding that much, or had it crept up on her?

"What about the Demons?" Nicki asked, cutting into his thoughts. "The Fae? The Sídhe? The Old Ones? What happens to them now?"

"Paths will be opened for them, if they wish to leave the Iron Realm, as the worlds heal."

Yeah, Bran thought bitterly. Wrapping everything up in a little bow. It would never be that simple. He stared at the Iron Soul, trying to gather some semblance of calm. The Iron Soul met his gaze briefly before nodding to the portal. Nicki and Aiden didn't move towards it, their eyes on him.

"I'll be right behind you," Bran promised again. If he was smart, he'd leave now, but he didn't.

Aiden and Nicki saw too much. Their expressions were too sad, too kind, and he hated it. Nicki hesitated, opening her mouth and struggling with what to say. A deep, lost sigh escaped her. Keeping her eyes down, Nicki closed the distance between them and gently pulled the canteen with Morgana's ashes from his hands.

"We'll be waiting for you," Nicki whispered. "Don't stay too long."

Canteen in hand, Nicki returned to Aiden's side. He wrapped an arm around her shoulders and hugged her close. They both trembled. Bran's anger faded a little. It wasn't just him that was hurt. They were all being left behind. It wasn't just him that Alex hadn't warned.

"Thank you," Nicki finally said. Her voice was strong now as the Iron Soul regarded her. "For everything."

"You are welcome, Nicole."

Nicki shook her head at the words and took a deep breath. Twisting out of Aiden's grasp, she grabbed his hand and pulled him towards the portal. Neither of them looked back, but Aiden paused and waved casually over his shoulder to the Iron Soul. Something finally flickered in those metal gray eyes at the gesture. Bran gasped and stumbled closer, almost tripping on the discarded backpack as Nicki and Aiden vanished.

The Iron Soul's attention snapped back to him. A wave of dark gray sparks pulled the discarded pack out of the way, giving him space to recover his balance. He almost stepped on Galahad. The small act of kindness, maybe of worry, hit Bran all wrong.

"Alex?" he called.

"No. I am sorry."

He almost believed that lie. Straightening up, Bran glared into the gray orbs, willing for there to be a spark of Alex. Only seconds ago; he'd thought- he'd hoped.

"She can't-" Bran shook his head. Tears slipped from his eyes once again as anger crumbled away, leaving only the void below. "I..."

The Iron Soul reached out and cupped his cheek. They were too close now. Bran leaned into the touch without thought, but the familiar gray eyes remained distant. Then a thumb brushed away one of the tears, and there was a flicker of sorrow in those eyes. He wasn't wrong. He wasn't lying to himself. How did that make it all worse?

"You were loyal. Even through rebirth, you were always loyal, Brandon," the Iron Soul said. "We remember."

He opened his mouth to say something, but there were no words. His heart twisted in his chest, but his lungs wouldn't work. Bran tried to bring an arm up to reach for Alex, but he couldn't. Then a sob escaped him. The tears ran freely. Everything he'd never said hit him all at once, but the words wouldn't mean anything now. Or would they?

"I love you," he confessed.

Searching those eyes, he waited for a change, for Alex to come back. The Iron Soul smiled sadly at him. Their thumb brushed away another tear as the last flicker of hope died in his chest. The smell of ozone consumed his awareness. He could taste it on his tongue, feel it on his skin, and humming in his chest.

"She cared deeply for you as well," the Iron Soul said. "We loved you as Gofiben and Alexandra."

"Two missed chances then," Bran whispered. He didn't want to think about Gofiben, suddenly grateful for not remembering. Suddenly grateful that, as that Bran, he'd died at the same time as Gofiben. "Never could do anything right when dealing with romantic feelings."

The Iron Soul's soft smile fell away. Bran didn't like that. It was better than the expressionless being it had been, but he wanted Alex. Then the Iron Soul leaned forward, and before Bran could move away, pressed their lips against his. They were soft and warm. Magic danced across his skin, and he sighed. Another lie, but one he'd take. Closing his eyes, he inhaled the smell of the Iron Soul. It still smelled like Alex, but there was a dusty undertone now that ruined the illusion. Like an old library. Like time.

Pulling himself back, he ended the kiss, but kept his eyes shut. It did nothing to hold back the grief and the wave of tears. The Iron Soul said nothing. Their hand lingered on his cheek until he stepped back and pulled away. Immediately, his skin was cold, and he missed the hum of the Iron Soul's magic and the illusion of Alex.

"I never wanted anyone." Bran shook his head as more tears pricked at his eyes. "Only Alex." The Iron Soul knew. He shook his head and backed further away, needing distance to breathe. "She wasn't a lie," Bran said firmly. "She wasn't. None of them were."

"We know," the Iron Soul assured him. Then they smiled. This time the smile lit up their face and eyes. For a moment, he could believe it was Alex, just Alex smiling at him. A shaky breath escaped Bran. He basked in the warmth of the smile. "We know, Brandon Fisher."

No one called him that. He was Bran. He'd always been Bran. Swallowing, Bran told himself to let go.

"Merlin and Morgana are gone." Bran exhaled and straightened his shoulders. Meeting the steely gray gaze of the Iron Soul, he raised his chin and said, "I volunteer to take their place." When it didn't answer him, Bran pressed on. "You may have the solution to the Darkness, but beings are still living in the Iron Realm and causing magic. Even if you open paths for them, not all will want to leave Earth. To some, it is home. Some of their descendants may become threats in the future. Someone needs to be ready for that, to train any future mages that may be born."

The Iron Soul studied him. They weren't surprised; they weren't worried or happy. They didn't seem to be anything. Holding his breath, Bran met the stare and fought not to flinch. He already missed Alex's stormy gray eyes. They were dark gray now. Like iron, hard and firm in the face of anything he could say or do. The memory of the dead Sídhe world rested heavily in his gut. The Iron Chalice's magic would heal it eventually. He had faith in its power, but the animals were long gone, and the buildings buried. He stood by his statement and knew that this was not the end of all the magical troubles.

"I still make the offer," Bran said. "Things won't resolve overnight." At least he couldn't imagine that even this being could work so fast. "It's going to be messy. There are thousands of years of resentment, and some worlds are already gone. Some species are gone. I stand by what I said. I volunteer to take on the burden that Merlin and Morgana carried."

Those dark gray eyes considered him. Bran did not balk. He did not hide from the Iron Soul. The weight of his words settled on his shoulders. Merlin and Morgana's burden had shaped them, changed them, and had led to Alex's change. It would change him. He would not lie about that, not to himself or the Iron Soul. Then, the Iron Soul held the Iron Chalice out to him, their left hand wrapped around the neck and fingers pressed against the Triskelion symbol.

Bran reached out to take the Chalice. His hand brushed against the Iron Soul's. They were so close. The smell of ozone taunted Bran. The energy of a building storm danced across his skin. Nonetheless, the Iron Chalice was comfortable in his hand.

"This belongs with you," the Iron Soul said.

Bran swallowed. Then the Iron Soul knelt and picked up Galahad with tender hands. They said nothing, but cradled the stuffed dog in their arms. His throat closed. The Iron Soul had Galahad, and the photos Alex had packed were only a few feet away in the backpack. Maybe it was only another illusion or another lie, but Bran appreciated it.

Dark Gray magic spun through the air and vanished into the pocket of the hoodie around Alex's waist. The Iron Soul did not move. They pulled a cloth bag forth in the wave of magic and brought it towards him. Bran remembered Alex pocketing it from Morgana's gear, but he hadn't thought about it. There had been too much else to concern himself with. The fabric was a rich purple color, but the drawstrings were fraying at the ends. It floated in the air before him.

"This is the mirror that Morgana used for much of her three thousand years," the Iron Soul said. Maybe it was his imagination, but their voice seemed softer now. "It carries a strong imprint of her magic and her desire to protect the Iron Realm. The mirror might not be iron, but her intent is fused within the metal. It will serve you well."

He took it from the air. The bag was heavy in his hand. Bran swallowed, trying to figure out how to respond. The Iron Chalice in one hand and Morgana's mirror in the other. One a symbol of healing and his past life and the other of the role he would now hold. Magic stirred in his chest. He didn't have to ask to know that the deed was done. There were no fireworks, no elaborate displays. It simply was.

"Thank you," was all that came out.

"You are welcome, Bran."

The sound of his name gave him pause, but he nodded. Bran turned towards the portal. His tongue was heavy, but no longer burning. The first steps were hard. He glanced back and found the Iron Soul once more holding Galahad. They were looking at the stuffed dog with softer eyes. Bran almost spoke again. He almost did a lot of things, but he reached the portal. Closing his eyes, he held his breath and stepped through.

The scent of Earth met Bran like the open arms of his mother. It surrounded him as his feet touched down on the other side of the portal. Bran had no idea if he was safe or not, but he kept his eyes closed and inhaled the smell of his homeworld. Tears were stinging his eyes, threatening to overwhelm him again.

Had that really just happened? Was Alex really.... He couldn't even finish the thought. It was terrifying and horrible. It was too big. Bigger than anything he'd feared would come out of this, and now there was an aching void in his chest that his magic couldn't fill. His fingers tightened around the round shape of the mirror, reassuring him it was very real.

"Bran?" It was Nicki's voice. "Bran, honey, are you okay?"

Hands with small calluses on the thumbs and index fingers touched his face. He could feel her moving in front of him. There was a murmur of voices, and he heard Aiden and what sounded like Jenny. He should open his eyes and join them in the explanations. The grieving that was sure to come.

"Bran," Aiden said gently. A hand fell on his shoulder. "We're back."

"Yeah." Bran heard his voice break. He opened his eyes. "She- they sent us back."

"You left two days ago," Jenny said. She was beside him, throwing a blanket over his shoulders. "You're in the backyard of the house."

"We would have left Wales recently," Aiden offered. "Not sure with the time difference..."

"The others said what happened, Bran. Keep breathing," Lance said firmly. He was on Bran's other side, a warm hand on his shoulder. "Come on, let's get inside."

He blinked as the words slowly sank in. Tilting his head, he peered beyond Nicki and found that indeed, their house was only a few feet away. It was a gloomy day, and he was standing in snow with the winter chill trying to cut through the blanket and his coat. But it wasn't really the winter making him cold. Jenny's eyes were red, and Lance kept swallowing.

"I'm alright," he lied. "I'm alright. Just need some sleep."

They didn't believe him. Bran didn't blame them for that. Glancing over his shoulder, he was both relieved and sad that the portal had already closed. He knew where the Iron Soul was. They were in the light in the trunk of the Tree of Reality. Maybe they were the light. They had forged themselves, both at the beginning and now at the end.

Bran sighed and looked into the sky. The sun was coming up on the horizon, casting shades of pink across the clouds. It was another dawn. People were getting ready for their days already, not knowing anything about what had been given up to keep them safe. The morning was calm and still. There wasn't even a breeze to match his storming mood. Earth had just lost- shouldn't there at least be a thunderstorm rolling in to mark that Alex was gone? Lightning had always been her thing.

Bran tightened his grip on the Iron Chalice and the mirror and followed the others inside the house. There would be many years ahead of him to understand. He didn't need all the answers this morning.

The Iron Realm was safe, and there was hope for many who had been hopeless. Bran could live with that.

www.ingramcontent.com/pod-product-compliance
Lightning Source LLC
Chambersburg PA
CBHW071402200726
48294CB00002B/273